PRAISE FOR *EYE CONTACT OVER TRUK*

"Woodman's **empathy and insight** will move readers to tears." — *Booklife*

"A **heart-wrenching and insightful** exploration of the social and psychological cost of war wrapped in an **entertaining and well-crafted story…**" — *Reedsy Discovery*

"One of those **stories that will linger in the mind and memory** of the reader long after the book itself has been finished and set back upon the shelf." — *Midwest Book Review*

"…a **perfect story** of emotions, past trauma, healing wounds, and learning to live with your trauma…The descriptions were **incredible**, and the imagery of the lagoon was **breathtaking. I loved each moment of the story and highly recommend it.**" — *Readers' Favorite*

"…it is **surprisingly lovely and even uplifting to read.**"
— *Matt McAvoy Book Review*

"…**a powerful** message about **forgiveness, healing,** and rediscovering **the joy of living.**"
— *The Historical Fiction Company*

"The characters are so meticulously developed that their emotions resonate deeply with the reader…is a novel that **will touch your heart and leave a lasting impression.**"
— *The Coffee Pot Book Club*

STEPHANIE WOODMAN

EYE CONTACT OVER TRUK

Vortex Publishing

Library of Congress Control Number: 2024904636 | ISBN 9798989940615 (paperback) | ISBN 9798989940608 (e-book) | ISBN 9798989940622 (audio-book)

FIC014050, FIC115000, FIC080000

Author: Stephanie Woodman

Cover design by: Steven Novak—Novak Illustration

To my dad, Stan, and Bill for your help and support.
I hope you both are enjoying your next great adventure.
To Nick, for always listening.

Part I – Nick

Sometimes, to see the light, we have to step into the dark.

One

August 14, 1985 - Ventura, California

The end. Everything ends. Days end. Jobs end. Friendships end. People end. Nick Mitchel had lost count of how many endings he'd lived through, how many people he had lost. Lost. What a stupid word; as if they could be found. Though some people in this world were found, not in Nick's. Death was not recoverable. With their deaths came burials on land and sea. Memories buried as well.

This was different. Nick had known this day would come. For three years, cancer had slowly, menacingly, insidiously eaten at her body. His shoulders slumped over as he sat in his living room chair, holding the little crystal clown fish Jeanne loved so much. A down light shined on their family photo mounted above the fireplace. The picture was a few years old, taken on the rocks at Ventura Beach with the waves crashing behind them. Nick had his arms around Jeanne as they leaned back on a rock. She was the picture of health. Anthony stood tall behind them, and Dana sat on the sand, leaning against Nick's legs. It was the four of them, as Dana hadn't married or had his sweet granddaughter yet. The light seemed to focus on Jeanne, her smile, her sparkling, happy eyes drawing her up. Nick rubbed his eyes, irritated at conjuring such a thought. *My beautiful Jeanne. When she d... is gone, how do I stay? She is my wife, my love, my best friend. She knows me better than I know myself. I've shared everything...almost. Maybe I'm not meant to go on. I don't deserve to go on.* Nick stopped this thought. Now wasn't the time to go down that black hole. She still needed him, and he would continue to take care of her until he fulfilled her final wishes.

Unconsciously, his fingers twirled his wedding ring around his finger as he tried to reconcile his prayers. He had to find the strength to pray for what would be the best for her, causing the worst for him. "Lord, it's been long enough. Please end her pain," he said.

"Dad," said Dana, choking on her words.

Nick knew it was coming. He took a deep breath and got up to face his son and daughter. His wasn't the only heart breaking. He peered into the eyes of his children, who had said goodbye to their mother.

"Mom wants you," Dana said, her voice barely a whisper, tears rolling down her face. Nick nodded to her. He saw his son fighting for control. Nick gave them both a quick hug. Forcing himself to stand up tall, he took another deep breath, walked into the bedroom, and sat down on a chair by the bed.

Jeanne lay on her side, eyes open, staring with the same vacant expression she wore for the last several days. Those eyes that had been so vibrant, so intense, now outwardly blank. Whatever held her vision was now internal and didn't live in Nick's world.

"Yes, my love," he said. With shaking hands, he moved her dry gray hair back behind her ear, then he took her hand in his. "Can I get you anything?"

With effort, she focused her eyes on him. "I told the kids, I want you to take my ashes to Hawaii."

Nick nodded.

Jeanne struggled to take another shallow breath. "It's time, Nick. You have to let me go," she said in a soft, frail voice.

"You can't ask me to do that," he whispered, shaking his head, fighting desperately for control, as the tears welled up again. Nick gazed into her eyes, the pecan color that had captured him so long ago.

"I can't stay," she said, taking a breath. "Nick, you can't follow me to the afterlife. If you do, I won't talk to you there."

At those words, Nick actually smiled. "Yes, you will. Wherever we are, we will be together."

"I'm not...going to...be there," she said. Jeanne's chest barely moved as she strained for more air. "I believe...in rein...carna tion....I'm coming...back a fish." She gave a slight smile.

Nick's mouth trembled. "What kind of fish?" he asked.

"Clown fish."

"No, my love. You are too strong and elegant. You will be a manta ray or an eagle ray."

"I...like...eagle...rays."

"I know." I know everything about you, he thought. I know you can't pass a lavender bush without feeling the leaves and sniffing its scent. I know how you smile when you see a yellow finch. I know where you keep your secret stash of semisweet chocolate chips.

"Nick...hold me."

Nick stretched out beside her, as he had done daily for forty years. As tenderly as he could, he rolled her over so her head rested on his shoulder, wrapping her, protecting her in his arms. She felt so fragile to him, almost as brittle as dried twigs.

"I've...always...loved your...strength."

But it's of no use now, he thought. Nick kissed her hair. "I've always loved your strength as well." She couldn't see his face, so he didn't try to control the tears, not that he could have.

"You have...to let...me go." Each word wheezed out, grew fainter and fainter.

"I don't know how." His heart beat faster and his whole body shuddered.

She inched her hand to lay over his heart. "You have to...say goodbye." He didn't answer her. "Nick...our paths...part...here. You...have a...different journey...to take."

"What journey could I ever take without you?" he asked, trying to keep her talking.

"You have...to go back...you have to...feel it...You have...to say...goodbye."

Nick's lungs burned with each of her breaths. He couldn't help her, couldn't stop this. His world was collapsing down on him.

"I will be...right here." She rubbed her fingers over his heart. "Promise me!"

"I promise." He tightened his hold on her, knowing what was coming.

"It's time." She closed her eyes. "Goodbye...Nick Mitchel."

Tears overflowed, running down his face. "Goodbye, Jeannette Crawford Mitchel."

She took one last, deep breath.

It happened. He knew it had happened. His arms cradled her body, but it wasn't her anymore. He felt the moment her spirit left, the void back-filled with some invisible mass. What was he supposed to do now? Their bedroom was the same. No, it wasn't. A putrid, sweet odor articulated death's victory. In its last act, death took his heart, leaving a mechanical pump in its place. Why the hell couldn't it have taken him? What was the purpose of staying?

"Dad," said Anthony in a whisper, "I called Christine. She said Hospice would help with..."

Nick opened his eyes. His son stood at the foot of the bed, his arm around his sister, while she cried. Nick nodded. A task had to be performed. Duty called him into action and he grabbed it as the life ring it was. Gently, he rolled Jeanne back over, kissed her forehead, and stood up. Jeanne lay there like she was asleep. How many times had he watched her nose twitch and eyelashes flutter while she dreamed? How many times had he softly kissed her awake until she was fully alive in his arms? This time, he fell back into the well-ingrained habits of the last couple of years and quietly turned away, not wanting to disturb her. After he wiped his eyes, he pulled both kids into his arms for a tight hug. "Let's go to the living room," he said in a low voice.

The doorbell rang, and Anthony went to answer it.

"Dad," said Dana, wiping her own eyes, "I'm going to bed. I want to make sure Jani doesn't wake up and comes out. I don't want her to see—"

Nick nodded.

Christine, from Hospice, arrived, followed by two men from the mortuary. Nick did his best to talk coherently with them, answering their questions, agreeing with schedules. Part of him wanted to yell, *GO AWAY! She's just sleeping!* The robot part of him held control, clinging to the tasks that had to be done. He directed the men to the bedroom.

As Jeanne's illness had progressed, his mind had projected to her death, probably some self-protection mechanism to prepare him. Whatever the reason, it had been a complete and utter failure. But in all his projections, this moment, this scene, this agony never showed itself. She wanted to die in her own bed, and Nick made sure she did. Yet, it never occurred to him what it would feel like to watch her carried out with a blanket over her head. This is something seen in movies, not real life. Until this moment, he could pretend. God, he wanted to scream at the men to stop, leave her! Take me instead! She would wake up and then bring him the death certificates. He wanted to grab her from the gurney and pull her into a dance around the bank accounts. Lose himself in her beautiful eyes. Make love to her under the obituary. Ripped in two, he was half heart and half robot, and they raged against each other, neither containing a brain. With every step the men took, his shell cracked, his will crumbled.

The final nail was in place as he stood there, staring at the closed door. His legs, somehow rigid enough, kept him standing. Nothing made sense. His mind reeled, while his head rolled like a bobble-head doll.

"Dad, are you okay?" Anthony asked, putting a hand on Nick's shoulder.

Nick didn't move. *If you can't let him go, bury your emotions. Bury them deep.* Where did those words come from?

"Dad?"

Nick's eyes narrowed, then he shook his head to come back from some place, long forgotten. He took a deep breath and turned to his son. "I'm alright. How are you?"

"Not sure." Anthony gave a subtle shrug, lowering his arm. "I feel like I've been run over by a truck." He paused, his shoulders slumped like a helpless man adrift without a rudder. "What do we need to do now?"

Anthony stood eye to eye with Nick, the same build, the same straight nose, but he had his mother's eyes. Nick gazed into those eyes and saw the mixture of Jeanne's spirit and Anthony's confusion. Putting an arm around his son's shoulders, he squeezed. "We go on." His voice went down an octave. "That's what your mom wanted. We just go on." Nick took another deep breath and put on a slight smile. "You've missed a lot of work. Why don't you go home, get a little sleep, then check in with your office?"

"But I can help you."

"There isn't much to do." Nick shrugged. "Your mom was clear about what she wanted. I'll take care of...the arrangements this afternoon. And at some point, mow the grass. The neighbors have been very patient with me. This morning I'll try to catch up on some sleep." He saw Anthony's uncertainty. "I'll call you when I need help, I promise. The best thing we all can do right now is to get back to our routine. Activity helps."

Anthony's face showed his uncertainty. "Alright. How about I come over this weekend and help you tackle the gardens?"

"I'd appreciate that. Thank you." Nick wrapped his arms around his son, trying to give strength as much as he was needing some as well. When they broke apart, Anthony gave a shallow smile, then left.

Nick walked back to the living room and sat down in his chair. For all his words to Anthony, Nick was wandering in an abyss, a fog. *We go on.* How? There were no immediate demands, no orders, no missions. A vacuum sucking him down to some deep hole.

Little Jani ran past him into his bedroom, her soft stomps rushing into the bathroom. She came back out, looking as lost as he felt. "Why did grandma have to go to heaven?" she asked. Jani stood in her butterfly pajamas that no longer fit growing legs. Her eyes, that hadn't completely woken up yet, welled with tears. Early morning light peaking around the drapes cast a diaphanous glow around her tangled blond hair.

Nick didn't think he had enough heart left to feel, but something tore inside him. He opened his arms. Clutching her little stuffed red bear, she ran to his lap. He pulled a soft baby blue blanket over and wrapped her up in it, then gave her a corner to rub against her cheek. Nick hugged his granddaughter close to his chest, resting her head next to his heart. In the desolate sink hole he was existing in, this little body with little arms and little ears brought a little ray of light. The two sat there in silence, listening to the soft ticking of the anniversary clock on the mantel. A tiny silver thimble wedged between the fibers of the carpet behind his foot. He breathed in her wonderful tiny child's sweet smell, as a drowning man tries to breathe fresh oxygen. Why? That was the question. *How do I explain this to a four-year-old when I don't understand it myself? How do I help her accept that her favorite person in the world is gone? And so is mine. That Wednesdays won't be grandma day anymore. They won't make play dough animals or finger paint pictures together. How do I fill this void in her life when I am a void?* There was no way to understand when love is ripped away. He sat there, trying to find the words that she could understand.

"It was grandma's turn to be an angel," he said. "So she can help other people who need her."

"But I need her," Jani said, her voice as small as she was. Her body shuddered against him.

So do I. He gently rubbed the blanket covering her back.

"Oh, Sweet Pea," he said, "Grandma is going to help people who don't have anyone else. She will always watch over you as well. Every time you see a butterfly, it will be Grandma coming to see you." As Nick hoped, at the idea of butterflies, Jani calmed down. "We still have each other, and your mommy and daddy."

"And Uncle Anty?" she asked.

"Yes," he said, smiling, "Uncle Anty as well. And you have red bear." She pulled the stuffed toy up to rest on Nick's chest. The bear was well loved, with one particular ear more loved than the other. His bow tie was undone, again.

"Will I be an angel?" she asked, with a bit of fear in those words.

"No," he said quickly. The mere idea of losing Jani caused a brief panic attack. "Not until you are very old." His arms pulled a little tighter.

"You are very old. Are you going to be an angel?" she asked, the worry still there.

Nick smiled again at her honesty, though words failed him. It made sense that Jeanne, with all her love and kindness, would be an angel, but Nick knew he didn't qualify. "No, Sweet Pea," he said, "I'm not going to be an angel."

Two

August 15, 1985 - Davenport, Iowa

Natalie Thornton, her hands deep in a sink full of dishes, watched fat rain drops pelt the window. The clanging of her gate told her she hadn't shut it. That could wait. She didn't mind summer storms. They never lasted long and her yard needed the water. Dark black clouds seemed appropriate today. The heavens should be crying and howling. Today was a day for such sadness. Natalie had cried herself out last night.

When the phone rang, she shook off the suds, dried her hands, and reached for it. "Hello?"

"Nat, it's me." The voice was a plaintive whisper.

"Nick," she said, pressing a hand to her heart. "Are you doing okay?" she asked the required, yet stupid, question.

"Yeah, I'm alright. Who called you?" he asked, his voice cold and raspy.

No, you're not, she thought, but there was no need to state the obvious. "Dana called last night. I was going to call you tonight. I know last night was hell." She listened, but no response came. "Nick?"

"I'm here." Natalie could hear the tremble in his voice. She sat down at the table, pulling an arm around herself. A calming tea tree scent infused the air from a votive candle on the table next to a vase filled with white and red carnations. She had picked them up yesterday, trying to bring some beauty at this horrible time. They didn't work.

"How did you make it after Carl died?" he asked.

Her yellow short-sleeve shirt she was wearing should have been warm enough, yet she shivered. Not from cold, but from memories. *How do I explain the un-explainable? That your mind has complete clarity on what happened, yet no longer functions properly? Your life is torn in two, diametrically pulling you apart. Both lives are only shells, facades, with no heart. Simultaneously living and dead. That you want to scream at people at their oblivion of the magnitude of what's happened. No, words are useless. Experience is the only way to understand this part of life.* Instead, she shared the practical activities. "There was so much I had to do right after he passed I went from task to task for a while. When those ended, I threw myself into work."

"How did you make it through the nights?" She could hear that fear in his voice at this question. "During the day, I can find things to do or get in the car and drive."

"The nights are the worst," she said. "Some nights, I held his pillow and cried. It still had his smell and when it wore off, I splashed a little of his English Leather aftershave on it. Other nights, I couldn't face the bed, so I slept on the couch, usually with the TV on. I wasn't getting much sleep, anyway."

"She was sick for so long," his voice rose, "you'd think I would've been ready for it."

Natalie's heart broke for him. "You're never ready for it. It will get better. Keep breathing. Go through the motions of life for a while. When you find yourself with time, try to remember the happy times when you laughed together. Those memories are your salvation." Nat listened, but there was only silence. The wind died down so that the ticking of her wall clock was the only sound. "Nick? Are you still there?"

"Yes," he said. Nat held the phone closer to pick up each word. "I don't know if I can make it." The words shook out of him.

"Yes, you will," Nat said with determination. "It was Jeanne's time to go. Not yours."

"I know, I'm just tired." Something in his voice made her uneasy. Considering what he was going through, he would sound odd. She shook off the feeling.

"I know, three years is a long time to battle. It's going to take a long time to heal and get your bearings again," she said. "When's the service?"

"A week from Saturday," he said, his voice a bit stronger. "Are you going to be able to make it?"

"Of course. I'll actually be there the day after tomorrow. I booked my ticket right after Dana called."

"You can have the guest room, if you want it. Jeanne's sister will stay with Dana."

This was the Nick she knew, on top of details. "That works, thanks. How's Anthony doing?"

"Not well. He's not saying much."

"I wonder where he picked up that trait."

"Yeah, like father, like son."

That made her smile. "I can't count the number of times I heard Jeanne say that." Again, there was silence on the line. This time, she waited. A crumb leftover from her toasted cheese sandwich sat on the place-mat. Three pictures she had brought over from the fireplace mantel this morning stared back at her.

"She wants me to go back," he said, his voice barely audible.

"I know. She and I talked about it a while back." That something in his voice was back. Nat was very glad she would be there soon. "Don't think about that yet. Let yourself be for a while."

"Okay," he said, sounding like he'd been given a reprieve.

"Nick, if you need to talk before I get there, or just need to hear another voice, call whenever, day or night. I never sleep through the night, anyway."

"Thanks Nat." The line disconnected.

Natalie stared at the phone. Her heart aching for him. Nick was special to her, like a brother from the time she was a little girl. He always referred to her as his little sister. Secretly, though, Nat had had the biggest crush on him. So tall, so nice, so happy. No matter what he and her brother James were doing, Nick made time to talk to her and ask about her activities. When she'd had her piano recitals, he came with James to watch. Never missing any, until they both left for the war.

She'd held out hope that, after the war, Nick would fall in love with her. But nothing ever goes as planned in a war. Her wonderful brother died. When Nick came home, he was different. Still nice and thoughtful, but a part of him had died too. Or maybe it was the kid in him that had died, as it had in all of them. Also, Nick came back in love with Jeanne. When Nat first heard this, she'd been overcome with jealousy and anger that this woman had destroyed her little girl fantasies. Meeting Jeanne changed her mind, though, as Nat loved her as well. Jeanne became the sister she'd never had. There was also a nagging belief that Nick's love for his wife was what brought him back.

The picture of her and Jeanne was about twenty years old. They were on a friend's sailboat in Ventura Harbor, posing like sun goddesses, holding up their glasses of frozen strawberry margaritas, laughing as they almost always did together. That was a good day, sailing in the morning and having dinner on the boat that evening. *Back when I actually looked good in a bathing suit. I could be myself with Jeanne. No artifice, no judgment.* Kindred spirits, friends, sisters. How much fun they had together and with their families. Her death caused a hole that Nat knew would never be filled.

She picked up one of the other pictures, a very old black-and-white photo of a trio of beautiful boys. James, Nick, and Tony, laughing in their khaki Navy uniforms, were home for only a day before heading to their next level of training. Nat was young enough to see it as an adventure they were going on. Nothing bad could happen to them. So strong, so confident, so invincible. Young heroes. It wasn't until she saw her mother and saw the fear etched on her face that the possibilities entered Nat's consciousness. She quashed them, telling herself that her mother was being a worrywart. After the boys left, life continued its routine. Until one day, about a year later, a telegram came. Her mother's legs gave out, and Nat caught her to break the fall. While on the floor, she glanced up as her father read. "We regret to inform you that your son, Lieutenant James Steven Carson, is missing in action." Nat watched the light in his eyes die. It was then that reality hit her. Fragments of hope lasted until they received the letter from Nick.

The photo next to that was of her wedding day to Carl Thornton. Another casualty of the war. He survived, but never got over it. That war took so much.

Three

September 3, 1986 – Ventura, California

Nick's head thrashed back and forth. Eyes wild under the closed lids. Bombs exploded. "NOOO! Tony, pull up, pull up!" someone screamed. "Get us the hell out of here!" came over the radio. "Torpedo away." So cold. Each exhale fogged his windshield. "There's one behind us." "Keep the canopy open," the commander ordered. "Let's get a table. Where's Tony?" "Bull's-eye, bull's-eye." "He's late. He saw Jeanne off at the train." A little boy, in a boat, stood with his arms out. James flew ahead to the right and yanked his plane up. "You want a beer?" Nick saw it, but the stick wouldn't move. It blew, throwing the plane to the right. "We're hit!" Danny yelled. "Jason's hurt." Engine stalls. Tony walked in, smiling a big grin. No power. "Guess what? Jeanne and I are engaged." Jeanne's beautiful face stared back at Nick from the picture jammed in the control panel. The cabin reeked of burning fuel. Beer ran down his neck, filling his suit. Arms froze, the stick froze, the plane froze. Nothing worked. "Nick, what are you doing? Pull up, pull up! Do something!" James sat beside him in the one-man cockpit. "I'm sorry, Nick. I'm so sorry. I should have taken that shell." Explosions all around. Jeanne's soft voice whispered in his ear. "It's okay Nick." The radio broadcasted the guys screaming their pain. Cold air whipped around his face. The nose slowly began to move down. Gravity took control. Nick watched, fascinated, as the view ahead changed from the beautiful blue smoky sky to green burning islands, then to blue gray burning water. Huge waves rolled in the cold. A tropical storm brought in the cold snow. The plane picked up speed, faster, faster, faster as it raced toward the wall of water, the end, the finish, the termination. Picket boats are too far away to make it in time. Climb out on the wing. Nick tried to wrestle free from his straps. Nothing. He lost all feeling in his legs, welded to his seat. "Am I hit?" Ahead JC's eyes grew larger and larger, head nodded the invitation: join me. Falling, falling, falling, falling. Why isn't my life passing before me? Isn't that part of the process? This is it! He closed his eyes, threw his arms up in front of his face. Yell...

"NOOO!" Nick bolted up, struggling to breathe, eyes jumping around the living room. Furniture waves exploding up. Family picture above the instrument panel. His pulse raced as fast as he was flying. Anti-aircraft fire pushed him around. Empty plant pots strafing the table. His hands felt his gray sweat suit. His toes felt the carpet. Reality inched ahead in his mind. Home. His throat was dry and raw. Nick realized that he had screamed out loud. Tension in his shoulders eased as the nightmare cleared. He leaned his head back and rounded his lips to blow out, extending each exhale, calming his breathing. Moisture around his eyes felt cold on his skin.

His pulse and breathing returned to normal. Feeling more secure in his own recliner, Nick scanned the room. Jeanne's conch shell, with the dried fan coral attached, sat on one of the shelves. She had found it on a pile of shells in Tobago Cays. Board games stacked on the bottom, ready for the game nights they used to play. Little Jani sitting on his lap, as he tried to teach her Monopoly. But she wanted to play with the little metal game pieces, several of which went missing after that night. College graduation pictures of Anthony and Dana, many years old, gave evidence of fleeting time. Books and figurines collected through the years brought more comforting memories.

The mantel was built out of driftwood he'd found after a storm. He remembered the hours he had spent planing one side to get it flat enough. On it stood the antique brass anniversary clock and the box of Jeanne's ashes. A brass plaque on the front of the box stated her full name, a name that he uttered only twice. Her parents called her Jeannette, but to Nick, she was Jeanne. A thick, fat dust bunny leaned up against it. Nick knew what he needed to do, but doing it was another thing. He peered at the family photo, confused by his own smiling face. Why was it so hard to remember being happy? Memories confirmed that man had been happy, yet now he felt no connection to those feelings.

Nick's stomach growled, motivating him up and into the kitchen. He opened the refrigerator door in the hopes that it was fuller today than yesterday. No, the food fairy hadn't come. An old jar of mustard, two dehydrated carrots, a tub of butter, a bag of moldy lettuce, and a shriveled cherry tomato stuck on one of the wire shelves were the only options. Opening the freezer would be equally useless. Nothing to eat. Cold air floated around him. "I need to go to the store and get a rotisserie chicken," he said to no one. "Anything, something. Nothing sounds good. I don't want to cook. I don't want to eat. I don't want to go," he yelled, then exhaled, deflating his anger.

"Yet I don't know how to stay either." Nick finally uttered the words that had been hiding under his surface. "I don't want anything. I don't want to have to think. I don't want to feel. I don't feel. I'm numb. For three, no, four years I lived in hell watching her waste away. What's left to feel about? She's gone and all I have left are the bombs!" he yelled again. "She took the only good part of me with her. I want out. I want to sleep, to escape. But there is no escape. They come when I sleep. I left them. It's over. Why are they coming now? What the hell am I supposed to do?" He stopped and waited for an answer, but the hum of the refrigerator gave no guidance.

Nick slammed the door shut and turned to examine the kitchen. "Empty. The whole goddamn house is empty. My life is empty." Leaning back against the door, he slid down to the floor. A bottle cap sat under the cabinet. "I guess I'm supposed to pick that up," he said. "Who the hell is going to care? Who the hell is going to even see it?" The kitchen was dark. The drapes closed off everything that could be light, that might spark life. Pops and crackles came from the refrigerator compressor. Nick noticed the stains on his sweatpants. He couldn't remember when he'd changed his clothes last. *What's the point?* He sat there and noticed a smell. *What the hell is that?* He leaned forward enough to realize the stench was him. "I could take a shower. For whom? I could change my clothes. For whom?" He leaned his head back and closed his eyes. A pair of eyes stared back at him. He couldn't get away from them. Wherever he went, they followed.

He opened his eyes again. A dark, dusty, lonely house. "I could go to work, but I don't have any ideas. I'm as useless there as I am here. I have to do something, but what? I have no goal, no destination. I'm a dead ship, floundering in this house. Can a person release their past? Can I say 'abracadabra' and everything that happened is no longer? If I do that, then I have to release the good as well, and I don't want that part to go. I want what I had." Futility summed up his life. "I can't have what I want. What the hell is left?" He covered his face with his hands, massaging his forehead, then ran his hands up through his hair. "Jeanne, what the hell do I do now?" Jeanne's words came back to him. *You have to go back. You have to feel it. You have to say goodbye.* "How am I supposed to go back? They're all gone. I don't know how to do this."

A hushed, rhythmic sound came from the other room. "What the hell?" The pattern became clear. "Oh no." Anger exploded in him as he jumped and almost ran back to the living room. The anniversary clock rang out its Ode To Joy chime, mocking Nick with its dulcet tones. Nick grabbed the clock with both hands, raising it above his head. "I have no control over anything else, but I damn well don't have to take this from you!" His target was the brick fireplace. He moved his arms down to launch the missile, then stopped, closing his eyes. Jeanne was there, in Paris, smiling as she listened to the beautiful chime. She loved Ode To Joy. It was one of the songs played at their wedding. Nick brought the clock back down, knowing it wasn't to blame. Killing it wouldn't solve anything, nor would it make him feel better. Instead, he shut it off, sentencing it to permanent silence. Nick placed it back on the mantel, then blew off the dust bunny and rested his forehead against Jeanne's box. *Something is going to have to change.*

Four

September 10, 1986

Natalie paid the driver and got her bag. The house appeared the same as it had when she came for Jeanne's funeral. However, the yard was neglected, the flower beds overgrown, and the grass was dropping its seeds. Nick used to pride himself on his beautiful yard. Maybe Dana had been right when she called to ask for help. Nat had come out to see for herself, as well as help if he needed it. The question was: what help did he need?

She came up the stone walk entrance, both sides lined with lovely tall red canna lilies. Unfortunately, dead flowers cluttered the weed-infested ground. At the door, she rang the bell and admired the detailed carved dark wood depicting a giant bird of paradise blooms. After several moments, she rang it again. Dana had said Nick would be at home, but maybe she should have called first.

Finally, the door opened.

"Surprise!" she said. Smiling, she let out the breath that she didn't realize she had been holding.

Nick stood in the open door, his eyes not recognizing her. Finally, he reacted. "Natalie! What are you doing here?"

The instant she saw his face, she knew he was in trouble. He sported a heavy beard and his clothes were not only a mess, but looked two sizes too big. His normal salt and pepper hair was now very heavy on the salt. The real alarm was his sagging blue eyes, very dark and very lost.

"It's nice to see you, too. May I come in?"

"Oh yeah, of course," he said, backing up to let her in. "It's good to see you. Why didn't you call? I could have picked you up at the airport."

"I wanted it to be a surprise. I flew in about an hour ago and took a cab. Do I get a hug?"

"Yes," he said. Nick stooped down a few inches, then pulled her in for a big hug.

Natalie balanced up on her toes to meet him halfway and held on a few extra seconds. She felt far more bones in this hug. She pulled back to smile at him and tried to hide a cringe from his odor. "You always give good hugs."

"You look good, Nat," he said, and his eyes seemed to mean it.

"For an almost sixty-year-old woman, you mean?" she laughed. "Thank you. I'll take the compliment. It's starting to get cooler back home, so I thought I would treat myself to a vacation in sunny Southern California. I bought some new shorts and covered up most of the gray hair with auburn, hoping that would make me feel a little younger. Unfortunately, I can't seem to get rid of the wrinkles. Oh well. Mind if I put my suitcase in the guestroom?"

"I didn't expect you, so it isn't clean," Nick said, then took her bag for her. "Here, I'll put it in there for you."

"Thank you and don't worry about the room. I'll clean it." Now inside, she stopped, disappointed at the dark gloomy room. Nick designed this house and made the far wall full-size windows that normally showcased the spectacular view. When opened, the interior and exterior spaces merged, summoning everyone out to the patio and a beautiful ocean view. Natalie took the opportunity to glance around, noting the thick dust everywhere, but also the suspicious absence of anything that should have been here. No newspapers spread about, no cups, no books.

Nick came back and studied her intently under heavily guarded eyes. "Nat, it's not like you to spring up like this without letting me know. What are you really doing here?"

"Are you seriously asking me that?" she asked, with her hands on her hips. "What do you think I'm doing here?"

"Dana called you, didn't she?" Shaking his head, Nick walked into the living room, turned back around, planting his legs, preparing for battle. "Well, I'm fine. I don't need you here," he said.

"Oh really? Look around, Nick. This place is filthy." She wiped her fingers on the table, holding them up to produce the evidence. "Obviously, you need help cleaning, or is your goal to plant grass all over the house? You know, there is a wonderful invention called a vacuum cleaner. Or better yet, pick up the phone and call a cleaning service."

"There is also something called a hotel. There are lots of them around, with a nice comfortable one by the airport. If you want clean, go there!" He stormed off into the kitchen.

Nat smiled, relieved to see some emotion out of him, which meant he wasn't completely lost. All she had to do was get him upset enough to break through the wall he'd built up and, she thought, turning around until she spied the side table, head off his escape routes. She grabbed his car keys from the small tray and stuffed them in her pocket.

"First things first," she muttered, then went and yanked the drapes open. A dust storm blew up, forcing her to step back to breathe. Now she could admire the beautiful view. The house sat on top of a hill overlooking the endless blue. Glancing around the yard, it was clear that Nick wasn't the only living thing needing tender loving care. Turning back around, the house cheered up a bit in the light. When Jeanne was well, there used to be beautiful floral arrangements everywhere. White was the predominant color scheme for the furniture, tile, and walls. Dramatic seascape paintings depicting waves crashing, thunderstorms, and sunsets hung around the walls. The floral arrangements were her other passion to splash color around. Roses, lilies, carnations, hibiscus, everything grew here. With Jeanne gone, the home had lost its color, its soul.

Nat took a deep breath, drew her shoulders back, and followed Nick into the kitchen. "Well, I knew this room would be cleaner, since you've given up eating," she said, as she surveyed the room, then opened the refrigerator. "I guess we'll be going out to eat." Nat turned back around to him. "Oh, and don't blame Dana. I heard from Anthony as well."

Scowling at her, he grumbled, "If you're going to follow me everywhere, I'm going to leave."

"Since I took your car keys," she said with a gloating smile, "you'll have to walk, and I'll follow."

Nick glared at her. "What do you want?"

"Come with me," she said and led him back to the living room. Nat sat down on the couch. "Please sit down."

Nick hesitated, then sat in his chair. "Fine. Now tell me what you want, then get out."

Natalie cocked one eyebrow and stared intently into his eyes. "Oh, make no mistake about this. I am not leaving anytime soon."

Nick took a deep breath. "What do you want?" he repeated.

"I want you to grow up and stop behaving like a scared little boy!"

"What?" Nick yelled, then grabbed the arms of the chair. "Of all the ridiculous things to..."

Natalie immediately cut him off, yelling louder. "Jeanne died. She's gone. You lost your wife, the love of your life, your best friend. Now, you're wallowing away."

"I am allowed to grieve, aren't I?" he said, turning his head away.

"Grieve, yes, waste away. No! It's been over a year. It's time to begin to get on top of this."

"I'm fine." He threw his hands in the air. "Why won't anyone believe that?"

"Really? You think you're fine? Look at yourself! How much weight have you lost? Your clothes don't even fit you anymore. Those pants would never stay up if you didn't tie the drawstring. This house is absolutely arctic. Who the hell lives in sunny California with the air set at freezing, drapes closed, wearing a sweat suit? Your yard is a mess. Inside is a dust bowl. You're turning into ZZ Top, and you stink."

"Big deal! I can gain back the weight or I can buy new clothes. And you came unannounced and uninvited, so you get what you get."

"You yelled at Anthony for caring about you!" Natalie saw the regret briefly pass over him before he could fight back.

"I'm his father," he said, his jaw muscles flexing. "Yelling at him when he steps out of line is in my job description!"

"Oh, that's pathetic. He tried to help you and you intentionally drove him away because you're scared." Natalie jumped up and walked to the fireplace, lowering her voice. "And this Nick?" she asked, placing her hand on the box of ashes. "When Jeanne lay dying in your arms, did she specifically ask you to keep her ashes on the fireplace mantel?" Nat steeled herself when she saw the anguish in his eyes, loving him enough to keep going.

"That's a low blow, Nat," he whispered, rubbing his hands on his thighs.

"If I went into her closet, I'm going to bet that all of her clothes are still there as well. Dana said you wouldn't let her go through them. She actually could wear some of Jeanne's clothes and I promise you that Jeanne would like that. Is keeping them around helping you to pretend that she isn't gone?"

"I'll deal with them when I'm ready," he said very quietly, looking down.

"And when will that be?" Nat asked more gently. "What's going to be different in your life tomorrow or the next day?

You've withdrawn from life and are only existing here. Jeanne would be furious at you for taking this lovely home and turning it into a mausoleum!"

"You don't understand…"

Natalie came over and knelt by Nick's legs. "You know damn well I do. I watched Carl go through this for years before he finally died."

"I'm not drinking myself to death." Nick shifted in his chair, rubbing his hands together.

"No, you've picked a different poison, depression, and it's eating away at you. I will not allow you to do this anymore. You have too many people who want you back. Good God, even little Jani is asking what's wrong with grandpa? She lost her grandma, now she's afraid to lose you. Anthony and Dana don't know what to do with you. And now I hear you're going to retire and sell your business? Have you lost your mind? You've loved being an architect." Nat stayed there with her hands on the arm of the chair, waiting.

"Did you come all this way to yell at me?" His eyes shot daggers at her.

"No, it's just a bonus," she said, smiling again.

"God, you're a pain in the ass!"

"That's what sisters are for, and you aren't getting around me!"

"What do you want me to do?"

"Stop hiding! Do what Jeanne asked you to do. Spread her ashes, say goodbye, then let her go." Nat could see his face contort in pain. She softened her voice. "Nick, it was her time to go, not yours. I'm convinced you two are soul mates, so you'll see her again. But it's time to let her go. After that, you have to go back somewhere and you know it." Nat watched Nick's face turn white.

"I don't want to do that," he said in a whisper.

"Of course you don't want to do that! No one in their right mind would want to do that. But you're a grownup and we grownups have to do what's necessary, not what we want!"

"Stop treating me like a child!"

"Stop acting like one! Something happened to you during the war, and you never dealt with it. You tried to forget it, didn't you? However, you can't, can you? Now your life has been turned upside down. You're in between chapters and the past came back. You won't be able to go on with life until you face whatever it is. Carl had the same choice, but he gave in and you know how his life turned out. That war never ended for him. He suffered those nightmares for thirty years, until he became one more casualty. Is that what you want? How long are you going to suffer? Will giving up your life make Jeanne happy? Will it actually help anything from the past?"

"It's my life, my choice!" Nick jumped up, walking away. Nat fell back on her hands.

She scrambled to her feet and followed. "You don't even know the choice you're making, so let me lay it out for you. Your kids are grown, your wife has died, and now you're willingly giving up your passion. You aren't playing golf or going out at all. You've clearly stopped eating anything of substance. No wonder you're all messed up. You've come to a fork in the road. You have to choose between living, which means doing the hard things to deal with everything, or death. So, as you said, it's your choice." When no response came, she continued. "Well, which is it going to be? Are you going to be a man and deal with all this, or are you going to continue to commit suicide until you're successful?"

Nick's mouth dropped open, then his eyes narrowed. "You're being melodramatic..."

Natalie cut him off again. "So you're choosing suicide. Fine, I'll notify the kids. Dana has a responsibility to protect Jani, so she won't allow her to see you anymore. I'll tell Anthony not to come over as well. If you want to speed things up, stop drinking water. It's faster than not eating. Of course, you could just get a gun and blow your brains out. That would make it really quick. If you choose that route, let me know. I don't want Anthony to have to find you that way."

Nick's mouth dropped open. "I'm grieving for my wife, and now you have me dead. I think you're the one who's crazy."

"You chose the road. I'm only helping you see the end of it. Or are you going to choose to live instead? That road starts ugly, but in the end it's a beautiful ride."

Nick slumped back down in his chair. "You can't understand, Nat," he said.

"You're right, I wasn't there. I didn't experience the horrors that you, James, Jeanne, and Carl did. But war isn't the only hell on earth."

"I'm not saying it is."

"You still haven't answered my question."

"I've lost my ideas. That's why I'm retiring. I have no passion for it anymore. No, I've been thinking about this for a while. I talked with Jeanne about my work, showed her my drawings, she always had comments, a balanced perspective. I can't go on with my life the way it was, because every routine thing I do reinforces that she isn't coming back." Nick's shoulders sagged down, defeated. "I have to change my life, and I don't have the foggiest idea of how to do that."

Nick had always been in control, caring for others. Admitting this impotency cost him dearly. Nat knelt down on the floor next to him again and took his hand in hers. "That I do understand. But you're going about it the wrong way. You can't move on until you close the two chapters of your life, Jeanne and the war."

Nick nodded, dread covering his face.

"Where do you need to go Nick?" He sat there for so long Natalie began to wonder if he heard her.

"Truk."

Natalie sat there, stunned. In her mind, she figured it would be Okinawa or some other place. Not Truk. She knew that was where James was shot down. He and Nick had been such close friends, but she didn't think that was what haunted Nick. No, something else, something bigger, must have happened there.

"It's going to be a tough trip," she said.

"Yes."

The idea came so quickly she didn't think. "Would you mind if I went with you?" As soon as the words were out, she question herself, but thinking more about it, she liked the idea. Nick didn't respond at all. "So you haven't said a word."

His brow wrinkled as he looked at her. "I'm surprised. Why would you want to go?"

"I know it's sudden and I've never thought about it before. We never had a grave at home to visit James. The last day I saw him was when you two stopped after CQ training and that was an unhappy visit. Truk is really James' last resting place. Going is sort of my chance to say goodbye to him." Nat got up and sat down on the couch again. "I know this sounds strange because you told us about the crash, but part of me always hoped that he was still alive somewhere. Mom, Dad, and I never had a service for him. We just all hoped without ever talking about it. I never closed that chapter. I guess you could say that I acclimated to him being gone. If you don't want me to come, tell me, and I won't."

"I don't know. I hadn't anticipated that you'd want to. But I can see why you might." He ran his hand through his hair. "Are you wanting to dive?"

"It's been a couple of years since I was diving, but yes, I think I will."

Again, Nick sat there in silence.

Natalie shook her head and sighed. "Nick, I don't know what happened to you during the war. Lord knows you didn't talk about it anymore than Carl did. So if you're going back to Truk, it isn't only for James. If you let me go, I promise, I'm not going to play mother hen with you. I realize that this is sudden, but I want to go for me. I never got to say goodbye to my brother, and I never got to understand what Carl went through. I know he was never at Truk, but I'm not going to Okinawa. I see this as a way of finding closure for myself. So, what do you think?"

"Okay, I get it."

"When do you want to go?"

Nick closed his eyes. "February."

The two were quiet for a few minutes.

"What are you going to do with Jeanne's ashes?" she asked. Now that he moved on one area, she had to keep pushing to get him moving on the other.

"I'm pretty sure the flights to Truk will have to connect in Hawaii. I can go a day early and place them on the reef she loved so much. It's what she wanted."

"Do you want me to go with you?"

"No, she asked me to do this. It will be our last dive together."

"If it's alright, I'll fly with you to Hawaii and you can go on your own to place her ashes. I'll be fine by myself. Then we can go from there."

"Alright."

"What are you going to do until then?"

"I have to resolve the business."

"Nick, are you really sure about that?"

"Yes." His voice sounded a bit stronger. "I'll let you know when I have more details." He stood up. "I'm going to take a nap." He gave her a small smile. "Afterwards, I'll take a shower." Then he walked off.

After he left, she sagged back against the couch cushions, drained but relieved. She hadn't expected him to be this far gone, which scared the hell out of her. Now that he seemed to break out enough to make decisions, she felt a bit better. Nat had never seen him like this. Nick had always been the strong one, the one who quietly took charge. Today he seemed so defeated, far more than the normal grieving process, if there was a normal grieving.

Truk was a surprise for her. This needed some actual thought. Truk was not a spur-of-the-moment getaway. She hadn't been on a dive recently, so she needed to schedule a refresher. Nat knew a lot about Truk, though. When Nick had gotten home from the war, he told her and her parents a brief version of what happened. When the discovery made the news, she did a lot of research on what was there and watched the Jacques Cousteau show about it. A slim hope existed that she might see James' plane, but then would she want to? That reality had her shaking her head. Definitely not!

Although she said she wouldn't play mother hen, part of her wanted to go for Nick. Jeanne had told her about how Nick would withdraw periodically. That scared Nat. She had watched her own husband do that for years, until one day he never came out of it. Nat knew that, without Jeanne, Nick was vulnerable to do this as well. She wasn't planning on losing another brother.

Part II – Junichi

"How much more grievous are the consequences of anger than the causes of it."   Marcus Aurelius, Meditations

Five

October 5, 1986 - Kyoto, Japan

The streets of Kyoto were quiet this early in the morning. The sunrise failed to break through the heavy, moist clouds that had moved in, painting the valley in a deep dark gray. Some clouds broke free to sink below the surrounding mountains. Junichi Takahashi glanced up to see parts of the beautiful Kiyomizu temple peer out from under its gray blanket. There would be rain today. He could smell it in the air, feel it on his skin, and knew it in his heart. When this ended, would the rain help wash the bad away and bring a fresh start? He knew the answer to this.

Junichi continued to walk down the street. The casual black slacks and white button-down shirt he wore might, at a quick glance, indicate that this was a businessman out for an early morning stroll. But his gait gave a different impression. With a strong and determined stride, his eyes looked down at the road as his every step pounded down on it. Anyone watching this man would see his dark expression, his anger, his frustration in his walk, in his face, in the rigid set of his shoulders. Anyone peering into his dark brown eyes would see the sadness, the pain.

Junichi checked his watch, relieved to see it was not his turn yet. His father's care was shared between him, his mother, and his wife. He still had more time and kept walking. Junichi knew fear and terror, and he knew death. He had seen it, he even stared it in the eyes. His grandparents, on his mother's side, died when he was very young. In fact, he was uncertain what happened to them, but unfortunately, he had a good idea. His other grandfather passed a few years back; which was sad, but the man had a very long life. Now, however, it was to be his father, and this was different. This was complicated.

Frustrated with himself, he took a deep breath. He was forty-six years old, a grown man, a father to a nineteen-year-old son. Yet when he sat before his father, he became the frightened seven-year-old boy he was that day they met, so many years ago. A man shouldn't feel this way. He was being ridiculous. He was an adult, a successful businessman. He walked faster.

When his father died, would the complications die with him? No, Junichi admitted, the problems weren't between him and his father. Their relationship had not had the often dominant father expecting his son to follow the path he set and the subsequent teenage rebellion to assert independence. His father had been loving and supportive. They had actually never argued and disagreed only once. Even at the height of Junichi's anger, he could never bring himself to take it out on his father. Kaito Takahashi had always suffered, not only from the physical impairments inflicted on him but also by painful emotional scars from the memories, realities, and disillusions of his world. Junichi stopped and turned back toward the house. No, today would not end the complications. He was going to have to find another way.

When he reached the house, he saw his wife, Shoko, standing outside. Her smile was sad, but her eyes were loving.

"Is he...?" Junichi did not dare finish the question.

She shook her head, no. "Your mother is with him, but she asked for you come in as soon as you got back." Junichi nodded and headed into the entrance to take his shoes off before going into the house.

His mother met him at the bedroom door, tears on her face. "Junichi, it is time." The news punched him in the gut. He fought to take a breath. He immediately looked at his father lying there on his futon, covered in a thick white blanket, and went to sit by his side. Although his eyes were closed, Junichi knew he was still awake. Part of him wanted to ask him what he was thinking, but the other part did not want the words spoken out loud. Thoughts were one thing; memories were definitely another. Junichi knew what was going on. His father had been on this slow road for a very long time; a road that, once a person traveled, had only one exit. Junichi's body made it clear that knowing this was coming did not prepare one for it.

"Junichi," his father said in a frantic whisper, holding his hand up like a child wanting to be held. The old man had suffered, his body now mostly a skeleton under the sheet, showing the very last bit of holdout from the endless pain.

Junichi quickly took the frail, shaking hand between his own, willing his strength to extend to his father. "I am here." Junichi would not cry. He would not show weakness.

"I am...sorry...I could not...be the...father...that you...deserved."

At those words, the river broke free from the control and ran down Junichi's face. "No, I have always been honored to be your son," he whispered and kissed the old man's hand.

Kaito struggled to open his eyes, gazed at his son with all the love he had, silently moving his mouth trying to form the words. Junichi bent down to hear his father's last words. "Junichi...my...son." Kaito Takahashi took one final deep breath.

"Goodbye, Papa." Junichi stayed, holding his father's hand to his cheek, desperately wanting his grip returned, but knowing it never would be again.

At some point, Junichi became aware of a gentle hand on his shoulder. "Come, Junichi," his mother said.

Junichi gently laid his father's hand on the bed, taking one last look at him, poised in endless sleep. He got up and left the room with his mother.

In the next room, Junichi pulled his mother into his arms. The two of them had been through this entire journey together. Kana Takahashi wrapped her arms around him, both drawing comfort from each other. She was so small, at only five feet. Junichi towered over her by a good ten inches. He willed his strength to go to her now. She smiled at Junichi, putting a hand up on his cheek. He saw the resigned acceptance in her exhausted eyes. Her tight smile also showed a bit of relief. Then she walked back in to her husband.

His wife, Shoko, came and wrapped her arms around him. Junichi held her tight. She pulled back. "Junichi, go out to the garden for a while. I will help your mother prepare him," she said.

Gratefully, he nodded to his wife and went to the garden.

The karesansui garden, sometimes called a Zen garden, was one of Junichi's favorite places. He built it many years ago for his father. This type of garden intentionally had no water, but rather was designed to give the impression of water through the use of gravel, which could signify water, and larger rocks suggesting islands. He patterned part of this design after a garden at one of the sub-temples in the Daitoku-ji complex, which was his father's favorite. A larger gray-brown rock formed an island at the far end, with smaller rocks jutting out like a peninsula. Junichi lovingly tended to it, pruning the weeping cherry tree, if needed, re-raking the whitish gravel into curves resembling gentle waves surrounding the little islands, and generally cleaning up around the moss and rocks. The leaves of the cherry tree were now the color of rust for fall. He knew the pale pink blossoms his father loved so well would be back in the spring. A small bamboo tube dribbled water over several black rocks, completing the serene sanctuary. Not a particularly big garden, nonetheless, it did provide a refuge for mediation and inspiration.

Now Junichi sat there alone. He would never talk with his father again. Kaito was at peace. Or will be soon. Junichi would see to that.

Not sure of his feelings, of course, there was always anger. He resented that the responsibilities fell to him. There also seemed to be a gaping hole in his life, yet partially filled with relief for his father, as he was now free from pain and, ashamed to admit, relief for himself. Junichi had watched his father's slow inevitable death, from almost the first day he met him, almost forty years ago. Now Kaito was gone. The funeral would be soon. After that, he had only one more task to finish for his father.

Six

July 14, 1986

"What are you thinking about, Father?" asked Junichi. Kaito, wrapped in his favorite lapis blue kimono, had been quiet, staring out to the garden. His body was very thin and frail.

"Time," Kaito said. "Time is both our greatest ally and our most unforgiving adversary."

Junichi glanced at the paper and pencil on the table. "Is this what you are writing about?"

Kaito stared down at the paper. "No, I was writing about what I will say to my friend when I join him."

Junichi's eyebrows shot up. His father had not left the house in several months, nor asked for any friend to come to visit. "Who is the friend you wish to see? I will invite him over for you."

Kaito did not look up. "His name is Takeo," he said in a quiet voice, "and you can not invite him here. I believe he died many years ago."

Junichi did not ask his father why he was uncertain about a death. Thousands, if not millions, of people in Japan disappeared during the war. However, his father had never mentioned this friend before and Junichi was a bit hurt his father had never shared this part of his life with him.

"May I ask who Takeo was to you, and how do you think he died?"

"Takeo was in the navy with me, and I believe he died in battle."

"What do you wish to say to him?"

"I wish to explain what happened during and after the war."

Junichi's mouth fell open. "Father," he said, "I believe his soul already knows what happened."

Kaito glanced over at Junichi and smiled. "I am not crazy, my son. I believe that as well. However, this is for me. My time is ending very soon. Having this knowledge makes me think through my life, see the choices I made, what I accomplished, what is left unsaid, and what is left undone."

"May I read it?" Junichi never realized that his father had not resolved this and wanted to know his thoughts. The war was one subject his father never brought up, and for his own reasons, Junichi did not ask about either.

"Yes, you may, when it is finished."

Junichi sat there, frustrated by his own impotence. The older his father got, the less power Junichi had to help alleviate the pain, the inevitable. "Is there something that you wish to do? I will help you."

"There is somewhere I should go, but it is a trip that I can no longer take."

Junichi understood this, as his father's health had deteriorated rapidly these last few weeks, and he had grown weaker. Soon, Junichi would have to help him move from room to room. His mother did not have the strength for that. "Where do you want to go?"

"The island of Natsu-Shima."

"Natsu-Shima...I mean..." Junichi stammered, then shook his head. "Father, I am surprised. Why would you want to go back there?"

"Want is not the correct word. I am compelled to go, but there is no desire. I have many memories from there. Some good, some bad." Kaito became quiet again.

"Father," Junichi asked, "did you want to go to war?"

"At that time, yes. I, like many of my friends, believed in our invincibility. When the war started in 1931, I waited impatiently for eight years until I was old enough to join. When it was my time, I wanted to go into the navy. I had always dreamed of the ocean, and that was my chance to experience it. I was assigned to the Heian Maru, a submarine tender, so we were part of the support fleet in battles, never in the actual fighting. I met Takeo on the ship. We shared the same dreams and became very close friends. We sailed over much of the Pacific. I loved it.

"My favorite base was on Natsu-Shima. In my off hours, I would swim and see the sharks and rays. Other days, I would walk and explore the islands. I met friends at restaurants or Saki houses to share our stories. A couple of friends, from the tankers Nippon Maru and Shinkoku Maru, had been at the attack on Pearl Harbor. It was thrilling to hear their stories of the great victory. The town was a proper town that many of the other navy bases did not have. There were shops, barbers, post offices, movie theater, and, of course, comfort houses."

Junichi glanced at his father, the unspoken question in his eyes.

Kaito smiled. "No, I did not go to those."

Junichi smiled as well. "As her son, I am glad. As a man, what stopped you?"

Kaito pulled out a very old photo from the pocket in his kimono and handed it to Junichi. "She did."

The black-and-white photo, badly warped and creased with torn edges, showed Kana on her wedding day. "She was beautiful," Junichi said, smiling at his mother's picture.

"Yes, she is. I love your mother very much. I was the luckiest man in the world when she agreed to marry me. Both of our parents wanted the union. She, of course, would never show any emotion to me before the wedding. After though, she told me I was the one she wanted." Kaito took the photo back. "I carried her photo in my pocket every day. I do not know how it survived."

Junichi watched as his father's eyes darkened and wanted to see him happy again. "I remember the day you came home. Her smile radiated in a way I had never seen, pure happiness."

Kaito smiled at the comment, then his face turned serious again. "She deserved so much more than I became."

"No..."

"Yes," Kaito said emphatically. "That battle, those two days, the next two and a half years..." Kaito fell silent.

Junichi watched his father's face tense, not knowing what to do to help him. In all the years they had talked, Kaito had never gone into detail about what happened during the battle.

"After the raid started, the captain ordered most of the crew off the ship. He was concerned a bomb could explode the torpedoes we had in the ship holds. Takeo and I were part of the skeleton crew kept on board. She was such a massive ship, an easy target. When the planes came for us, I jumped on one of our guns and started firing. A dive bomber got us, and the explosion blew me off the ship. My leg was badly cut and broken. I was able to swim to shore, crawled out, and took cover wherever I could. I found some pipes to help me walk. The bombs kept coming. It was hard to find a break to make my way to other shelters.

"At one point, one of the officers ran up to me. I thought he would help me, but instead he started beating me, yelling for me to get a gun and start fighting. I limped over to a bunker. One of the men inside helped me wrap up my leg. I spent the rest of the battle shooting and hiding from the bombs. After the raid was over, there were so many more severely wounded, as well as hospitals damaged, that in the end my leg was never set properly."

"Did no one help you?" An image of his father laying somewhere wounded with no help turned Junichi's stomach.

Kaito smiled. "Yes, a local man, native to the islands, helped me. He found me under a tree. I had developed an infection and was very sick. The man carried me back to his family. They used coconut husk fibers to stitch up my leg and coconut sap to treat the infection. He also made a better splint. We became...friends. I..." Kaito shook his head. "I have to think on this."

Junichi had watched his father's face reflect each of the varied emotions as the memories came. He did not want to upset him further, but he needed to fully understand. "And Takeo?" he asked softly.

Kaito's shoulders slumped with a long exhale. "That morning was the last time I saw him."

He stared at the ground for several moments, then looked up at Junichi. "Natsu-Shima was the war for me. I left it there, but never ended it. I have a request of you, my son. After I am gone, take the trip that I could not. Resolve this for me. There it will end for me. Then I will be at peace."

Seven

October 6, 1986

On the day of the funeral, Junichi left early for the crematorium to meet with the priest and ensure everything would be ready. Though not as devout a believer as his father, Junichi appreciated the formality and pageantry of the Buddhist ceremony, as it was designed to transition the soul from this world to the eternal. The rituals were a well-established and easy process to follow, which was helpful. Despite watching his father's long decline, Junichi was far more affected than he had anticipated.

As he was walking, a physical pressure bore down on him. The sky filled with clouds, heavy with moisture, yet not enough to release, weighed on his shoulders, increasing with each step. Approaching the building, he noticed a repugnant, almost sweet smell hung in the air, encircling him. A cold sweat engulfed him as his body racked by uncontrollable trembling. *No, I cannot get sick now!* He staggered over to a tree, falling to his hands and knees. Revulsion took over his body, vomit exploded to empty whatever was inside. As the retching continued, Junichi heard his grandfather, long dead, yelling at him to wake up.

Eight

March 9, 1945 - Tokyo, Japan

Junichi jumped up, awoken by his grandfather yelling. A strange noise blared so loud, he looked around to see where it was coming from. "What is that noise, Mama?"

"Sirens, Junichi. They mean airplanes are coming." She bent down and put her hands on either side of his face, making sure she had his full attention. "You have to stay right by my side. Do you understand me? Right by my side!"

"Yes, Mama," he said, still confused, his heart pounding. His mother grabbed his hand and pulled him up. Both gripped tight as they rushed from the bedroom to the outer room, his grandfather's workshop.

"Put your shoes on, Junichi, quickly!"

Junichi sat down and picked up his sandals, then noticed that his grandfather's lathe was still running. "Mama..."

"Hurry," his mother yelled. Then she grabbed his arm and pulled him up and out the door.

The moment they met up with his grandparents outside the house, a massive explosion occurred far down the street. Terrified, Junichi jumped at his mother, wrapping his arms around her waist. After that, every few minutes, a new explosion occurred.

"They are bombing the Shitamachi District," his grandfather said. He glanced around his workshop, then back to Kana. "They are after our small factories."

Junichi had no idea what that meant. They heard many more planes overhead. He raised his face to see more explosions and fires, burning buildings and homes.

His grandfather whipped around, grabbing his mother's shoulder. "Kana, my child, take Junichi and go. Run as fast as you can! Follow the river!"

"But you and Mama will come, too!" Her voice cracked as the words came out.

"Kana, nothing is going to stop that fire! I will take care of your mother, now GO!"

Junichi watched her nod to her father and her mother. She grabbed Junichi's hand and pulled him. "Junichi, we have to run, run fast!" The wind whipped around them, pushing them as they ran. They weren't the only ones running.

Bombs were now dropping every minute, bringing more fires, more screams. The heat was inexorable. The center of the inferno instantly incinerated anything it touched. Tokyo had descended into hell.

They ran as fast as they could. His mother pulled him to the left to try to get closer to the river. Another bomb exploded, its force throwing them to the ground. Junichi peeked behind them. The fires had merged into a single wall of flame racing toward them. The wood and paper houses provided the perfect feast for the ravenous inferno.

Even in the dead of night, the massive fire lit up the scene, forever burning the images into his memory. He watched his house consumed by flames; his grandparents were nowhere to be seen. "Junichi, go!" his mother yelled as she yanked him up.

They were surrounded by people now, all running and screaming in desperation. Windows exploded from the rising heat, throwing their molten shards like tiny burning daggers at anyone within reach. A couple of people fell down in front of them. His mother stopped to help them up. Junichi glanced back again to see a monstrous demon. The swirling vortex of fire sucking up everyone and everything near it. He saw people screaming as they were pulled in and devoured. Junichi tried to scream for his mother, but the essential breath wouldn't come. His body couldn't move, his eyes frozen open. Human debris circling, forming eyes for the demon, staring at him as it marched confidently, menacingly at him. He was to be the next meal.

Another bomb exploded, this time next to the demon. Only it seemed to have greater power as it redirected the demon in another direction. His mother yanked him again, this time toward the crowd that was heading for safety in the river. Their screams halted his mother, causing him to run into her back. He stared in horror at the people in the water, desperately trying to crawl back out. The water churned not only from their desperate movements but also from bubbles jumping around. The river was boiling from the heat of the fires, cooking the people to feed the demon.

Another bomb exploded, throwing a woman and her child into him and his mother, knocking them down. The woman was wailing in pain as much of one side of her was gone. She pleaded to his mother, holding her daughter up. "Haroko, take her, take her!"

His mother took the crying infant. Junichi watched as the woman's hands fell down, her screams silenced forever.

"Run, Junichi! Run!" cried his mother, holding the baby with one arm, pulling Junichi with the other. "Don't look back, just run straight down the road!"

And he ran, too terrified to think. His shirt, the only thin protection he had between the heat and his skin, was searing his back. His feet burned from the heat of the road under his shoes. Yet he ran. The new explosions seemed to be far behind them. Junichi didn't stop, terror providing the strength to run on. The screams behind slowly faded away. The winds still blew, but this time in their faces.

He didn't know how long they ran, but at some point, his mother slowed, as did the others around them. The bombs exploding far in the distance. Only the glow of the fire was still visible. They walked parallel to the river, which was full of charred bodies giving off the most repulsive, sweet stench.

The group finally stopped, and everyone collapsed to the ground, exhausted and quiet. He and his mother looked at each other, then she glanced down at the silent infant in her arms. Tears gushed from her eyes. Junichi looked at the child, her tiny eyes open, her body not moving. He didn't know what to do. He had never seen his mother cry. The sight of her sobbing so hard was almost as frightening as the fire. Instinctively, he got up and put his arms around her, as she had held him before. He buried his face in her neck, moving back and forth with her while she rocked the child.

A few other people saw what was going on, dug a shallow grave, and took the tiny infant from Kana's arms. His mother immediately pulled Junichi on her lap, rocking him while they both cried as little Haroko was buried. Afterwards, Kana and Junichi lay down while exhaustion took over.

Nine

Rain brought Junichi out of his memories. Wiping tears away, he regained control, but sat there, confused. He had buried these memories long ago, or so he thought. *What brought this on?* Then he smelled the air again. The crematorium, burning flesh. Closing his nose, Junichi took several deep breaths through his mouth, trying to calm his stomach.

He and his mother never saw his grandparents again after that night. Never had any word if they made it. Estimates of the death from the Tokyo fire bomb ranged between 100,000 to 300,000 that night, with many more following. Junichi later learned an estimated one and a half million people lived in the sixteen square miles that burned down. While some had already left the city, many had remained. Entire families perished that night with no one left to bear witness to their lives. The real death toll would be impossible to determine. That night of black snow, as it came to be known, was the single most deadly air raid in the history of mankind.

Junichi rolled to his knees and leaned on the tree to get up. He steadied himself, then went into the crematorium to find a bathroom. He needed to clean up and call his wife to bring him some clothes.

After the funeral, friends and family gathered at the house to share support. Once everyone left, Shoko took over cleaning up and shooed Junichi out to the garden.

Closure, conclusion, ending. Why had these not come? Funerals were supposed to bring them. Junichi paced around the garden like a penned-up leopard, not knowing, not understanding how he felt, what he wanted. His father's was the first death he had experienced in his adult life, as well as the first funeral he attended. Now what? Go back to work? No, he needed to stay and help his mother for a few more days.

Junichi stopped pacing and peered at the garden. The earlier rain had cleared, leaving only a few billowy clouds. Though the ground had dried, the stagnant humid air was heavy and oppressive. Leaves scattered over the rocks by the storm needed to be picked up. The stone path should be swept. Tasks. He could do tasks, but none of them made any difference to him. What about me? I've done tasks all my life! Is that really all a life is—tasks, responsibilities?

Now he also had to go to Natsu-Shima. Junichi knew what was there. The news reported the discoveries. It was also the last place he wanted to go. Though he and Shoko loved scuba diving, neither one of them had wanted to go to those islands. His hands balled into fists, longing to hit something. The knowledge that the tomb of so many of his countrymen was now a popular vacation spot for scuba divers turned his stomach. What sort of sick people would happily explore the graves of others?

Glancing around the garden showed nothing he could hit without destroying it. He paced again. With each step, the tension in his arms eased. Where does joy, laughter, and happiness come in? Precious few of these existed in his life. In their place had been fear, terror, and anger. Always anger, always work.

The funeral stressed peace and calm, yet during the service, Junichi felt like an actor playing a part, the dutiful son, honoring his father, becoming head of the family. Afterwards, friends stayed on and talked of Kaito's life. How casually everyone discussed how Junichi met his father, as if on that day, their relationship magically cemented, instantly forming one big happy family. It had not worked that way. Kaito left for the navy before he knew Kana was pregnant. When he came home, he was just as much a stranger as any other new face was. It took a long time for Junichi to get to know Kaito. Though, did he ever really know him? His father would not speak of much of his life. But then, neither did Junichi share all of his own life. It seemed that the two of them usually spoke of tasks. Not of nightmares, nor of dreams. Inserting Kaito into the calm life that came after the war changed so much. A new room had to be partitioned for Junichi, as he could no longer share a room with his mother. When he had nightmares, he had them alone. Early in life, circumstances forced Junichi to learn independence, and he learned it well.

Junichi sat down in one of the wooden chairs, not bothering to dust it off. A small torn piece of paper stuck out from underneath a candle on the oval wood table between the chairs. The soothing rhythm of the babbling water calmed him. To be fair, Kaito had tried to be a good father. He was a kind man, never angry, always supportive. Love grew between them.

Kaito was not well the day he came home and never really recovered. Regardless of the extra work having him home caused, his mother had been very happy at Kaito's return. They were at this house, and his grandfather had still been alive.

Ten

November 11, 1946

Junichi sat on the ground by the chicken coop, enjoying the rare warm sunshine in November, warm enough that he ran around in bare feet. He picked up a feather and brushed its softness on his toes. No clouds, no wind. It was a nice day. Taking care of the chickens was Junichi's biggest responsibility, and it was an important job because his mother traded the eggs for fish, meat, or anything they needed. They had many chickens: nine hens, one rooster, and six young hens, that were not really chicks anymore. The hens were nice, but the rooster could be mean. Junichi fed them all, cleaned up after them, and of course got the eggs every day. Two of the hens laid light blue eggs. The chickens were not pets, his mother told him, but they were to Junichi. Secretly, he named them all and, when he was alone outside, he talked out loud to them. Junichi liked it best when the baby chicks were born. He and his mother would have to gather and separate them from the older hens so that the babies did not get picked on. Junichi fiercely protected the babies. They were not big enough to protect themselves. The chickens were his friends. He did not play with other children. Although the war was over, everyone stayed close to their own homes, working.

Kana tended the garden, pulling weeds, and mixing the dried leaves into the dirt. She said it helped prepare the soil for next year. Junichi thought the mix of clucking, crunching leaves, and the thump of the falling dirt made interesting music.

"Kana," a man said.

Junichi glanced up when he heard the strange voice, then stared at the man standing by the door. He leaned heavily to one side, supported by a cane, and wore a dirty uniform that had many holes in it. His grandfather was standing in the doorway, oddly smiling and crying at the same time. Junichi watched as his mother gasped and dropped her hoe. Her fingers touched her open lips. She stood frozen, her eyes wider than Junichi had ever seen.

"Kaito?" she asked in a soft voice. Junichi knew Kaito was the name of his father. The man nodded and started crying, then Kana ran and threw her arms around the man.

Junichi stayed where he was and watched. No man had ever held his mother that way. The only person who had hugged his mother was Junichi. Now the stranger kissed her. He wasn't sure how he felt about this, but it was not good. The three adults were smiling and crying. Junichi could not feel either emotion. Tears were for sadness and smiling was for happiness. This was strange.

Then the man, with his arm still around his mother, turned toward him. "Junichi," he said whispering.

Junichi did not move. He did not know this man; he was a stranger. How was he supposed to be happy?

"Junichi," his mother said, "come here." Kana extended her hand out, her fingers bending in invitation. For a moment Junichi stared at her, as her face radiated sunlight, her eyes sparkling in the wet joy. Seeing his mother so happy brought a warmth inside him. Yet there was also a sadness that Junichi never made her this happy. He got up and slowly walked to them. His young heart began to pound. How was he supposed to act? What was he supposed to say?

His grandfather brought a chair over and Kaito sat down. The man's tears continued to flow. "Junichi," he said in a clearer voice, then took Junichi's hands in his. "I am your father."

Junichi stood there and stared at the man. His grandfather had told him once that he looked like his father. Junichi wondered if he was going to have such a long thin face and so much gray hair.

"For so many years, I have pictured in my mind what you looked like. The real you is so much better. The thought of you and your mother is what saved me." His father was crying harder now. "I love you, my son." Then he pulled Junichi into his chest and held him for a long time.

Eleven

Kana came out, sat down in the other seat, and took a long, deep breath of air, letting it out slowly. "It's always so peaceful here. Your father loved this garden so much. Thank you for taking care of it all these years." She had changed into her white kimono and looked exhausted.

Junichi was quiet. This day had been far more difficult than he had ever imagined.

"When will you go?" Kana asked quietly, staring at the water flowing.

Junichi knew what she was asking, but did not want to think about it. One more task. At least this would be the last task he ever did for his father. This thought was selfish and petty. Kaito had not chosen his fate. It was not fair to feel this way. He was the son. It was his responsibility. "February," he said, then turned to her. "Will you come?"

"No," she said, shaking her head. "I made my peace. Take Shoko with you. The trip will be good for her as well." Kana handed an envelope to Junichi. "He left you this letter, but asked that you not read it until you are there."

His face tightened as his lips pressed together. "Why?" He took it and squinted at the envelope. *What now? Why? Why could he not tell me himself?*

"Junichi, look at me," his mother said in a surprisingly strong voice.

He turned to gaze into her loving eyes.

"Junichi, you had to become a man when you were only a boy. Your father and I hated what you had to do, but he and I are also so proud of your strength, your honor. No son could have been better. You have accepted one last task to bring him peace, and I know that you do not wish to go."

Junichi looked away, not wanting to upset his mother. Her hand covered his arm and squeezed. Turning back, he saw love shine in her eyes and felt its warm comfort flow into his arm.

"You hide your feelings well, my son, but never from me. I know you want to be free, though you are not yet clear on what you want freedom from. Go on this trip. Go and see it all. Be your father's eyes, both the young and the old. Maybe there you will find what you are seeking. It is time for you to find peace."

His face relaxed, and he nodded in agreement, knowing what she said was true. How was the bigger question? His mother always knew how to calm him down. It struck Junichi that she, who had just lost her husband, was thinking about him. Then he realized that the two of them never sat here together, never talked about her life. Both had shared part of the joyous burden of taking care of his father, but his mother's portion was much larger. She also shouldered the burden of raising him for the most part on her own. Junichi really looked at her now. The wrinkles around her mouth and eyes, overwhelming gray in her hair. Physical exhaustion in her slumped shoulders, the loss of hopes and dreams in her caramel eyes. Her small body began to display the weakness of a much older age brought on by years of endless work, yet he still saw her strong spirit.

As he verbalized his thoughts, his voice shared the awe of his realizations. "You and I never sat out here talking. You were always working, taking care of father, taking care of grandfather, taking care of me. I never said thank you." His tone deepened at his thoughtlessness.

Her eyes grew large. "Junichi," she said, shaking her head, "you do not have to thank me."

He ignored her protest, his eyes never leaving hers. "Your determination that night saved our lives. You were willing to stop and help those people when no one else would. You took that little girl to try to save her. You pushed us to get to Kyoto. You were always there for me, always there for father." He reached for her hand, feeling the softness, the frailness of it, almost for the first time. He kissed her hand. A new resolve came over him, his voice stronger. He gazed into her shocked, tear-filled eyes. "You are right that I need to find peace. That has to start with me telling you how much you mean to me, how much I admire you, and that any good that I am is because of your support and guidance." He smiled at her, his eyes full of all the words he could not say. "You are not alone. I will always take care of you, Mama."

Part III – The Journey

"No man ever steps in the same river twice, for it's not the same river and he is not the same man."   Heraclitus

Twelve

"You'll call me, won't you, dad? I promise not to keep you for long. I just need to know that you are alright," Dana said. The four of them stood at the gate, surrounded by a lot of excited people all dressed for a tropical destination. LAX was a beehive of activity, as usual, even at this ridiculously early hour.

Nick smiled down into his daughter's worried eyes. "Yes, I will. However, I probably won't be able to call when I reach Truk." It never ceased to amaze Nick how Dana's expressions and mannerisms were the same as Jeanne's, except her eyes. She had Nick's eyes. "Don't worry about me. I'm fine."

"I do worry about you. This isn't a regular vacation." Dana reached down and ran her hands over the box her brother was holding. "It's like we have to say goodbye to Mom all over again," she said. Tears formed in Dana's eyes, tearing at Nick's heart. He gathered her in a big hug, wishing he could make it all better, but he was feeling the same way. Nick glanced up at his son, who was standing very straight with rigid shoulders, trying to maintain control.

"I can still go with you...if you want," he said.

"Anthony, I'm getting ready to board the plane."

"You know very well that I can take another flight and meet you there."

Nick released Dana, straightened up and gave a confident smile. "I know you can, but your mom asked me to do this."

"You'll call me?" Dana asked Natalie.

"Yes," Nat said, then gave her a hug.

"Now," said Nick, "you two need to stop worrying. I'm fine. Really. We're going to two different island paradises, and we'll be able to relax in the sunshine, dive on some beautiful corals, drink pina coladas, and listen to the ocean. Actually, in many ways, I'm looking forward to the break. Plus, Nat will watch out for me, won't you?" Natalie nodded. He could see that neither of his kids believed him, but he kept the smile plastered on his face.

"Final call for flight number 3267 to Honolulu, now boarding gate 53," came over the loudspeaker.

"That's our flight." Nick reached to take the box from Anthony and handed it to Natalie. "This will be a quick trip. We'll be back in a week and a half. You two take care. I love you both so much." He pulled them both to him, letting his arms communicate how much they meant to him. "See you soon," he said, as he stepped back, his voice low and gruff. Nick took the box from Nat and turned quickly to board the plane.

He kept up his composure until he found his seat. Then he let his shoulders slump. Maintaining control was for the kids' sake, but he was tired of being strong. In fact, he was just tired. He placed Jeanne's box under the seat in front of him. It turned his stomach, knowing that his wife was sitting on the floor with a broken pretzel on the floor next to her. That thought process wasn't helping, so he focused on getting situated for the long flight.

Once settled, he leaned back and closed his eyes. *I am so full of shit! I don't want to do this!* Relaxation, enjoyment. How could those words actually come out of his mouth? Burying his love, saying goodbye, going back to memories he'd intentionally forgotten. *Damn it, Jeanne.* She knew what she was doing when she made him promise. How could he say no? Though it took Anthony and Natalie to move him into action.

Reluctantly, Nick admitted Natalie had helped him. She'd stayed for three weeks, because, according to her, that was how long it took to set new habits. Part sister, part friend, part drill sergeant. She made him do things. Together they cleaned the house, opened the drapes again, bringing light back into his life. She ordered Nick and Anthony to clean up the yard, as well as the patio furniture. He ate, he walked, he cleaned himself up. All the planning details for the trip were Nick's responsibility, though Nat checked in on his progress like a teacher hounding him to do his homework. The activity was good, it gave the impression of purpose.

The hardest part was when she convinced him to let Dana and Anthony clean out Jeanne's personal items. Nick stayed outside that day. Dana kept most of the jewelry, except for Jeanne's engagement and wedding rings. Nick gave those to Anthony, so that he could give them to someone special if he wanted to. Jani also had the opportunity to choose some of grandma's items. She took the seashells and crystal fish from the bottom shelves, which surprised Nick until it dawned on him those were the items she saw as she played on the floor.

Another blow hit when he walked back into his bedroom that day. Her clothes, shoes, jewelry box, all gone. Her end table emptied. The cookbook that sat for so long on top disappeared. Jeanne had wanted to learn to cook Moroccan food and asked for a Tagine for Christmas. The romance novels reread and dog-eared were her go-to for light, feel good reading. Sudoku puzzles to clear her mind. In the bathroom, lotions, a glass jar of cotton balls, removed from the vanity. Her bottle of Joy perfume, that Nick always bought for her, was now missing.

Just stuff, irrelevant, inanimate objects, yet personally selected by Jeanne. But they weren't irrelevant. Each was a puzzle piece of her life. Some held the meaning of an enduring passion, others a frivolous passing fancy. Holding on to her things, her ashes, all helped the illusion that reality was the true fraud. Absence of her belongings couldn't be ignored. Nat said that grief was acclimating to the new life, not getting over the absence of the old. One thing was perfectly clear—change sucked!

Now he was on a trip to who the hell knew. Trepidation filled every cell in his body. For the last several months, this trip was the future. Boarding the plane brought it to the now. He knew what he had to do in Hawaii. He didn't want to do it, but it was clear. It was a task, and he could complete tasks. Going on to Truk wasn't clear. It was an abyss, and always with this thought, eyes popped into his head. *I know I'm coming, but not yet.*

Nick opened his eyes and saw the final passengers board. A woman tried to herd her three little kids as they bounced down the aisle. The man that followed, heavily weighed down by bags and small cartoon backpacks, wearing no smile, was obviously the father. A smiling young couple in T-shirts and shorts still held hands as they walked single file, stealing glances at each other.

"Do you think they're on their honeymoon?" asked Nat.

Nick nodded as he continued to stare at the couple, but he saw himself and Jeanne when they were that age, boarding a plane to Hawaii for their honeymoon. It hit him that this was the first trip he wasn't taking with her. He wasn't part of a couple anymore. After forty years of marriage, he didn't know how to be a single. With Nat next to him, he could pretend he wasn't alone. Turning to her, he gave a slight smile. "I'm glad you're here."

Nat smiled and reached to squeeze his hand.

The flight attendants closed the door and prepared for take-off. Once completed, the engines revved up, and the plane pulled back from the gate. While they taxied to the runway, a flight attendant demonstrated the safety features. Nick flew enough he could recite the speech himself, so he closed his eyes and let his mind wander. Exhaustion took over, and the attendant's voice faded.

***

When the ship's loudspeaker shouted, "Pilots, man your planes," Lieutenant Nick "Gent" Mitchel, and Lieutenant James "Tom Cat" Carson jumped up to join the others running out of the room to the flight deck. Once he reached his plane, he walked around, inspecting the exterior of the TBM Avenger, then put his head inside to check in with the radioman/bombardier. "Jason, did you verify the ammo for both fifty caliber wing guns?"

"Yes, sir. I also verified my thirty caliber ventral gun. I'm going through the rest of my checklist now."

"I've got my ammo as well, Skipper," said Danny from the gunner's turret.

Nick climbed into the cockpit, stowed his plotter board, and began his interior checklist. After a few minutes, both the radioman and gunner completed their lists. The announcement came through the ship's loudspeaker. "Pilots, start your engines." After the deck crew signaled they were clear, Nick started his engine. A crewman held up the final check board and gave Nick taxi instructions. Once in line for takeoff, he lowered his wings and, with the aid of the deck crew, he confirmed the aileron, rudder, and elevator controls were free and the flaps were set for takeoff.

When it was his turn, the deck hands guided his plane to taxi out and hooked up the catapult. The Avenger was the largest of the attack planes, with a 54-foot wingspan and, when loaded with the almost 2000 pound torpedo, the plane weighed over 20,000 pounds. Although Nick didn't like the G forces from the catapult, it did make it easier to get this heavy bird up.

"Ready to launch." Nick went to full throttle, revved the single engine to 2600 rpm, forced his head back against the rest, held the stick tight and jammed his elbow in his gut to ensure he didn't pull the stick back during the launch. The signal flashed, and the force sucked him further back into the seat cushion. It only took 150 feet to reach seventy-five knots and clear the deck.

<hr>

"Nick," said Natalie as she elbowed his arm.

He opened his eyes. It took a moment to register that the plane was in the air and that Nat was looking at him.

"Are you with me?" Her eyebrows were drawn down, concern in her eyes. Nick was thankful she didn't ask anything else.

"Sorry, I must have dozed off." Nick shook his head awake and pushed himself up in the seat. He reached up and opened the air vent full blast to counter the sweat under his navy blue golf shirt. The plane had reached its cruising altitude and the flight attendant pushed the breakfast cart down the aisle, offering coffee, tea, or juice with the small pancake breakfast.

"You know, I never asked where we're staying. I feel bad that I left all the arrangements for you."

Nick cocked an eyebrow and pursed his lips. "No, you don't," he said. "You've been bossing me around for months." He then saw one corner of her mouth turn up. "Since it's only one night, we're staying at a little motel next to the airport."

Nat's shoulders dropped as she turned away, frowning.

"Ha, serves you right, leaving everything to me."

She turned back around. "Very funny, you twerp." Her eyes lit up. "Where are we really staying?"

"The Royal Hawaiian."

She lifted her hands in question.

"The pink one," he said, "on the beach."

"Really?!" Nat almost jumped out of her seat. "Thank you."

Nick had to smile at her excitement. "Well, we don't have much time, but you should do it right your first time there. We get in pretty early, and I have to go to the marina right away, so you can take the bags and drop them off. They'll hold them until check in. What are you going to do then?"

"Are you kidding? I'm from Iowa. Of course, I'm going to the beach. Unless..."

Nick immediately shook his head and his smile vanished.

"Okay, then I plan to be a tourist all day. I'll be back for dinner if you want to meet up then."

"Maybe. I'll leave you a message if I do. Otherwise, I'll see you in the morning."

"Alright." Nat rummaged in her bag and brought out an envelope for Nick. "I forgot to give this to you earlier. I didn't think you had a copy." Nick opened it and pulled out a heavy gray paper folder. Inside was a black-and-white picture of James, Tony, and Nick in their khaki US Navy uniforms, taken a few minutes before they left for flight school.

Nat grabbed the little pillow and got comfortable against the bulkhead. "I hope you don't mind, but I have got to sleep."

"Not at all. I know how grumpy you get when you haven't slept," he said with half a smile.

"You're a real comedian today. Good night." It didn't take long, and she was out.

Nick shook his head, envying her ability to drop off that quickly. Nat was easy to be around. Even as a kid, she was happy and easygoing. Life had thrown her several challenges, and she'd overcome them all. Now at fifty-nine, she had a calm confidence about her, not caring what others thought, not stressing about little inconsequential issues. She was comfortable with herself, which was an incredibly attractive trait. Her auburn hair, mixed with a fair amount of gray, cut short and curling around her face. A few more wrinkles, though she called them laugh lines, darted from her eyes and mouth. Her smile made them disappear. It's so sad James couldn't have lived to enjoy his sister. After Nick got back from the war, he doubled his efforts to keep up with her, for James' sake, as well as his own. He and Jeanne became aunt and uncle to Nat's daughter, Alex. It had been a joy to watch her grow up. Natalie had been an aunt to his kids as well.

He gazed down at the picture, running his fingers over the other men, his friends. How he missed them. His Mom would say, go out and play and come back for lunch. Nick joyously loved the freedom and went to meet up with James and Tony—the Three Musketeers. They spent their days fighting bad guys, always winning and saving the day. Little Natalie would try to play, and they would save her from the bandits, but she would get bored when the boys focused on the fighting, hiding in the bushes, planning their strategy.

As they got older, they planned their future. When it came time for them to do their part, they enlisted together. Tony didn't want to fly, but Nick convinced him it was the best chance for the three of them to stay together. It worked for a while.

Thirteen

December 1942 - Glenview, Illinois

What a cruddy day to fly. Not that he had a choice, Nick thought. Hopefully, they would be done quickly. What he really wanted was a cup of steaming hot coffee, which was out of the question, since they would be in a plane for several hours.

"You know, Iowa has cold winters, but the wind coming off Lake Michigan in December is ridiculous," said James. Tony pulled his jacket tighter.

This was the final stage of their training, Carrier Qualification (CQ), practicing taking off and landing from the deck of an aircraft carrier. They had done it on land earlier with normal land-based runways painted to look like the deck of a carrier.

This morning, the three joined the other pilots for a pre-flight briefing by Commander Bennet. "Good morning, gentlemen. You've finished your class work and practicing on the fields. Today, you will be introduced to our Corn Belt Fleet, where you will get the feel of taking off and landing on aircraft carriers. Understand that these ships, the USS *Wolverine* and the USS *Sable*, are really just retrofitted steam ships that traveled around the Great Lakes. The deck you will be landing on today is 550 feet long. Which is about a third shorter than the real carriers and is only twenty-six feet off the water. On the big boys, you'll be at least forty feet higher. In short, if you can land on *these* ships, you'll be able to handle the real ones.

"As you have been instructed, your flight group consists of six planes and will leave from Glenville. After you reach the shore, the flight group leader will radio the *Wolverine* and follow the air controller's direction from there. You will land and then go through your rotations from there. Your goal is eight completed patterns. The faster you're done, the faster you will get back here.

"Things to keep in mind today. The weather is slightly better than yesterday, but still pretty damn cold. Despite the temperature, you will need to keep your canopy open. This is necessary to enable you to get out quickly if you have to ditch the plane. There will be Coast Guard Picket boats out there to pick up anyone who has to ditch. If possible, get on top of the plane as fast as you can and stay there as long as you can. The water is frigid and hypothermia is a very serious threat.

"Also, the winds are blowing pretty strong, which will help takeoffs, but are causing some big waves. You'll have to time your landings, which, I appreciate, will not be easy. This is where the phrase 'controlled crash' comes from. Remember to watch the Landing Signal Officer, known as paddles, for your landing signal. Whatever happens, you are required to follow his signal. Failure to follow his signal will result in immediate court-martial. Gentlemen, you are being trained for combat operations. You have to follow all signals, period! Any questions?"

No one raised their hands.

"Alright, man your planes and good luck."

They got in their planes, started the engines, and moved into the line. Tony was fourth in line, then Nick. James was last. As their signals came, they took off. In the air, they fell into formation and flew out toward the lake. Nick could hear on the radio when their flight leader contacted the *Wolverine*. The wind was freezing, which was extra motivation to make sure every run was a success. He wanted to get out of the damn cold!

When they came parallel to the *Wolverine*, they began the first landing attempt. In thirty second increments, they each broke formation. Nick watched the flight leader turn into the wind. He got the signal from the paddles and landed successfully. Nick couldn't see the next two pilots as he was now ahead of the carrier. When it came his turn, he broke formation and turned back into the wind. Tony was ahead of him trying to time his landing on the ship as it rolled on top of the crest. *Yes!* Tony's hook snagged one of the arresting cables.

Now it was his turn. Dropping, he lowered his flaps, wheels, and finally, the hook. The ship was down low in the trough of a very big wave when the paddles flashed the signal to land. Nick had to get the plane down low enough to land, but also stay high enough to ensure the hook didn't catch the tail of the ship as it was rising on the wave. His heart beat fast and hard, while his stomach rolled as violently as the water. He cut his engine back, dropping abruptly. The rising deck slammed up against his falling plane, competing forces compressing his spine and rattling his head. He held his breath, hoping to catch one of eight arresting wires. Suddenly, he lurched forward. Success! He let out the breath he was holding. *Good lord! No wonder they call it a controlled crash!*

All six pilots made the first landing. But there was no time to celebrate, as they immediately received the signal to take off and do it again. *Good, let's get this over!* He watched ahead as the flight leader took off and banked left. They were to take off, move into formation, then circle the ship until it was time to land again. One by one, they took off. Nick watched Tony get his signal and take off. He got up and was well into banking left when the plane dropped. "Pull up, pull up!" Nick screamed. He sat there frozen, watching as time slowed to ensure his eyes would see every detail as his friend fell.

"Mitchel, your signal!" came over the radio. Nick's eyes stared ahead, registering the signal. His training took over. Like a robot, his body launched the plane; his eyes watched his friend. Tony's plane fell nose down and slammed into the water. Nick's heart stopped. "*NOOOO!*" he cried. It couldn't be real. As Nick banked his plane, he could see one of the Picket boats racing toward Tony's plane. He flew out of sight so he didn't know what happened. Nick's heart hurt. His hands shook. He was in shock. His mind picturing Tony in the cockpit, unhooking the straps, climbing out, swimming up to the surface. His radio came on with the order from the flight leader to prepare to land again. Again, his training took control: keep flying, stay in formation, watch for signals.

Rotation after rotation, they all flew as the day wore on, but no mention of Tony. Nick was in shock, yet functioned as a well-trained pilot. Nick missed a few of the landings, and so did James. . By the end of the long day, the group completed eight practice runs and then received orders to return to Glenview.

When they landed and taxied to a stop, Nick got out as fast as he could. He saw Commander Bennet and ran to him. "Sir, Ensign Tony Misner..."

Bennet held up his hand. "I'm sorry," he said. "Ensign Misner didn't make it. When his plane went in, he, for whatever reason, couldn't get out of the cockpit in time. The plane sank quickly and, with the waves, the salvage crew couldn't stop it. Misner went down with his plane."

Nick stood there. James put his hand on Nick's shoulder. "Thank you, sir," said James.

Commander Bennet's eyes softened. "I hear Misner was a friend of yours." Nick and James nodded their heads. "Listen to me..." Bennet said sternly, "both of you." Nick looked up into Bennet's eyes. "With war comes death. It's a horrible reality. He was your friend, but you have to let him go."

Rage burned inside Nick, his clenched fist desperately wanting to hit the Commander.

"If you can't let him go," Bennet continued, "bury your emotions, bury them deep. You can't let yourself get distracted up there." Bennet's voice softened. "Tony..." he said to Nick, "wouldn't want to be the cause of either of your deaths, would he?"

Hearing the Commander call him Tony had the desired effect. Nick understood. *No, Tony would not want that.*

"You both passed CQ today and will be shipping out tomorrow. Your orders will soon arrive, so pack your bags. Good luck to you both."

Fourteen

February 11, 1987 - Honolulu, Hawaii

A sleek white fifteen-foot motorboat quietly left the harbor. Nick headed straight out for a while before he turned east to ensure the boat didn't cause any problems for the early morning surfers. He stood at the wheel, under a white canopy, and gunned the motor. It had been years since Nick drove a boat and with the calmer morning water, his energy surged with the motor. He glanced back at the Honolulu skyline and noted several new high-rise buildings built since his last visit, which bore evidence of Waikiki's popularity. Up ahead was Diamond Head. Just the thought of it brought a smile at one of his happiest memories, the moment he met Jeanne, which was always followed with laughter over the crazy turn of events that night.

The boat rounded the island and turned northeast. Soon he passed Koko Head and Hanauma Bay. Here, he had to search for certain rocks as landmarks. His memory was a bit fuzzy, but then he saw them. He positioned the boat down current from the sight and set the anchor. The waves picked up some, but still not bad.

Earlier at the dive shop, he had changed into his swim trunks. He brought his own scuba gear, so he only needed to rent an air tank. Now he sat in the boat, rocking with the swells, not in any rush to get into his gear. It was a peaceful, crisp morning. Mother Nature cooperated as well. There was a little breeze, so the water was, relatively speaking, very calm. Sitting on one of the cushioned seats, Nick looked back toward land. He and Jeanne had spent a lot of time in Hawaii exploring every island. The lush beauty of the islands, the warm trade winds, and the slower island life helped bring a calm to Nick. Tension in his shoulders that had been there for longer than he could remember began to ease. Tightness in his chest loosened. Nick took in the whole panorama, thinking of the many happy times.

The sound of a ship's horn in the distance startled him. He glanced around, but there wasn't any boat nearby that needed help. His eyes spied the box containing Jeanne's ashes. His happiness faded as his mind came back to what he had to do today.

Nick dropped a drift line in the water that fortunately moved slowly. The current didn't appear to be too strong and there was good visibility. Scuba diving alone wasn't a particularly smart thing to do, but he had been to this dive site many times and it wasn't deep, nor was it in the usual lane of boat traffic. This was something he had to do alone, and somehow knowing Jeanne would be his dive buddy today was a talisman to his safety.

Oh, how Jeanne had loved to dive. It was one of the many passions they'd shared over the years. When scuba diving became a safe and popular sport, they both took lessons. After their kids grew up and left home, their vacations were all based on diving. Nick's favorite was diving the giant kelp forests off the California coast. He loved swimming through the tall greenish brown strands that spanned the sea floor to the surface. A hundred feet tall strands were not unusual. It was common to see sea lions, bright orange Garibaldi fish, electric rays, and, if lucky, sea otters. But Jeanne had trouble with the cold water, so they spent more time traveling to tropical waters and, since they'd met in Hawaii, it was their favorite. Nick leaned his head back, closing his eyes and smiled at the memories of their last dive here.

⸻⟡⸻

"Come on slowpoke," Jeanne called up to him as she dunked her head, then came back up smiling. "The water is glorious. It makes me feel so free."

Nick was still getting his gear on after he had secured the anchor. "What, do you feel like a prisoner the rest of the time?"

Jeanne laughed. "No, but don't you feel it? All our normal responsibilities and commitments aren't part of this world. The only pressure I feel is the water, which I love. And time, it's not relevant here."

"Maybe not to the fish, but it still matters to us. We need to breathe." Nick smiled, as she was so animated in her thoughts.

"Always the pragmatic," she said. "What I like the most is the diversity on the reef. Anemones, corals, big fish, little fish, turtles, and they all live so cohesively."

"Except at dinnertime," he said, his eyes twinkling.

Laughing, Jeanne splashed him. "Stop it."

Nick rolled back into the water to join her, both bobbing on the surface. "I know what you mean. For me, I like that there are no walls, no boundaries, an almost endless sea with a few islands scattered about. Are you ready?"

Jeanne swam up close and pulled him in to touch her lips to his, a kiss to share their joy, their happiness, and their love. "Lead the way, my captain."

⸻⟡⸻

Nick's eyes dropped back down at the box, acknowledging what he needed to do, but delaying the end. A box of ashes was no substitute for her touch, her voice, her energy, but it was all he had left of her, and today would be the end. For the last year and a half, he had subsisted in the parallel universe that came after a death. Half of life, rote motions in an auto pilot existence. The other half, both numb and stupefied, fighting against acceptance of reality. Finality had now arrived.

This is what she wanted, to finish her life on a coral reef. *Take my ashes to Hawaii and put them on a reef. My body won't be of any value anywhere else. Let me be part of that life cycle. It will be our last dive together.* It was time. Nick got up and put on his wetsuit and dive gear. He posted the dive flag up high on a pole, so that other boats would know that a diver was under the water. He placed the regulator in his mouth and closed his eyes. Hugging the cardboard box, imagining her in his arms, he rolled back into the water.

Down he swam, against the current, the short distance to the reef, which was healthy and vibrant. *Pretty little reef* was how Jeanne had described it, *and it will grow here, far enough from the shore and pollution.* Nick floated over the several small fields of coral, reminding him of adorned cities that never slept. Closer to one, he watched the small and tiny fish moving in and out of the coral like little children on a playground. Up off the coral, schools of larger fish swam and moved together in such perfect unison as if the action were a well-rehearsed choreographed performance.

Reverberations suddenly hit his back and echoed through his chest as the distinctive sound rang in his ears. Nick whipped around in time to see an enormous mother humpback whale gliding in the distance while a young calf worked to keep up. Never had he seen a whale, which was something to do on his bucket list of life. Such magnificence, such grace, such elegance. The mother continued to emit a variety of grunts and clicks mixed in between her melody. Though he would never know exactly what she said, he flashed back to a time when Anthony was little and Nick had to remind him to keep up and not wander off. Maybe all parents speak the same language. Nick watched, spellbound until they were out of sight.

A calm enveloped him like a warm blanket. This was the right place, the right time. He dropped to swim through a small tunnel to find an area surrounded by hills of colorful, soft pink and green corals. This was a beautiful, peaceful spot, protected from the ocean's harsher surges and teaming with life.

Nick took a deep breath and opened the box. Gently, by handfuls, he spread her ashes about, ensuring not to bury any of the young coral. Several brave little fish came to see what Nick offered. Nick looked at the now empty, soggy box and pulled off the small brass plaque:

Jeannette Crawford Mitchel, (1LT, USANC)
1922 to 1985,
beloved Mother, Wife, and Friend
"It was love at first sight,
at last sight,
at ever and ever sight."
—Vladimir Nabokov, Lolita

Raising it to his mouth, removing his air regulator, he kissed the plaque. Replacing his regulator, he took the plaque and wedged it between some of the hard coral. He knew over time, the coral would grow over the plaque, but that was okay. Jeanne wanted to be part of the reef.

Nick leaned his head back and blew air from his nose into the mask, displacing the tears that collected. Floating up from the reef a bit, he viewed the sight and burned the image in his memory. *I love you, Jeanne, and I always will.* Turning his face up to the surface, Nick swam to the boat.

Once back on board, he took off his gear, then fell back in a seat and let out a deep breath. It was done. Now all he had were his beautiful memories. Just as he did in the war, before a battle, he let his favorite memory of Jeanne play out. A slow, deep smile formed and sent warmth down into his heart.

Fifteen

September 1943 - Honolulu, Hawaii

"May I have the next dance?" he asked, before her partner could whisk her away.

"Yes." Then she turned to her previous partner and smiled. "Thank you for a lovely dance." The guy shot Nick an angry look, but politely left.

As Nick took her hand, electricity shot up his arm. The brunette jumped as she felt it, too. Glen Miller's *You'll Never Know* played. Nick pulled her into his arms, as close as he dared, for a first dance, amazed at how perfectly she fit. "Hello, I'm Nick Mitchel. What's your name?"

"Jeannette Crawford," she said.

Her piercing dark brown eyes gave Nick the impression that she saw down into the very depths of his soul. She was lovely, though not in the glamorous sense. Her honey brown hair wasn't cut in the latest style; however, it suited her perfectly as it curved down to her shoulders. Her light blue dress, also not the current trend, accentuated the gentle curves of her body. A perfect balance of curves, he thought. She swayed to the beat of the music—quiet elegance summed up what he saw. The only jewelry she wore was a thin gold watch and a necklace with a gold pendant holding a single black pearl.

"Hello, Jeannette Crawford. It's very nice to meet you." They continued to stare into each other's eyes, both smiling.

"Hello, Nick Mitchel. You're a good dancer."

"My parents loved to dance together and made me take lessons. Now I'm very glad they did." As they danced, Nick glanced up to see Jeannette's previous partner watching them. "Jeannette, may I call you Jeanne?"

"Yes," she said, still smiling.

"Jeanne, before someone comes to steal you away, would you do me the honor of having dinner with me?"

He could almost see the gears turning as Jeanne made her decision. "Yes, I'd like that."

A warmth emitted from his heart into every vessel of his body. "Would tonight be good with you, or would you prefer another night?"

"Tonight is good."

Nick's eyes lit up. "Wonderful. If you give me a moment, I'll call a taxi for us."

"You don't have to. I have a friend's car, so I can drive us. Do you have a place you want to go?"

"Actually, I'm sorry to say I don't know of any place. I've only been here a couple of days and haven't had the chance to explore." Nick said, kicking himself for not being better prepared. *Smooth, Mitchel, way to impress the lady.*

"It's alright. I've been here awhile and there is a nice restaurant on a beach, about a ten-minute drive, if that's alright?"

"Sounds great." He pulled her a bit closer while they finished the dance in silence. Once the music ended, Nick stepped back, and, keeping his hand on the small of her back, led her through the crowd and out the door. He came to this party with James, but now didn't bother trying to find him. He would figure it out.

Once out the door, Jeanne led the way to the car. Nick smoothed his hair down again and checked his uniform. "Have you been here very long?"

"Almost six months now. I've been lucky enough to have explored quite a bit of Oahu in my off hours." She started the car, then left the busy neighborhood. As she turned onto

Kalanianaole Highway, Jeanne described Koko Head Crater and the beautiful flowers that they drove past.

Clearly intelligent, she didn't just tour the area; she actively learned about it. Somewhat intimidated by this, Nick pulled out a cigarette. He only smoked when he was nervous. "Do you mind if I smoke?"

"No, go ahead."

He offered her one, but she shook her head. "No, thank you."

He lit a cigarette and turned his body a bit to confidently lean on the door, listening to her talk. After he took a few puffs, Nick casually tossed the cigarette out the window. The butt immediately bounced off the glass and landed back on his lap. Nick jumped in his seat, slapping his lap, trying to put out the burning embers. Surprised, Jeanne quickly pulled the car off the road. Nick yanked the door open, falling out of the car, furiously wiping the cigarette off of himself.

"Are you alright?" Jeanne asked, trying very hard not to laugh, but failing miserably.

Nick's face flushed hot as he looked sheepishly back. *So much for suave*, he thought. "I forgot the window was closed." Thoroughly embarrassed, but he still laughed at himself.

"Yes, I noticed that. Are you ready to keep going?" she asked, still laughing. Nick nodded and climbed back in.

After driving another few minutes, Jeanne pulled into a gas station. "I'm sorry, but I need to use the restroom. I'll be just a couple of minutes." She quickly headed to the side of the station. Nick sat there, embarrassed by his stupidity. *What an idiot. How on earth did you not know the window was closed? Great first impression, Mitchel.*

After about ten minutes, Nick began to worry about Jeanne, as she hadn't come back yet. This is her car, so I know she didn't leave me. Do I go and check on her? Do I just pound on the ladies' room door? I'll give her a few more minutes. Maybe she isn't feeling well. Nick got out of the car and started pacing. "That's it," he muttered and went around to the ladies' room door. Tentatively knocking, he called to her. "Jeanne, it's Nick. Are you in there?"

"Nick!" she yelled back. Her voice was higher and panicky. "Yes, I'm fine, but the door to the stall is stuck and I can't get out."

Relieved, Nick yelled back. "I'll get help." He ran around into the station and found the manager, who grabbed the spare key. As they started to open the door, Nick warned, "Jeanne, the manager and I are here and coming in."

"It's alright, come in," she answered. "The stall door is the one that is jammed. Can you open it?"

The manager tried the stall door, but it was jammed tight. "Do you have a crowbar?" Nick asked. The manager nodded and ran out. He returned and Nick took the crowbar from him and wedged it into a small opening. "Stand back," he yelled, and both men pulled. The stall door popped open. Nick reached in and pulled her out.

"I'm so sorry, miss," the manager said. "I've been meaning to get this fixed. Are you alright?"

"I'm fine, really I am," she said, then turned to Nick. "Let's leave, please."

Nick took her arm and escorted her to the car. They sat leaning on the side of the car for a couple of seconds, gazing at each other, then they both burst out laughing, shaking their heads.

"Well, I think suave and sophisticated are out for tonight. What do you think?"

Jeanne nodded. "Thanks for rescuing me." As they smiled at each other, the nerves were gone. Nick took her left hand, running his thumb over her soft fingers, stopping at the third finger. Possibilities turned to probabilities and a warm contentment settled the decision. "Let's go get something to eat."

Sixteen

February 12, 1987 - Honolulu, Hawaii

Nick met Natalie in the lobby the next morning, giving her a big hug. He was nervous about what was coming and was glad she was there. "How did you sleep?"

"Not great," Natalie said, yawning. Nat was dressed in a well worn running suit. "If I have to be on a plane for eight hours today, I'm going to be comfortable. How did you sleep?"

Nick shrugged. "Not great, either. So I'm hoping to sleep on the flight. I wish I brought my sweatpants."

"I'm looking forward to landing in Truk tomorrow and not getting on another plane for a week. Sorry, I never sleep well the first night away from my own bed," she said, mustering a small smile.

"Come on grumpy. Let's get some food. You'll feel better."

"Okay. I at least need some coffee to wake up."

Nick directed her to the hotel restaurant. Each ordered a good breakfast, needing to fill up before the flight. Airplane food was unreliable.

"So how was yesterday?" she asked between bites of French toast with blueberries on top.

Nick always appreciated Nat's directness. "It was alright. Not as bad as I thought it would be. I found the spot she loved so much. It was beautiful, and it almost felt like I was bringing her home. She'll be happy there." Nick wasn't ready to share the whale experience yet. It felt like a wonderful secret he shared with Jeanne. Then another memory popped in and he smiled a bit. "Although by now, she's probably already reincarnated as a fish."

Nat laughed. "What?"

"Oh, it was what she said she was going to do after she died. She was going to come back as an Eagle Ray."

"Wait a minute, Eagle Ray is the name of the live-aboard we're staying on. Did you pick it because of the name?"

Nick didn't respond. His face turned a shade of red.

Nat started laughing again. "You did, didn't you? That's great."

Nick grinned as well.

During the rest of breakfast, Nat regaled her adventures, exploring Honolulu, at least the shops and the beach. Afterward, they collected their bags and headed to the airport. Once done with checking in and security, they boarded the long flight to Guam. Nick gave Nat the window seat again, and he took the middle. Luckily, no one sat in the aisle seat, so he moved over to give them both some extra room.

As soon as the plane took off, the apprehension came back. Gone was the clarity of tasks, gone were the happy memories of Jeanne and the wonder of the whales. Now the plane was literally forcing him on to the unknown. *No*, he stopped these thoughts. Whatever was coming soon enough.

When the flight reached its cruising altitude, Nick leaned his seat back and tried to get into a position to sleep. It was just before noon and the cabin was filled with sunlight. All the surrounding passengers were wide awake and many talking. Nat, however, was unusually quiet. Nick glanced over to see her, deep in some thought, her face pinched with furrowed brows.

"What are you thinking about so hard?" he asked. "You look almost scared."

"Oh, I was wondering about what condition the wrecks would be in now. Probably pretty broken up. I mean, obviously they sank, and it's been four decades of corrosion and coral buildup. It's just...Carl had periodic nightmares of the bombings in Okinawa, for years actually. I'll never forget how he reacted, throwing his arms over his head, thrashing around so much that I couldn't hold him." She shrugged her shoulders, shaking her head. "All I could do was watch. I know that those nightmares, as bad as they were, didn't come close to the real thing. Now that we're getting closer, I guess it's starting to become more real, and I was thinking about how it might have felt, fully realizing that I will never be able to imagine it." She stopped, realizing who she was talking to. "I'm sorry Nick. I shouldn't have brought it up. Forget I said anything. I think I'll try to nap for a while."

Nick nodded and watched her get comfortable to nap. Forget about it. That's what he had done all those years ago. He didn't say anything, but he had begun to think about the wrecks as well. But these thoughts jumped to Okinawa.

At that point in the war, the Japanese had lost almost all offensive abilities and their defenses had become more desperate, less organized. The battles were more brutal, more protracted. Most of the horrific aspects of the war fell with the ground forces, but the navy wasn't immune to them. Nick had built up a form of protective shell, a numbness. It became routine when he returned from his missions to find out which pilots and crew didn't make it back. He saw mangled planes and mangled bodies return from battle. All horrible, but understandable from a perspective of cause.

However, he saw something in Okinawa that he could never understand. They had been flying daily missions, supporting the landings. The Japanese had hidden themselves in caves that were not easy to destroy. It was slow and hard work to get a foothold. It was at this point that on one mission, Nick saw civilians ahead on one of the cliffs. It was a family with a couple of little kids. Nick watched in horror as together, they jumped. Nick flew past, knowing that there was no way they could have survived. For several days, many of the pilots reported similar suicides. Nick could never understand why, nor could he forget.

Nick shook his head, trying to clear that memory. Out the window, there were a lot of clouds, with only a few breaks. In those breaks, he could see they were over water. So many times he had flown in and out of clouds over this Pacific Ocean.

The memories returned. What had those people been so afraid of that suicide was better? Most likely helplessness and fear. He had experienced both in Okinawa. When he was flying, he had some control. His instincts, his reactions, had played a part in saving his life and that of his crew. But there was a day when he had no control. That day he experienced the briefest sense of the hell it must have been like for those under the bombs he dropped. The helplessness, fear, and memories that no one should have, but so many did. Nick closed his eyes and let the memories come.

Seventeen

May 11, 1945 – USS Bunker Hill

"How did we get so lucky?" Danny asked sarcastically.

"Lieutenant, did you make someone mad?" Jason asked, only half joking.

"Stop grumbling guys. We'll take our hops this morning, then we can relax this afternoon." Nick understood their complaints. They had all been in combat for almost two straight months. Every day, they supported the landings at either Iwo Jima or Okinawa. The grind was taking its toll. Today the carrier took a little break, though they stayed in the area with the other ships. Many of the men who had been at their posts were allowed to relax. Unfortunately, Nick was one of the unlucky pilots that still had to fly that day. That meant his crew did as well. "Come on, let's get to the plane and go through the checklists." Nick led them out to the flight deck. Jason and Danny crawled inside and Nick began his routine of walking around, inspecting the outside of the plane.

Nick jumped as the ship's guns started firing. "What the hell..." His eyes followed where the guns were shooting and saw the Zero diving straight at the ship. "Guys, get out of there!" Nick yelled. Jason jumped out, but Danny had fired his gun at the plane. Nick glanced at the parked airplanes, each loaded with fuel and bombs. He yelled at Jason, pointing forward on the deck. "Run!" Then he yelled inside. "Danny, get out of there." The plane got closer. Nick helped pull Danny out, then glanced up to see the bomb released. The bomb hit behind him, the force sending Nick flying forward. As soon as he hit the deck, he heard and felt the concussion of the explosion. He rolled over in time to see the Zero plow into the middle of the parked aircraft. An instant relay of explosions transformed the deck into a solid wall of fire. Nick got up and ran further away from the planes.

"There's another one!" someone yelled. Nick's eyes shot up just in time and saw a dive bomber drop his bomb. Nick ran as fast as he could, then threw himself on the deck. This time, the bomb detonated on impact. The shock waves rippled through the deck. Immediately followed by another explosion, as the plane flew into the ship's island. The heat from the flames was searing his flight suit. A succession of explosions continued on the stern of the ship.

Nick couldn't hear anything, but he felt the reverberations from the ship guns, so he knew they were still firing. The fire crews immediately got the hoses out and began to spray water, which helped to contain the spread of the flames. He looked back at the planes, then saw a guy who was trying to crawl out from the inferno. The fire crews sprayed water on the man as Nick ran to help. Pulling the guy's arm around his own head, he half dragged him clear. The man was badly burned and fortunately, fell unconscious. Jason and Danny ran up to help carry the man to the medics.

At some point, Nick realized that the ship's guns had stopped. However, on the ship, chaos ensued for the next several hours. Other ships came in to help hose down the flames and take on the injured. Nick spent those hours moving the injured and helping the fire crews. No one knew the full extent of the damage and wouldn't until the flames were extinguished. Fires and flooding were the ongoing risks to the ship.

It took five and a half hours to get the fires out and stabilize the flooded compartments. Then the next horror began. Giant holes permeated the flight deck. Gaping caverns filled with ripped, torn metal lie underneath. Several full of water. All evening and night, they faced the painstaking task of sifting through the rubble to find everyone—alive or dead. As soon as the wreckage of the kamikaze plane had cooled down enough, it was moved, so Nick and several others began to descend into the ship. The dark hallways, full of smoke. He shined his flashlight ahead and stopped. His heart dropped, tears falling. Bodies packed the hallway leading to one of the pilot ready rooms. "Oh, God," said Danny.

Nick took a deep breath, then coughed from the smoke. "Let's get the stretchers. We can't get any farther until we get these guys out." The group turned around. Nick reported what they found to one of the Commanders. The others got lights and stretchers.

It took all night. No one slept. All the seriously injured were transferred to other ships. Everyone else searched to find the rest of the crew. The medics had the difficult task of identifying the dead. Some were easy because of the dog tags, but many could only be identified by dental records. By dawn, everyone that could be identified had been. There were still around twenty men missing, probably thrown overboard in the blasts.

That morning, they began the process of burial at sea. Normally a short ceremony, but due to the sheer numbers of dead, it took almost eight hours. Total death count came around 393, which included the missing men. This was about fifteen percent of the crew aboard the ship. Some men couldn't stay to watch the burials, overwhelmed by the ordeal. Nick stayed, though. It was all he could do for them now. Each man deserved the acknowledgment of their service, their sacrifice. Nick didn't know most of them, but he knew the pilots. All brave, good men. He stood saluting each man as the twenty-one gun salute played over and over.

The body of one of the kamikaze pilots was also found. The ship's captain ordered that he be given a proper burial. The pilot's Japanese flag was also found, and a medic wrapped it around his body. Nick watched as the pilot was placed on the stretcher. He saluted him as well.

After the ceremony, the ship began the long trip back to Pearl Harbor for repair. That evening, most of the men were quiet, each dealing with the shock in their own way. Nick sat outside on the flight deck with several other pilots and crew.

One of the guys sitting there verbalized what so many of them felt. "I can't believe the Captain gave that Jap the same military funeral as our guys. That bastard murdered so many. We should have thrown him over the side like the garbage he was."

"Why did the Captain do it?" asked Jason. Then he turned to Nick. "Why did you salute him?" he asked almost accusingly.

Nick could feel several of the others turn to stare at him. "Because I won't treat them the way they've treated so many of our guys. That man did his job to the best of his ability. He bombed his enemy to try to protect his country. It's the same job that we've been doing. And he gave his life doing it." *God, I'm tired of it all.* With that, Nick got up and walked away.

Eighteen

February 13, 1987 - Weno, Chuuk State

"Good morning, welcome to The Archipelago Hotel."

"Hello, we have a reservation under Takahashi," said Junichi.

"Yes, sir, I have you here for one night," the clerk said, as he dealt with the paperwork.

"When I made the reservation, I asked for a guide today. Is one available for us?"

"Yes, sir. After you settle into your room, your guide will be waiting here in the lobby. Is this your first trip to Chuuk?"

"Yes, it is." Junichi signed the room form and took the key.

"Your room is down that hall on your left. Please let me know if there is anything we can do to make your stay with us more comfortable."

"We will, thank you." Junichi glanced around the hotel. It had been there for a while. He could see the wear; however, it was still inviting. The windows were open, with a lovely breeze flowing through.

He and Shoko went to their room and dropped off their luggage. Shoko turned to get ready, but Junichi walked to the window. "Do you want to cancel the tour today?" she asked.

Junichi continued to stare out the window, then took a deep breath. "Yes, I do, but I will not. I wish I could be someone who finds all this interesting. For me, this represents pain and anger." He turned to her now. "Do not be surprised if I end the tour early."

Shoko nodded.

They both changed into shorts and comfortable shoes, sturdy enough for hiking rougher terrain. Shoko stuffed a few things into her shoulder bag, then grabbed a hat. They headed back down to the lobby.

Standing by the counter was an islander dressed in black shorts and a tropical patterned shirt roaring in laughter at something the desk clerk said. Junichi grimaced, assuming this was their guide, and he was in no mood for joking around. The man was a little taller and bigger around the middle than Junichi, and was maybe a few years younger. The clerk looked up. "Mr. and Mrs. Takahashi, this is Nekiniuo, your guide for the day."

Junichi bowed, then met the man's gaze. "It is a pleasure to meet you, Nekiniuo. Please call me Junichi and this is my wife, Shoko."

"Hello, it is nice to meet you both. I'm happy to be your guide for today. Please let us sit over here for a few moments and talk about what you wish to see." The hotel lobby had a few well-worn cushioned chairs spaced between big, green leafy plants. Deep tones from a long bamboo wind chime that hung near a window provided a calm, serene ambiance.

"Nekiniuo, my father served at the naval base here during the war and told me much about it. We would like to see the island of Tonoas, which I believe was where the main base was located. Is this correct?"

"That is correct. Your father probably referred to it as Nat-su-Shima."

Junichi nodded.

"It has also been called Dublon. Once Chuuk regained our independence last year, we changed all the names back to what they were originally called long before the Spanish invaded. Now it is called Tonoas. This island used to be called Moen, though the Japanese called it Haru Shima, it is now known as Weno.

"We will take my boat over to Tonoas, which is only about a ten-minute ride. We will arrive at what was the seaplane base and walk from there. The island is only about three kilometers wide by three kilometers long. Once we get there, you can decide how much hiking up the hills you wish to do."

"Thank you. Can we get some water to take with us?" asked Shoko.

Nekiniuo held up his backpack, smiling. "I have already done this, and I brought lunch for us as well."

"Thank you, that is very kind of you," said Shoko, smiling her appreciation.

"If you will follow me, please." Nekiniuo led them out of the hotel and down to an old wooden dinghy tied to a small dock. "Please be careful getting in." Once they were settled, he untied the boat, pulled the cord, starting the motor and set off toward Tonoas Island.

It was a beautiful day. The sky was a vivid blue with white puffy clouds scattered about. The soft trade winds blew between the islands, causing only minor waves for the boat to cut through. The water was a greenish hued turquoise near the islands, turning a deep dark blue as the ocean floor became deeper. Turning his attention to their guide, Junichi saw he didn't wear sunglasses, or a hat, and his feathery brown hair floated in the breeze. Nekiniuo's muscular arms had no trouble controlling the boat. He appeared to be a man very comfortable in his element and, thankfully, was not the joking sort Junichi had feared.

Talking louder to get over the sound of the motor, Nekiniuo described the lagoon. "In the lagoon, we have many islands of different sizes. The largest and tallest islands are part of an old volcano. The other smaller islands were formed from coral. Our people live on most of the islands except a few of the smallest. The big island far on your right is Tol. It has the highest peak in the lagoon at well over 500 meters."

"Nekiniuo, were you born here on one of the Islands?" asked Shoko.

"Yes, my family lives on Tonoas."

"You don't look old enough to have been here during the war," said Shoko.

"Thank you, but yes, I was here. I was six years old when the battle occurred."

Junichi turned back to Nekiniuo, realizing they were the same age. "That must have been very frightening for you at that age."

Nekiniuo's dark brown eyes stared intently back at Junichi. "Yes, it was." With that, Nekiniuo continued the tour. "The navy base had five air strips spread across several islands. Japanese military personnel were located on all the biggest islands and many of the smaller ones as well. The navy had the majority of its operations on Tonoas. We are approaching the northwest tip of the island. Over there is where the submarine base was located. There is also a large bunker where they kept the suicide torpedoes."

Junichi and Shoko glanced at each other. Up until then, thinking and talking about visiting the island had given Junichi the image of old war relics, historical and not personal. Suicide torpedoes were personal, both weapon and coffin.

The dinghy continued along the shore, then rounded the southwest tip of the island. After a few minutes, they turned toward the shore. "This is the seaplane base. We will get out here." Nekiniuo hopped out of the dinghy to tie it up to a tree. Junichi and Shoko got out and stood on a very large ramp, built for the seaplanes. "As you can see, without war, the island's plants and trees have fully re-grown. As we walk, you may not see all the remains of the war, as much of it is now hidden by the thick plant growth."

Junichi viewed the area and saw various metal remnants scattered around, with only the tops of them peeking out through the trees. A short distance from shore, the water softly lapped against the decaying metal of some shipwreck. The corrosion was so advanced, it would be difficult to determine what boat it had been.

"If you will follow me," Nekiniuo said, "we will head down this path. There is much to see on the island, so it would be helpful if you can tell me generally what you are interested in."

Junichi spoke as they walked. "My father was assigned to one of the ships. Before the battle, he would come into the town here. However, after the battle, he was on this island until he came home. He spoke of digging tunnels. I would like to see those types of areas. I know that the defensive guns are up in caves on the hill, but I do not wish to see those."

"That is good. Then we will walk east on the south side of the island. Most buildings were constructed with concrete bases, timber walls, and metal roofs. As you will see, most of the buildings did not survive the bombings. After the war was over, and the Japanese and Americans left, the islanders disassembled many of the damaged structures to reuse the wood and metal." As they walked, they came up to a reinforced concrete building where a family was now living. Several little children were playing around the building and laundry was hanging out to dry.

"This was the communications building for the seaplane base. It is a very heavily fortified concrete building. There was much damage from the bombs, but the building still stands. The family that now lives here has a strong roof to protect them."

The children stopped playing when they saw the visitors. They smiled and waved. Junichi and Shoko smiled and waved back. The children's mother came outside. Like her children, she pleasantly accepted them.

"Shoko," Junichi asked, "will you please give me some of the candy in your bag?" Shoko handed him a few pieces, and he approached the mother. "Hello, I apologize for interrupting you."

"Hello, you are welcome here," said the woman. She smiled and gestured with her hand that they could come in.

"Thank you. May I offer you and your children some candy?" Junichi asked, but made no move to enter.

"That is kind of you. Thank you." The mother called to her children. Two little girls and a little boy ran over.

"For you," Junichi said, smiling as he handed out the candy to each of them, then more to their mother.

"Please come in." She gestured again with her hand.

"Thank you, that is very nice of you, but we have much to see today. We must go," Junichi said.

"Thank you for the candy," the oldest girl said.

Junichi knelt down to eye level with her, smiling at her. While looking at her, a vague memory of an American GI with a chocolate bar briefly formed in his mind. "You are very welcome. Goodbye." He got back up and waved as they walked off.

A short distance from the building, Nekiniuo stopped to consider Junichi. "You could have gone in, if you wished, to see the inside. The family would not have minded," Nekiniuo told them.

Junichi shook his head no. "I would not have felt right. I want those children to know their home as a home with their friends and family visiting. I do not want them connected to a war," said Junichi, his voice low but determined.

Nekiniuo stared a few more seconds, then nodded. "Let us continue." As they walked down a wide, well-worn path between the trees, Nekiniuo pointed out the bombed-out power plant. Then they turned toward the hill to find a very large bunker, measuring thirty meters by thirty meters by seven meters tall, buried in the hill. "This housed aircraft and people after the battle. Chuukese laborers worked for a year, digging this bunker by hand with picks and shovels." Junichi heard a sharper tone in Nekiniuo's voice and glanced at him. Nekiniuo had his hand up on the surface of the tunnel and his face was rigid as he glanced around the cavernous bunker.

Nekiniuo seemed to pull himself from his thoughts. "Come, we go on." He then led them by old underground fuel tanks. "Some of these tanks are now used to store water. We go now to Kokuso Dock. If your father worked on a ship, he might have been on this dock at some time." Little remained of the dock. Part of a heavily corroded boom section of a large crane laid half submerged at the end of the dock.

"Ahead is the main dock used for the largest battle and merchant ships. It was longer by about fifty meters during the war and was bombed heavily. As you see, it was rebuilt a few years ago to service fishing boats."

Junichi walked on the dock, feeling certain his father had been here, yet this was rebuilt so not the same. He had been quiet so far during the tour. Part of him was viewing ruins of history and part of him imagining what it might have been like when his father was there. But of course, he knew his images were his creations. His father had never gone into detail about how it looked, only of its existence.

Junichi's stomach had been uneasy all morning at the thought of visiting these relics, these reminders of a horrific war, a horrible time. *What are you searching for? He didn't die here. There are no answers here.* He thought about asking if there was anyone on the island that knew of the battle. *But for what purpose? Even if we could find them, why remind someone of that time? What could they tell me about my father that I don't already know?*

Junichi jumped at Nekiniuo's voice. "If you would like to see the town area, it isn't far. This would be a good place to take a break with water and food." Nekiniuo kept the explanations going, pointing out the municipal building that was once a school before the Japanese took it over. "Here is a memorial to Mori Koben, who was a Japanese pioneer in this area. He lived here when the Germans invaded our islands and was well respected among my people."

Junichi turned to Shoko. "I have never heard of him. Have you?"

Shoko shook her head.

They both spent several minutes reading and inspecting the memorial.

When they were done, Nekiniuo directed them on. "This area to our right was the town. Before the battle, it had many buildings: restaurant, laundry, barber shop, radio station, movie house, hospital, and more. As you can see, most buildings were either destroyed in the bombing or taken apart after. One building that remains is now a home to a family. Come, we can sit on these to eat."

He led them to some chunks of concrete under the trees. Nekiniuo pulled bottles of water out of his bag, as well as containers of food. "One of the restaurants made these. They are rice and fish bowls." He offered them to Shoko and Junichi. They both took them and sat down.

"Thank you, Nekiniuo, this was very kind of you," said Shoko, as she started to eat.

"Yes, thank you, Nekiniuo," said Junichi. He opened his water bottle and drank it down, but made no move to eat.

"Junichi, are you not hungry?" asked Shoko.

He shook his head no, then got up and walked around.

"Nekiniuo," said Shoko, "how did you become such a knowledgeable guide?"

"My uncle was a guide for many years, so I began to join him when he led the tours. As you can imagine, we have many Japanese coming here. But we also have people from all over the world that come to tour as well."

Junichi finished walking around and came back. "Nekiniuo, you said you were here during the battle. Would you be willing to tell me about how it was when you were young? Please."

Nekiniuo's thick eyebrows lowered. "When the Japanese come here, they do not ask about my people. Why do you wish to know?" he asked.

Junichi understood the wariness he saw in Nekiniuo's face, so he softened his expression, trying to be as honest as he could. "I am trying to understand that horrible time from all perspectives." Junichi lowered his voice. "I need to understand."

Nekiniuo regarded him for a few moments, then nodded his head. "As I said, my family lived here on Tonoas. We had a home and a farm..." He took a breath, collecting his thoughts. "No, I need to start much earlier. My country," his hands spread out, indicating all the islands, "and my people have been invaded four times in the last 120 years. First by the Spanish, then the Germans. After World War I, my country was handed over to the Japanese, as if it was someone else's right to do so. We were not included in those decisions. The Japanese saw this atoll for its strategic benefit and began to build a very strong base with many amenities.

"During that early buildup, the Japanese Navy was very respectful of my people. In fact, many of the elders say that was the best time in our history. Life here was smooth and happy. That changed a year before the battle. More homes were taken over. More labor was needed and my people were expected, demanded actually, to provide that labor. The aircraft bunker we were in..." he said, waiting until Junichi nodded, "my father was one of those laborers who hand dug that enormous bunker, using only picks and shovels." Nekiniuo shook his head. "My people knew of construction equipment that would come on the ships, but for some reason, they never allowed their use for that bunker." Nekiniuo stopped to take a drink.

"Once the Army came in, more homes and farms were taken, my family's included. We were told to leave but had nowhere to go. We went to the hills searching for caves, but the military soon took those as well. This was common among many of my people. We were left to find shelter under thick trees. News began to spread that they were expecting an attack.

"When the attack came, my family was able to make it to a very small island. When it was over, everything became very bad. There was not enough food for everyone here. Every possible area of land that could be used to grow yams or anything else was used. My people were..." Nekiniuo stopped, his jaw clenching. "My family lost several members to starvation."

Shoko gasped.

"The war ended, and the Americans brought food. Then, a year later, everyone left. Once again, without involving my people, my country was given to the Americans, though this time they did not invade us as the others had. They sent money, but had no other interest in us. My people are peaceful. We did nothing to prompt that war, yet it was fought on our soil. Again, we were insignificant, irrelevant. So, no one has helped us recover." His gaze flowed over the island, while he thought.

"But time goes on and for the first time in over a century, we were left alone to work with some of the other islands to plan our own path. We have achieved our independence again." Nekiniuo ended his story with a smile.

Junichi was confused. "That family back there was welcoming and friendly to us. You have been kind to us. How is it that you do not blame us for what happened to your family?"

Nekiniuo smiled. "We may be a small country, and larger countries have deemed us irrelevant, but we are a proud culture that existed long before the Spanish invasion. No matter who was here, we kept our culture. I learned we can never change the past, but life has many sunrises. It is up to each of us to decide when to enjoy them. We treat you the way all people should be treated."

Junichi and Shoko were quiet as they considered this simple, yet very powerful, statement.

"Are you ready to go on?" Nekiniuo asked.

"Yes," Junichi said quietly. "Are there any tunnels nearby?"

"Yes, this way." Nekiniuo led them, still continuing with the descriptions. "This path to the right leads to the causeway that the Japanese built to make a faster connection to another part of the island, which is where fleet headquarters, a bank, and another hospital were located. Up ahead on this hill is another tunnel. In reality, there are many tunnels in these hills. After the battle, everyone began digging bunkers and tunnels in the hills, so they had some safe shelters." They came to the opening of a very long tunnel. "This tunnel is about a hundred meters long and over 3 meters tall. During the battle, the Japanese moved their communication and command here. You can see the remains of old generators over there."

Junichi observed the dark tunnel for only a few minutes, then began to feel weak, sweating, like the tunnel was closing in on him. He abruptly left to go back out into the sunshine. Shoko came and put her hands on his shoulders, gently rubbing, calming him down.

Nekiniuo followed them out. "Not too far from here is a cemetery and shrine. Would you like to see it?" he asked.

Junichi knew he didn't want to see it, but he needed to honor his countrymen. "Yes."

This time Nekiniuo led the way without saying anything, no descriptions. They found the cemetery and shrine. Junichi and Shoko took their time walking through it, reading the headstones. Most had Japanese names, but other names were probably Chuuk natives. He admired the shrine. *Brave men, I hope you are at peace.*

Junichi led the way out of the cemetery. "Nekiniuo, you have been a wonderful tour guide and I very much appreciate your help. I realize that I scheduled this for an entire day, but

I would like to go back to the hotel now. I will pay you for the whole day, as we agreed."

Nekiniuo tilted his head, considering Junichi for a few moments. "Junichi, I would like to show you something. It has nothing to do with the war and is not part of any tour. It is, however, up this mountain. Would you trust me?"

Junichi, intrigued, glanced at Shoko, who was nodding. "Yes," he said.

Nekiniuo smiled. "Good, please follow me." They walked a path up the hill, ducking under tree limbs and stepping over rocks. The path became switchbacks to traverse the hill. After many minutes, Nekiniuo stopped to check on them. "Are you both alright?" he asked, reaching into his backpack for more water bottles.

Junichi and Shoko drank liberally. "Yes, we are fine. The brush is getting thicker."

"Yes," Nekiniuo said, "this is the main path up the hill, but we don't cut too much of the bushes and trees because they provide shade from the sun. Ahead, we will pass a couple of caves with guns in them, but we are not stopping there." Junichi nodded, and the group walked on.

As Nekiniuo stated, they did pass the guns along the way. Junichi and Shoko glanced at them, but had no desire to inspect them.

Nekiniuo kept a brisk pace up to the last cave where the trail ended. This cave also had a gun in it.

Junichi frowned. "The trail ends here."

Nekiniuo smiled. "No, the path ends here. Most people who come on this path want to see the guns. That is why the path ends, but the trail goes on. From here, the hike is much harder. We walk slower, holding on to tree limbs. The ground is wetter as the foliage is thicker, hiding the sun." He turned and walked to the bushes at the edge of the cave. He pulled them back and stepped over the trunk. Junichi and Shoko followed. They climbed some rocks, stepped over more bushes, ducked under more trees, and walked through mud. Then Nekiniuo stopped, pulled back another bush which revealed the entrance to a cave. "Please go in," he said.

Junichi and Shoko smiled at each other, sharing the discovery, then they walked over to the bush and entered. The cave was large enough to fully stand in. It had two other openings that were covered by bushes and trees. Junichi glanced questioningly at Shoko, who subtly shrugged her shoulders. Neither could see the attraction here.

"Junichi, will you please take that rope over there and pull it back, tying it on that rock?" asked Nekiniuo, as he grabbed another rope. When they both pulled, the bushes parted to frame the most breathtaking view. This side of the cave faced the East. They could see small coral islands below, the outer coral atoll with the waves crashing, then the endless blue ocean, topped with the heavenly blue sky. While the view mesmerized Junichi and Shoko, Nekiniuo pulled on ropes on the opposite side of the cave.

"Look over here."

They turned around to see another equally spectacular view. To the West, Tol's peak stood tall surrounded by many big and little emerald-green mounds dotting the turquoise waters of the lagoon, with the ocean behind.

"Was it worth the hike?" Nekiniuo asked.

Shoko nodded at him, her eyes glistening. "Thank you for sharing this with us, Nekiniuo."

Junichi's eyes narrowed, pulling his eyebrows together. "Why did you share this with us?"

"Because you asked about my people. You gave the simple act of kindness of giving the candy to the children. You saw that building not as a museum to be toured, rather, as those children's home. To you, we are not insignificant. And I brought you because you said you needed to understand. This might be a good place to start." Nekiniuo, seeing Junichi's confusion, explained. "Because of the wrecks, tourism is one of our main industries right now. We see so many people from all over the world. Every year the number grows. The people who come here are interesting and all are intelligent people with the money to afford such a trip. Most are respectful of the sites and the people. However, it is very interesting to see how many of these intelligent people look at so much, yet see so little."

Nekiniuo glanced around the cave. "My uncle found this cave after the war. He trimmed some of the bushes and put in the ropes. The ropes are the only man-made items we allow to stay here. It was many years before he showed me. He waited until I was old enough to understand. When I am down below and life becomes difficult, I look up at the hills and they are like my problems. Some big, some small. If they are islands, I can go around them. But if they are problems, I have to get on top of them or forever be in their shadow." He walked to the edge, facing out to the ocean.

"But when I come here," his tone of voice changed, softer, "I see a world so large and powerful. A world with endless, indescribable beauty and full of possibilities. I realize that although I am small, I am still part of that power, that beauty. My problems become much smaller and I have the power to solve them."

Nekiniuo looked back at Junichi. "You trusted me to come here. I am trusting you to keep my secret. Please enjoy it as long as you wish. When you want, I will take you back." With that, he sat down, leaning against a rock, and closed his eyes.

Shoko took Junichi's hand and led him to the edge. They sat down on the ground, dangling their feet over the edge, and took in the view.

Junichi stared out at the immensity, the magnificence of the view. He closed his eyes, feeling the breeze across his face, the ground he sat on. Hearing only the gentle rustling of the leaves, he freed his mind of everything, except this moment. Taking several deep breaths and with each slow exhale, the tension in his shoulders eased little by little. He opened his eyes again and contemplated the expanse.

Time became irrelevant, no longer controlling their world. At some point Junichi's vision changed. He stopped gazing at the view and began to see his world, its radiance, its glory. Vibrations slowly flowed through his limbs. A calmness enveloped him. He felt his connection to power. No longer bound by his day-to-day responsibilities or pulled by continuous man-made distractions, he silenced the nagging of his problems. In doing so, he found his strength.

A smile from within formed and took over his face. He took a deep breath and noticed that Shoko had a smile on her face as well as tears freely falling down. She met his gaze, her eyes reflecting the beauty she felt. He raised her hand, kissed it, his eyes radiating the love he shared with her.

"Are you ready?" he asked in barely a whisper. Shoko squeezed his hand and nodded. The two got up and turned to Nekiniuo.

"Good," he said. He nodded and then went to untie a rope. Junichi helped with the other. Nekiniuo then led them back down to the dinghy, no one saying a word.

Once back at the hotel, Junichi paid Nekiniuo and added a generous tip. "Thank you, Nekiniuo! What started out as a difficult day ended a special day that I will never forget." Junichi and Shoko bowed to him.

"You both are very welcome," Nekiniuo said, smiling at them, then he turned and left.

Shoko took Junichi's hand. "Come, let us clean up, have a nice dinner, then walk on the beach watching the sunset."

Junichi walked with her to their room, appreciating her more with each step he took. Always present, always strong. Quiet, but when she spoke, she was always wise. When their door closed, he pulled her into a long hug.

"If we are lucky," he said, kissing her neck, "maybe we can find a secluded, romantic spot on the beach where I can hold you in the moonlight." Then he gazed deeply into her eyes, noting the small flecks of gold that shined when she smiled. "Thank you for being with me."

"Always."

Nineteen

February 14, 1987 - Guam

Nick followed the slow line of people down the aisle. Natalie was up ahead. They wouldn't be together on this flight. She was energetic and fully awake after a good night's sleep. Nick envied her energy as he had tossed and turned all night. Fortunately, this was the last leg of their journey, and it was a relatively short flight. When he reached his row, another person was sitting in his seat. He stood there staring, then shook his head. "Excuse me, but I have the window seat," Nick said to a young blond woman.

"Oh, hi," she said, smiling. "Sorry, I wasn't paying attention. Give me a second," she said and got up to let him in.

Nick saw that Natalie got settled several rows back, then stowed his bags up above and took his seat, not paying attention. "Ow," he said, after the thump. Then he sat down, rubbing his head.

"Are you alright?"

"Yes. This plane is just smaller."

"Hazards of being tall. I don't have that problem. I'm Sarah," she said.

"Hello, Sarah. I'm Nick." They shook hands. She was a pretty young woman with a bright smile in her green eyes and a cute button nose. Her bubbly energy and smile reminded him of Jeanne when she was that age.

"Since you're flying to Truk, I'm assuming you're a diver as well?" Sarah said.

Nick nodded.

"Where are you staying?"

"I'll be on a live-aboard called the *Eagle Ray*. A friend of mine, Natalie, several rows back, will also be on board."

"Do you want your friend to sit with you? I can change seats with her."

Nick smiled. "That's nice of you to offer, but I'm sure Nat is already well into a conversation with whoever she is sitting with, and she makes friends easily."

"Hey, guys," Sarah called over the seats in front of them, "meet Nick. He'll be on our boat. Nick, this is Frank and Ray."

Frank looked back and offered his hand. "Hi, Nick, it's nice to meet you." Then Ray offered his hand as well. "Hi, Nick."

"It is nice to meet you both. Where are all of you from?" Nick asked Sarah, as Frank and Ray sat back down.

"We all work at the same company in southern California and, obviously, we're all divers. A friend told me about Truk, and I wanted to come. After I told these two about it, they wanted to come too. How about you, Nick?"

"California as well. Ventura actually."

"It's so beautiful up there, but I don't like when the fog comes in the summer."

"Me neither," said Nick, "but it only stays for a while."

The flight attendants were going through the cabin and getting everyone settled. Sarah began talking to her friends through the seats, so Nick tried to relax. He glanced at the three young people and wished he had their energy. He glanced around the plane, assuming most people were divers, and wondered if there was any other business on the islands?

"So, Nick, what do you do for a living?" asked Sarah.

"I'm a newly retired architect."

"That's interesting. My father was also an architect. Did you specialize in commercial or residential?"

"Residential, custom homes, mainly. I did some commercial buildings, but I much preferred homes."

"That's what my dad did as well. All growing up, we would spend several hours on weekends walking through houses. It was very interesting. I liked the houses when they were still studs and the drywall wasn't up yet."

Nick smiled. "I walked my fair share of those. What do you do?"

"I'm an engineer. We all work for a pharmaceutical company. The guys are in sales and marketing."

Nick was impressed. "Do you enjoy it?"

"Yes, we all work an incredible number of hours. The company is still young and dynamic. We've got a few very good products on the market and in development. We're also lucky, so far, that the CEO is focused on the patients first, which means we do what is right, no cutting corners in any aspect. It's nice to know we're helping people. It makes the long hours worth it. I know one day it'll change and some executives will come in and only care about the money they make. I think we're all enjoying it for as long as we can—before the greed takes over."

"I'm surprised that you see the reality so clearly."

"I've worked for other large and established corporations, so I see where we'll eventually go. I have no illusions about the greed and questionable ethics of corporate America. But for as long as we can, we'll enjoy what we have. So, you mentioned that you're newly retired. How does that feel?"

Nick tilted his head and grimaced. "Different! I'm not sure about it yet. It gives me too much time to think, which isn't good for an old man like me." Nick laughed at himself.

"You don't appear old to me. You're going on a major diving trip so you can't be too old. Do you do much diving?"

"My wife and I dove the kelp beds off California quite a bit. But she much preferred warmer waters, so Hawaii and the Caribbean were our favorites. How about you?"

"I learned to dive in those kelp beds and love them, but like your wife I'm a cold-water wimp. I've been to the Great Barrier Reef, which is absolutely amazing. Didn't your wife want to come on this trip?"

A pang shot through him, dimming the beautiful day. "I lost her a year and a half ago." The words bit at his throat. After he said them, it hit him that his life, up till now, had been surrounded by people who knew about Jeanne. He left the comfort of his sanctuary, so now more strangers would inevitably ask.

"I'm so very sorry, Nick. This trip must be difficult for you."

"Yes, it is," he said, touched by the caring in Sarah's eyes. "What exactly do you do as an engineer?"

"Well, I'm currently heading a couple of teams that are responsible for the operations side of a few of our products. This includes manufacturing, logistics, and quality assurance. Some of the products are already on the market, some are still in development."

"That's interesting. What type of products?"

"There's a variety that our company deals with. Mine are therapies that help people going through chemotherapy."

"Which ones?"

Sarah told him the name of the product currently on the market.

"That's a good drug. My wife was..." Nick stopped, his jaw muscles began to flex.

"I had a good friend on it as well," she said softly.

Nick looked back at her. "Did she..."

Sarah gave a sad smile and shook her head no.

"I'm sorry," he said.

"I'm sorry too."

He gave her a rueful half smile. "It's hard, isn't it?"

"It's horrid," Sarah said.

"Have you lost others?"

"Yes, unfortunately, I've lost several people I love. A couple to cancer, my dad being one of them, and a very close friend to a heart attack."

"That's a lot to deal with."

"The one thing I've learned is to take the opportunity to tell people what they mean to me. When my friend died of a heart attack, it was unexpected and immediate. We were so close, sisters really. We supported each other through so much—work, family…" She shot Nick a smile mixed with false anger. "Men." Nick smiled. Then she continued. "But I never told her I loved her."

"I'm sure she knew."

"I'm sure she did, but I always regretted not saying it. For years, I had the opportunity to tell her, but never did. Then that door closed in an instant. I had the opportunity with my dad to tell him how much he meant to me and say goodbye. That helped as I didn't have any regrets. It was just so hard to watch him suffer."

Nick closed his eyes, nodding his head. "That was the hardest part with my wife. I couldn't do anything. I couldn't stop her pain. I couldn't protect her. All I could do was watch and hold her. I've never been so useless in my life."

"Nick," she said gently and waited until he looked at her, "by holding her, you were giving her your strength when she no longer had hers. You couldn't stop her from leaving, but you did give her the one thing she needed, and that was the strength to go."

Nick smiled, his eyes glistening. "Thank you!" He leaned his head back and closed his eyes.

Several minutes later, Frank popped up. "Hey, I was reading about Chuuk, though it's still routinely called Truk. It got that name from the Germans who mispronounced Chuuk, which is supposed to be pronounced Chook. The islands are the remnants of an old volcano that formed, then sunk a little. After that, the weather started to eat away at the lava, leaving the islands that currently exist as well as new ones formed by the coral.

"Excuse me for a second. Does anyone know what time it is?" asked Ray.

Nick glanced at his watch. "I believe it is 12:36 pm."

"What day is it? Didn't we pass the international date line sometime last night?" asked Sarah.

Nick responded again. "It's Monday, the fourteenth."

"Wait a minute," Ray said. "We left on the night of the twelfth and now we are here on the afternoon of the fourteenth. So does that mean we left yesterday but arrived tomorrow and missed out on a today?" Ray said, laughing.

Sarah, laughing, hit Ray with a pillow. "Stop, you're hurting my brain. Frank, have you learned anything about the wrecks yet?"

"Not yet, only that we bombed them for two days and sank a lot of ships. I'm sure we'll learn a lot more in the next few days." Frank saw the flight attendant with the beverage cart, so he sat down and ordered some coffee.

The flight went on smoothly, with the three Americans either talking or reading. Nick's own thought dominated his mind as he sat back and stared out the window. *Bombed them for two days and sank a lot of ships,* he repeated to himself. His gaze fixed on the little islands scattered ahead, yet his vision reflected memories of what lay just beyond. A coral ring surrounded lush green mounds. Shivers racked his limbs as he flew around and around the ring.

⸺⸻◦⸻⸺

The air group circled the outer reef, eyeing potential targets. Nick radioed back to his crew. "Guys, we're staying with the main formation. Jason, get on your ventral gun and keep an eye out below. I don't want any Zeros surprising us from behind."

The fighters were chattering that there didn't seem to be many Zeros left, but there was plenty of anti-aircraft fire from the guns hidden in the hills. The fighters then saw a Jap destroyer trying to escape through the North Pass. The air group leader sent a few of the Hellcats and a couple of Avengers to go and sink it. Over the radio came the flight leader's voice. "Gent, you and Tom Cat take that tanker ahead. The rest of you follow me. We're going after that big ship to the right."

"Roger." Nick dropped down with James behind on the left. They had a couple of fighters up ahead strafing the ship's guns. With this protection, Nick radioed his wingman. "Tom Cat, I'm going lower to drop my fish."

"Copy, I'll follow."

Nick began a downward wide sweeping S maneuver. At the end, he could see the broadside of the ship straight ahead. Sighting his target, he aimed for the middle of the stern. Regardless of any variance in the torpedo's path, it would still hit. His plane was about twenty feet off the water and the torpedo was set for a six-foot running depth. "I've got you," Nick muttered to himself. "Then..."

"Sir," said the flight attendant.

Nick jumped, his heart still racing.

"Will you please put your seat up? We're landing in a few minutes."

"Of course." Nick shook his head and raised his seat. Landing. *Oh hell.* He closed his eyes and focused on deep, even breathing. *This is it, JC. I'm here.*

Twenty

Nick peered out the window at the very lush island of Weno, covered in dense green foliage. The plane taxied to the airport terminal. After Nick got off, he waited for Natalie on the tarmac.

"How was your flight?" she asked when she caught up. "I saw you talking with those young people."

"Yes, three Americans, and they'll be on the Eagle Ray with us. You'll like them. How about you?"

"Oh, it was very interesting. I met a very fascinating man from Chuuk. He's part of the local government and works with the neighboring islands, as they develop a more uniform, economical approach. He said it's hard to be such a small country and, by building collaboration with the other countries in the region, they can be stronger among themselves and in the world economy."

"I knew you would find someone interesting. Let's get our bags and go through customs."

They walked into the terminal. Calling the building a terminal was a generous description. The walls were concrete with glass-less windows and covered by a sheet metal roof. Inside was divided into two rooms, incoming and outgoing. With only the one plane, customs didn't take long. A bored man in a uniform briefly glanced at the bags, stamped their passports, and the formality was over.

The churning in Nick's stomach shifted into high gear as he put on his sunglasses and walked out the doors, then stopped. His gaze wandered around and saw quite a few people. Odd, considering the lack of air traffic. Visitors were easy to pick out from the crowd. The islanders were plentiful. A Chuukese woman wearing a red dress with large white flowers walked by, casting a glance at him. Two men sat on a bench to the right side of the door talking in their native language, a few men waited with their taxis, several others sat looking the new visitors over. Some of the other incoming visitors passed him with their bags in tow. Green foliage with pink and white flowers grew wild around the airport, with no manicured gardens here. Like the terminal, the other amenities were sparse and limited. The parking lot, paved with crushed lava rock and full of muddy holes, was small, yet probably large enough for the limited population.

Nick breathed in the floral scented salty breeze. This wasn't what he expected, though he didn't have enough clarity to know what to expect, nor had he ever been on the islands before. The hills before him were lush and so dense only a machete could get through. Colorful birds hopped from tree to tree, chirping and squawking to each other. Heat from the intense sun warmed and calmed him down. Knots in his shoulders that he didn't know he carried, released. It wasn't a disappointment, but for some reason he felt let down, but from what he had no idea. For decades, he'd built a shell to protect himself from...what? All he saw was a tropical island. No carnage, no angry mobs, no pretty girls with leis welcoming the visitors. Such an anticlimactic arrival disorientated him. Inevitably, his eyes moved to the sky. A few clouds, but nothing else. His memories weren't from down here, but his imagination...

"Nick," said Natalie, as she put a hand on his arm. "Is everything alright?" she asked.

Nick slowly brought his gaze down at her. In the sunlight, her auburn hair took on a golden hue. Nat was a friend, a familiar part of his life, which was comforting and brought him back. "Yes, just looking around."

"Our van is over there." She pointed her thumb to the left.

Nick followed her, seeing the sign that read *Eagle Ray*. An Asian couple stood by the van. The gentleman was lean, yet muscular. His short jet-black hair was slicked straight back and his eyes hid underneath dark sunglasses. Though he watched them walk up, there was no welcoming smile. The lady, on the other hand, gave a pleasant smile.

"Hello, my name is Natalie Thornton, and this is my friend Nick Mitchel. We'll be on the *Eagle Ray* as well."

"Hello," said Nick, putting out his hand. The man glanced down at it, then back up, bending his head back a bit to meet Nick's eyes.

"Hello, I am Junichi Takahashi and this is my wife Shoko," Junichi said, as he took Nick's hand.

When they shook hands, Nick felt the hard, calloused skin. Whatever the man did entailed physical work. Junichi's grip was steel, borderline challenging. Nick strengthened his own grip to match. Junichi's sunglasses were too dark to see his eyes, but his face showed no tension or challenge. Yet, for some inexplicable reason, Nick felt as if this man actually looked down his straight, thin nose at him. When the two let go, Junichi turned away.

"It is very nice to meet you both," said Shoko. She also had the same black hair, but hers was shoulder length and curled under her chin, framing her pretty porcelain face and gentle smile.

Nick watched as the other Americans came up to introduce themselves, pleased that everyone was engaged in conversation and that he didn't have to participate. Still unsettled about meeting Junichi, Nick watched him until he realized that the man wasn't any more welcoming to the others. Nick shrugged off his illusions. Maybe the guy wasn't feeling well.

A driver loaded all the bags, and the group piled into a gray van that had seen a long and very rough life. Nick's seat had generous amounts of tape holding the torn fabric together, but no springs dug into him, so the ride was comfortable enough. The drive to the docks only took about ten minutes. It wasn't that far, but the roads were in desperate need of repair. The quick trip through the town revealed one gas station, two buildings, and a few houses. One of the buildings had a sign that said Hospital. Its outside dilapidation did not instill confidence. The van swerved several times to miss various potholes or other cars. Finally, they made their way to the docks, where a couple of launches were waiting to take them to the ship. They loaded their dive gear, bags, and themselves, then took off.

During the twenty-minute boat ride to the ship, Nick took in as much of the Lagoon as he could. Luscious emerald-green islands of various sizes scattered around the lagoon. In the distance, the white, sudsy waves crashed onto the outer coral atoll. Inside, the water was a bit choppy when they were out in the open, but calmed when they were protected by the leeward side of an island. It was a beautiful lagoon, very serene, and very different from the last time he was here. Nick took a deep breath, exhaling slowly.

Nat leaned over. "Are you doing okay?" she asked into his ear.

Nick turned to her and gave her a slight smile, nodded, then turned back to continue his exploration.

The *Eagle Ray* was a beautiful ship with crisp white and royal blue highlights. About 150 feet long, she appeared to be sturdy and welcoming, with one full deck wrapping around her and two partial decks above.

Once they docked to the big ship, Nick followed the rest up the stairs. The guests were directed to the upper deck while their dive gear was unloaded. The ship's captain was waiting at the top of the stairs to greet the new guests. Others had already arrived and were mingling about.

"Welcome, I'm Thomas Forsey, Captain and owner of the *Eagle Ray*. If you will all make your way into the salon, Mary, my lovely wife, will direct you to your cabins and give you the schedule for the week. Please settle in and review the schedule. We will have a briefing meeting in the dining room in one hour. I would appreciate everyone attending. Thank you."

Nick stood back, letting everyone else go ahead. The *Eagle Ray* had seen many voyages, but the captain took care of her. She was sleek and clean, with ample use of well-oiled teak wood. Although a working vessel, she presented herself as a comfortable and inviting home. This covered deck had some bench seating toward the stern, with other chairs spaced around.

Several accents and languages were spoken around him. Besides him and Nat, the guests consisted of the three young Americans, four young Germans, a couple from Scotland, and the Japanese couple. The Germans were all young men, joking and laughing with each other. The couple from Scotland were quiet with broad smiles as they were looking around. It would be interesting getting to know these people.

The last person Nick wanted to watch was the captain. When Nick turned to observe him, he found himself under interested scrutiny. Both men smiled, acknowledging the mutual interest. Thomas was in his early fifties and in pretty good shape. He had a little gray mixed in with his blond hair and the wrinkled tanned face of a man who had been at sea for many years. His gray eyes were penetrating, yet softened by an easy smile. Nick had a feeling he would get on well with Thomas.

Nick followed the line into the salon, ducking a little at the door. Here he found a large space with many built-in couches, covered in nautical blue canvas, and a few comfortable striped tan and blue chairs. The room looked like it may have been custom decorated to service pleasure-type cruises. The front of the salon had a bar on the left side of a hallway that led to cabins. Behind the bar, next to the various bottles of alcohol, was a mini store for the guests with a selection of snacks, toiletries, books, postcards. On the bar sat a large container of water and a tray covered with fruit. The wall on the other side of the hallway held a large television fixed to the wall, above a well-stocked bookcase, with a variety of videotapes and books.

He turned his attention to Nat and Sarah ahead of him. They were both talking away. It wasn't surprising that those two extroverts hit it off so quickly.

Natalie smiled up at him. "This is a nice surprise; Sarah is my roommate on the ship," she said, then followed Sarah to their cabin.

"Well, they are becoming friends."

Nick turned to the woman who spoke.

"Hello, you must be Mr. Mitchel. I'm Mary Forsey," she said, as they shook hands. Mary had a lovely welcoming smile, with very round deep blue eyes, and Nick guessed to be in her late forties. She wore little makeup and instead sported a healthy tan. She was dressed in casual white shorts and a long pale pink T-shirt, her brown hair pulled back under a white headband. She gave an aura of happy and comfortable.

"Yes, I am, but please call me Nick."

"It is lovely to meet you, Nick. You are in Cabin 5, down the hall on your right. Here is your schedule for the week detailing the available dive times each day, as well as the dining schedule. Thomas has assigned you to dive with the other Americans, who are all experienced divers, and your friend Natalie. It says here that you brought your own diving equipment. We do, however, have gear on board. If you find yourself in need of anything, ask your dive master. Well, then, when you get settled, please go down to the lowest level, which we call the dive deck, and the staff will show you to your gear station. Up one deck from there, you will find the dining room where you will have your briefing in an hour. Do you have any questions?"

"Mary, you are quite efficient. May I also say how lovely and inviting this salon is? Thank you for sharing your home with us."

Mary's smile brightened. "Thank you for saying that. Not very many people see this as our home."

"If you don't mind me asking, from your accents, I assume you and Thomas are from England, but I was curious. What part?"

"The southern tip, Cornwall."

"I haven't had the pleasure of visiting Cornwall, but I have heard it is very nice."

"Yes, it is. I hope one day you will be able to see it. I loved it there."

Nick smiled, then went the short walk down the hall to his cabin. He booked a cabin for himself—he was way too old for roommates. The cabin was, of course, small, but he had been in far more cramped quarters. It had two berths opposite each other, with a short dresser between, and a narrow closet at the end of one of the berths. The attached bathroom was compact, with a sink and toilet. Nick was very happy to see a shower head on the wall and drain in the middle of the floor, indicating that the entire enclosure made a shower. Testing the bed, he found it was comfortable enough. The round porthole showered the room in light while he unpacked the few things he brought. Nick knew how to travel light. When he opened the closet, the sunlight reflected off something on the floor. Reaching down, he found a one peseta coin. Maybe a prior occupant was from Spain. Nick dropped the coin back down for someone else to discover. Then he hung the few nicer shirts and shorts he brought and put the rest in the dresser.

The briefing wasn't for a while, so he took this opportunity to lie down. This had been a very long journey and his old body worn out from the flying, but so much more by the emotions that brought a myriad of memories, both good and bad. Now that he was finally here, he didn't know what to feel or what to think. *JC, what in the hell am I doing here?*

Twenty-One

S ilhouette shadows crossed his walls as people passed the porthole. Curious, Nick sat up. Then it struck him that he actually felt curious about anything. This trip might be the break he needed to be able to start to feel again. Now wasn't the time to lose himself in thoughts or sleep, no matter how enticing that was. That would have to wait til another day. To be ready for diving tomorrow, tonight would need to be an early night. Nick got up, stretched his tired muscles, and left to join the others.

Heading down first to the dive deck, he saw sixteen air tanks spaced apart on each side of the boat. "Excuse me," Nick said to the crew member filling tanks, "my name is Nick Mitchel, and I was wondering which station would be mine."

"Hello, I'm Eonin, one of the dive masters. Let me see what group you are in." He picked up a clipboard with a list of names. "And here you are, Nick. Ben will be your dive master, and your station is number 9, right over there. Your dive bag should be underneath. Let me know if you need anything."

The first thing that Nick noticed about the man was his piercing yellowish-brown eyes under an almost continuous eyebrow. Eonin was a short man with a heavy-set barrel chest, a full face, and the same light brown skin of the Chuukese people. Nick wondered why he didn't wear a hat to protect his bald head. Creases on his forehead, probably from squinting in the sun, and wrinkles around his eyes showed he wasn't a young man.

"Thank you. I do need a weight belt."

Eonin reached up to get one of the belts hanging on the wall. "You can use this one. Over there are the weights, so pick out whatever you need."

"Thank you," said Nick, then picked the necessary weights and went to his station. His tank was already pressurized, so he slipped on the buoyancy compensator (BC), and then attached his octopus, which was the common term for the full assembly that connects the primary and backup breathing regulators, a pressure gauge, and the inflator hose. Once connected, he opened the valve on the tank and, while under pressure, inspected each mechanism. No air leaks confirmed the gaskets were sealed. He took several breaths through both regulators, then filled and deflated the BC bladders.

Glancing up when he heard footsteps, he saw Junichi coming and smiled at him. Junichi, acknowledging with a nod, but no matching smile, then turned to talk with Eonin. Not a friendly guy, Nick thought, then went back to checking his equipment. His dive computer turned on immediately, and everything worked fine. Nick shut off the tank valve, disconnected the octopus, and did a final check of his mask, snorkel, and fins. Once finished, he headed back up the stairs.

The wonderful smell of freshly baked bread led him to the dining area. When he got there, the room was full. A couple of booths were built in on opposite walls, and four tables sat between. A long table stood near the front of the room with a door to the kitchen behind, which was open, emitting appetizing aromas. Overhead lights weren't on, as enough light came in the windows lining three sides of the room. Like the salon, the color scheme was tan and marine blue, with drapes depicting sea life patterns. Nick spied Sarah and Natalie sitting at a table, laughing at something. Sarah waved him over to join them.

"Hi, Nick, how is your cabin?" asked Sarah.

"Very comfortable, thank you. And yours?"

"Great," said Sarah, "tight space, but everything fits."

"If I could have everyone's attention, please," said Thomas. He stood at the front of the room and waited for all the conversations to be quiet before he started the briefing. "Again, welcome to the *Eagle Ray* and to Chuuk Lagoon, historically referred to as Truk Lagoon, however Chuuk is the proper name. You are in for an amazing diving experience. Nowhere else on earth will you find an array of shipwrecks to parallel this experience. I won't even try to find words to describe what you will encounter, because there simply aren't any." Thomas stopped, allowing his gaze to spread around the group. "Now, I do have a rather long list of important information to share with you, so please honor me with your complete attention and I will make this as quick as possible.

"This entire lagoon has been designated a Historical Preserve by the local government. It is against the law to take any artifacts. As you can understand, this area is visited annually by thousands of divers, and the temptation is very strong to take home a souvenir. However, as divers, we also know that if everyone did that, this site would quickly lose its value. As it is, most of the valuable artifacts have already been taken officially or unfortunately through plundering, which is why the law was enacted. Therefore, I am sure you understand and will respect the historical significance of these wrecks and the growing marine life by not disturbing these sites in any way. Although I am also sure it is unnecessary, I will formally state that I will most vigorously enforce this law, with no exceptions." Again, Thomas slowly glanced at each person.

"Now, you will have seen on your schedules that I have assigned you to a dive group for the week. Also on your schedules are the times for all available dives, as well as the location to meet your group and dive master. Please understand that these dive masters are well trained and experienced divers. They know these waters and dive sites very well. Their job is to get you to the sites and bring you back here to the boat. But, unlike many recreational dives around the world, these dive masters are not your guides. How you explore the wrecks is completely up to you. Your dive master will, however, set the general schedule for the dive and is a good source of information about these sites.

"You were told, at the time you booked this trip, that diving in Chuuk is *not* for novices. Thus, your safety is *your* responsibility, not your dive master's. You are all certified, experienced divers. Dive within that experience level, not beyond. This is *not* a place to get yourself in trouble. The closest hyperbaric chamber is in Guam, a two-hour flight from here. If you need that chamber, you will die a very painful death well before you could land in Guam. Also, you may have noticed the hospital on your drive from the airport to the docks. Hopefully, you could see that this is not an adequate resource for emergency medicine. So, plan your dive and dive your plan.

"The shallowest dives are approximately fifteen meters. For you Americans, multiply that by 3.3 to convert to feet. Most of these wrecks are deeper than this. There is still plenty to see for normal recreational divers though. If you are a certified deep diver, over forty meters, and want to do these deeper dives, please meet in the salon right after this briefing, so that we can set these up for you.

"We offer repetitive dives for the next few days, then a rest day before you fly. Repetitive deep diving brings more vulnerability to decompression sickness, the bends. Therefore, we add in an extra safety stop before surfacing. Please understand that the dive masters also experience the same repetitive deep dives. I remind you of this, so that you understand that if you get into trouble, the dive masters cannot jeopardize their own lives, nor the lives of the others, to rescue you. You are on your own. However, the dive master will hang an extra air tank down to five meters. This is *only* reserved for emergencies and should not be relied upon so that you can extend your bottom time." Thomas stopped and took a drink of water.

"In the salon, we sell the book *Hailstorm Over Truk Lagoon*, by Klaus Lindemann, which has detailed descriptions of each of the wrecks. This is a wonderful resource to plan your dives, as well as a thorough historical record of the military battle known as Operation Hailstone. These wrecks are still in very good condition, but the salt is beginning to take its toll on the metal. Additionally, unlike ships sunk intentionally, these wrecks do not have their hatches welded open, nor have the hanging pipes and wires been removed. It can be very easy to get caught by something sticking out. Be very careful when you are swimming through tight areas, as well as around the jagged metal.

"Also, as you can imagine, the silt buildup is deep, so if you are planning to penetrate the wrecks, do so slowly and calmly to minimize disturbing the silt. Remember to kick your fins gently outward, not up and down. If disturbed, the silt can reduce clear visibility to zero in a manner of seconds. Once churned up, silt does not settle quickly. Therefore, penetrate with a clear plan on how to exit in the event you lose your visibility." Thomas took a breath and waited until everyone was looking at him.

"Now one last, but equally important, item. Please remember that these wrecks were not sunk to entertain divers, nor with the intent of promoting marine growth as an artificial reef. As alluring, mysterious, and beautiful as the wrecks are, they are first and foremost tombs to those who died in the battle. Most of the human remains have been removed, but not all. To the families of the men who died here, visiting this site is the same as visiting a gravesite. This is especially important to understand this week because Thursday and Friday will be the anniversary of the battle. Every year we expect some families to come here to pay their respects to their lost loved ones. Some might put wreaths on the water. As you can imagine, the families find it difficult to understand that this grave site is a vacation spot to you. We ask that when you surface from a dive, that you look up as you are ascending, which you should be doing anyway, to see if any other boat or activity is happening on the surface. If so, please swim over as close to your boat as possible before surfacing. If in doubt, watch for signals from your dive master. If you see anyone on the surface in mourning, please respect them and their loss.

"With that, this briefing is complete and, for those of you who aren't too tired from traveling, there is an afternoon dive shortly."

"Natalie and Nick, are you both going on the dive?" asked Sarah.

Natalie shook her head. "No, I'm going to wait until tomorrow. How about you, Nick?"

"I'll pass today. I'll relax in the sun until dinner. Have fun."

"Alright, see you later."

Nick watched Sarah walk out. Nat followed his gaze. "She's a lovely girl."

"Yes, she is," he said, still watching, even though Sarah was out of sight.

"Did you notice?"

"Of course. I saw it on the plane."

"Does it upset you?"

He shook his head. "No, it's actually nice. I find I want to tease her to see that lopsided grin again. Except for the hair and eye color, there are a lot of similarities between them."

"I've seen them too. It's a little... Anyway, how are you doing?"

Nick smiled at her. "I'm fine. Thanks for asking. How are you?"

"Good. I'm going to set up my gear, then I'll be in my cabin. I need a little nap."

As Nat got up to leave, Mary came by. "Did I hear a nap is in order?" Mary asked. "I'm envious, so enjoy it for me as well."

Natalie laughed. "I will."

Mary turned to Nick. "Is your cabin satisfactory, Nick?"

"Yes, very comfortable, thank you. By the way, do you do the cooking? The smell is wonderful."

"It will be even better when you taste it. I don't cook anymore. I did when we first started the business, but now we have a very talented culinary staff. We have also been fortunate through the years that many guests have shared some wonderful recipes, like tonight's meal, from all over the world. We've incorporated many to diversify the menu. The staff appreciated that. We have also had some repeat guests who brought special spices for us. So, our kitchen is rather well stocked. Before I forget, I wanted to ask you if you are comfortable with the Americans in your dive group?"

"Oh, yes, Natalie and I have been diving together many times, and I met the others on the flight in from Guam. They're a very nice and happy group. I envy their energy." A crew member motioning for Mary caught Nick's eye. "Mary, someone needs you over there."

Mary glanced behind her. "Yes, it seems I am. Well, I hope you have a lovely afternoon, Nick. Please let me know if there is anything I can do for you." She then hurried off.

Nick decided to tour the *Eagle Ray*. He went back down to the lowest deck, the dive deck. This time, he surveyed around the equipment area to see a couple of air compressors and a variety of tools, all necessary to support the diving operations. Further exploration found the crew quarters and engine room. The next deck up was again the dining room with an associated kitchen. However, there were also additional passenger cabins farther in front. Back up on the upper deck, he found the German boys engaged in a lively discussion in German, so Nick had no idea what they were discussing. Through the salon, passing his own cabin, as well as a few others, he saw the captain's office and the bridge. Exiting a side door, he found stairs that led up to a smaller top deck area that was partially covered with a blue awning.

Here, he had an almost unobstructed view of the lagoon. The deck space was big enough for four white lounge chairs. He chose one in the shade, then squirmed a little to move the chair's plastic straps around to get comfortable. Taking in the stunning view and feeling the soothing, gentle breeze, he decided this was his favorite part of the ship. This area provided a bit of quiet and solitude from the general socialization on the deck below. Nick closed his eyes and took a deep breath of the tropical salt air.

"Am I disturbing you?" asked Thomas in his low-pitched baritone voice.

Nick opened his eyes, surprised to see him standing at the railing because he never heard any footsteps. "No, I was enjoying the smells and breeze. A true tropical paradise."

"I may not use the word paradise," Thomas said, laughing as he sat down.

"That's because you work here. I get to...play."

If Thomas noticed the hesitation, he didn't let on. "That is true. But, in reality, I do love it here." Thomas smiled, looking out over the water, then brought himself back to Nick. "How were your flights getting here?"

Nick laughed. "Long! But actually, I flew into Guam last night, so I was able to catch up on some sleep. I plan to have an early night tonight and catch up on the rest." One of the dinghies drove past with the German boys, heading to their dive site. Nick gestured with a slight jerk of his head. "Somehow, I don't think those German boys will be sleeping as much as I will."

Thomas laughed. "No, I can tell you most emphatically that they will not. All four of them were here last year and, no, sleep was not their priority. They did fall in love with the adventure of wreck diving though, and are all very competent divers.

They came back again to see some of the other wrecks. It takes many trips to explore everything here. I haven't done it all yet."

"Mary told me you both are from Cornwall."

"Yes. My family was in commercial fishing. I grew up around the sea."

"How did you get from there to here?"

"When my son grew old enough, I turned the business over to him and we came here. I heard of the discoveries and started dreaming about them. I came out to dive and fell in love with the place and the people. I convinced Mary to take the adventure. I knew a man in the Philippines who helped me find this boat. We bought her, fixed her up as a more comfortable live-aboard, and sailed her here. It has been good. Mary and I experienced a few rough spots, but we worked those out and are now doing very well. It is difficult to believe that we have been here almost six years."

"Do you still dive much?"

"Every opportunity I can. I convinced Mary to learn to dive as well. She prefers exploring the barrier reef areas. There are many beautiful, solid coral reefs out there. I prefer the wrecks, so we compromise and take turns. "

"Has there been much of a change in the wrecks since you've been here?"

"Yes, gradually they are decaying, but the reefs are thriving. Also, the popularity of the site is wonderful for my business. Unfortunately, all divers are not as careful with the sites. Damage occurs from...call it 'foot traffic' for want of a better term. I suppose with all things come good and bad. What about you, Nick? What brought you out here?"

"Well...I too love diving." Nick said, while trying to suppress a yawn.

"You will not be disappointed," said Thomas, as he got up to leave. "I believe you might benefit from a short nap."

"I think you might be right." Nick closed his eyes again and was asleep within seconds.

Junichi called to Thomas as he was entering the Salon. "Hello, Thomas. I was wondering if I could speak with you."

"Of course, please come with me." Junichi followed Thomas to the room at the end of the hall which had a name plate—Captain Thomas Forsey—on the door. "Have a seat."

Junichi took one of the two sturdy wooden seats, each with a detached tan cushion to sit on. The first thing to catch his eye was the window behind Thomas' desk that showed the ship's bridge, then through the front window to the ocean beyond the bow. The rich brown teak wooden wheel shined with polish. A pair of black binoculars sat on the control panel.

Inside the office, a magnificent piece of art caught his interest. "That is stunning," said Junichi, as he got up to admire the two-foot wide by one-foot high wooden carving depicting a sunrise with islanders fishing above the waterline and the large ocean creatures below. "The detail is meticulous, and the different shades of brown are beautiful."

Thomas glanced over at the artwork. "Yes, it is. A very talented friend, over on Palau, gave this to me. It's called a Storyboard. He told me that the Japanese brought in this type of art when they took control of the islands before the war."

"It is a treasure," said Junichi as he sat back down.

"Now, what can I do for you?" asked Thomas.

"I was reviewing the dive schedule for my group, and I have a request. I very much wish to dive on the *Heian Maru* this week and I did not see it on our schedule. Would it be possible to replace one of the existing dives with this ship?"

"Yes, we can do that. May I ask why you want the change?"

Junichi pursed his lips, then sighed. "My father was on that ship during the battle."

Thomas' eyebrows shot up. "Did he die on the ship?"

"No, he was one of the survivors and stayed here until after the war. However, he did pass away in October."

"I see." Thomas' surprise changed to concern as he lowered and softened his voice. "My sincere condolences for your loss. I have lost my own father and know how hard it can be. I am concerned, though. Won't diving on the wreck be difficult for you? Diving that far down is a very dangerous place to be overwhelmed with emotions."

Junichi maintained his stoic expression. "I appreciate your help and your concern. My father was ill for a long time. I have had much time to deal with his passing."

Thomas studied Junichi, deciding whether to believe him or not. "Alright, I will make the change and redistribute the schedules."

"Do you think the Scottish couple that we are diving with will mind?"

Thomas smiled. "They are on their honeymoon, so no, I do not believe anything is going to upset them now."

Junichi gave a small smile as well. "Thank you, Thomas. I appreciate your help."

Twenty-Two

Nick woke when he heard the flapping of flip-flops coming up the stairs.

"Hi, Nick, you look comfortable," Sarah said. She chose a chair in the sun and wrapped herself in a big thick towel as she sat down, then tilted her face up.

"Hi Sarah, I'm glad you came. Otherwise, I would have slept here all night." Nick sat up, adjusting the back of the lounge chair. "How was the dive?"

"C-c-cold!" she said through chattering teeth.

"Really?" asked Nick.

"Well, it's my own fault. Tropical waters, close to the equator, sounded so warm that I didn't wear a wetsuit. At first it was heavenly, but we were down for over forty-five minutes, so even eighty-two degrees isn't warm enough for that length of time. Tomorrow I'm wearing my wetsuit."

"Sorry you're cold. I'll make sure to wear mine as well. What was the dive like?

Sarah's brows lowered as she thought. "Interesting. It was an Emily Flying Boat at around forty feet. It's odd to say that it was both pretty broken up and more intact than I anticipated. A lot of coral growth. It wasn't what I expected, though I can't really tell you what I expected either. It was just..." Nick watched her eyes and mouth change as conflicting thoughts ran through her head. "I guess the word is eerie."

That word had a sobering effect on Nick's mood.

Sarah's face converted into a smile. "Oh, don't mind me. The cold got to me and my imagination. However, you're going to like Ben, our dive master. He's a really big guy, but seems to be like a gentle giant, and has been diving for over ten years now. He's from Australia and has a home on Weno, where he lives with his wife." Sarah loosened the towel. "The sun heats up fast."

"Sounds like you got his life story," Nick said, smiling at her energy and quick change of topics.

Sarah laughed. "Well, I'm sure you've figured out that I like people and their stories. I'm going to clean up. All the salt water is drying and stinging me. See you later."

Nick watched Sarah leave, then turned to gaze out over the water. The wind was picking up, bringing in big puffy clouds, dark with moisture. I guess our weather is changing, he thought. Glancing at his watch, surprised to see it was dinnertime and that he was hungry. As he stood up, a strong gust of cooler wind hit him. Living in California, he missed the variety of weather that he had growing up in Iowa. Maybe the soothing sounds of rain tonight would help him sleep. He headed to the dining room, and, once there, he found Natalie sitting at a table with Frank and Ray.

"Ah, these are the rolls I was smelling earlier," he said as he sat down next to her.

"Wasn't it heavenly? My mouth has been watering all afternoon. This also smells good. I wonder what it is?" asked Natalie.

Sarah sat down on the opposite side and picked up a small stand with a notecard from the middle of the table, and read it out loud. "Aubergine Stew, from Ghana. It has beef, eggplant, and okra, all served on couscous; fresh baked rolls; and for dessert we have Ko'n, from Chuuk, which is breadfruit with coconut milk."

Natalie took a bite, savoring the flavor. "Interesting. I've never had it, but it's very good."

"Anyone going on the night dive?" Frank asked, eating fairly quickly.

"You're on your own, Frank," said Sarah.

"Well, I'm going," he said and pushed back from the table.

Mary stopped by their table. "How was your meal? Did you get enough to eat?"

"Excellent," said Natalie. "My compliments to your chef."

"Thank you, I will pass them on."

"Mary, I particularly loved the rolls. The aroma filled the whole ship," said Sarah.

"I do, too. You will smell those several times this week. Divers are hungry people, so we need plenty of food to refill what you will be burning off."

"Let's go watch Frank off," said Sarah, and the others followed.

Nick joined Sarah, Natalie, and Ray at the railing, watching Ben load the boat, then he and Frank took off.

Sarah shook her head. "Frank is nuts. You couldn't pay me enough to go out there now. The only lights that exist are those little dots on that island way over there."

"I might do a night dive while I'm here," Ray said, as he yawned.

Sarah laughed. "You mean if you can stay awake?

Nick smiled at their banter and took in the view of the lagoon at night. The lights of the *Eagle Ray* spilled onto the ocean around the ship, but only for a short distance. Once the little boat ventured beyond these lights, it was completely dark. The clouds covered up the moon, if it was there, and the wind continued to blow, churning up the water. Although Nick loved to dive at night, this total darkness gave night diving a whole new meaning. He was used to the black veil under the water, seeing only what your dive light let you see. However, there were always lights on the boat as you went in and as you were coming up giving a feeling of confidence, or relief. In this case, the little boat didn't even have running lights. "How are they going to find the boat when they're done?" he asked out loud, to no one in particular.

"How in the world can Ben find the mooring to begin with?" asked Natalie.

Nick made a mental note to ask Frank about his experience when he returned. He smiled at the fearlessness of youth. For himself, today had been a good day. Taking the catnap on deck had refreshed him a bit. Socializing in the salon and having a nice drink before crawling into a comfortable bed was a good plan. "I'm heading to the salon for a drink. Would any of you like to join me?"

Ray yawned again. "I'm sorry, Nick, but I'm heading to my cabin for an early night."

Natalie glanced at Sarah in silent question, who nodded, then turned back to Nick. "We'll go with you. I actually snuck a nap in my cabin. Otherwise, I'd be crashing now as well."

When they walked into the salon, Eonin was at the bar pouring drinks. The four German guys were talking and laughing loudly. The party was in full swing.

Eonin called over to them. "What can I pour for you?"

Nick gave it a quick thought. "Scotch neat, if you please. Sarah, Nat, do either of you want anything to drink?"

"No thanks, I'm good," Sarah said, then went to get a seat. Nat shook her head no and followed Sarah.

Nick smiled at Eonin. "I gather you moonlight as a bartender?"

Eonin laughed. "Sometimes I do. I live on the Eagle Ray and help out whenever I can. Also, I made friends with the German guys when they were here before, so I know to pour the drinks a little weaker for them since they will party for several hours tonight."

"You're a good friend, then. Were you born here in Chuuk?"

"Yes, and I fell in love with diving, so I was very happy when Thomas hired me. I've been working for him since he started his business. I get to do what I love and get paid for it."

Nick raised his glass to toast him. "Smart man. Thanks for the drink." Nick went to sit near Sarah and Natalie, who had joined Thomas, Junichi, and Shoko.

"Thomas," Junichi said, "it seems amazing to me that the wrecks are still in such good condition after such a long time. Do you have any idea why the salt has not devoured the metal?"

"Actually, the salt water has done quite a bit of damage. It is not that obvious yet, though. In many cases, the corrosion is almost hidden by marine life. The coral is beginning to support some of the structures that they have taken over. In another forty years, we expect large sections of the ships to begin collapsing from the corrosion. However, the deeper structures are more protected than the shallow ones, as there is less oxygen in the deeper water. That will slow the corrosion for some of the wrecks."

"What about the large marine life, Thomas?" asked Sarah. "I realize I've only seen one of the wrecks here so far, but it seems strange that I've only seen a reef shark. Where are the larger marine animals?"

"The battles drove most of the larger animals out. Afterwards, the Japanese supply lines to the islands were cut off. The schools that remained were heavily over-fished, as that was one of the few protein sources available. In addition to the citizens, there were approximately 40,000 Japanese personnel stranded here with no supplies. According to the locals, it was a horrible situation of starvation for everyone."

Shoko grabbed Junichi's hand and squeezed.

Thomas continued. "For fishing, the Japanese used any explosives they had. The concussions from the blasts were the easiest way to get the quantities of fish they needed. That drove out schools of fish." Thomas stopped and quickly glanced at Junichi.

Nick wondered what stopped Thomas and watched Junichi for some indication. However, the younger man didn't show any reaction except a slight clenching of his jaw.

Thomas now struck a positive tone in his voice. "Now the reefs are established and growing, the big schools are back, and the larger animals are coming back as well. The whole ecosystem had to reestablish itself."

"I find it strange," Sarah said, "that I never heard of this battle growing up. We heard of so many, but not this one. It seems that the shipwrecks are more well known."

"Yes," Thomas said, "for some reason, it is considered the Pacific's forgotten battle. Which I agree is odd considering the importance of it. The atoll made it impossible for the Americans to land and 'take,' so it became the first real battle that showed the strategic value of carriers and their planes as the ultimate weapon rather than aiding a landing."

Nick thought it was so odd to hear Thomas referring to the 'Americans and Japanese' with Americans and Japanese sitting in front of him. Though, in light of the topic, this was the safest way to talk about the battles. He wondered if Junichi and Shoko felt this oddity as well. Nick took another quick peek at Junichi, but his averted eyes and expressionless face gave away nothing of his thoughts.

Nick wasn't ready to go to bed, nor was he in the mood to participate in this particular discussion or the other group party. He was content to sit back and be entertained by the young people with all their energy. It seemed like yesterday that he could party most of the night and still dive the next day. Not a particularly smart thing to do, but it was fun. An occasional drop of rain hit the window behind him. The wind was howling harder. Hopefully, Frank and Ben wouldn't get caught in anything big. Then again, Ben was undoubtedly very experienced, so Nick was sure they'd be fine.

Thomas got up and put a videotape into the VCR player and turned on the television. Nick was curious for a couple of minutes as a black and white newsreel began. Suddenly, Nick's stomach dropped as the video began to show planes taking off from an aircraft carrier. Nick recognized the ship.

His heart began to pound, his whole body started to sweat. The narrator's words hit him like a punch in the face. "...the finest planes and the greatest pilots in the world..." Everyone else was mildly interested in the video, not comprehending the significance of what they were about to see. Nick knew. His hands grabbed the arms of his chair in desperate need of stability. He didn't watch the video. He didn't need to. He had lived it and tried to forget it. Now that time came rushing back, refusing to stay buried any longer. Vague and clouded mental images that had laid dormant for so long, cleared into memories sucking him back to 1944. Old memories from Truk played in slow motion for Nick to relive...

Twenty-Three

February 17, 1944

The air group circled the outer reef, eyeing potential targets. Nick radioed back to his crew. "Guys, we're staying with the main formation. Jason, get on your ventral gun and keep an eye out below. I don't want any Zeros surprising us from behind." The fighters were chattering that there didn't seem to be many Zeros, but plenty of anti-aircraft fire from the guns hidden in the hills. The fighters then saw a Jap destroyer near the North Pass. The air group leader sent a few of the Hellcats and a couple of Avengers to go and sink it. Over the radio came the flight leader's voice. "Gent, you and Tom Cat take that tanker ahead. The rest of you follow me. We're going after that big ship to the right."

"Roger." Nick dropped down with James behind on the left. They had a couple of fighters up ahead strafing the ship's guns. With this protection, Nick radioed his wingman. "Tom Cat, I'm going lower to drop my fish."

"Copy, I'll follow."

Nick began a downward, wide sweeping S maneuver. At the end, he could see the broadside of the ship straight ahead. Sighting his target, he aimed for the middle of the stern. Regardless of any variance in the torpedo's path, it would still hit. His plane was about twenty feet off the water, and the torpedo was set for a six foot running depth. *I've got you.* Then

Nick pulled the lever. "Torpedo away," he called and angled the plane up.

Ahead, Nick saw the Japanese captain standing on the ship, watching the incoming torpedo. As Nick flew over, the captain glanced up. Their eyes met. Their mutual glance momentarily welded together as their destinies collided. A single moment in time causing one life to end, the other to be forever altered.

It was odd how clarity could come in an instant. Nick understood, no longer naïve, living the little boy's game of war. No matter who died, everyone still went home for dinner. Mr. Talon, his old physics teacher, came into view. With every action, there is an equal and opposite reaction. The soft dawn sky was a mix of blue hues outlining the lush green islands spotted around the lagoon. The smell of fresh-baked cookies filled him, replacing the salty ocean breeze. Nick remembered his grandfather's eyes right before. The silence was deafening, the recesses of his mind knowing there should have been engine noise. His plotting tablet stowed, a ticket stub attached, showing the directions back to the carrier, back to safety. No one there to give comfort. Jeanne's picture, jammed in the control panel, smiled at him. The captain stood tall and proud, impressive in his black uniform, his eyes accepted. Nick wondered what the man was thinking, remembering, wishing. Did he have a wife? Did he have children? There would never be answers, but the captain did nod his head, acknowledging the kill.

Nick's plane safely cleared the ship when he heard the explosion, pulling him back to reality. The anti-aircraft guns on the islands started to fire. The enemy had gotten over their surprise. Five-inch shells raced toward him. "We've got fire, fellas," Nick called back to his crew. He yanked the plane down to the right, hoping his guys were strapped in. An explosion pushed the plane further down. Nick spun to the right to miss another shell.

"Tom Cat's hit, they're going down," yelled Danny.

Nick pulled the plane around, hoping to help his friend. Instead, he watched it smash into the water, nose in. "NO!" he yelled. James 'Tom Cat' Carson, his best friend, was gone. Nick's mind would not accept what his eyes told him. No. They shared a room together. This morning, James brought him a game of catch in the backyard. They climbed trees, talked about how to meet girls. He can't be gone. He had to be there. I need him here. He's my connection to home, my anchor to a world not at war. A world of love, laughter, family. James can't be part of the dead. The cockpit closed in, stifling the air. A nauseating stench of burning fuel and bodies filled the cabin. His flight suit soaked in sweat. Nick's heart pounded against his chest, straining for release.

Nick was inside James' plane, watching it go down, trying to pull up, but the plane wouldn't respond. The nose hit the water, crushing the plane, ripping off the engines, sinking to the bottom. James dead in the cockpit.

"Skipper, we've got a Zero coming behind us," called Danny.

Nick pulled the plane back around, all guns firing. He felt the vibrations when the plane got hit, but it wasn't the cockpit. "You guys okay? Did we get hit?" No response. Nick's heart dropped. Panic seeped in. Nick had to yank the plane left to miss another shell. "Guys," he yelled desperately, "can anyone hear me?"

"Sorry," Danny responded. "Jason got hit, but it's not bad. Only a few holes. They didn't get anything important. Don't worry, just get us the hell out of here!"

Relief buoyed Nick into action. He pulled up again to dodge more flak, and that got them out of range. "How's Jason?" His crew was his responsibility, and Jason had gotten hit.

Jason came on the interphone. "I'm okay. I hit my head, and Danny came down to wrap up my leg. I'll be fine."

"Glad you're still with us. We're heading back." Nick's mind was overwhelmed; his training took over almost as an autopilot. Nick formed up with the rest of the squadron to head back to the ship.

On the flight back, Nick kept his eyes ahead, but his mind was numb. James was gone in an instant, just as Tony had. The same with that captain. He didn't try to look back for the ship. He knew it was gone. His mind could see it in its final sail, sinking slowly and settling on the bottom. No more movements, now lifeless. A tomb to the ghost of the Japanese captain and his crew.

Twenty-Four

The video continued in the salon, though Nick heard nothing. It showed the planes as they dive bombed the Japanese ships and airfields. The narrator talking about the brave American and Allied naval aviators in their fierce battle against the Japanese Empire. How the tides of the war in the Pacific had turned in the Americans' favor, and now they were pushing the Japanese slowly, but surely, back to their own beaches. He went on to say how the American and Allied soldiers were winning the fight against the Nazi occupation in Europe. As the video ended, everyone in the salon was completely silent.

After several minutes, Heinrick, a very proud German, broke the silence. "Well, that was propaganda," he said to no one in particular.

Another German, who wasn't about to let this party get philosophical, spoke up. "Gentlemen, what we need is more beer and a hot tub." And their party got underway again, as the four moved out to the deck.

Natalie stood up and quickly walked out of the room.

Mary glanced around at everyone in the room. She met Thomas' eyes briefly, then left the room.

Junichi sat in shock after watching what his father had gone through. He noticed Nick was still sitting frozen, staring at the television, engrossed in his own thoughts. It was then that Junichi realized that Nick had been personally involved. He was about the right age, and his reaction to the video left little doubt. Rage began to grow. How dare he come back here!

He glanced at Sarah, who returned his gaze with a sad smile as she got up to leave. He then glared at Thomas, who was watching Nick closely. Shoko pulled at Junichi's hand. He got up to follow her out, leaving the two men alone in the salon.

Thomas jerked his head at Eonin, indicating for him to leave. Eonin nodded, glanced at Nick, then left. Thomas took a bottle from the bar and poured Nick a drink. "How about another drink, Nick?" Thomas said, as he took the empty glass from Nick's hand and replaced it with the full glass. This brought Nick out of his memories. He stared down into his drink.

Thomas sat down across from Nick. "You know, I have had this ship here for many years now and have had a lot of people on board. I have shown this video to every group for years. I do not even watch the video anymore; I watch the people. Most of the reactions are the same. The young ones find it vaguely interesting. Some people react more if they lost a family member in the war. Usually, the video does give people a better sense of the significance of the wrecks. They take more care diving on them." Thomas took a breath. "You, however...saw a ghost." When Nick didn't answer, Thomas prodded. "Do you want to tell me about it?" Thomas sat back in his chair and waited.

Nick took a long drink and a deep breath. He stared at his drink for a while. "It was unnerving to see the battle in front of my face. I had forgotten that some of our planes had cameras mounted on them." Nick got quiet for a few minutes, then continued. "I thought, or hoped, some old memories got pushed out by the new memories of life. But, in reality, they're buried only to return when they decide. The video, seeing the planes from that perspective, brought old memories out." Nick took another long drink and sat quietly. Thomas patiently waited. "As you have figured out, I was here during the raid on Truk. I was one of the Avenger pilots." Nick admitted, deciding what to say.

"We were all so young. Blissfully, naively focused only on the victory. That's the way all wars are fought, by brave, naïve young people who don't know what they are doing, but follow orders well. I had been in battle before and after, but this raid was different.

"You know most of it. We caught them by surprise and pretty much blew up everything." Nick was quiet for a few moments. "Did you know that we dropped fifteen times as much firepower here as the Japanese dropped on Pearl Harbor?" He drained his drink. Thomas came over and refilled his glass.

"It was a beautiful day. We left the carrier before daybreak. The islands were silhouettes in the distance. I was so determined and exhilarated. This was our chance. We came over the islands and I got my signal to go in. The ship was sitting there waiting for me. There was so little anti-aircraft firing that I was able to come in..." Nick stopped in mid-sentence, then continued. "I dropped my torpedo and left. On the way out, we had to fly through heavy anti-aircraft shelling. I was soaked in sweat, holding my breath." Nick's eyes clouded. "My friend and wingman got hit. He and his two crew went down that day."

Nick downed the rest of his drink in one swallow. He looked at Thomas. "When I got back to the carrier, I had to report my mission, but I've never talked about it since then." Thomas was still focused on Nick's story, so it took a couple of minutes for this comment to sink in.

"Never, not to the guys you served with, not even to your wife?" Thomas asked.

Nick shook his head. "No, my wife had been a nurse during the war. She saw her own horrors, so we never talked about it." Nick started to shake his head, smiling. "I never knew how, but she always seemed to know things, though. Shortly after the wrecks were discovered here, she asked me when I was going to come."

Thomas had sat there listening to Nick, then finally spoke. "Nick, why did you come here?"

He thought for a moment. "I suppose, for the same reason any veteran visits a battle site from their past, to find closure."

"Do I need to be worried about you? This is not like walking around a field or touring through the remains of a building. This is underwater."

"It will be good to see the marine growth take over the ships. Life goes on, beauty covers destruction."

"That didn't answer my question, Nick."

"No, you don't have to worry about me. Now, we both need to get some sleep." Nick got up and put the glass on the bar, then turned back to Thomas. "Thank you for listening."

"Nick, wait. I have to ask. Do you know which ship you sank?"

Nick shook his head. "No, I don't. Good night." He left to walk the short distance to his cabin.

He collapsed down on his bed, thinking about his discussion with Thomas. Nick couldn't bring himself to give Thomas all the details. Those eyes! So many memories buried, yet he was never able to bury those eyes. Jeanne said eyes were the windows to the soul. What did those eyes convey: defeat, death, the end? That man's life ended that day, but the unanswered questions lived on.

A banging rang through the air as the wind whipped some rigging on the ship. Hard rain pelted the porthole as the clouds finally burst. So much for the soothing rain.

Nick bolted up when he heard the loud knock, rubbing his hands down his face. Taking a deep breath, he composed himself. "Come in."

When the door opened, two very cold and angry dark eyes stared down at him.

Twenty-Five

Junichi glared down at him through narrow slits. Drawn down, his eyebrows formed a sinister 'S' shape. His forearm muscles delineated as he clenched the door handle.

Completely confused, Nick turned and put his feet on the floor, but didn't stand. Junichi quietly closed the door, then turned back to face him.

"You were here, weren't you?" he said with all the loathing that burned inside of him. "Were you one of the pilots?"

Oh no. It never crossed Nick's mind that anyone other than Thomas saw his reaction to the video. He let out his breath slowly. "Yes."

"Would you like to know who else was here?" Junichi sneered, then didn't give Nick a chance to respond. "My father."

"Oh, God," Nick said in a barely audible whisper.

"That's right. Just think about this. There is a definite possibility that you were the one who bombed his ship."

Nick's stomach dropped. There was nothing he could say to counter that thought. So many possibilities existed. How could...

Junichi continued. "Oh, he didn't die here. No, he was blown off the ship. He made it to shore, crippled for the rest of his life. He was one of the people Thomas spoke about tonight, the ones that starved for two years. You have no right to be here!" Junichi yelled. "You have no right to come here and enjoy a vacation! Do you get some sick pleasure out of enjoying the tombs of the men you killed?"

Nick jerked back, throwing his hands up. "Junichi, it isn't like that." His voice hardened at the accusation. "I didn't come here for fun..."

Slashing his hand, Junichi cut him off. "Of course not. You, by chance, happened on this dive site. It is so close to your home," he spat out the words. His chest heaving, he took a step closer. "Of course you came for fun."

Knowing that Junichi was well past rational thought, Nick didn't respond, but he saw Junichi's hands clenched into fists. The younger man wanted to fight, and any movement on Nick's part would be all the provocation needed. Never breaking eye contact, he stayed seated.

"Which ships did you bomb?"

"I don't know."

"Liar." Junichi stared at him. "Did you bomb the airstrips and bunkers?"

"Yes."

"Do you know what I saw on that video?" Junichi yelled, pointing to the wall leading to the salon. "I saw his ship...on fire! From your planes! I heard the bombs that caused my nightmares for years! Do you know that all the years I grew up, I had to keep quiet at home because of what loud noises did to him?" Junichi took a step closer, looking down at Nick. "Are you going to stand and face me like a man?"

"No." The two stared at each other. Junichi's jaw muscles clenching.

Junichi lowered his voice to a whisper. "Were you in Tokyo?"

This question completely shocked Nick. "No!" Nick saw the raw pain on Junichi's face and remembered the fire bombings. "No," he said again, louder. "Those were B-29s. I flew Avengers."

Junichi didn't say anything.

"Were you in Tokyo when it was bombed?" Nick asked gently.

The answer flashed in the younger man's eyes.

Nick's shoulders dropped. *Just a small child.* "You had to be so young."

"I do not need pity from a murderer."

Nick held his breath, reading the conflicting emotions in Junichi's eyes: anger, sadness, fear, remorse. After several minutes, Junichi turned and left the room. Reeling from the confrontation, Nick fell back down and stared at the ceiling. *What in the hell...*

Twenty-Six

Junichi walked back through the salon and out to the deck. Rain was pouring on the overhead covering, and the wind gusts blew some in. He leaned over and put his hands on the back of a lounge chair and lowered his head.

"Junichi," Thomas asked quietly from behind him, "are you alright?"

Junichi stood up, but didn't turn. "Yes."

"I owe you an apology. I should have warned you about the video. I always show that to the guests and did it without thinking. It must have been a shock. I am extremely sorry."

Junichi nodded, but still didn't speak. Thomas continued gently. "I have never been in a war. I did my National Service after the war, stationed in Singapore. I cannot even imagine the horror that was experienced, the positions that men were put in, the decisions that had to be made, and the memories that had to be lived with. Nor do I know what you experienced. But I do think you know that you can't hold Nick responsible for your pain."

Junichi continued to stare out over the lagoon, not replying to Thomas.

"Do you want to talk?"

"No."

Thomas stood there for a moment, then sighed. "Alright, I'll leave you alone."

As he heard Thomas' footsteps fade, Junichi exhaled, letting his shoulders drop. The video had been a shock. However, his anger at Nick was even more of a shock. His reaction was completely visceral without any rational thought. The video had shown a small portion of what his father went through, which brought a form of reality to the images that had formed based on his father's descriptions and Junichi's own research. This reality was hard to face, reinforcing his father's pain.

But it was the sound of the bombs that triggered his own memory, forcing him to relive that night in Tokyo again. How many times would that nightmare replay, bringing back the fear? Junichi sat down on one of the chairs, wrapping his arms around himself, trying to stop the shivering. He relived it all over again: the wind whipping around him, the glass shards hitting his body, the screams, the stench of burning flesh, the feel of the burning shirt and shoes, the eyes of the little girl, his mother's sobs, the vortex chasing him. In the solitude of the night, Junichi cried the fear, the anger, the frustration, the impotence, the grief. He cried for his mother, for what she must have gone through to save them both. He cried for his father, for his physical and emotional pain and the life he could never have. And now, as a father would, he cried for that little boy.

Twenty-Seven

Mary found Natalie at the bow of the boat, leaning her arms on the rail and her head bent down. This part of the ship was dark, but there was enough shine from the masthead light for her to see that the woman's shoulders were shaking. The rain had calmed to a slight drizzle, which was enough to soak Natalie's shirt and hair.

"Natalie, are you alright?"

Nat jumped up and wiped her eyes and nose. Clearing her throat, she responded in a husky voice. "Yes, I'm fine." She didn't turn around, though.

"If you're fine, why are you out here crying?"

"Ah...it was...the video. I didn't expect it. That's all."

Mary moved to the railing, where she could see Natalie's face. "Why did it upset you?"

"My brother, James, was here during the war. He was a pilot, like Nick was."

Mary's eyes widened. This explained Nick's reaction as well. "What happened to your brother?"

Natalie closed her eyes. "Shot down during the battle. They never recovered his body."

"Oh, no. How awful," Mary said and, for a moment, thought back to her uncle's funeral after he died in battle. Mary could not imagine how difficult it would be to be left wondering, without closure. Wanting to console her, Mary reached up to touch Natalie's shoulder, but stopped her hand.

Having met the woman so recently, the gesture may not be welcome.

"I am so sorry. Is that why you came here?"

"Yes." Natalie's voice grew a little stronger. "Nick was coming here, and I asked to come with him. He has his own past to deal with, but I wanted a way to say goodbye to James. The last time I saw him was after his training, before he went to battle. Then later, all we got was a telegram and a few personal belongings.

"James' death almost killed my parents. We couldn't have a real service for him. There was no real way to say goodbye to him. It was like he disappeared. Mom wouldn't allow any changes to his room for a long time. We kept the door shut, but once in a while each of us would go in, just to sit and cry." She stood up, turning into the wind to blow her hair back out of her face. "I'm sorry, Mary. I'm being ridiculous."

"That must have been very hard," Mary said, ignoring Nat's apology.

"It's been so long ago, I didn't think I would be this emotional. However, seeing that video, I mean it was from a pilot's perspective, what James saw, what he had to do." Nat wiped her eyes again. "I'm alright Mary. Thank you for listening. I'll see you tomorrow."

Natalie knew she left abruptly, but hoped Mary would understand. She walked to the other end of the ship, relieved to be alone. Someone's hat was lying on the deck. Holding onto the rail, she rode the rocking of the ship, more pronounced at the back of the boat, away from the anchor. Salty spices mixed in the damp air, while goose bumps formed on her arms from the memories that flooded back. She sat down on the deck, ignoring the puddles of water. The bulkhead protected her against some of the wind, and she wrapped her arms around herself as her mother's eyes came into view. The mother she'd known had never come back after James' death. For years, Natalie didn't understand this. She grew angry at James for dying, for taking that part of her parents with him. Yet she was old enough to feel guilty about these feelings. Holidays were perfunctory in nature. Gone was the joyful, spontaneous laughter. She and her parents existed mechanically for years. It wasn't until she had her own child that understanding came. James was her brother, but he was her mother's son. Children shouldn't die before their parents.

Twenty-Eight

The next morning, Thomas sat at his desk facing Mary and Ben, who were seated across from him and Eonin leaning against the door. "Thank you, Ben, for getting here a little early today. I need to let you know that we have a strange situation with this group, and I would like your help with it. Nick Mitchel was one of the US pilots during the raid on Truk, and Junichi's father was on one of the Japanese ships, though he did not die on it. I do not know the story."

Ben gave a low whistle. "Well, this could get uncomfortable."

"It already has," said Thomas. "Junichi confronted Nick last night, and he was very angry."

"How did Nick react?" asked Mary.

"I don't know. I overheard Junichi yelling, then I tried to talk to him. I decided not to talk with Nick about it last night. Ben, will you please keep an eye on Nick? He says he doesn't know which ship he bombed, and I don't know how he is going to react to the wrecks."

"Sure, I'll watch him today. He and Natalie didn't dive yesterday."

"How were the other Americans?"

"Very competent. They're a conservative lot. Respected the site. They all have their gear well secured, nothing dangling. They worked together and had a plan with a maximum depth and stayed generally together. We dove on the Emily Flying Boat yesterday. Sarah made sure she was the first in."

"She went in? Did she stir up the silt?"

"No, in fact, I think that's why she went in first. She hardly stirred up anything. She controlled her depth with her breathing and used her hands to swim through, never her fins. She explored, then came out and let the others have a go. Frank and Ray were very controlled as well. Frank was also great on the night dive last night."

"Good to hear. Eonin, how did your group do yesterday?"

"Fine. All four of them are good divers. They dove as couples, but have similar styles. Junichi and Callum are more adventurous than their wives, but the men stayed with the wives. They all did light penetrations. The guys poked around a bit more. All were respectful of the site, managed their air well, all in all very competent.

"Good. Thursday, keep an extra eye on Junichi, please. The *Heian Maru* was his father's ship. He told me that his father was very ill for a long time and that his death a couple of months ago was expected. He said he is comfortable diving. I want you to know and watch out for him."

"Wow, I haven't had this before. So, his dad was one of the ones stuck on the island after the battle? This is going to be hard on Junichi. Of course, I'll keep an eye on him."

"Thank you. Gentlemen, please keep this to yourselves. This is private information and not the business of the other guests. Also, I am hoping this will all blow over and everyone can have a good experience with us."

"Thomas," said Ben, "another thing, compressor number one is acting up. I don't think it's filtering properly. Can we send it to the shop?"

"Yes, I'll call and get it scheduled. Eonin, will you please disconnect it when you go down next and let's only use compressor number two to fill tanks until number one is fixed, alright?" The men nodded and then left the office.

"Those two will keep an eye on things," said Mary. "Thomas, you should also know that Natalie's brother was a pilot during the raid and was shot down. She came to say goodbye to him in some way. I was thinking on Thursday, I would offer to help her."

"That would be nice to do. Do you think she's alright to dive?"

"I think so, but I'll keep an eye on her as well as the others. Now I have to go to oversee breakfast." Mary gave him a quick kiss and left.

Thomas sat there, thinking about the turn of events. High emotions and scuba diving were a bad combination. Although each guest had been told their safety was their own responsibility, Thomas never forgot that these dive masters could be put into dangerous positions if problems came up. When divers were properly trained and dived a site intelligently, the experience is smooth and enjoyable for everyone. When someone was overly confident or forgot something, the situation could instantly turn life threatening. Emotions could cause a diver to forget something important. Fortunately, no major issues had ever occurred. Nonetheless, Thomas never took safety for granted. Eonin and Ben had worked for him for many years and had become part of his family.

Twenty-Nine

Nick bolted awake, momentarily confused about where he was. Still in his clothes from yesterday. Morning light came in through the porthole, but the sky was still cloudy and the rigging still banging. He knew he did get some sleep, but it sure as hell didn't feel like much. Standing up, he stretched, then went to take a shower to wake up. Warm water hit the top of his head and ran down the length of his body, helping him fully wake up.

Thoughts of what Junichi had said last night came back. Nick had felt bad for him when he said his father had died and even worse was the thought of a boy in the fire bombings—if that's what happened. But Junichi wasn't a boy anymore, and the last thing Nick needed was someone telling him he had no right to be here. The more he thought about that, the angrier Nick got. *I never wanted to come here. Either time! Who the hell does he think he is? The only reason I'm here is because of that damn war that his country started!* He shut off the shower and yanked the towel off the hook. *And what was his dad doing on that ship? At that point, probably shooting at me.* Nick finished drying off and went to get dressed. *I'm here for a reason, which is none of his damned business, and I'm not going to let him stop me.* Having made that decision, Nick felt more in control and went to breakfast.

Most people were already in the dining room. Nick was both irritated and relieved that Junichi wasn't there. He joined his group and took a seat next to Frank. "Frank, I have been wanting to ask about your night dive last night. How was it?" Nick inquired as his breakfast was served—sausages, rolled omelets, and grilled tomatoes. Pushing his food around, he ate a bite of the omelets.

Frank turned to him with his eyes big and laughing. "The dive was interesting, as well as absolutely terrifying! I've never experienced such a dive before and I don't think I will want to again for quite a while. There is no way to describe that much black!" Frank's arms and hands moved around, animating his tale. "We motored for a while and then Ben slowed down and stopped. He looked to each of the islands, for what I'm not sure, and then moved the dinghy a bit more. Then he stopped, went to the front of the boat, reached the pole down and scooped up the mooring. The mooring wasn't even on top of the water. It was pitch black out there. How he found it, I'll never know.

"We found the ship about sixty feet down. I was planning on casually exploring the deck area, but *no*, Ben taps me on the shoulder, shines his light on himself, and motions for me to follow him. Then he began swimming. I wasn't too thrilled to follow, but I had *no choice*! He was the only one who knew where the dinghy was." Frank took a quick bite of his food and launched into the tale again. "We entered through one of the doors and swam down a hallway. I was following, so I can't tell you how relieved I was that Ben was so calm and didn't stir up the silt. I'm sure I did." Frank was laughing at it all now and at himself. "I don't mind admitting I was scared to death. We toured a few areas of the ship and then went up and out through the bridge.

"We did our safety stops, which were also an adventure. I had to focus on the dive lights to keep my perspective. For some reason, the theme from Jaws kept playing in my head. The whole time, I'm praying Ben knew where that dinghy was, which, of course, he did. I've never been so glad to get out of the water."

Nick was laughing with Frank. "I'm very glad I didn't go."

"Frank, did you get back before the rain hit?" asked Sarah.

Nick smiled at her with a twinkle in his eye. "I certainly hope so. He wouldn't have wanted to get wet."

Rolling her eyes, Sarah laughed. "Oh, very funny."

Natalie joined the table. "Sorry I'm late."

"Now that we're all here," said Sarah, "should we plan our next dive? This one is going to be deeper."

"Alright, how do we want to do this?" Frank asked.

"To be honest," said Sarah, "as exciting as this adventure is, I want to take a conservative approach. I mean, I'm not going to take any big chances. We have a lot of dives this week and we're going to Palau to dive next week. If I penetrate, it's only going to be in a place that is very clear how to get out."

Ray joined in. "I agree. I bought one of the books, as well, and as I read through it, most of these dives have deeper parts to them and we are diving repetitively every day. I think we should set a depth limit for each dive and stick to it. Sarah, what do you think?"

"I agree. I also think we should dive as a group. We can spread out down below as long as the visibility is good, but in general, I think we should stay as a group. Frank, what do you think?"

"I agree as well. Nick and Natalie, I don't know what your plans are, but do you want to join us?"

Nick focused on Natalie as she took a bit of sausage, then she nodded. "Yes," said Nick, "we would appreciate that. Thank you. I agree with the general strategy."

"Alright then," said Frank, "Today's first dive is on the *Shinkoku Maru*. It's a tanker about 500 feet long, a big ship. The top of the bridge is at forty feet and the propeller is 125 feet. Anyone want to set the depth of this dive?"

"How about a hundred feet? This gives us a little leeway up and down," Ray suggested. "I personally haven't experienced nitrogen narcosis yet, and I don't really want to push it on this trip. At a hundred feet, we should be able to see a lot of the ship and not get narced."

"At that depth, we will have roughly forty minutes of bottom time," Sarah added after she glanced at the dive tables.

"Looks like we have a plan. Shall we go?" Frank asked the group.

Everyone agreed, and they headed down to the dive deck to meet up with their dive master.

"Hello, good morning," the large man said to the group, then turned to Nick and Natalie. "Hi, I didn't meet you yesterday. I'm Ben, and I'll be your dive master. We'll see a few of the wrecks here over the next few days. It takes many trips to explore them all. The ones we'll see represent a very interesting variety from a diving perspective. While I am not your guide, I have been on each of these wrecks many times and can answer any questions you have."

Nick glanced over as Junichi, Shoko, and another couple came down the stairs. Junichi glared at Nick for a moment, then turned away. His eyes were again hidden behind his sunglasses again, so Nick couldn't read any expression. Just as well.

Ben also saw the group. "Let's go over here to talk about the dive." He led them over to the side, out of the way. "You may have seen that your tanks are charged to 3000 psi. We need to build in time for two safety stops. The first one will be for five minutes at fifteen meters. Which, for this wreck, is next to the smokestack and mast, so there is plenty to see. The other safety stop will be for three minutes at three meters, so we hang there." Ben stopped his explanation. His eyebrows drew down. "To make sure, are you all proficient talking in meters or do I need to convert to feet?"

"We're all fine with meters," Frank said. As he confirmed with the group. Everyone nodded yes.

"Good," said Ben, and then continued. "I want everyone to start ascending with about 1000 psi left in their tank. I realize this might seem somewhat early, but safety has to be our first priority. We want to surface with about 500 psi remaining. Again, this is for safety purposes. Is everyone in agreement with this plan?" Ben waited until everyone nodded their agreement. "Have you had a chance to read up on this dive?"

"Yes," said Frank. "Our plan is a max depth of a hundred feet, I mean thirty-three meters, and generally we'll dive as a group."

Ben turned to see Nick and Natalie nodding their agreement. "This is good. I'm very pleased that you have a plan. Do any of you plan to do deep penetrations of the superstructures?"

"Ben, I'm guessing the superstructure is the part of the ship that sticks up like a multilevel building. Is that correct?" asked Sarah.

"That is actually a good explanation. This area houses the bridge, crew quarters, offices, galley, medical spaces, etc."

"For this dive, we aren't planning on deep penetrations," said Frank.

Ben nodded and continued. "Visibility will be approximately twelve meters, so you should see the wreck quickly as we descend. Since this wreck is a little farther out from the island, there will be more choppy water, as well as a surge down below. Hopefully, it won't be too bad.

"You'll have a good opportunity to penetrate because there is a very large torpedo hole that is easy to get in and out. Even with a wetsuit, pay close attention to staying away from the corroded metal. Also, because much of this wreck is fairly shallow, there is an impressive coral buildup, and the marine life is plentiful. In your reading you saw that this is a large ship, so because of its size we'll have a second dive on it in a couple of days. Don't try to see everything today. If we're ready, do your buddy checks here, then take your gear to the dinghy."

When Ben left the group, Sarah spoke up, "Natalie, will you do my buddy check for me?"

"Sure, will you do mine?" Natalie asked, as she began to check Sarah's equipment.

"Of course, then I can do yours, Nick, if you want. Or you can get one of the guys to do it."

Nick smiled. "Thank you, Sarah. I would appreciate that." Nick felt warmed by this group, making sure he was included. He put on his dive knife and wrist computer, then began to check his own gear while also discreetly watching the others, and was pleased to see that they all seemed to be thorough. Once finished, they moved their gear over to load onto the dinghy. Frank and Ray, very gentlemanly, helped the women carry their tanks. Before Nick climbed into the dinghy, a tingling up his spine made him turn back to find Junichi watching him. Their glance held for a moment before Junichi broke it off.

Once on board, Ben directed the dinghy away from the *Eagle Ray*. The little boat jumped and lurched in the chop. Nick noticed Sarah staring at the horizon. "Sarah, are you alright?" he yelled about the motor noise.

"Yes," she shouted back, without looking at him. "I get seasick, so watching the horizon keeps it under control."

The boat ride took a good twenty minutes, but when they stopped, there wasn't anything to see. The group watched as Ben moved to the front of the dinghy, put on a mask, grabbed a rope, and then jumped in the water. A moment later, he pulled himself back on board. "There we go, all tied on."

Ray peered over the side into the water. "How on earth did you know where the buoy was?"

Ben laughed. "It took a long time to learn. I have to visually triangulate sites from the surrounding islands. It's a lot harder at night. We only go to a few of the wrecks at night because those are the only ones we can find. Any last-minute questions? No, alright, let's get going."

Sarah already had her gear on and fell back into the water. Nick was ready as well and followed her in.

"Feeling better, Sarah?" he asked when they surfaced.

"Yes, I do better with bobbing in the water rather than on the boat."

The others joined them, then they deflated their BCs and sank down. Since the top of the wreck was about forty feet, Nick saw its shadow almost immediately. The water, more murky at the top, was very clear about twenty feet from the wreck. The surface chop subsided and now there was a swell gently pushing him forward, then pulling him back. The ship was huge, by a diver's standard. Blue corals and green leafy plants already encrusted the still-standing King post. Small white Sergeant Major fish, adorned with their black vertical stripes, were out guarding their homes and feeding in the flowing water.

Further down, the colors were all a dull blue-gray to Nick, as the water filtered the sunlight. Even with the clouds, enough light made it through so that at close range he could see the most spectacular yellows, reds, emerald greens, and royal blues of the growing plants and animals. Fish in vibrant hues darted in and out, animating the tapestry. It was magnificent, and it gave Nick a heightened feeling of being alive. The top areas received the most sunlight and had become breeding grounds for this organic growth. The growth gradually slowed as the depth got lower, but it didn't stop. Over time, nature would overwhelm the exterior of the ship.

Once down on the wreck, Nick stayed up off the deck to take the whole site in. He watched the others as they began to explore. Natalie was inspecting the Staghorn coral. Ray had found a red feather starfish. Frank was headfirst in an opening, not penetrating, but shining his light inside the ship. Sarah, like Nick, had stayed back and also seemed to be taking in the ship as a whole.

Nick noticed Ray and Frank disappear over the side and followed them down. When he caught up, Nick saw they had found the large hole in the side of the ship. The opening was at least fifteen to twenty feet in diameter. The edges were torn and ripped. The guts of the ship were open to the water. The others had entered the wreck, but Natalie and Nick stayed out, hovering about forty feet out from the ship, staring at the hole.

The torpedo had hit its mark. The ship could never have survived this blast that instantly converted a crowded engine room into a large gaping cavern. It also tore through many surrounding walls, eliminating barriers that may have briefly hindered the inflow of the water.

Nick gazed at the hole. He had never seen an actual torpedo hole. He had...his vision became hazy, his mind's eyes took over, transporting him to the top of the ship, eyes watching the torpedo in the water, heading toward the ship. A massive explosion, deafening all sounds, a great concussion hit his chest. The power of the blast instantly...The pounding of his heart brought Nick back. He saw the hole, the others inside. He was still hovering; he hadn't moved.

Nick glanced at Ben, who was staring at him, showing the diver's okay sign. Nick automatically formed the sign communicating that he was alright. But was he? *Get yourself together, Mitchel!* He wanted to leave, but something pulled him in. Slowly, Nick kicked his fins and swam into the wreck.

Inside, Frank had found a diesel engine stuck down in the silt. Ray was inspecting a fuel injection pump and its pipes that were still mounted on the wall. Sarah was up by the first of two levels of catwalks. Nick turned to find Natalie hovering at the entrance, taking it all in.

Nick began to survey the area, hanging pipes and metal debris strewn around. It would take incredible power to rip this apart. A human body would not stand any chance against such a force. Uncontrollable shivers took over his body as his mind began to see the crew working here, the explosion blasting them apart. Others in the surrounding areas, still alive, fighting the immense torrent of water rushing in. The strength of the massive ship, useless against the pull of the weight of the water below, starting to sink, drawing in even more water from on top. He heard the cries, the screams of men swallowed by the overwhelming volume of water.

Something touched his arm. His eyes cleared to see Natalie looking at him, questions in her eyes. He nodded at her and swam out of the ship. *Get out of here.* Still shaking, he had to surface. As he exited the ship, an eagle ray swam by. Magnificent and elegant. Nick calmed down and watched the ray swim. He followed it a short distance. It turned to him and Nick felt her. *Jeanne, you're here!* The ray turned back and swam away. Nick watched until it disappeared.

You're losing your mind. Get a hold of yourself. You're creating images that aren't there! After several deep breaths, he regained control again. Still trembling, but not as much, he glanced at his pressure gauge and found he had used more air as he was going crazy, but still had enough to finish the dive. Then he checked his computer to see his depth, but nothing was showing. Tapping the screen didn't help. Nick couldn't understand it. He remembered turning it on and checking that it was functioning. *Hell!* Repetitive dives were a lot easier with the computer. First, he'd lost his mind, then he'd lost his computer. What next?

Natalie swam over, her eyes conveying her question. Nick pointed to his computer, and she looked down. She nodded, then signaled for him to follow her. He turned back to see the others exiting the hole and swam to join the group. They all began to explore the marine life. Nick took another deep breath to calm himself down. *Things happen.* After this, he was able to focus back on the dive.

He joined Natalie exploring at the sea fans, large oysters, leafy green plants, and orange sponges that were all flourishing on the ship. The sunken vessel provided the needed foundation for the artificial reef to grow. A sort of symbiotic relationship, the ship providing structure for the reef and the reef providing structure for the decaying ship. In time, the ship would fail, but the reef would protect part of it.

Sarah motioned to the group and pointed out away from the ship. A Black Tip Reef Shark swam by. Nick estimated it to be about five to six feet long. After it passed, he swam back to the wreck and ascended up to the deck area and watched as Frank and Ray immediately swam over to inspect a rusting gun, mounted on the poop deck, which was substantially covered in marine growth. Nick joined Sarah by a light pink sea anemone with a couple of clown fish swimming in and out of the anemone that somehow was safe from the anemone's stinging tentacles. Sarah looked at him, her bright eyes filled her mask. He signaled to follow him and swam over to inspect the ship's ventilators with their trademark curved cowls, which were now filling up with red soft corals and orange sponges.

The group continued their exploration until they reached the very top of the smokestack. This height gave Nick a very good vantage point to view the aft portion of the ship. It was obviously a shipwreck, but with the impressive marine growth and only a few straight edges could still be seen. Destruction and thriving life made a stark contradiction.

Ben knocked on his tank to get everyone's attention. Nick turned to see Ben give the okay sign, thumb and first finger touching, to form a circle with the other three fingers pointing up. Nick responded with the sign. Ben then put his hand out, showing three fingers. Nick followed the group, ascending up to the next safety stop. The wreck was now only a vague shadow. Turning his face up, Nick saw the surface shimmered, distorting and playing with the view of the clouds beyond.

Once the safety stops finished, they surfaced and got back on the boat. Nick helped the ladies with their gear. Ben unhooked from the mooring and started the dinghy, bouncing its way back to the *Eagle Ray*.

"Wow, that was amazing!" Ray shouted above the motor noise. "I didn't expect that much coral growth."

"The wreck is still in great condition," said Frank. "Are you alright, Sarah?"

"Yes, it was incredible, but I'm going to focus on the horizon for a few minutes," she said, staring out in front of the small boat.

Frank turned to Nick. "What did you think, Nick?"

"The marine life was spectacular." Nick glanced at Natalie. Her eyes conveyed a deeper understanding of the wreck and regret. She gave him a sad smile, then turned to gaze out over the water.

The chatter died down and Nick thought about what happened. None of his reactions made sense. Seeing the ray swimming and thinking it was Jeanne, then his imaginings of the horrors of the bombing, shaking his head as he watched the tranquil islands pass by.

Once back at the *Eagle Ray*, Eonin was there to help everyone unload. Nick immediately took his gear to his station, then inspected his computer.

"Nick, what happened to your computer?" asked Natalie.

Ben overheard her. "Nick, do you have a problem?"

Nick took it off his wrist, examining the back. The battery compartment cover was loose. "Water got into the battery compartment. It's through."

"I'm so sorry Nick. That was new, wasn't it?" asked Nat.

"Yes, it was," he sighed. "Ben, do you have one that I can rent?"

"I'll have to check. Eonin," Ben called, "do we have any more computers?"

Eonin checked, then came back over. "Sorry, I didn't find any. What happened to yours?"

Nick handed it to him.

"Sorry, Nick, this can't be fixed. This is tough, though it happens pretty often, especially to people who travel the farthest and are tired. Something gets missed. Make sure to follow the tables or stay close to your group on the rest of your dives and you'll be fine," Eonin said, then went to refill air tanks.

"Sorry, Nick," said Ben. Nick nodded.

The rest of the group headed to the upper decks to the lounge, but Nick went to his cabin.

After Nick closed his doors, he heard a knock. Opening it, he found Natalie.

"I wanted to make sure you were alright. You seemed upset a couple of times."

For her sake, Nick tried to smile. "Thanks, Nat, but I'm fine. I'll admit that the destruction got to me for a few minutes. Then I saw that eagle ray swim by, and I felt better."

Nat smiled at that. "Maybe Jeanne was there. I know I was surprised. I didn't expect the wrecks to still look so...new. It all began to get to me as well." Natalie tilted her head. "You know, big brother, I've got strong shoulders too. I also know talking isn't your strong suit, but if you want to, I'm here."

Nick nodded, but didn't say anything.

Nat smiled. "Glad you're okay. I'll see you at lunch."

Nick watched her leave, appreciating her thoughtfulness. Once he closed the door, he changed into dry clothes, then sat down to think. He was certain that he had tightened the housing, but then he was tired, so maybe he only thought he had. It wouldn't have been like him to not tighten it, though. Then he thought about how he'd lost his mind on the wreck. Why the hell had his mind created those images? He had no way of knowing what had happened, but for some reason, his brain conjured up that horror. *This is silly.* Nick got up and splashed cold water on his face. What he really wanted was oblivion, but every time he closed his eyes, another set of eyes stared back at him.

Thirty

Nick was a little late joining everyone for lunch. He spied an open seat near Sarah and Natalie. "May I join you?" he asked the table in general.

"Please do," came the reply from Shoko. Junichi didn't acknowledge him.

Nick sat down and turned to Shoko. "Did you enjoy your dive today?"

"Yes," replied Shoko. "We dove on the *San Francisco* and it was very beautiful. So full of coral and fish. Your companions here were telling us about your dive."

"I'm sure they told you it was on the *Shinkoku Maru*. It also had a substantial and beautiful reef buildup."

"Junichi," asked Sarah, "what part of Japan are you from?"

"We live near Osaka, but I also spend much time in Tokyo for business. I am a building contractor."

"Oh, Nick's an architect. You two have some things in common."

Junichi glanced at her, still refusing to acknowledge Nick. There was a dark intensity in his eyes; while not anger, it was clearly not welcoming. "Yes, he and I share some similarities, but differing...perspectives."

Shoko stared at Junichi, then her eyes shifted quickly and met Nick's, then she turned away. She seemed to pick up the note of tension. Fortunately, Sarah didn't. Natalie, however, was gazing at Nick.

"Shoko," Sarah said, "I must say, you both speak perfect English. If you don't mind me asking, where did you learn it so well?"

"Junichi and I both learned English in Japan. Additionally, we have traveled to the United States extensively, which allowed us to practice. We have spent much time on the west coast and Florida, as the weather is very nice in those locations. Sarah, how long have you been diving?"

"About seven or eight years. I fell in love with the sport."

The ladies continued their general polite conversation as the meal was served. None of them gave any indication that they were aware that neither Nick nor Junichi were participating. As before, Sarah read the menu card out to the table. "Paella, from Spain. It includes shrimp, clams, chicken, rice, corn and peas. One of my favorites, by the way. We're also having Jekaro Brioche bread, from Chuuk, with coconut sap for dessert."

Nick focused on his plate. Breathing in the rich paprika and oregano aroma soothed his queasy stomach. The German boys were at the next table having a good-natured argument about something. Though the words were in German, their hand gestures conveyed their feelings. Sounds of dishes and glassware gently knocking around came from the kitchen. He resolved, again, to ignore Junichi and enjoy his meal. A couple of sample bites confirmed the food tasted as good as it smelled, allowing him to relax and enjoy the dinner.

Thomas and Mary finished their meals and began to circulate through the room, checking on people to ensure they were content. "Nick," Thomas said, "Ben told me that you needed a computer. I have a spare you can use."

"Thank you, Thomas. I appreciate it."

For the first time, Junichi spoke to Nick. "Your computer looked new. Did it malfunction?"

Nick considered Junichi, trying to figure out why he would care about this. "The seal failed."

"That is unfortunate. Accidents do happen, though," Junichi said as he stood up.

"I suppose they do."

"I do hope," Junichi said, "that it does not spoil your lovely vacation." With that, he turned and walked away, leaving Nick staring at him.

⸻◦⸻

After lunch, Shoko and Junichi walked back to the cabin. Once inside, she turned to face him. "What is wrong?"

"Nothing."

She knew him for too long to accept that. "It is unlike you to be rude."

"I was not rude, nor did I feel the need to participate in the discussion. If you will excuse me, I am going to take a walk on deck. I will return in a little while."

Shoko's mouth hung open as she watched him leave the room. Junichi never elaborated on his feelings, but this was the first time he completely shut her out.

⸻◦⸻

Nat followed Nick to his cabin. "What was that all about?" she demanded as soon as the door was closed.

"What do you mean?"

"You know exactly what I mean. The tension between you and Junichi could have been cut with a knife." When Nick didn't respond, she prompted further. "Are you going to tell me what is going on?"

"No. I'm going up on top to read. See you later."

He walked out and shut the door. Natalie stood there. "Do I kill him now or later?" She shook her head, then went to her own cabin.

Nick stopped to purchase the Lindemann book and took it up to the top deck to enjoy the down time and begin his research. Fortunately, the winds had died down to an acceptable breeze, but clouds still filled the sky. Soft slapping of flip-flop shoes on the stairs announced Sarah's arrival.

"Hi, Nick. Are you reading about our next dive?" asked Sarah. She had changed back into her bathing suit with a large white floral T-shirt over it, wearing a gray baseball hat with a skeleton in scuba gear on it.

"Not yet. I'm still following the map, trying to figure out the position of the islands in the lagoon."

"I bet when you go into a shopping mall, you immediately go to the directory and look for the 'You Are Here' sign," said Sarah, laughing.

Nick had to smile at the comment. "Yes, I actually do. But I think you do as well."

"Yes, I do. How did you know that?"

"The way you approached the wreck this morning. Like me, you stayed back, hovering and observing."

Her expression showed obvious surprise that he'd noticed. "You're right. I need the overall context first, then the details make sense."

"Sarah, may I ask you a personal question?"

"Sure."

"You're a beautiful, intelligent young woman. Why hasn't some man snatched you up yet?" As soon as the words were out, Nick was appalled at his presumption. "Sarah, forgive me, that was inappropriate of me to ask."

"Oh, Nick, don't apologize, and thank you for the compliment. It is a perfectly normal question. After all, I asked about your wife on the plane. I was involved with a guy for a couple of years, but it ended last year."

"He was a fool to let you go."

Sarah shot him a beaming smile. "Thank you. I thought so too. There was, of course, drama that occurred. But he was a nice guy. After the emotions passed, I realized that the true issue was that our core values weren't the same, so the relationship fell apart on the first significant challenge. In the end, he wasn't the right guy."

"What are you looking for?" he asked, intrigued.

"That's the burning question. I asked my dad once how he was able to design homes for people—he was an exceptionally talented architect. He told me people had a hard time telling him what they wanted, so instead, he asked them what they didn't like about their existing home. While they talked, he drew. In the end, he eliminated everything they didn't like, so they loved the final design. That relationship I was in helped me see what I don't want. So, I think now I am in that stage of figuring out what I want, or maybe I should term them my non-negotiables. I'll find him one day. I've at least learned that passion without compatibility doesn't last."

"He'll be a lucky man when you find him."

"Again, thank you. You were married a long time, weren't you?"

"Yes, I found the right girl when I was twenty-three. You are right about the core values. Ours were the same. Which is why our relationship lasted through all the challenges."

"She was your love, your lover, and your best friend. You were very lucky to find her so young and have so much time with her."

Nick nodded. They were both silent for a few minutes, then Nick glanced at his watch. "We have another hour of surface time before our next dive. What are you going to do?"

"I hope you don't find me unsociable, but I think I'll nap in the nice breeze."

"Not at all. Enjoy yourself."

Sarah reclined back, pulled her hat down over her eyes, and relaxed. Nick was glad she wanted to nap. It was nice to be with someone, yet still alone with his thoughts. She was right. He was very fortunate to have found Jeanne, but he also thought of the war and how very lucky he was. What he couldn't figure out was why. He had survived all the battles, the training, married the most wonderful woman, and fathered two loving kids. All the challenges that came his way, he made it through. Why was he so fortunate, but others weren't? Those eyes immediately came into his mind, pulling his attention back to where he was and the book on his lap.

A quick scan of the table of contents showed it contained the Japanese record of the events, as well as a very detailed list of the US activities broken down by ship and by mission. Jumping ahead, he found the records for the Bunker Hill carrier. How odd it was to see a historical account on something he'd actually lived.

Flipping to the back, he found the maps and began to put together how Operation Hailstone played out, where the strike force was located, and how the planes came in. The advantage of being on a live-aboard vessel, instead of a land-based resort, is that Nick could sit here on deck in the lagoon, away from the islands, and envision what happened from the lagoon's perspective. As his vision began to form, he glanced back down to the map to begin to fit the location of the wrecks as they existed during the raid, this time from the pilot's perspective. He repeated the up and down process many more times until his image became clear. *This area!*

"Is Sarah sleeping?" asked Natalie.

"Not anymore," Sarah replied, still hiding under her hat. "Is time really up?"

Nick closed his book and checked his watch. "That was a fast break."

"It's about time. Frank and Ray want to meet up to plan the next dive. Are you both up for that?"

"Here we are," said Ray, as they came up the stairs and sat down.

Frank again took the lead. "Our next dive is on the *Heian Maru*. It's the largest ship in the lagoon, so I asked Ben and he said we would be diving on the fore ship area."

Sarah interrupted. "Excuse me. Fore ship? I have to say I'm getting confused about the ship's language. So, if I have this right, the bow is the front, the stern is the back. What is the fore ship?"

Nick explained. "A ship has three sections: the front, middle, and end. These three sections correspondingly are called fore-ship, mid-ship, and aft-ship. The very front of the boat is called the bow. Bow to your front is how I remember it. The very back is called the stern. Finally, the left side is called port, as in the sailor left the port. And the right side is called starboard. Does that help?"

"Yes, thank you. And while we are at definitions, I know what a mast is on a sailboat, but what does a mast and king posts do on a steam vessel?"

Everyone glanced at Nick. "The mast will typically have running lights, radio antenna, flags, or anything else that needs to be held up high. King posts, or when double and connected are called goal posts, are used for crane type actions, such as loading and unloading the cargo holds or supporting fuel lines."

"Ah, thanks again. Sorry, Frank, I needed a little clarity. So, we are diving on the front of the ship?"

"No problem, Sarah, and you are correct. The strange thing about this wreck is that it lies on its side, so it will be a little weird diving on it."

"What's the depth?" asked Natalie.

"Forty-five feet to the side that's up, known as the starboard beam." Frank grinned, showing off his knowledge. "And it's 110 feet to the seabed."

"How about we sort of split the difference and call seventy-five feet the max depth?" offered Natalie.

"Sounds good to me," said Frank.

Nick spoke up. "I hope you all enjoy the dive. I'm going to take a break and have a nap. Then I'll be ready for the next dive."

"Okay, see you in a while," said Frank.

As the others headed down the ladder, Natalie turned to Nick. "Why aren't you diving?"

"I thought you said you wouldn't play mother hen?" he asked with a smile. "Don't worry, I'm alright Nat, just tired."

She rolled her eyes at him. Though unconvinced, she nodded and left to catch up with the others.

Relieved to be alone, he needed time to think about how his imagination was getting away from him. *This is ridiculous. I'm far too old and too experienced a diver for this silliness, losing control like that, going into a panic. It made no sense.* Of course, the wrecks he dove on before were either much older and far more decomposed, or much younger, having been sunk intentionally, but that didn't mean that he hadn't anticipated the damage of these wrecks. *Why had he created illusions in his mind? Why attempt to mentally recreate the horror of it all? Am I losing my mind?* Fortunately, the eagle ray had come by and distracted him. *I can't keep having these reactions underwater!*

Then there was Junichi. *How did he know my computer was new?* Junichi knew which station was Nick's. Could he have been the one to loosen the computer housing? *Why ignore me only to comment on the destroyed computer?* None of this made sense. A voice of reason, deep inside, reminded him that he was very tired and could easily have forgotten about tightening the cover. But then...

Enough! Nick stood up and went down to the next deck to walk around. Sitting there questioning his sanity wasn't getting him anywhere. The wind whipped back up and sprinkles began to fall. Nick climbed back up the stairs and put his towel over the book. Thunder rumbled in the distance—a sound he hadn't heard in a long time. Thunderstorms were rare in California.

Nick went to the railing and watched the dark clouds rush in. Energy charged the oppressive air as the wind excited a force field around him. Mother Nature was angry. "Are you angry at me too?" he shouted to the sky. "Are you telling me I shouldn't be here?" Lightning backlit the dark clouds, its vibrations flowed through him, and its sound exploded in his ears. Nick closed his eyes and lifted his face to the heavens. "Do what you want to me. Finish this one way or another." The hard rain began to slap him. Wind found every opening in his shirt, flowing down the neck, inflating up from his sleeves. Exhilarated in a frightening way, he held fast to the wet railing. Legs spread apart, knees rigid, he rode the growing waves with the boat. Groaning sounds from the bow grew as the anchor chain stressed, but held. He opened his eyes just enough to see the spectacular display of power. Every form of energy in use at Mother Nature's will.

How long he stood at odds with the force, he didn't know. Then, without announcement, the squall stopped. Nick turned his face up to see the dark gray giving way to lighter shades. Silly as it was, he felt triumphant and alive in a way he hadn't experienced in years. The warming sun began seeping through the clouds. Nick, completely drenched, pulled an equally wet chair into the sun and lay down. Placing his wet hat over his face, he slept.

Nick stirred when something shook his body. Pulling off his hat, he found Natalie staring down at him.

"Good afternoon, sleepyhead. You were really out."

Adjusting the chair up, he blinked several times. "Hello."

"Nick, why is your backside all wet?" Natalie asked, pushing his arm forward to feel his shirt.

"The storm. Did you all get caught in it?"

Nat shook her head. "No, it must have hit while we were down. What did you do, stand in it?"

"Yes, actually," he said, his mouth grinning wide, "I did, and it was great."

"Okay," she said, laughing, "whatever makes you happy. Also, where did you get that green fishing hat? I thought your dad was sitting here."

"It's my dad's hat." His voice softened. "I took it after he died. I never wore it before because Jeanne and Dana told me I looked goofy in it."

"Don't worry, it's an acceptable goofy. Your dad would be very happy that you're wearing it."

Nick's smile widened. "Thanks. How was the dive?"

"Very interesting. The ship was huge, and it was on its side. So I had a hard time reconciling myself as we swam through it. I was glad to come back." Nat got comfortable and leaned back to doze.

Sarah came up the stairs, wrapped in a towel, dripping a trail of water behind her. "Hi Nick. I'm back to disturb your solitude." She laughed. Settling in a chair, she propped herself up to read.

"I welcome the company." Nick got up to get his book, that was now covered with a wet towel. The cover and the edges were wet, but the rest was fine. Sitting down, he opened it and read about the individual wrecks.

After a while, Nick realized he hadn't seen Sarah turn any pages. He glanced over to find her staring out at sea. "What are you thinking so hard about, Sarah?" he asked quietly.

"Oh, I was thinking about diving on these wrecks. I've never been interested in going to see a ghost town before, yet that's what I'm doing here. The only difference is that this seems to be a ghost fleet. It's odd." Sarah shook her head and tried to read her book.

A ghost fleet. Such an apt description, Nick thought. Turning his focus back to the book, he flipped the pages back and forth, confirming each wreck's location on the map. Realization exploded in his chest. *Oh lord! I did that.* Nick's hands shook as he picked up the dive schedule. His hands dropped. He took a deep breath, exhaling slowly. *Thursday!*

Thirty-One

An hour later, the group assembled on the dive deck with Ben. "Have you determined your strategy for this dive?" Ben asked.

Ray responded for the group. "We need to talk with you about that. The *Hoki Maru* is another long ship, at about 450 feet, so we need to know where we're going to plan our strategy."

"Excellent point. We will be diving around the stern, also referred to as the aft-ship. This is the only real part of the ship left. The front two-thirds of the ship was almost completely destroyed in a massive explosion. We guess that one of the bombs that dropped subsequently exploded existing bombs on board. You will see a metal flagpole at the stern, which is severely bent by the power of that blast. The depth of the deck is right at thirty meters. That said, the holds are very open. So, if you want to explore the holds, exterior of the sides, or the stern damage, you will drop quickly. The seabed is sloped here, and the aft is higher than the bow. Seabed in this area is still 45 meters; too deep if you are not specifically trained.

"Another thing to consider is our bottom time, which, if you all manage your air well, is going to be about thirty-five to forty minutes. Since this is a deeper dive, it will take about five minutes to get down to the deck and then another five minutes to come up. Add that to the eight minutes of total safety stops. We will only have a maximum of twenty minutes on the wreck."

"How about we make the maximum depth a hundred feet," said Ray, "and only plan very quick drops for anything interesting?"

"Sounds good to me," said Sarah. "I may want to drop into the hold, briefly anyway. But I don't think I want to go over the side on this one."

The others murmured their agreement with the suggestions.

Ben continued. "That sounds like a good strategy. Dropping down into the holds can take you much deeper. Have any of you been narced before?" Everyone shook their heads no. "In that case, let's review this. Nitrogen narcosis is also called 'rapture of the deep.' Certain gases under pressure, nitrogen in this case, can cause an anesthetic effect to the human body. This results in a feeling of euphoria, which is sometimes called the martini effect. It alters the reality of a diver, impairing his vision and mental capabilities. Deep divers train to learn when and how nitrogen narcosis happens to them.

"Since none of you have experienced this before, you have no idea of the depth that this can hit you. Exploring the holds can add up to fifteen meters to your depth. You need to be very quick in your exploration and *do not* go in alone. Have a buddy nearby, watching to ensure you don't get into trouble. Also, keep in mind that nitrogen narcosis can also occur if you ascend too quickly. In either scenario, the narcosis doesn't last, and reverses when the pressure is reduced. Any questions on this?" Ben took a breath and glanced around.

Everyone shook their heads no.

"Now this site is also farther out and won't have the islands to protect it from the trade winds. This means more chop in the water." He glanced at Sarah, smiling. "You may want to make sure you're ready out there."

Sarah grimaced and nodded.

"The choppy surface will subsequently cause more surge down below. I don't think the surge will negatively affect visibility though. We usually get about fifteen meters. This wreck is deeper, so we won't see it until we're down quite a ways. After we're all in the water, follow me down, because we won't follow the buoy line. When you get in the water, check your time. At twenty-five minutes, start your way back to where I am, and we'll ascend together. Now we can go and have some fun."

Everyone loaded their gear on the dinghy and set out for the site. Once again, Ben seemed to magically know where to stop, this time using a pole with a hook on the end to grab the submerged buoy. As soon as he said they were connected, Sarah, with fins in her hand, rolled back into the water.

Nick watched her fall in. "She's quick."

Natalie laughed. "Better quick than sick."

Once they all got in the water, Nick released the air from his BC, and descended headfirst, pausing every three feet or so to equalize the pressure in his ears. Swimming down, he experienced the odd feeling of dropping down into nothingness. Above, he saw the shimmering surface and the sky beyond, but down below there was nothing except tiny particles floating in the water. Nick checked on his partners to ensure they were alright, then continued down waiting for something to appear.

An image began to emerge, faintly at first, but gaining in detail the farther down they went. The ship was large and the undamaged portions were well-preserved. While Nick hovered, an image formed in his mind. He was flying and up ahead, he saw a monstrous explosion followed by several instantaneous explosions, feeling the reverberations in his chest. Working to hold his plane steady, he saw a massive ship blown almost out of the water, with the smoke and flames shooting hundreds of feet in the air. Nick shook his head, clearing his vision to see the wreck below, wondering if this was what remained of that ship?

Stop it! I'm not doing this again. With that resolve, Nick swam down to catch up with the group. As they reached the ship, they began to spread out for their exploration. The surge wasn't bad, but still enough to push Nick around. For every five feet forward, he was pushed four feet back. It wasn't powerful enough to slam him into anything, but he had to work to ensure he didn't hit anything, either. Floating up off the deck and away from the coral, the surge eased to a gentle rocking back and forth, which allowed more relaxed observations. There was sufficient sunshine to light the wreck, yet it was filtered enough that there weren't as many corals or sea fans down at this depth. This wreck appeared to be much closer to how it had been the day it went down.

From his reading, Nick knew it used to be an old New Zealand freighter that was captured by the Japanese in the summer of 1942. Most of the crew were sent to prisoner of war camps. Several crewmen died from the horrid treatment. Fortunately, though, most survived. The ship's engines were foreign to the Japanese; therefore, the Chief Engineer and several other crewmen were forced to stay on board to operate the equipment. The Chief and crew conspired to sabotage the ship, burned blueprints, pumped fuel out of the ship, threw necessary tools overboard, and caused damage to many of the working mechanisms. The Japanese never realized that the prisoners caused the damage. Their shipyards were able to make sufficient, although not complete, repairs. It was put back out to sea to deliver fresh supplies to Truk in January 1944, only to be sunk a few weeks later.

Sarah and Natalie were down on the deck inspecting the hold area. The large wooden hatch covering the hold had decomposed, leaving rows of steel beams about four feet apart. Sea grass, as well as various forms of leafy algae, had begun to establish themselves on these beams. Nick swam down and joined them, then examined a sea anemone and a large school of tiny fish swimming around their homes in the grass. Sarah motioned at Nick and Natalie, then gestured that she wanted to go down into the hold. Natalie indicated that she was staying up on deck. Nick glanced into the hold, then at his gauges, surprised to see he didn't have as much air as he expected he would at this point. Still no danger. He pointed to Sarah, then held up three fingers, indicating three minutes. Sarah held up the okay sign. Nick glanced at Natalie. She gave the okay sign, so Nick followed Sarah down into the hold.

With the hatches gone, there was enough sunlight to see most of the space. Nonetheless, Nick pulled out his dive light to shine in the corners and under debris. The hold was huge and held a treasure trove of large vehicles. There were a couple of large bulldozers, multiple trucks, and tractors. Other than the substantial silt buildup, most of these vehicles were in almost perfect shape. Their exterior metal sides were, for the most part, still intact, with only small portions eaten away. There wasn't any bombing damage to be seen in the area, yet it was clear that the vehicles, still upright, had shifted and moved around quite a bit as the ship rocked from explosions and sank. There was no marine life of any nature in the hold. A thick layer of silt covered metal gray equipment in a silt-covered metal gray hold. A very eerie setting, conveying the impression of what it was, an underwater tomb. Shivers ran up the base of his neck. Images of the crew working in the hold formed. He could feel the vibrations of an explosion further in the ship, the tilt of it as it began to sink, the machinery sliding. Terrified crew trying to get out. He jumped, imagining one of the bulldozers sliding toward him. Silt billowed up around him. Shaking his head, reality came back. He had sunk down into the silt on one of the bulldozers. The gray cavern was as it had been. Nothing had moved. Nick partially inflated his BC and rose above the silt. His breath was racing as fast as his heartbeat. He had to calm himself down. *It wasn't real.* He repeated to himself. *Only my imagination.*

Nick checked his depth. At 130 feet, he was way too deep. Kicking his fins hard and stirring up the silt, he swam up. Checking his gauges showed that time was up and he was already down to the safety limit on air, but still had enough to do the safety stops. He shined his light to get Sarah's attention. Sarah gave a thumb up sign and inflated her BC. Nick also inflated his BC and kept his movements slow and controlled. When he came out of the hold, he felt a little better. Natalie gave Sarah and Nick the okay sign and both responded with it. All was good. They all checked their gauges again. Nick had lost more air.

Ben banged on his tank and pointed his thumb up. Nick inflated his BC more and began the ascent to fifty feet for their first safety stop. He knew to control his ascent so that it was gradual. This allowed his body sufficient time for the nitrogen that he had absorbed going down to transfer back from the tissues to his bloodstream, then into his lungs to be exhaled out. If Nick ascended too quickly, the pressure would be relieved too soon. The nitrogen could then expand rapidly, creating bubbles large enough to block blood flow anywhere in the body. The last thing Nick wanted was the bends.

During the ascent, he watched the wreck disappearing into what seemed like a dense fog. Something caught his attention, however, when he faced forward, he couldn't see anything, truly nothing! Confused, he looked back down at the wreck, but it too was gone! There was nothing to see. Overwhelmed, his head began to spin, yet he knew he wasn't moving. He jerked his head up, expecting to see the surface. Nothing! His eyes registered only an abyss, void of everything. Panic grew. He had no point of reference, nothing anywhere to see. *The others!* Nick whipped his body around, but no one was there. Then he felt something pulling him up. Glancing up, he saw Ben above him, pulling him up to the others. Nick kicked his fins and Ben let go.

Something wasn't right. He was sinking again, so he re-inflated his BC. After a moment, he started to sink again. He was using more air than he should be. His BC wasn't holding his air. Ben gave him the okay sign in question. Nick shook his head to indicate there was a problem. Pointing to his BC, then showed Ben his air pressure gauge showing low air. Ben swam around him, tugging at the BC. When he was behind him, Ben tugged at the BC. Ben swam back, pulled out a slate and wrote:

BC leaking. Stay with me.

Ben inflated his own BC and grabbed hold of Nick to help pull him up to finish the safety stop.

Natalie swam over to Nick. Her eyes held the question, so Nick showed her his air pressure was getting very low. Natalie pulled out her secondary regulator and offered it to him. Nick hesitated, then she held up her air gauge that showed she had plenty. He took her spare and started breathing, using his little remaining air to continually refill his BC.

They hung there for a couple more minutes. Though he had to work to stay at this level, he calmed his breathing. Nick turned to focus on Frank and Ray. Ben was trying to show them how to blow their exhaust bubbles in the form of a ring. Ben had mastered it, as his bubble rings were perfect. Frank and Ray had a long way to go.

They finished the five minutes and inflated once more to head up. During the last three-minute stop, Nick kicked as hard as he could to stay up. He began to wonder if he should drop the weight belt, but Ben swam over and helped hold him up.

Once on the surface, Ben told Nick to get in the dinghy first. Once in the boat, Nick helped the others with their gear, then pulled off his BC to inspect it. "Ben, where did you see the leak?"

"It was in this area. The bubbles were small, but it was a steady leak." Ben turned to start the motor and direct them back to the Eagle Ray.

Natalie leaned over to his ear. "Are you alright?"

"I have a problem with my BC," he said.

After they returned and unloaded, Nick sat down to inspect his BC again. He found the hole. It was small, but that's all it needed to be.

Ben came over. "The bubbles merged with your exhaust, so I didn't see it until I swam behind you. I wondered why you were using so much air."

"What could have caused such a hole? It worked fine on the first dive."

"I don't know. Did you bump into anything diving in the ship's hold?"

"No, I took a lot of effort to ensure that I cleared the sides."

"What about the surge? Did it send you into any part of the ship?"

Nick shook his head. "I didn't hit anything." As Nick sat there, he was becoming more frustrated and angry by the minute. "Well, I'm going to need another BC. Do you have one I can rent?"

"Yes, we've got a good one. I'll talk with Thomas about not charging you. I'm sorry, Nick. I guess it was a weak spot and, for some reason, chose that point to fail."

Nick turned to see Junichi's dive group arriving back and unloading their gear out of the dinghy. Eonin walked over to Nick. "Hi Nick, do you have a problem?"

Nick nodded, watching Junichi, who was staring back with an inscrutable expression.

"Sorry, Nick, you seem to be having a run of bad luck," said Eonin.

"Or it's a sign telling me I shouldn't be here."

Junichi turned to put his gear away.

Eonin patted Nick on the shoulder. "No way, man. Just one of those things. Dive gear is great, but they're mechanical, so stuff happens."

Nick glanced at Ben. "I'll get the BC later." Then he left to go to his cabin. Natalie, who had listened to the entire exchange, followed him.

"Alright," she said, after the door shut, "tell me why you think Junichi had something to do with this?"

"I didn't say that."

"No, but your eyes were very clear. What's going on?"

"Fine. After the newsreel the other night, Junichi came to see me. He demanded to know if I was one of the pilots. After I said yes, he became very angry and told me his father had been here during the battle. Then he said that I had no right to be here. Since that time, I've had a run of bad luck with my gear."

There was a knock on the door. Natalie opened it to find Thomas. "Hi. Nick and I were discussing his trouble with his BC. Come in."

"I'm sorry, Nick. I wanted to see how you are and to tell you I won't charge you for a rental."

"How am I? I'll tell you how I am. I'm mad as hell."

"Ben said he wondered if you thought Junichi had something to do with this."

"He would be right, I do wonder. He made it clear to me that he felt I shouldn't be here."

"Nick," said Natalie, "his dad died here. He's upset and taking it out on you."

"His dad didn't die here," said Thomas. "He died a few months ago."

"Oh, that's even harder," said Natalie. "Nick, don't you see? This has got to be such a hard trip for him. You've seen his face. He's angry, upset, grieving. You know how that feels."

"Nick, I don't think he caused these problems," said Thomas. "I saw the BC and I've seen holes like that develop. It may have gotten hit during the flights you took and there was enough pressure on this dive to cause the final failure."

Nick contemplated one, then the other, knowing neither was going to believe him. Maybe Nat was right. Maybe Nick's own emotions were making him blame Junichi the same way he was blaming Nick. "You may be right. I'll calm down. If you don't mind, I'm going to rest before dinner."

Nat and Thomas both nodded and left. Nick sat down and thought back. He knew he didn't bump into anything, and he knew he packed his equipment very carefully, as he had done countless trips before. There was no proof, but a gut feeling told him this wasn't bad luck.

Thirty-Two

Nick walked down the stairs to the dining room and turned, stopping just before he collided with Junichi.

Startled and irritated, the younger man looked up, his eyes narrowed at the sight of Nick. "You are in my way."

"You've made that clear." Nick's shoulders pulled back, lifting his head to his full height so that he stared down at the other man. He had given up the power role last night, but not again.

Junichi's eyes noted the change in roles. His jaw muscles flexing repeatedly. "No, I made clear that you should not be here at all."

"Junichi, I heard from Thomas that your father's death was recent and undoubtedly hard on you. Out of compassion for your loss, and as a father, I am trying very hard to be patient with you. I think it is best that we avoid each other. However, since we both have to eat, let's try to ignore one another in the dining room. We only have a few days left. Then we never have to see each other again."

"I do not want your fatherly compassion or patience. I do not want anything from you." With that, he moved around Nick and went into the dining room.

Nick rolled his eyes and waited a few seconds before he followed.

The dining room was completely full when Nick arrived late again. Pleased to see the others saved him a seat, and that

Junichi was across the room, Nick sat down just in time for a crew member to hand him his dinner. Natalie read out the menu card. "Coconut Curry Chicken, from Chuuk, served with rice and salad. For dessert, we have Uter, which is also from Chuuk, and it is taro and coconut balls. Interesting."

Sarah started with dessert. "Yum! I need to ask Mary for some recipes. Although, can we get taro at home? Hey, Nick, this is Helen and Callum McCleland. Callum and Helen, this is Nick Mitchel."

Nick and Callum shook hands. "Hello, it is very nice to meet you both. Where in Scotland are you from?" Nick asked.

"Helen is from Edinburgh and I am from St. Andrews. We both live in Edinburgh now. Sarah said that all of you are from California. We haven't been there yet, but hope to. We have friends who say it is very pretty."

"It is. I have been to St. Andrews many years ago. I was able to play the New Course. I didn't have a handicap that qualified me for the Old Course," Nick said.

Callum laughed. "Don't you love how the New Course was still built in 1895? I played it once myself. It's not easy."

"Shoko mentioned that you both are on your honeymoon. Congratulations," said Nick.

Callum's smile radiated happiness. "Thank you. Yes, we are. We met while diving in Australia, and since we both have limited vacation time, we decided to take our honeymoon on a diving trip. Last week we were in Palau, this week here. Sadly, we go home next week. But it has been truly wonderful."

"How was Palau? We're going there next week," said Sarah.

"Amazing!" Helen responded. "I hope you go to Jellyfish Lake; it was my favorite. The lake is in the middle of one of the small islands, so you have to hike into it. The island rose quickly a long time ago, trapping some ocean water with jellyfish there. We snorkeled with them and could touch them. We were told that their stingers were gone, so they were harmless to humans. It was incredible!"

Nick's attention was drawn to his meal. After the exertion today, he was ravenous, and the food was wonderfully flavorful. He had to force himself to slow down and not devour it. "Well, that was wonderful. Mary," Nick said, as she passed the table. "This coconut chicken curry is very good."

"Thank you. It is one of Chuuk's specialties."

"Hey, Nick, Natalie, we're heading into the salon. Do you want to join us?" asked Sarah.

Natalie tried to repress a yawn. "I know I'm not. I'm heading to bed."

"Thank you for the invitation, but I'm a bit tired for a party tonight. Have fun though," said Nick.

Everyone pushed back from the table and headed in their different directions. Nick hung back to ensure that Junichi was well gone before he made his way up to the top deck. Once there, Nick got comfortable in one of the lounge chairs and adjusted the back down. The clouds from earlier had cleared out, leaving a blanket of stars covering the sky. At home, only the brightest stars shone through the city lights. Here, the stars had no competition, nothing to filter their glow. What an awe-inspiring display.

"Good evening, Nick. I see you've found my favorite spot."

Nick turned to find Mary standing by the stairs. "I was so mesmerized by the stars that I didn't even hear you come up." He tilted the back of the lounge chair up a little.

Mary pulled a chair out from under the canopy and sat down, staring up. "You would think living here I would take them for granted, but how could I? They never cease to amaze and humble me."

"I was thinking along those same lines. We get so caught up in our own world, yet how insignificant it is in the immense universe." Without the moon's glow or the boat light, shielded by the canopy, Nick shared the dark space with Mary, but couldn't really see her face.

"True, but our own world is all we have. We cannot travel to the ends of the universe. Not yet anyway."

"At home, in the city, I normally see the Big Dipper. Here I see the rest of Ursa Major, the Great Bear. Then on the left over there, next to Orion's Belt, we can see the rest of the constellation. See the bow out to the right and up a bit?"

"Yes, I do. I admit that my knowledge of the constellations is woefully lacking. I do, however, know the Milky Way on the left."

"Amazing. It's been a very long time since I saw that." A memory, standing on the carrier deck in the middle of the night, came to mind. Most of their raids started at sunrise, so he had to be up in the wee hours of the morning. Coming out to view the stars, before all the activity started, was his way of connecting with home, with Jeanne. She had suggested it to him in a letter, reminding him that they shared the same sky.

"I come sit up here whenever I can," Mary said. Her voice reminded him of where he was.

"I imagine that you don't get to do that as much as you might like. Is it hard to share your home with so many people?"

"It definitely took some time to get used to it. However, we found a bit of a rhythm in how to do it successfully. If, for whatever reason, it gets to me, I can go to the island. We keep a small home on Eten. It comes in handy during major storms or if either of us needs some space."

"I've known other couples who worked closely together. It takes a special sort of relationship for a marriage to survive that much togetherness."

Mary nodded. "Yes, that was, in fact, the biggest challenge we had to overcome. When we first got started, Thomas wanted to be involved in everything. That didn't work for our marriage. So over time, we split up the work so that he has his job and I have mine. He manages the business and mechanical aspects. I manage the food and cabins. I guess you could say the comfort aspects. That separates our day-to-day responsibilities, which saved our marriage."

"Let me tell you that you do a wonderful job—you and your staff, that is. Was it hard to come here from England?"

"Our son grew up and joined the fishing business with Thomas. Over time, Thomas needed a change and our son needed to take over running the business on his own, away from his father's influence. It was best for both of them. Thomas loves the sea and loves to dive, so this worked well for him."

"What about for you?"

"When Thomas first broached the idea, I was not...thrilled. When I saw him so excited, I began to see this as a bit of an adventure. Which it has been. Once we sorted ourselves out, I started enjoying it. I am able to meet people from all over the world. I love that part. On the one hand, my personal time is more limited, on the other I make many new friends from all over the world. I like people. We talk and sometimes dress in different clothes, yet in the most basic sense, though, we are all the same."

"You are living an adventure that few people ever have."

"What about you, Nick? Do you have children?"

"Yes, I have a son and a daughter. My son recently became engaged. His first marriage didn't work out, but this time I think he chose very well. My daughter is happily married and has the most precious little girl, my granddaughter." The mere thought of her made Nick smile.

"What about your wife? I see you are wearing a ring?"

Nick was silent while he touched and twirled the gold band. His ring was as much a part of him as the finger it circled. He couldn't remember the last time he had taken it off. "I lost her a while back to cancer," he said in a low voice. "It never crossed my mind to take it off. I still feel married..." *but I guess I'm not.*

"I am so very sorry, Nick."

"Thank you. She would have loved this place. Jeanne liked adventures. I think the two of you would have enjoyed getting to know each other."

"I bet we would have. What do you do for a living, Nick?"

Nick appreciated the change in subjects. "Well, I was an architect. Now I'm retired."

"Why architecture?"

Nick smiled. "My mother was an artist and my father was a home builder. I got a bit of both of them."

"The homes I lived in were rather old and not too interesting. I don't know much about what being an architect does, beyond the obvious."

"It's actually much more than drawing up construction plans. Done right, the house should be fitted to the property. When people spend money to buy property, they choose it for a reason. Our homes are our refuges from the world—the place where we are truly ourselves. My goal, as the architect, was to give them the home that accentuates the very reason they bought that property. It might be to enjoy the view, have the right spaces for children, have an amazing kitchen, merge the living with the surrounding property, comfort, etc. Done right, it's so intensely personal." Nick stopped and laughed. "I'm sure that's a lot more than you wanted to know."

"Actually, I find it rather interesting. I never thought about it, but I can see your point of view. If you don't mind me asking, why did you retire?"

"After Jeanne passed, the designs stopped. My ideas dried up. She was the foundation that I created from."

"Would Jeanne agree with that?"

Nick considered the question for several minutes. "I don't know."

"Ask her."

Nick whipped around to Mary, his eyebrows drawn down. "Excuse me?"

Mary smiled. "I get the impression that you two were married for a long time. You were obviously close. I imagine that you talked with her daily. When you get home, look through your past designs and talk with her about it. She is still very much with you, even if not physically. You might be surprised at what you hear if you listen with your heart."

The German boys came out to the lower deck, talking and laughing.

Nick smiled at Mary. "Our quiet solitude has ended. I think I'll turn in for the night. Thanks, Mary."

"Good night, Nick, I hope you sleep well."

Nick went down to his cabin and got comfortable on the bed. He thought about what Mary had said. However, he admitted to himself that there was more behind his retirement than what he had shared with her. Nick glanced at the Lindemann book he bought earlier. The events of the last couple of days began to replay over and over in his head. He began to wonder if he would be able to sleep tonight. In the background, the gently cadenced sounds of the water splashing against the boat and the subtle rocking motion lulled him to sleep.

Thirty-Three

Junichi stood by the railing in the bow section, absorbed in the view.

"Hello," said Thomas. "How are you tonight?"

Junichi jumped at Thomas' voice. "Hello, I am well, thank you."

"Were your dives today enjoyable?"

"Yes, very interesting." Junichi sat down in one of the white metal chairs surrounding a round table.

"You didn't want to join the party in the salon either?" Thomas asked as he took one of the other chairs.

"No, I am beyond the party stage. It is nice here in the dark," he said, gazing out to the lagoon. Subtle waves sparkled up to the edge of the ship's light. At that line, darkness took over, with only a few small lights scattered on the distant islands. A soft evening breeze minimized the residual humidity from the earlier storm.

"Junichi, I was wondering what made you go into construction."

"It is all I have ever known. I have been doing it since I was ten years old."

"Ten! That's very young!"

Years ago, Junichi had accepted that most people he came in contact with would never be able to understand that his childhood was not like theirs. "Yes, it was," Junichi agreed. "My father was unwell when I grew up. He could not do any physical work, so he took in bookkeeping for a few businesses, but not too many. He had to rest often. My mother always worked and never once did I hear her complain. One night, I overheard them talking about doctors' bills. After that, I saw the strain on her face and in her shoulders when she did not know I was looking. I am very close to my mother. As the son, it was my duty to take on some of the responsibility. My father never asked me to do this, but I had to. I walked by a construction site one day and thought maybe I could do something there."

Junichi smiled at the memory. "I was so nervous, a skinny little boy. I was determined, though, so I walked straight into the little shed that was the office. Two men were inside. One of them asked me if I wanted something. 'Yes, sir,' I said, 'I would like a job.' The other man started laughing. I was so embarrassed, I almost ran out the door. However, the first man just stared at me. He had such intense eyes. I was scared, but I stood my ground, never breaking eye contact. 'Come with me,' he said. I followed, and we walked around the site. He showed me an area with a pile of debris, then asked me if I could sort it. I said, 'Yes, sir.'" Junichi smiled. "In reality, I had no idea if I could or not, but I was not going to say that." The memory played in his mind. His shame when the man asked if he had long pants and good shoes and he had to say no. The man gave him some money to buy some.

"What happened then?"

Junichi shook his head to clear it. "I worked every day after school. I did not tell my parents until I brought my first pay-check home. They were so shocked. My father said very little. It was later in life he told me how humiliated he was that his son had to work at such a young age.

"The next day when I went to work, I saw my father talking to the owner. I was scared he was going to take me home. When he was done, he...he limped over to me, put his hand on my shoulder and told me that I was a good son, then he left." Junichi's smile faded. "But I was not always a good son."

"Why do you say that?"

"Construction was a good job for me as I grew older and stronger. It was physical. I needed the physical exertion as an outlet for my anger. I resented working, but I could never tell anyone this. My family depended on the money. There were always doctor's bills.

"Why were you angry?"

"I was a teenager, angry at my father for not being a father. Angry at my country for what they did to my father, and to so many others. Angry at the lies told to my people before and during the war. Angry at our history." Then he turned to Thomas, "And angry at the Americans for what was done to my father."

Thomas didn't say anything, so Junichi continued to talk.

"I worked hard and, eventually, I quit going to school. The owner, Mr. Tanimoto, knew it, but he also seemed to understand that I needed the physical outlet. It was the only way to get my anger out. I could not talk to my mother or my father. None of what I felt was either of their fault and I could not cause them more problems. I could see the shame in my father's face, although sometimes I was not sure what caused it, not until later.

"Junichi, when your parents found out that you had stopped attending school, were they upset?"

"Yes, they wanted me to go back. By that time, though, I was older and stood firm. There was nothing they could do about it. It was my decision.

"One day, Mr. Tanimoto came by while I was working. He asked me if I was through yet. I was so confused. I held up what I was working on and said that this would take several more days to finish. Then he looked deep into my eyes and said, 'I am not talking about this task Junichi, I am talking about your anger. Life is never fair. You, however, have the strength and power to make it better. You have been shouldering a man's responsibility in a boy's life. You are no longer a boy. Now you have to decide if you are going to keep a boy's anger in a man's life.' Then he walked off."

"He must have really cared for you," said Thomas.

Junichi nodded. "It took a long time for me to see this for myself, but slowly I started to grow up and returned to school part time. Then, I began asking questions about the business. Mr. Tanimoto answered my questions and showed me how to run the business. I never knew during those early years that he had lost his son to an illness not long before I showed up. He retired several years ago and sold me his business. He and I are still close."

Junichi stopped, embarrassed by all he had said. "Thomas, I am talking too much. I have described a bleak picture. My life was not as bad as I am portraying. I am letting emotions overwhelm reason. We had many happy, laughing times. I loved my father very much and respected him for how he handled his past. He never complained. It simply was the way it was," Junichi said. "I cannot think why I told you this tonight. You must think me weak."

"No," Thomas said quickly. "I think the opposite, in fact. Sometimes talking to a stranger can help. You can express what you have kept inside with no possibility that your family will ever know. Junichi, you say that your life wasn't as bad as you portray. However, you were very young, in a terrifying time. You had to grow up far too fast. I imagine that your life was much more difficult than you have allowed yourself to acknowledge. You had to be the man of the family and your life didn't allow you to finish being a child. You can be proud that you were a good son and did what you had to do. Knowing that, though, doesn't wipe away the scars. We men feel, we just tend to bury those emotions and go on with our lives, but they don't go away."

Junichi glanced at him. "Thank you, Thomas."

"You're welcome. I'll say goodnight now."

"Goodnight." Junichi watched Thomas leave, wondering why he had told that story. He'd never intended to tell anyone. Yet, it was a relief. All these years, Junichi had suppressed memories and moved on with his life. In reality, though, he only moved on with some of his life.

Junichi thought of his own son. How would he have helped his own son if he had gone through the horrors that Junichi had? As his father, he would have held his son through his nightmares. Junichi's mother had done that. He would have been there to listen. His mother would have been there for him as well, but he never went to her. He had been too young to understand from an adult's perspective, yet old enough to recognize what he saw. As well, the world was different then. He had loving parents, but life was hard for all of them. Everyone was in a state of shock; nonetheless, there was work that had to be done to survive.

Tonight, he had shared some of those childhood memories, but he'd done it from a child's perspective. Even verbalizing that small amount had given him some slight relief.

Thirty-Four

Nick woke up early the next morning and realized he'd slept for almost nine hours in his clothes! Invigorated from such a sound sleep, he stood and stretched. Waking early was a habit set by years of working. Although it frustrated him on the weekends when he wanted to sleep in, he enjoyed getting up early on vacations. After changing his clothes and freshening up, he went on his first mission of the day, a cup of tea. For Nick, coffee was to be used to wake up when he had to work. However, to leisurely enjoy the morning, nothing beat a warming cup of tea with a little milk and sugar. Success. The staff had the coffee and tea service ready in the salon. Faint sounds of an air compressor wafted up from the dive deck. The crew was already hard at work filling tanks. No one else seemed to be out yet.

He took his tea and made his way to the top deck to enjoy the islands in the morning. The horizon was just beginning to turn red, inspiring a new beginning, bringing light, color, hope. Mother Nature overseeing her creations, nurturing them to wake up and start anew. The islands were so crisp and tranquil. The quiet, so noticeable. Island life was much more relaxed than what he had been used to. Distant clouds floated in the sky. Nick watched as the sun slowly rose behind the puffy clouds. Several wide rays burst forth in a circle, cutting through the clouds. It was an image he had seen before, but couldn't place. Then it hit him: *the Japanese flag, the Rising Sun*. This was it, before him proclaiming a new day.

A new day. I wonder what today will bring? Yesterday was hard. The destruction of the wrecks, evidence of the horrors of war. His imagination followed suit and the issues with his gear...he stopped. *I'm not going there now. I'm going to enjoy my morning.* There were good spots in the day. Nat was a rock, as she always was. The three Americans were easy and enjoyable to be around. Their enthusiasm was contagious and distracting. The marine life was beautiful. Jeanne would have loved the coral yesterday.

Jeanne. He smiled. At the thought of her lovely, beautiful face, the tension in his shoulders deflated. He thought of how strong she was. After the initial shock of the diagnosis, her resolve, her strength, began to shine. Even as the illness progressed to the point of the inevitable, Jeanne's will never faltered, never hiding from her reality. *I'm not afraid to die. I'm only sad to leave you and the kids. This is just my time,* she said, one night when they lay in bed together, wrapped in each other's arms. She had seen the coming conclusion of her life and made peace with it.

It struck Nick that this was the first time he wasn't completely desolate at the thought of her. Numb ever since her diagnosis, he had pushed that aside to take care of her. As her cancer progressed, he watched her waste away, yet he always kept a strong resolve in front of her. Then her death. All through that time, everything had been about her. Jeanne was now where she wanted to be. Nothing was left for him to do.

Now it was all about Nick. His life hadn't been turned upside down, as someone once told him. No, his life, as he had known it, had ended. This was a new experience, this complete lack of responsibility, of purpose, and it was frightening. Like a leaf blowing in the wind with no control and no idea of where he would land. Everything in his life that he had to think about, that grounded him, was gone. Now his actions were based solely on the immediate situation and his thoughts went where they wanted to go. He could stop them for a little while, but they came back. Which brought him here to Truk. *Why did I really come here?* That question plagued him, yet he knew the answer. *JC.* What scared him the most was not knowing what was going to happen. The decision to come here, and all his actions since, were driven more by some subconscious plan rather than any recognized goal.

The sound of a motor brought Nick out of his mental wanderings. The four young German boys and their dive master headed out for an early morning dive. His stomach growled, demanding food, which Nick took as a reason to escape from the question he had no answer to.

***

Shoko was trying to decide how to approach Junichi. He could be such a stubborn man. He came in late last night and did not want to talk, so she decided to wait till morning. She was waiting when he came out of the bathroom. "How did you sleep?"

"Fine." He focused on dressing, so he could not see her roll her eyes.

"What were you doing last night?"

"Talking to Thomas."

She took a deep breath. "Are you going to talk to me about whatever is happening between you and Nick?"

"It is nothing."

"I saw his eyes, and I saw your reaction. It is not nothing. Other people are noticing as well. Has Nick been unkind to you?"

"No. We are having a slight disagreement about something. It does not concern you or anyone else. However, since this upsets you, I will try to stay away from him. You go to breakfast. I am not hungry."

Shoko sat studying him for a moment. Yesterday she was shocked, today she was becoming angry. She decided it would be good to be away from him until she calmed down. "I have decided not to go on this morning's dive. I will see you later." She left with the satisfaction of seeing his shock.

"Good morning, Shoko," said Mary, as she saw Shoko coming down the hall.

"Oh, good morning, Mary. How are you today?"

"I am very well, thank you. Are you going to breakfast?"

"Yes."

Mary could tell from Shoko's face that something was wrong. "Isn't Junichi joining you this morning?"

"No!" she said sharply, then sighed. "I decided not to go on the dive this morning. I think I will enjoy the sun and read a book."

"Well, I believe you will be happy with breakfast and the weather is beautiful right now, so you will have a nice day to relax."

"That will be nice. Thank you."

Mary watched her walk away, wondering...

Shoko joined the table with Nick, Frank, and Ray.

"Good morning. Nick, I see you did not join the early morning divers either." Shoko said as she sat down.

"No, I wish I still had their energy. I've hit an age where my old body seems to have more influence than my heart's desire," Nick said, smiling. "I see you didn't make it out early, either."

Her eyes narrowed. "No, we did not." Shoko pursed her lips, then took a breath and relaxed.

Though Nick wasn't happy she was upset, he did feel little relief that he wasn't the only one upset with Junichi, then immediately chided himself for his childish thoughts. Nick smiled at her. "Well, we can enjoy the breakfast. I was up on the top deck when the heavenly aroma drew me down." He reached for the note card in the center. "Mary is smart to put the meals on these cards. This morning we are having grilled sea bass with rice porridge from Japan, and uht sukusuk, from Chuuk, which is boiled bananas with coconut milk." As Nick finished, the plates of food were served.

"I love rice porridge and Mary has furikake seasoning as well," Shoko said, shaking some over her porridge. "That was kind of her."

"What is furikake seasoning?" Nick asked.

"It contains dried seaweed, sesame seeds, bonito flakes, and other seasonings. It tends to be more salty, savory."

Frank picked up his spoon and sampled the uht sukusuk. "This is wonderful. I don't know if it's proper, but I am going to mix this with the rice porridge." Once mixed, he took a sample, his eyes lit up. "Oh, that's good."

Nick consumed the fish first, enjoying the light garlic flavor, then turned back to Shoko. "Are you going on any night dives while you're here?"

"Possibly tonight. I enjoy diving at night very much. The beautiful corals bloom, which, of course, means they are eating, as they are not a flower. I am fascinated by the change in the reefs that occur at night. Nocturnal creatures are usually out of their hiding places. The colors are even more amazing, due to our lights. Junichi and I do many night dives. I like finding the bio-luminescent algae or features in some of the marine life."

Sarah had joined the group in time to hear Shoko's comments. "I agree that night diving is very interesting, but it's also scary!" Everyone laughed. "I gather from everyone's empty plates that breakfast is good?" Sarah asked as her plate was served.

"Is Natalie coming soon?" asked Ray. "We want to plan our next dive."

Sarah paused before taking another bite. "No, she is going to skip this next dive."

At that, Nick glanced up.

"She's fine Nick. She wanted to enjoy a peaceful morning." Nick nodded.

"What are we diving on?" asked Nick

"The Betty bomber," replied Ray.

"Oh, that should be interesting," said Sarah. "How deep is it?"

"Only fifty feet, so we should have a longer bottom time and we don't have to worry about limiting our depth," said Ray.

"Frank," said Sarah, "does the book say if it was shot down during the attack?"

"No, it said that it is very close to one of the landing strips. Apparently, it crashed as it was coming in, but there isn't any information to tie it to the battle or, for that matter, any cause for the crash."

"At that depth, there will be a lot of coral. You guys can go. I'm almost done."

Nick smiled at her. "Don't rush Sarah. We'll wait for you."

⸺◈⸺

Nat sat back in the lounge chair, holding the romance book that she had borrowed from the ship's library.

"Not going on this dive?" asked Mary.

Nat turned to see Mary come up the steps. "Good morning. No, the wrecks are interesting, but also a bit hard to see. This view, on the other hand, is heavenly."

"I know what you mean about the wrecks. I've seen many of them, though I prefer to dive on a coral reef. I like to see life growing on something other than a grave." Mary's eyebrows shot up. "I have an idea. If you are interested, later you and I can go to my favorite little reef. It is so beautiful and only about thirty feet down. It's next to a small island where we can have a picnic lunch. But of course, if you would rather not, I completely understand. This is your vacation, so you should do what you wish."

"Mary, I would love that, actually. I need to get away from these wrecks for a while, and that would be a true escape. Thank you."

"Natalie," she said softly, "may I ask you why you used the word escape?"

She didn't say anything for a few moments, trying to decide what to say. The truth won out. Turning back to the water, she explained. "These wrecks are a vivid reminder of a horrible time. My husband, Carl, was also in the war, as a marine. He was part of the landing force for many offensives, the most important of which was Okinawa. The problem was that he never dealt with those experiences. During the day, he worked hard, outwardly seemed happy and content. Only I knew he wasn't. He was old school. The man had to be strong, never show weakness. Unfortunately, over time, he started drinking. I had to research a lot about Okinawa to try to understand. What I learned was truly horrid, and *I* didn't live through it."

Natalie sat the book on a table. "The first ten years or so, after the war, we were happy, living on his farm. Then things began to slowly change. He spent more time thinking. Then he began to attack the physical work on the farm almost like a demon, trying to escape his memories of God knows what.

This, of course, started to take its toll on him. Then the nightmares started. He wouldn't get help from anyone, including me.

"Life began to spiral downward for him. His body couldn't take the abuse, so the farm work started to suffer, not bringing in enough money to hire some help. He didn't want to admit he needed help on the farm or anywhere. Our daughter and I did as much as we could, which also reinforced his, I guess, failures to him. We argued more because he shut me out.

"After that, I had to go to town to get a job to pay the bills. That was the final denigration, and he started drinking. Over time, it got worse and worse, until one day, his body couldn't take any more."

"How did you and your daughter deal with that?"

"We had very good friends. Carl never took out his anger or problems on the two of us. The only person he wanted to destroy was himself. Something happened to him during that battle, something he did that he couldn't forgive, or some hell he saw that he couldn't forget." Nat sat there shaking her head. "That war destroyed so many lives and even after it was over, it still kept taking more."

Mary sighed. "I can't make sense of it either. I've often wondered if we humans are, in reality, the stupidest of all the species on the planet."

"That is a very good question."

Mary thought for a moment. "Natalie, I was wondering, Shoko decided to skip the morning dive as well. I don't know why, but I'm thinking that she might also need a break. How would you feel if I invited her to go with us?"

Natalie immediately smiled. "That's a great idea."

"Good. Give me forty-five minutes to get everything ready, then meet me on the dive deck. It should be clear by then."

"Would you like me to invite Shoko?"

"Yes, thank you. She was heading to the stern deck."

As Mary left, Natalie thought this might be interesting to see if Shoko knew of the confrontation between Junichi and Nick. Nat hadn't spent much time with Shoko, but she had watched her eyes and knew that she picked up on the tension. Then again, it might be wonderful to have a day away from men. Smiling at that thought, she went in search of her.

Natalie found Shoko sitting in a chair, reading. "Good morning, Shoko. Am I disturbing you?"

"Not at all. I heard that you are also taking a break from diving this morning."

"Not from diving, but I did need a break from the wrecks," Nat said, smiling. Shoko cocked an eyebrow in question. "Actually, that is why I am here. Mary has invited both of us to join her. She is going to, in her words, her favorite little reef; which she said is about thirty feet—I mean about ten meters—down and that it is next to a beautiful little island. She is organizing a picnic for us. Would you like to go? The decision is yours, though it would be nice if you came."

"Yes, I believe I would like that," Shoko said, her eyes showing her intrigue.

"Wonderful. Mary said to meet her on the dive deck in about forty minutes."

"I will be there."

Thirty-Five

"So, are you ready to dive on an airplane?" Ben asked as he met the group at the bottom of the stairs.

"We are," said Nick. "Natalie isn't joining us for this dive. She wants to relax this morning. Is there anything specific we need to know?"

"Not very much this time. The plane isn't deep, so we don't require our normal second safety stop. However, we should limit our bottom time to about fifty minutes. We will only have about fifteen meters of visibility, which is still sufficient to see the entire wreck. Important to remember, though, is to go gently into the wreck. It's open, but if we disturb the silt, it will no longer be any fun inside. There is plenty to see around the whole area, so you may want to take turns in the wreck. If everyone is ready, let's go."

It was a short and smooth ride out to the site. Nick got his gear on quickly, momentarily irritated that he had to use the borrowed BC. He forced himself to let that go, then fell overboard to begin the descent. He was surprised to see Sarah actually descend first, with everyone else following. They came down behind the plane.

For a crash site, the plane was far more intact than Nick expected. The Betty Bomber was actually a Mitsubishi G4M bomber, commonly known as a Flying Cigar. Her fuselage was longer, with unprotected fuel tanks. Originally, it was successful for the Japanese, but as the US planes developed, the bomber became an easy target. The twin engines lay nestled in the sand a few yards ahead of the plane. The tail fin and rudder sections lay mangled on the sand. The wings, spanning over eighty feet, appeared amazingly unharmed by the crash.

As usual, Nick hung up away from the wreck and watched Sarah immediately penetrate the fuselage, entering through the gunner's bay window. Ray wiped silt from the pilot seat a few feet from the plane, then swam to an engine with all three blades intact, with one partially buried in the sand. A three-foot floral display of leaf coral and orange sponges, molded to the contours, encrusted the engine housing. Frank was inspecting oysters that had taken over an air intake manifold on the plane. Ben was floating around, watching everyone.

In the distance, Nick saw movement, and a sea turtle slowly swam closer. It was big at almost four feet long. Its gentle rhythmic movement was amazingly graceful. Nick watched, transfixed, as the turtle swam past. He turned to follow it for a little while, then swam back to the tail of the plane.

Nick put his hand on the tail, running it back and forth over the metal. He hadn't flown a plane since the war. On his very first flying lesson, his instructor'd had him hold out his hand, then asked him what he held. Nick looked at his empty hand and said he held nothing. His instructor said no, there was something there. Nick then realized he was holding air. Exactly, replied the instructor. Flying requires air, an intangible gas that can never be seen, is periodically felt, usually taken for granted, but has the power to kill in an instant. Once he learned not to fight the air, instead to work with it, using its power, he fell in love with the freedom of flying, the feel of riding the waves of air.

He also learned about the mechanical wings of the bird he flew; inspecting every aspect of the plane before each flight, no area overlooked. The old routine subconsciously took over. His hands ran along the tail, checking the elevators, which, of course, no longer moved. The surrounding metal on the tail had spots of marine growth. It seemed harder for corals and plants to attach themselves to smooth surfaces.

The torn metal, where the tail section broke free, had considerable growth. A small stag horn coral grew on a piece of metal that was swinging back and forth in the surge. The little black-and-white striped Sergeant Major fish were in a constant game of catch up with their swinging home.

Continuing the slow inspection of the exterior of the plane, almost as if he was inspecting it before takeoff, his eyes ran over the riveted seams along the fuselage. Feeling along the wings, attempting to move the frozen flaps. He inspected a cannon laying on the wing, chunks dug out of it from rust. To the side of the cannon were a couple of sea cucumbers inching their way over the wing. Nick glanced at the machine gun in the sand as he passed over it, then stopped to inspect a section of gauges that was sitting on top of the plane. Nick made his way around to the front of one of the wings, slowly caressed his hand over it. His mind blurred and merged with what he saw in front of him and his memories of a previous plane—his Avenger. Felt her wings. She was strong... *Stop it.*

Nick shook his head to clear his mind, then swam over to one of the engines to feel the propeller. This one missing one of the three blades, but also encrusted with a large hard coral formation surrounded with leafy green algae and purple soft corals. Small Zebra fish danced in and out of the coral.

He swam back over the wing to see Frank inside, then disappeared, only to have his head pop up in the gunner's turret. Then Frank swam out of the plane, leaving it open for Nick. He entered through the window, gently pulling himself in. The interior space was too small to use fins, so he only used his arms to swim through. He also ensured his buoyancy was neutral, so he controlled his height by breath alone. Glancing toward the back of the plane, he saw three Lionfish swimming. Fortunately, when they saw Nick, they darted quickly away. Amazingly beautiful fish with red and white striped bodies, but equally dangerous, with their venomous spines sticking out like a porcupine.

Like the other wrecks, there was a layer of silt, but not as deep. His exhaust bubbles collided with the ceiling, disrupting a little bit of silt above. Much of the interior had been gutted for whatever reason. Nick, however, spied the radio on the side and momentarily stopped to inspect it. Though the letters were in Japanese, it looked similar to the radios he had used. Leaving the radio behind, he slowly made his way to the front of the plane, the area that had suffered the most damage. The cockpit was gone. In its place was a gaping opening.

Nick swam out of the plane and spied the twisted metal of what had once been the cockpit. The nose of the plane was destroyed, so it must have gone in nose first. He wondered if the pilot was able to get out. Nick couldn't stop his mind from envisioning the plane diving into the water.

His mental visions immediately converted to a memory. *Tony!* Those moments he watched his friend's plane go down played in slow motion through his mind. The splash after it hit. James' plane on fire, erupting more on impact. Nick's stomach lurched, his hands trembled. Is this what Tony's plane looked like after it crashed? Is this why he couldn't get out? Did he die on impact, or did he...? Nick's stomach started rolling, threatening to erupt. *Stop!* Nick shook his head. Then his mind pulled his plane around, a moment before James' plane hit the water, then he yanked his plane up to miss a shell. *Don't do this!*

Nick closed his eyes, sinking down into the silt. Bending forward, he tried to take deep breaths to calm his stomach, but the images in his head wouldn't stop. Stomach muscles cramped as the retch began. Grabbing his regulator, gluing it to his mouth, he heaved. Pushing the purge button, he blasted out the vomit. As he let go of the purge button, an explosion of air bubbles engulfed his head. The roar of the air erupting deafened one ear. He took a breath in, instantly stopping when he could feel the seawater rushing in. Nick yanked the regulator out and grabbed his alternate, only to find his air pressure plunging. He was about to make an emergency ascent to the surface when Sarah's face came into view. She pressed her spare regulator to his lips and he bit down on it, sucking in huge breaths of air.

Ben, Frank, and Ray also swam over. Ben took Sarah's pressure gauge to monitor her supply. Sarah put her hand on Nick's shoulders, squeezing to help calm him down. After a couple of minutes, his breathing calmed. Ben held up his thumb to everyone to ascend to the safety stop. He then offered Nick his spare regulator. Nick took it so that Sarah had enough air to finish the dive.

Once they surfaced, Ben grabbed Nick's arm. "Are you alright?"

"Yes, thanks," said Nick. "I have no idea what happened, but thank you." He then turned to Sarah. "Thank you so much."

She smiled at him. "That's what dive buddies are for. Let's get out of here."

While the others climbed in the dinghy, Nick rinsed out his mouth with sea water.

Once in the little boat, he pulled off his gear. "Wow," said Sarah, "here it is." She slid down the hose protector, revealing a deep gash in the airline that fed his primary regulator.

"How in the hell did that happen?" asked Nick. No one said a word.

"Let's get back to the Eagle Ray," said Ben.

When they got back to the ship, Frank and Ray immediately began unloading the gear. Nick took their help because he was still shaking from the ordeal. He stripped off his wetsuit, then sat down at his station with Ben and looked closer. After a moment, their eyes met, both understanding—this gash was manmade.

Ben immediately stood up, holding the full assembly. "Nick, would you mind leaving this with me? I'd like to inspect this more closely." Ben was staring intently at him, then he glanced at the others. "Why don't you all go and relax for a while before lunch?"

Nick understood Ben didn't want everyone to know what was happening. "Good idea."

The others agreed, but Sarah's face told him she had already figured it out. "We'll meet you up on deck later."

"We need to show this to Thomas," said Nick. Ben nodded and led the way.

Ben knocked on Thomas' door.

"Come in."

"Thomas, we need to show you something," Ben said as they walked in.

Nick immediately sat down. Thomas glanced from one to the other. "What is it?"

As Ben explained, Nick sat there staring out the forward windows. A column of gray clouds floated in the distance. He glanced back when Thomas reached for the assembly, inspecting it himself. After a few minutes, Thomas sat back. "The edges are too straight. This was cut with a knife."

Nick didn't respond to the obvious. His frustration grew by the moment. No one would believe him yesterday. Now they had no choice. He maintained eye contact with Thomas, waiting for him to verbalize what they both knew had to be done.

"You still think it was Junichi, don't you?"

"He's the only person I know that doesn't want me here. He made that completely clear two days ago."

Thomas took a deep breath. "Alright. We don't have actual proof, but we can talk with him. His group won't be back from their dive for another twenty minutes or so. Ben, will you go and bring Eonin up here once they are back?" Ben nodded and left. Thomas turned back to Nick. "I want to talk with him first to find out if he saw anything, or anyone. Then I'll talk with Junichi. After that, I'll let you know what I find out."

"No! I want to be there. I want to look into his eyes. I'm the one he's after."

"Nick, we don't have proof…"

"Either I'm here with you or I do it myself." Nick's eyes blazed.

Thomas took a deep breath, then exhaled. "Fine, but will you agree to let me do the talking?"

"Yes." Nick stood up. "I'll be in my cabin."

The adrenaline from the experience was wearing off. He took a hot shower, rinsing out his mouth, then brushed his teeth. Once in dry clothes, he fell onto the bunk. The dive began replaying in his mind. How could Junichi hate him so much to do this to him? Did he really want Nick dead? There was no proof that Nick attacked his father. *It's been over forty years since the war ended. What would be the value now?* Nick couldn't stop his brain. Every interaction with Junichi repeated over and over. No understanding came, but the anger was building.

***

When Eonin returned, he and Ben came to Thomas' office. "Eonin, there was an incident today. Nick Mitchel's air hose ruptured during his dive." Thomas handed him the hose. "It appears like it had been cut before the dive. Now we have to figure out who might be doing this."

Eonin ran his fingernail along the cut. "This is bad. Yeah, it's a straight cut. Did you call the police?"

"Not yet. I'm hoping to figure this out quietly. The last thing I need is for the other guests to hear about this or for it to get around the islands. I don't want to think about the damage to our reputation."

"The question is, who the hell did this?" said Ben.

"Have either of you seen anyone hanging around the dive deck?"

Eonin hesitated. "I don't want to cause him problems, because I never saw him around Nick's gear."

"Go on. Who did you see?"

"Junichi. I've seen him several times, actually. I thought he was just walking the decks."

"We're going to have to ask him," said Ben.

Thomas rubbed his forehead. "I know."

"Do you want me to get him?" asked Eonin.

"Yes, please bring him up here. But after that, leave. Ben, will you do the same with Nick? I want this to be as private as possible. I don't want Junichi to think everyone is against him. Also, I want you both to check everyone's dive gear before each dive."

The men left. A couple of moments later, Nick came into the office and sat down.

"Eonin is bringing Junichi up here. Remember, you agreed to let me do the talking. We don't have proof, so we are only watching for his reaction. Agreed?"

Nick nodded. He was so angry, he dared not say a word or he would explode.

"Come in," answered Thomas when the knock came. Junichi opened the door.

"Thomas, have you seen..." Junichi stopped when he saw Nick staring at him.

"Seen what?" asked Thomas.

"Shoko," he said, turning back to Thomas. "Eonin said you wanted to talk with me. What is this about?"

"Shoko went with Mary and Natalie to dive a little reef that Mary likes. They should be back soon. Please have a seat." Junichi hesitated, then sat down in the chair next to Nick.

Nick continued to stare at Junichi, but Junichi no longer acknowledged his existence.

"Well?" he prompted.

Thomas sat a little straighter in his seat, twirling a pen between his fingers, and took a deep breath. "We had an incident today with Nick's dive equipment and I have begun an investigation to find out what happened. I wondered if you had any information that might be helpful."

"What happened to his equipment this time?"

Nick stared, almost in shock that he had the audacity to allude to the other incidents as well. He noticed a cricket bat laying on top of the bookcase against the wall, with an almost overwhelming urge to use it on this man. Instead, he curled his hands around the arm of the chair to stop himself from moving.

"An air hose ruptured, but it looks as if it was cut with a knife before the dive."

"May I see the hose?" Junichi asked.

Nick watched Junichi for any sign, but the man was playing it very cool. However, Junichi's shoulders were tensing up. Thomas handed over the hose and Junichi turned it over, pulling the hose cover on and off.

"Yes, these are straight cuts at the edges." He handed back the airline. "I do not know how this happened."

Thomas nodded. "Do you have a dive knife in your gear bag?"

Junichi's eyes narrowed. "Yes, like every diver on board, I have one. Who else have you asked in your...investigation?"

"Ben and Eonin, of course, were the first."

"Which of the other guests have you asked? Such as anyone in his dive group who would have known Nick's diving schedule."

"You are the first guest I've talked to..."

"Talked to!" Junichi interrupted. "Do you not mean interrogated?"

"Crikey," Thomas muttered and threw the pen down on his papers. Taking another deep breath, he continued. "Junichi, you know that Nick was a pilot during the raid on Truk. Your father was on one of the ships during that raid. You were very upset after the newsreel. I could hear you yelling at him in his cabin. Do you have any vendetta against Nick?"

Junichi's face flushed red. He turned his body to face Nick. "You think I did this. You thought yesterday that I sabotaged your BC. So, because I am angry that you came to enjoy a lovely vacation at the expense of the men you killed, you are blaming me. I am Japanese, so I must be to blame!"

At this, Nick erupted. "How dare you suggest that I'm here for a lovely vacation! How dare you suggest that I created this so that I can blame the Japanese! You told me straight out that I shouldn't be here. Who the hell do you think you are to be telling me where I should or should not be? I never wanted to come here now or during the war. I came here because your people started a war. You dragged me here. You forced me to fight. You killed my friend!"

Junichi jumped up, yelling. "How dare me? How dare you say that I did anything to you! I was a child. I never forced you to drop your bombs. Those decisions were yours and yours alone. I am not going to stay and listen to this."

Nick jumped up and grabbed Junichi's arm. "You aren't going anywhere until you admit what you're doing to me." Thomas jumped up as well, but said nothing.

Junichi turned and came very close to Nick. "Listen carefully, Nick Mitchel. I hold a double black belt in karate. If you have proof that I sabotaged your gear, then call the police. Until you do, let go of my arm."

Their eyes locked. Nick didn't move for several moments. The wind began to howl outside, and the room darkened as the clouds moved in to shield the sunlight. How far did he take this? Did he really intend to physically hit this man? The dark eyes he peered into held such anger, yet a sadness briefly shone through. A drop of sweat ran down his spine. When it reached his shorts, Nick let go.

Junichi stepped back, never breaking eye contact. "If you ever touch me again, you will be very sorry." With that said, he left the room.

Nick fell back down in the chair.

"Well, that did not go well. What happened to letting me do the talking?" Thomas ran a hand through his hair and dropped into his chair. "Nick, please go and relax for a while, preferably away from Junichi, and let me think about what to do next."

Thirty-Six

Natalie sat at the bow of the little boat, the wind pasting her hair back, happily riding the jolts up and down over the waves. The breeze counterbalanced the warm sun to just the perfect temperature. They passed big islands, small islands, heading for a tiny island. This was her idea of an adventure, something she and Jeanne would have done together. A pang shot through at the bittersweet thought, though she knew what Jeanne would say to her—*don't get sappy, go have enough fun for me as well.*

Mary pointed out the different islands as they passed them, telling them which were inhabited and what grew on them. "We are going to a small, uninhabited island. It is my favorite place in the lagoon. It sits a little way behind Tol, the biggest island, and it's very protected from the wind. Only the locals know about it and, even then, most people don't have any reason to go there. It does have a few trees, so we will have shade for our picnic. The plan is to do two dives, then have a leisurely lunch. After that, we will come back to the ship. In the cooler, you'll find some food for breakfast. We'll be motoring for a while, so feel free to eat."

Once they passed Tol, Mary pointed ahead to a picturesque little island with several coconut trees on it. A postcard view of a lonely island with the endless blue background. "Oh, how lovely!" Nat said.

Mary cut the engine down, so talking was easier. "Nat, will you look down in the water? There is a small outer reef circling this island. Let me know when you see a break in it. I can motor through and run the boat onto the beach."

Once the dinghy was on the beach, Shoko hopped out with the rope and tied it to the closest tree. "There, isn't this wonderful?" asked Mary.

Shoko smiled, admiring the view. "It truly is beautiful. I can feel myself relaxing."

"You'll like the reef. It's well protected from much of the winds, but you'll still feel a bit of current when we're down there. It's not bad though. The current comes from two of the passes on the outer reef. Enough to feed the reef so that it grows, but not enough to damage it. It's only vulnerable to large tropical storms, which do happen, but not often. Let's unload the food and put it under the shade."

The three worked together unloading the boat. "You won't really need a wetsuit unless you want one. It's a shallow dive and we won't be down that long."

This thrilled Natalie. It had been years since she felt the freedom of diving in just a bathing suit.

"If you're ready, we can get our gear on. We'll leave the boat and dive from the beach." The women put on their gear and carried their fins to the water. "Follow me," said Mary, "we'll swim out that opening, then turn to the right, against the current. You will see the drop off, so the dive is part wall dive and part reef. It's not big, so explore as much as you want. There are several resident spiny lobsters and octopus, so peering into the holes is fun. I will bang on my tank about thirty minutes in, then we can explore more while the current carries us back."

About an hour later, they made their way back to the beach and took off their gear. Nat sat on a towel, letting the sun and breeze dry her, then pulled on a long cover-up over her salty skin. Mary reached in the cooler for the food and pulled it out.

"Mary, does an eel live down there as well?" asked Natalie, as she tied her hair back to keep it out of her eyes.

"Yes, it is a brown moray eel. Did you see it?"

"No, but a lobster in his hole had one antenna out and one pointing back in the hole."

"He was probably there. I've only seen one eel, and that was at night."

"Thank you for this. It was exactly what I needed." Thinking of this beautiful little reef brought Jeanne back to mind.

"You are welcome, but why are you sad?"

"I was thinking about Jeanne and how much she would have loved this."

"If you do not mind me asking," said Shoko, "who is Jeanne?"

"Jeanne was my friend and Nick's wife. She passed away last year."

"I am sorry for your loss. Death is hard."

Something in Shoko's voice caught Natalie's attention. "Oh, Shoko, I am sorry for your loss as well. I heard that Junichi's father passed away recently."

"Thank you. He was here in the navy during the war and asked Junichi to come here for him."

"That is sad. This trip must be hard for you and Junichi."

"It has been difficult for him, but his father was ill for a very long time. His death was not a surprise."

"Jeanne was ill for a few years as well, but that doesn't make death any easier, does it?"

Shoko shook her head. "No, it does not make it easier."

"Were you close to his father?" asked Natalie.

"Yes, he was like a father to me. I am close to his mother as well. They have always treated me as a daughter."

The three became silent for a while. Natalie felt a little uncomfortable knowing Junichi's father had been here during the war. She didn't want Shoko to know that her brother had also been here, on the opposite side. She kept quiet, hoping nothing would spoil their lovely outing. The rustling of the palm fronds was the only sound. Even the water on the beach lapped silently on and off, its force subdued by the coral ring. In the distance, the open ocean crashed against the outer atoll, flowing only through the passes. No other boat traffic around gave Nat the feeling they were completely alone on a deserted island.

Mary broke the silence. "What about your parents? Are they still with you?"

Shoko was silent for a moment, then said softly, "No, they are both gone."

"I'm sorry, I shouldn't have asked," said Mary.

Natalie immediately noted the change to Shoko's face, as if a shield had gone up.

Shoko smiled, although it didn't reach her eyes. "That is alright. The truth is, I am not certain what happened to either of my parents. It is not something I speak of easily."

"You don't have to talk about this if you don't want to. It is a lovely day and I wouldn't want you to be uncomfortable." Mary was clearly feeling bad about bringing such a personal subject up.

"Mary, please do not feel bad. It was a difficult time. I was young, but I still remember my parents. They were very loving, and we were happy. I had a younger brother as well. My father was called to the army. Where he served, I never knew. We lived in Tokyo and my mother worked in a store. She couldn't teach me because she worked, so when I turned six, she sent me to a school in town. My brother was small, so he had to stay with her. The school was still in Tokyo, so I was able to see her periodically.

"When the Allies began to bomb the mainland, my class was evacuated to a temple in the mountains. None of us were able to say goodbye to our families. After the fire bombings were over, we were brought back to Tokyo. There was no one from my family there to get me. I never saw my mother or brother again."

Natalie's eyes were huge when she glanced at Mary, who was also stunned by what Shoko said.

"What about your father?" asked Natalie gently.

"I do not know if he returned or not." Natalie's and Mary's faces showed their confusion. Shoko explained. "Much of Japan was devastated after the war. Millions of people were displaced from their homes. For many years, there were lists posted of people searching for family members. I would check often, but I never found either my parents or my brother."

Natalie's heart broke for Shoko, picturing her as a young girl, hope slowly dying. "How did you live? Who took care of you?" asked Natalie.

"I was taken to an orphanage, but I took care of myself." Her face took on a determination and anger. "Do you know no one helped us? The Government had many programs, many for the atomic bomb victims, but none for us. Even the Americans that came after the war, they did nothing for us."

"Shoko, I don't understand. What happened when you were sent to the orphanage?" Shoko hesitated, so Natalie prompted. "Please, we would like to understand."

"The fire bombings occurred in several cities. Tokyo was the hardest hit. The devastation was incredible. I know the atomic bombs were also horrid, but they got all the attention. So, the victims of the fire bombings were ignored. The orphanages in those areas could only hold about 12,000 children. However, there were over 120,000 of us.

"If relatives could be located, some children were sent to them. However, many of those children were treated very badly. There was much starvation at the time, so some families took care of their own children, treating the orphans as servants or field labor, or worse.

"In the orphanage, we were fed only one meal a day and sometimes not even that. I survived because I was smart enough to watch and listen. I was hiding one day and overheard a conversation. Two of the people, who were supposed to be taking care of us, were talking about selling some of the children to be farm laborers. I was still hoping my family might be searching for me, so I ran away from the orphanage. That way I could stay in Tokyo."

"Where did you go?" asked Natalie.

"Wherever I could. I found other children, older than I was, and I followed them. We would hide out in the train station many times, or under bridges. Being small, I could hide in many places. Some of the older boys would steal food and sometimes share. I watched many learn to pick pockets so they could buy food. Sometimes, the police would come and take as many as they could to jail. What happened to them after that, I never knew."

"How could people allow this to happen to children?" Natalie asked, horrified.

"My country was in a state of chaos. By that time, the war was over. There were millions of people needing help and children could not represent themselves."

"Again, how did you survive?"

"As I got older, I walked around the city more. I searched through the rubble and found parts of blankets, clothes, and other things to use. One day I smelled food cooking. The smell led me to a part of town that hadn't been destroyed. I hid behind some bushes and watched. There, people dressed well, smiling, laughing. I watched them go into a building and realized it was a restaurant. I walked behind the building and found their trash cans filled with uneaten food. I would take some, then go hide and eat it. The people who worked there caught me a few times. 'Kuzo' is what they would say to me."

"What does that mean?"

"Trash," Shoko said, when she turned to Natalie. "Although in a more refined company, the word was 'Improper' people. But I did not care. I was eating. One day, a lady came out and found me. She still looked at me like I was trash, but she asked me if I could wash dishes. I said yes and followed her into the restaurant. She told me to go to the bathroom and clean up. Then she wrapped a towel around me and I washed dishes. I was paid a small amount, but more importantly, I was allowed to eat properly. I still lived on the streets, but I worked there. Once I made enough money, I bought some new clothes, found places that I could clean up. At the restaurant, no one talked to me, other than to tell me what to do, but I worked hard. They let me start to wrap up the food that was going to be thrown out, and I shared it with other children on the street. Over time, I made enough to rent a room."

Natalie and Mary exchanged glances, horrified by Shoko's experience. Nat wanted to say comforting words, but Shoko was proud and might take this as pity. "You are a strong woman."

Shoko smiled at this. "We do what we have to do, do we not?"

"Yes, we do. How did you meet Junichi?" Nat asked, hoping to lighten the conversation.

Now Shoko's smile brightened. "When I grew up, I found a job at a little restaurant near the University. I knew there I could meet people closer to my age. Junichi came in one day and saw me. Then he started coming in daily. It was quite a while before I spoke to him, though. We began to talk and do things together. I fell very much in love with him, though I did not tell him of my past."

"Did you ever tell him?"

"Yes, when he wanted me to meet his parents, I had to tell him. I was so scared that day, because I knew that I had no records of my family to prove where I came from. This meant that I was not suitable to marry into a nice family." Shoko smiled again. "But Junichi convinced me that his parents were not like this, and he was right. Kana and Kaito, his parents, accepted me and took me into their family. They became my parents." Her eyes glistened. "So, my early life was not happy, but since I met Junichi, I have my best friend, parents who love me, and a wonderful son. Now I am very blessed."

"Shoko, you are the very definition of the word perseverance," said Mary.

"Thank you, I like that word." Shoko took a deep breath, letting it out slowly. "You know this trip has been very interesting and unexpected."

"How so?" asked Mary.

"For some reason, I am very comfortable with both of you, though I hardly know you. Mary, you brought us here, sharing this very special place with us. Thank you. This is the second special place I have been to during this trip."

"Where was the other?"

"Junichi and I toured one of the islands the day before we came to the Eagle Ray. Our tour guide was very nice and showed us his spot."

"Was your tour guide Nekiniuo?" asked Mary, smiling.

"Yes, do you know him?"

"Of course. Nekiniuo is wonderful, isn't he? I spend a lot of time with his wife, who is also lovely. So, he showed you his cave?"

"Yes, but he asked that we not tell anyone about it."

Natalie spoke up, "Don't worry about me. I'm not going to tell anyone since I don't have any idea what you both are talking about."

Mary laughed. "Nekiniuo has a very special place on one of the islands. He took me once to it. I can only describe it as stunningly tranquil."

"That is a perfect description," said Shoko. "We spent a couple of hours there. Nekiniuo was very kind and patient."

"Shoko, you and Junichi must have touched him deeply for him to share his cave."

Shoko answered the unspoken question. "I believe Nekini-uo saw Junichi's struggle and thought it would help. Which it did."

"If you don't mind me asking, is he struggling with his father's death?"

"Junichi doesn't speak of his troubles directly, but I believe he has yet to come to terms with his father's life and his own past. Junichi saw his own terrors from the war." Shoko stopped, clearly not intending to divulge Junichi's past.

Mary lightened the conversation. "You mean he's another man that won't talk about his feelings?" she asked. Her wide-eyed look had Natalie laughing. Even Shoko grinned.

"I gather Thomas will not either?"

"Are you joking? I firmly believe that Thomas has convinced himself that expressing any emotion will result in instant death."

Natalie and Shoko laughed, then Shoko turned to Natalie in question.

"My husband, Carl, refused to talk about his issues, and it cost him his life." She said the words lightly, but the mood darkened.

"Oh, I am very sorry to hear that," Shoko said.

"Thank you. I loved Carl dearly, faults and all. But I've let him go. I hope he's at peace now."

"And your friend Nick?"

Natalie smiled and nodded. "Yes, he's another man who won't talk about his problems. Oh well, he's a man, a good man, but still a man."

With that, the three women looked at each other and burst out laughing.

"Ladies, I brought a wonderful lunch and a bottle of sake. Do you want to dive again or..."

Natalie and Shoko didn't hesitate. Together, they yelled, "Sake!"

Thirty-Seven

Nick sat down in the chair, trembling from the confrontation, at a total loss as to what to do next. Should he just leave? But that only solved the Junichi problem, not his own. Did he dare dive again? If the trajectory of events continued, he'd be dead soon. Did he...

A knock came from his door, followed by Natalie's voice. "Nick, are you in there?"

"Come in," he yelled. Nick didn't get up when she came in. Clutching the arms of the chair was a good use of his energy. He knew if he stood up, he would probably throw the chair through the door.

"I just got back, and Ben said something happened on the dive," she asked. Her eyes grew wide when she saw him, then narrowed. "What happened?"

"Junichi struck again, that's what happened!" he said, pushing himself up to pace the room.

"And?" she asked, while her head tracked his path back and forth.

"He cut my air hose, enough so that when I was down there, it ruptured. Thankfully, the others were there, otherwise I would have had to make an emergency ascent, with no air!"

"I can't believe it." She sat on the other bed, shaking her head. "Did he say why?"

"No, he's still denying it." Nick continued to pace, his jaw muscle flexed in rhythm with his steps.

"Then how do you know he did it?"

"Who else is there?" He threw his hands in the air. Part of him knew that he needed to calm down, the other part ignored this. Nick couldn't remember the last time he had been this angry, or if he had ever been this angry. He desperately wanted to get his hands on Junichi. And then what? Strangle him, hit him? Nick hadn't hit anyone in his entire adult life, yet rational thinking was losing his internal battle.

"I don't know, but still, if there's no proof..."

Nick whirled around to face her. "Whose side are you on?"

"Yours, but I still believe in innocence until proven guilty. I gather you confronted him?"

"Yes," he said, resuming his pacing. "Thomas, and I did. He had the gall to suggest that I'm blaming him because he's Japanese. Me!" His hand slapped his chest. "I don't have a prejudiced bone in my body."

"Nick, will you please stop pacing and sit down? I'm getting a crick in my neck." She reached up to massage the straining muscles.

He let out a sigh and flopped back down on the chair, sending it sliding back several inches.

"Thank you. Now, can I say something without you biting my head off?"

"You don't believe me again!"

"Alright, bite my head off." Natalie reached over and took Nick's hand. "Nick," she said calmly, "I believe that someone is doing these things to you. I believe you have never been prejudiced toward anyone."

The touch of her hand and calm voice began to help Nick's shoulder loosen.

"I also believe that you were hurt by what Junichi said to you on Monday. You have always been a good man with a kind heart. I can't imagine what battle was like for you. The reason you came back here was because something didn't end after that battle. I'm wondering now how hard it is for you to come face to face with someone who is so connected to that enemy?" She stopped to let that sink in, watching his eyes thin. "If Junichi's father were here instead, how would you treat him? Would you blame him, or wonder if he was also a good man like you put in a horrible position? I don't believe you are prejudiced against the Japanese race, but have you truly forgiven your old enemy?" Natalie let go of Nick's hand and left him to think.

⚬

Shoko opened the cabin door to find Junichi lying in bed staring at the ceiling, strangling a pillow. "Are you unwell?" she asked and put her bag on the floor.

"No!" he said, snapping at her.

"Junichi!" she said sharply. Her own eyes narrowed. "These one-word answers have to stop."

His face lost its rage, shocked by her tone. "I have not heard you speak to me that way in many years."

Shoko was in no mood to be distracted. "I want to know what is happening on this ship between you and Nick."

He continued to lie there for several moments, then sighed and looked at her. "It appears someone is sabotaging Nick's dive equipment, and he is blaming me." Junichi went back to staring at the ceiling.

She started to sit on the bed, but froze when she heard those words. "Why would he suspect you?" she asked, then sat down.

"He does not suspect me," he said with a rising voice, "he stated out loud that it was me! Thomas believes him as well." Junichi slapped the pillow on his legs, then began to wad it up.

She recognized another question that he did not answer. Taking a deep breath to calm herself, she thought through the last few days. "You were upset with Nick after the first night. What happened that night?"

Junichi did not say a word, but his cheeks flushed red.

"Junichi," she said, but he would not look at her. "What did you say to him?" she asked gently.

Junichi let out another sigh. "I told him he had no right to be here, enjoying a vacation at the expense of those he killed."

Shoko placed her hand on his leg. "This trip is very hard for you," she said, "and it is very hard for Nick as well."

Junichi bolted up. "How can you say that? You have seen him smiling and laughing."

She began to gently run her hand up and down his leg, hoping to soothe him into a more receptive state. "You say that because you have not really looked at him. None of his smiles ever reach his eyes. Think about this. The war affected your father so much that he wanted to come back, but could not. This trip has been very hard on you because of your own nightmares, as well as your father's pain. Do you really believe Nick would choose this place to come for pleasure?" She could see these questions running through his mind. "We both know you are not the one sabotaging him. So, the most important question right now is who is responsible for the sabotage."

His shoulders slumped as her rational words penetrated his defenses. "I have been wondering that, too. If I am to clear my name, I will have to figure it out." He stood, holding his head high. "I am going to take a walk." Before he opened the door, he spun and pulled her into his arms. "I love you," he said, then kissed her and walked out.

Junichi walked around the decks, thinking. Everything was about the dive gear, which anyone on board had access to. He was gone many times during the days, so had no idea of who, besides the crew and guests, came on board. Delivery people might. But only the crew and the guests knew which gear was Nick's. Junichi did not know the other Americans very well. Each of them would know Nick's schedule and his gear. Natalie was not a real suspect, as she seemed to be a close friend. *Ben!* He had complete knowledge of Nick's dive schedule and equipment. Why he would do anything was not clear, but he was in a position to do whatever he wanted.

Junichi took the side stairs down to the lowest level, which brought him to the dive deck from the side, behind the mechanical area. No one seemed to be there. The clang of metal tanks stopped him from leaving. The hiss of air escaping meant someone was connecting tanks to the compressor. The sound of his footsteps was drowned out by the compressor motor. He moved up, then peeked around the corner. Eonin was filling a tank. Junichi almost stepped out to talk with him, then pulled back out of sight. When he heard the next tank connected, he poked his head back around. Eonin was filling another tank, but this time the sound squealed loudly. Again, Junichi jumped back. Regardless of what was going on, he knew that compressor should not be in use. He followed this pattern several more times, realizing that Eonin had used one compressor for most of the tanks, but had used the other compressor for only one of the tanks. Junichi softly walked back toward the side. He went up the stairs intending to tell Thomas, then stopped. He had no proof that anything was wrong, and there were too many accusations being made without proof. Junichi turned to walk to the central stair that led to the dive deck. As he descended, Eonin glanced up and greeted him with a smile. "Hi Junichi, out for one of your walks?"

Junichi studied him and saw something change in his eyes. "Yes, it has been a difficult day. I thought I would clear my head."

Eonin nodded. "I heard, man. It's tough," he said in a deadpan voice and continued to fill more tanks, but his hands fumbled with the connections.

"I think Shoko and I may leave tonight." Junichi used this ploy to keep him talking. Eonin dropped a wrench, and his hand shook as he picked it up.

Eonin's head jerked up, and his eyes flickered more yellow as he met Junichi's gaze. Just as quickly, he deliberately raised his mono-brow and the light in his eyes dulled. "I thought you wanted to dive on your father's ship tomorrow?" Even though the wind blew a cooler breeze, sweat covered Eonin's bald head.

"I did, however, I do not believe I am welcome to stay." Junichi watched Eonin take a filled tank and place it at a station. His jittery movements were more consistent with someone on drugs, or in withdrawals.

"No man," he said, waving a hand, "this is your vacation. Don't let anyone drive you away." Eonin picked up another tank, the one that had been filled by the noisy compressor, and placed it in Nick's station.

A knot grew in Junichi's stomach. This didn't make sense. He must have made a simple mistake, but then maybe not. "Eonin, you are correct. It is not I who should leave."

"That's the spirit," he said with a forced smile that caused an odd glint in his eyes.

"Eonin, it seems you seem to do most of the work around here. Why does Ben not work as hard as you do?"

"Oh, I don't mind. I told Ben to take a break. I heard their dive this morning was kind of rough."

"That was kind of you. Well, I think I will continue my walk."

"See you, man."

Junichi had seen enough. He went straight to Thomas' office.

Thomas was coming out of this office when Junichi walked up. A subtle jerk of his head told Thomas to go back in.

"What do you want to discuss?" asked Thomas, after he shut the door.

"I have a question about your air compressors. You have two of them, correct?"

"Yes, why would you care about this?"

"Are they both currently operational?" Junichi ignored the suspicion in Thomas' voice. Now was not the time to be diverted.

"No, the shop on Weno is coming to pick up one of them shortly."

"What is wrong with that one?"

"Junichi, why do you want to know?"

Junichi took a deep breath. "I started my own investigation, and I may know who is really behind these events. I went down to the dive deck, from the side stairs, and looked into the mechanical area. Eonin was filling the tanks. However, I watched as he filled one of the tanks from a different compressor than he used to fill the others. That compressor squealed too loudly to be mistaken. I also saw him put that particular tank in Nick's station."

Thomas' eyes narrowed as the implication became clear. Shaking his head. "Eonin has been with me for years. He wouldn't do that."

Junichi stared into Thomas's eyes, watching as he mentally ran through scenarios. "Thomas," he said gently, "there is only one way to know. Do you have a carbon monoxide analyzer?"

Thomas nodded, but didn't move. "He would not do this."

"Thomas, Eonin spends far more time on the dive deck than I ever could."

"Alright, but I am sure there is a mistake." Thomas picked up a radio. "Ben, are you on?"

"Yes, Thomas, I'm here," Ben answered.

"Can you meet me on the dive deck now?" asked Thomas.

"Sure, I'll be there."

Thomas put down the radio and got up. "Let's go."

"Nick needs to be there," Junichi said. Thomas started to say something, then stopped and nodded.

They went down the hall and Thomas knocked on the door. Nick opened it, then immediately scowled at Junichi. "Nick, this is important. Will you please come with us?" Nick saw Thomas' dark face and followed them.

Ben stood talking with Eonin when they got down the stairs. He and Eonin glanced at each other, then everyone watched as Thomas walked into the mechanical area, opened a cabinet and brought out a small case. Junichi watched Eonin's face turn white. Thomas went to Nick's station, opened the case, and began to attach the analyzer. The instant the valve opened, the sensor set off a piercing shrill, indicating a high concentration of carbon monoxide. Thomas closed the valve and turned to face Eonin. "Well?"

Thirty-Eight

"Hey, uh I...uh...it was a mistake..." Eonin stammered, then stopped. His face contorted into a maniacal expression as he turned toward Nick, then lunged at him. "You murderous bastard."

Junichi spun around, kicked up his leg and Eonin landed face down on the deck. Ben jumped on Eonin, who struggled, but Ben was larger, younger, and stronger. Thomas brought over some rope. Within moments, Eonin was still.

"Ben, grab his arm. We'll take him into his cabin." The two picked him up by the arms and Eonin walked, no longer fighting.

The cabin was small, with only a single bunk and no porthole. A musty smell matched the disheveled room. Clothes lay haphazardly around the room But the most notable aspect was the complete lack of anything personal. No photos, no knickknack collectibles, no books. Just a mess.

All five men crowded in. Ben shoved Eonin down in a chair. Thomas' shoulders sagged, his eyes crushed. "Why?"

Eonin looked up at Nick, his face still contorted, yellow flames burned from his eyes. "You killed my family. Your bombs destroyed them all. I went to see what the noise was. When I got back, they were all gone! All of them. My father, my...mother, my little sister." Tears streamed down Eonin's face. His voice dropped. "They didn't deserve to die. My father never did anything to you. I had to bury them all, the parts that

I could find of them. You don't have any idea of what that's like, do you? You flew in, dropped your bombs, then left. Did you even look back? Did you even think about what you did to us? But that wasn't enough for you, was it? You weren't satisfied with destroying everything. You had to cut the supply lines as well. You had to make sure everyone starved. Men, women, children." Eonin shouted the words as he jumped up, trying to kick at Nick. Ben pulled him back down and held him in place. "You had no right to come back here, enjoying a holiday. No right."

Although surprised at Eonin's story, Junichi felt a small sense of gratification when he heard the same words that he had said to Nick.

"I saw you smiling," said Eonin to Nick, "laughing. What sort of sick bastard are you?" Then Eonin turned to Junichi with the same hatred. "And you," he spat. "How dare you come here after what your father did?"

"What?" asked Junichi, completely caught off guard. "My father never did..."

Eonin interrupted him. "He wouldn't let us into the cave. When the bombing started, we all ran to the caves, but we weren't allowed in. He shoved a gun into my father's face and told us to leave, all of us. This was our island, our home. You were the visitors. All we could do was hide under trees!" Sobs wrenched from the man, clearly reliving that moment. "Afterward, he wouldn't share his food. He didn't starve. I had to stay awake at night to steal food from him to eat, knowing that if I got caught, I would have been killed, like many of my people were. After the war, he went home to you, his loving son. I had no one." Eonin closed his eyes, tears falling down his face.

Junichi stood frozen, unable to look away, not wanting to believe him. His father was a good man. He would never have treated anyone, much less a defenseless child like this. Watching this level of anguish was almost indecent, a violation. A strong man, close to his own age, reduced, destroyed in front of his eyes. How could he hold on to the past this long? The question ricocheted back to him like a punch to the face.

"Thomas," Nick spoke for the first time, "will you go check Junichi's tank, please?" His voice was quiet, yet clear.

Junichi glanced at Nick, but Nick was still watching Eonin with an inscrutable expression.

Thomas came back in and nodded. "I'll contact the police." Thomas' voice and face reflected the loss of a loved one, a friend, a brother.

"Junichi," said Nick, "you can do what you want, but I won't press charges."

"Nick," said Ben, "if you had used that tank, you would have died. Eonin meant to kill you."

Nick nodded. "I know, but putting him in prison won't solve anything. He needs help, the help he never got before. I won't be part of more suffering from that war."

"I will not press charges either," said Junichi. He did not know what he was feeling, stunned by all that he saw and heard.

Nick turned to fully face Junichi and took a deep breath. "I apologize for blaming you. I was wrong." With that, Nick left the room.

"Ben, will you please stay with Eonin? I need to call for some help," Thomas said as he left the room.

Junichi followed Thomas outside. "Thomas, is what Eonin said true? Were the natives denied food and shelter?"

"Yes. With the supply lines cut, there wasn't enough food for everyone. Most families had already been forced off their farms, and the Japanese made it a crime for the islanders to fish in the lagoon. And, yes, they did kill those who got caught. When the Americans came in and investigated, they charged several Japanese with war crimes like this, and other crimes against the POWs and some islanders. Those convicted were hung."

Junichi knew that desperate people did desperate things, but this intentional act, consistent with other atrocities he had heard about, was unforgivable. Is this what his father would not speak of? Could he have done this? No! "My father would not have done this," he said to Thomas, and to himself. "He could never have been so cruel." His face lifted, but his eyes held a question that would never be answered.

"Junichi," Thomas said, putting his hand on Junichi's shoulder, "there is no way for Eonin to have ever known who specifically did anything during those years." For whatever reason, Eonin snapped today and took out all his blame on Nick and your father, which translated in his mind to you. You know your father to be a good man, which means he did not commit these acts. Not all the Japanese were like this. I have heard many stories of Japanese secretly helping families."

"But it had to be in secret," he said, his jaw clenching.

"Yes. If found out, they would have been killed as well."

Junichi nodded and walked away.

Thirty-Nine

When Nick closed his cabin door, he leaned back on it, then his legs gave out and he slid down to the floor. More death, more pain. Eonin, an innocent child orphaned during the battle, had carried the pain, the anger, all these years. How could a child survive that hell? *Did my bombs kill his family? If they were near the airstrips, then it was possible.* Then there was Junichi, also a child who lived through hell. Nick knew he hadn't bombed Tokyo, but how many children's lives had he destroyed? He wrapped his arms around himself, suddenly very cold.

Shame washed over Nick. Why was he so quick to blame Junichi? Where had his compassion been for a man who had just lost his father? Had Natalie been correct? Did Nick still harbor resentment toward the enemy of old? Eonin and Junichi still carried anger and pain after all these years. Nick wondered what he still carried. When does a war actually end?

Tony's and James' faces came into view. Their airplanes crashing, his imagination picturing their deaths. Tony and James died so long ago. Why are they coming back? *Why can't I let them go?*

Jeanne's words came back to him. *You have to go back. You have to feel it all. Only then will you be able to be free.* Nick started breathing faster. He'd never said goodbye to Tony. He went down with his plane. There was no body, no service, no funeral, no pallbearer, no casket, no ashes. For James, there had been a small service on the ship, but no body. Another memory returned on the carrier, a seaman packing up James' possessions.

"What are you doing?" Nicked yelled at the young man.

The seaman spun around, immediately saluting Nick. "Sir, Lieutenant Carson's personal items need to be sent home to his family."

Nick closed his eyes briefly, then returned the salute, freeing the kid.

"Sir, you may go through them and take whatever you want."

Nick glanced at the items: clothes, hat, a couple of photographs, wallet, magazines, toothbrush, comb. He didn't want things; he wanted his friend. Nick shook his head, and the seaman picked up everything and left the room. Nick walked to the empty locker. At that instant, it felt as if his friend was somehow erased.

Here one minute, gone the next. No way to resolve, no way to end, no time! He had shipped out immediately after Tony's death and had to fly again not long after James died. Nick never got to say goodbye to Tony, to James, to so many others, to...JC.

The barricade to his hidden past came down. Nick leaned his head back against the door, closing his eyes and allowed the memories to come. He remembered watching the crash, knowing, but not believing; the laughter; the joy; the shared boyhood dreams. Then the full extent of the memories hit him. He relived it all. Now he understood what he had buried so long ago and why. It was his contribution to that horror. All those flights, all those bombs. He experienced only a small taste of what it felt like to be hit by those monsters. Multiply that by hundreds to get an understanding of the battle at Truk. Multiply it by thousands to see what it felt like at Iwo Jima and Okinawa.

How many monsters did he drop? He never kept count. How many hundreds, maybe thousands, of people did he kill? And in those numbers, how many were innocent civilians, women, children? While he flew, he focused on the flying, the dodging of anti-aircraft firing, shooting at other planes. He had tried not to look at the devastation below. But he had seen it. So many islands. Did he leave them in the same state that Truk had been left in? Did those islanders starve the way the people on Truk starved? Is that what that family in Okinawa faced? It wasn't fear and helplessness that made them jump; it was hopelessness. Did the parents see what would happen to their children if the parents died, or were forced to fight? Was death really better than their future? Was the nightmare so horrid that death was a relief? Did they jump to end this life in the hopes that the next would be better? Was Jeanne right in her belief in reincarnation?

Losing Tony in a training exercise was Nick's first interaction with death and the parallel consciousness that one exists through afterwards. It was also his first experience with the burial of memories and emotions. It was the first layer of his shell. The war provided many more.

Nick's skill as a pilot earned him distinctions and medals. His quiet acceptance was seen as humble acknowledgments of his just rewards. At first there was some honor in the awards. Until that day. It was that day Nick saw these medals only as gold stars he used to get on some of his grade school math papers. Get nine out of ten answers correct—get a gold star. Shoot a plane down—get a gold star. Kill a man—get a gold star.

He lost more friends, buried more memories, built more layers. War was a game of chess with millions of pawns. Nick continued to make his moves as one of those pawns. Be true to your soul, his father had told him. *What soul?* Forgive yourself for whatever you do, his mother had said. *How many whatevers can be forgiven?*

Now the question that had been building for years, no, it had been decades, became clear. How did he live with himself, knowing the full extent of what he had done to so many? How...

Part IV - It's time

When we face our greatest fear, we find our greatest strength.

Forty

Junichi and Shoko woke early to prepare for their early morning dive. Shoko rolled over and, seeing the question in her eyes, he smiled. "I am fine. It is time to do this," he said. The two got up and dressed, then he led the way down to the dive deck.

Thomas was there talking with someone new. "Good morning, Junichi. Good morning, Shoko. I would like you both to meet Jack, a friend of mine, who has agreed to be your dive master. Jack knows these wrecks very well. Also, I want you to know that he and I double checked all tanks this morning and I would like each of you to check your gear thoroughly. Is this alright?"

Junichi smiled at Thomas. "Thank you. Yes, this is fine." Junichi said, then turned to look up at Jack. "Hello, it is nice to meet you," he said as he extended his hand out. Jack was a tall man with a friendly, relaxed smile. There was just enough gray hair mixed in with his blond, that gave the impression that he was close to the same age.

"I'll leave you all to plan your dive," Thomas said, then walked off.

"Junichi," said Jack, "may I talk with you a moment before the McClelands come down?"

"Of course."

"Thomas told me what you have been going through here, as well as your father's recent death. First, let me give you my sincere condolences for your loss. Secondly, I want to make sure that you are alright to make this dive. This particular wreck is on its side and can be quite disorienting."

"Yes, I am fine." Junichi met Jack's gaze and saw only genuine concern in his blue eyes. After all that had happened, it felt both odd and quite nice to be on the receiving end of a kind smile. "Thank you for your concern. You do not need to worry."

"Alright, then I also need to know if you want the McClelands to know about this. I don't know how you all have been diving so far. It is a bit easier for me if you stay in a group. However, I can understand if you two want to go on your own to explore."

"I understand and do not mind telling them. I do not wish to upset their dive, so it would be best to work out a plan."

"Good, because they are coming down now." Jack tilted his head up, gesturing at the stairs.

When the group was together, Jack introduced himself, saying that Eonin had become ill and he would lead them today. Then he began to explain the dive. "The *Heian Maru* is a passenger ship that was reconfigured as a submarine tender. It suffered a hit on the first day of the raid and a massive fire broke out. It finally sank the second day. So, if you penetrate the bridge superstructure, which is an easy penetration, as there are a lot of windows to go in and out, you will notice that wooden floors and walls are gone. Also, this ship is on its side so it can be disorientating to navigate inside. We never have great visibility here, so expect less than ten meters. The water will be calmer today, both on the surface and below. Another nice aspect of this wreck is the top of it, or in this case, the starboard side, is about where we need to do our five-minute safety stop. It is best to save that area to explore at the end. Now, as a group, we do need to discuss something else." Jack turned to Junichi.

Junichi took a deep breath. "Callum and Helen, I need to tell you that I asked Thomas if we could dive on this ship today.

That is why you received an updated schedule. The reason for my request is that my father worked on this ship during the war and was here during this battle. He did not die in this battle," Junichi added, at Helen's stricken look, "but he did pass recently."

"Junichi, we're glad that you told us. I know we've been diving as a group so far, but if you wish to go on your own, we understand and can go to another area on the ship. However, Helen and I have no specific agenda with this dive, so would be happy to follow as well. Whichever you prefer," Callum said, and Helen nodded.

Junichi was surprised and rather touched at their under-standing. He had imagined that he and Shoko would be alone. "I appreciate your flexibility. It is easier for Jack if we stay together." He turned to Jack. "As you have been on the wreck before, could you suggest where might be a good place to start? I know my father worked on the ship for a long time, so I am sure he went everywhere. However, I am most interested in those areas where he probably spent most of his free time."

Jack thought for a moment. "It's a bit challenging because the ship is on its side. There is a hold area, with various items, like torpedoes and artillery shells. It's very dark though. The superstructure took the majority of the fire, so there are only a few cabins left, but they are still damaged. However, there are several passageways that are open and light. One in partic-ular has several spare periscopes lying on the bulkhead. Which would you prefer?"

Junichi thought for a moment. "One of the passageways. I would have no idea where his sleeping quarters would have been, but it is safe to believe he walked in the passageways. Let us go to the one with the periscopes."

Jack nodded. "Alright then, I'll lead everyone down there first. After you're finished, we'll make our way back up, and everyone can explore along the way."

"Thank you, Jack, that is a good plan," said Junichi.

Callum spoke up. "Junichi, please do not rush. What you are doing is very important and there is plenty of time." Junichi smiled and nodded his appreciation. That settled, the group loaded their dinghy.

Forty-One

As usual, Nick rose well before sunrise, both exhausted and relieved. The night had been long, with minimal sleep. Now he didn't think about the past. Today was about the dive this morning. An odd sense of nervous anticipation set in, yet also a calm comfort, that whatever was going to happen, it would finally be resolved today. Never acknowledging it to himself, but he'd been on a long journey to this day. No more waiting, no more wondering, no more exerting energy to forget. It was time.

Nick made his way to the salon and found the coffee and tea service set up. After he fixed his tea, he headed for the top deck, which was the perfect place to watch the sunrise in peace. However, someone beat him to the spot.

Sarah leaned on the rail, absorbed, staring out over the lagoon. She didn't hear him, mesmerized in thought. Irritated that he wouldn't have the place to himself, Nick almost left, but as he watched Sarah, he began to wonder why her eyes hung low, drawing down her thin brows. "Sarah," he said softly, not wanting to scare her. When she didn't turn, he said her name a bit louder. "Sarah."

At that she turned, and he could see the cloud in her eyes for a brief moment before they cleared and she smiled at him. "Good morning, Nick. How are you this very early morning?"

Nick smiled back. "Fine, thank you. I didn't expect to see anyone out this early."

"I love sunrises. For a short time, there is incredible peace and beauty not seen at any other time of day. It's the dawn of a new day, a new beginning. Another opportunity for the world to be right and good." She gave an embarrassed laugh, smiling at her verbal musings. "As you can see, I like sunrises."

Nick came to the rail. "If you enjoy the sunrise so much, what made you so sad?"

Sarah glanced up at him, then back out to sea, then took a deep breath. "I'm having trouble reconciling the in-congruencies of this trip." She was quiet again, but Nick waited, sensing she was trying to arrange her thoughts and wanting to hear them. "This trip has been full of almost opposites. I was so excited about it. I thought only of getting away and enjoying a tropical paradise, incredible marine life, adventurous wreck diving." Sarah stopped and her eyes took on the intensity again. "I naively never really thought of why this place has such appeal. It's built on wars, destruction, and death. A monument to man's stupidity."

Sarah smiled again. "Above the water are lush islands, populated by peace-loving people. Breathtaking sunrises and sunsets. This is a place infinitely suited to relaxation and tranquility." Then Sarah's brows came down. "But below the water, the scene is different.

"I've dived on wrecks before, but they were either boats that were sunk intentionally, or on wrecks so old that only part of the wooden hulls are still visible and all artifacts removed. These wrecks are still intact. The damage was man-made by bombs and torpedoes. The sites remain almost exactly as they were when they sank. Only some of the personal items have been taken and most of the human remains, but not all. This is a graveyard with no personal headstones.

"And yet," she said, her eyes gleaming, "incredible coral has grown, turning the decaying metal into a beautiful mass of color and life. Fish, turtles, sharks, rays all swim in and out of the holds and among the army field artillery that sit on the decks." Sarah looked at Nick in question. "Does life always find a way?

"Then on this boat we have people from Germany, Japan, Scotland, England, and the US. Not so long ago, we were mortal enemies, fighting to the death. Now we're all talking, laughing, and sharing an incredible vacation together." Sarah shook her head and questioned more to herself than anyone. "Is it like the old saying that time heals all wounds?" Then she let her shoulders sag. "I'm sorry, Nick. I was rambling and distracting you from a beautiful sunrise."

Nick had no answer for her. She had no idea how much her confusion paralleled his own.

The two were quiet as the sun peeked above the horizon, painting the sky red, fading to orange, then yellow as it rose. For a few moments, the sky was lit up like a rainbow as the sunrise backlit the wispy clouds.

"A new beginning," Nick whispered. Sarah smiled at him.

The sun rose above the horizon, and the sky turned light blue. "Nick," Sarah asked, "can I ask you a question?"

Nick's heart began to pound as he suspected what was coming, but he still gave a gentle nod yes.

"Why did you come back?" Sarah asked, gazing out over the water, then glanced up and saw the question in his eyes. "I was in the salon that first night. I saw your face. The rest of us saw a newsreel video. You relived memories," she replied to his silent question.

Nick turned his face out to the islands. "Did everyone notice?" he whispered.

"No, only Thomas, Mr. Takahashi, and me. Everyone else was wrapped up in their own feelings, their own reactions to the video."

The two were quiet for a few minutes, deep in thought. Sarah looked down into the water. "What are you hoping to find down there?" she asked. Before them, the lagoon was almost glass, with a mild shimmering reflection of the islands.

Off to the west, the small movement of the water was lit up like a million small diamonds in the rising sunlight. Birds sang softly in the distance. No other noise disturbed their song. Nick was quiet for so long, Sarah turned to leave.

The innocent, direct question shook him. Through the night, a variety of images came in and out of consciousness. The possibilities stayed in his mind, but the words refused to be spoken out loud. "I don't really know," he said. "I wish I did."

"I'm sorry Nick," Sarah said, with such regret. "I shouldn't have asked. It's none of my business."

"It's alright, Sarah," Nick said, to make her feel better. "I've been in a similar confusion. I wish I had answers for you, but I don't." Nick turned to Sarah and smiled until she smiled back at him. "I think we will both have to live with questions for a bit longer until answers wish to appear. Now we need to enjoy the gift of a beautiful new day. I'll meet you later for breakfast."

As Nick turned to follow Sarah down the stairs, he heard one of the dinghies leaving for the early dive. He glanced at the sound to see Junichi staring back up at him. They stared at each other until the little boat drove past.

Forty-Two

The noise from the motor was the only sound during the short ten-minute ride to the site. Junichi kept his gaze forward and tried to enjoy the view but failed. So many conflicting thoughts and emotions collided inside him. What he wanted was to finish this dive and go home. He had come here to find peace and found everything but that.

Jack stopped the little boat and hooked the buoy. The group put on their gear and rolled backwards into the water to begin their descent. Jack was right about the reduced visibility; nevertheless, they couldn't miss the wreck. It was enormous, at 12,000 tons and 510 feet long. Below the surface, the site was a huge green mass. As the group got closer, the details of the ship emerged to reveal its massive hull lying on its side with the top of the ship jutting out parallel to the seabed.

Jack led the way to the Bridge Superstructure, which resembled a four-story building with approximately twelve windows across. Its mammoth size made Junichi feel very small and insignificant. He hung over the wreck for several minutes to allow his mind to re-orientate to the ninety degree shift. The brain had such a clear vision of what it should look like, but the reality was in stark conflict with what the brain expected. Once he began swimming along the lines of the ship, everything made sense.

They entered the bridge through one of the windows. Of course, the glass was all gone, blown out by the blast or fire.

The bridge was on the top floor, but on its side, it was the furthest out from the deck. There was also a bridge wing that protruded out further. As they swam through, they saw the engine telegraph and some lights, glass still intact. The group exited the bridge through the back, then turned left toward the deck to enter the passageway on the promenade deck. Here they found an open and spacious passageway with plenty of sunlight. The only oddity to this area was the presence of several spare periscopes laying on the bulkhead. Each one was about twenty to thirty feet long and about ten inches in diameter. Jack led everyone to about halfway down the long corridor. He then stopped and indicated for the group to begin exploring.

Junichi scanned the area. This was light and open. It would have been a nice place to walk on board the ship. Yes, he could see his father here. He swam down the passageway, peering into the remaining doors and windows. The devastation from the fire was immense. He could almost imagine those remaining souls who had never escaped. He thought about the years of struggle that his father had endured.

Because of his injuries, Junichi had always seen his father's weaknesses. However, now seeing what his father went through, he recognized Kaito's spirit was very strong. He survived it all and came home. And at home, his father never wallowed in bitterness or anger. He dealt with his limitations with honor and strength. Regret overwhelmed Junichi. How foolish he had been, and now there was no way to rectify this with his father. Taking in all the destruction, it hit him how close he had come to never meeting his father.

A hand squeezed his shoulder. Junichi reached up and covered Shoko's soft hand. His mask slowly filled with tears, every breath stuttered from emotions. Closing his eyes, he took several deep breaths and calmed down. He turned his face up and blew air out of his nose, flushing out the tears. Blinking away the remaining tears, he could now see. Junichi turned to see Shoko's loving eyes, then nodded, leading her back to the others.

Jack was waiting for them on the bridge. Once he saw them, he swam out of the windows and toward the deck. Shoko and Junichi followed him. Shoko was immediately drawn to the marine growth. Small mounds of Brain coral were plentiful, but there were also several Elk-horn and Table coral growing. There were only a few soft pink corals to start, therefore the wreck didn't have as much of the vibrant colors yet. However, soft green leafy plants were well established and, through their photosynthesis, this area would continue to develop. Schools of little sapphire-colored fish darted around the plants. This wreck is providing a very strong foundation as an artificial reef, he thought, and it will be very beautiful in a few more years.

Junichi glanced around the deck area, spotting the spent ammunition by an old gun area—but the gun was missing. Close by were two large windlasses with their cables still connected. His mind envisioned them as they would have been with his father there, operating them, lifting fuel lines, hauling periscopes. Bringing his mind back, he appreciated that they were now providing a base for plants and a couple of oysters. The king post was sticking straight out from the ship deck, parallel to the seafloor. Light green leafy plants covered the post as well as what remained of the rigging. A variety of Pillar and Lettuce corals had chosen this as their home. Looking out further away from the ship, there was a very large school of a hundred or so Barracuda passing by.

A pale pink jellyfish swam by and grabbed his interest. Its translucent jelly body had a mushroom top head with a bottom like bell skirt with ruffles. The top pulsed in and out like a heartbeat, propelling itself through the water. It was a delicate pale orange color and beautiful to watch. Fortunately, this one didn't have long stinging tentacles yet. He followed it for a few minutes. It was a beautiful reminder of life. Turning, he headed back to Shoko.

At this point, they swam out to join Callum and Helen on top of the wreck—the starboard side of the ship. Here was a vast area spotted with small coral, like a town where the houses were spaced apart, but would eventually fill in as the population grew. A marking on the ship's hull captured Junichi's attention. Shoko followed him and they came to the name on the ship—*HEIAN MARU*—written in both Arabic and Japanese letters. At first that seemed strange, then Junichi remembered that this was a merchant vessel before the Japanese Navy took it over to support the war effort, so it sailed into ports of many countries around the world. He ran his fingers over the letters, softly wiping away the silt. This was the address of his father's past, and it was time to say goodbye.

Forty-Three

At breakfast, Nick took a seat next to Natalie. "How are you this morning?" Though not hungry, he did enjoy the aroma of onion, garlic, and soy sauce. He wasn't sure, but there also seemed to be a sweetness, with a little kick of some spice. Part of him wanted to taste it, but the other part didn't know if he could keep it down.

"I'm fine," she said. "I stopped by your cabin, but you were already gone."

"I got up early for the sunrise and met Sarah on deck." He reached for that pitcher of water and filled his glass.

Natalie lowered her voice. "How are you?" she asked, scanning Nick's eyes for the truth.

Nick returned her gaze with a smile. "Good. Really good," he added, when it was clear that she didn't believe him. Nat had always been there for him. He hated making her worry. But some things can't be changed.

The staff prevented Natalie from probing further as they began serving breakfast.

"This is a taco rice bowl," said Ray. "I've heard about this. It's from Korea. A restaurant began to make these for the American GIs. It was their cross between Mexican tacos and Korean rice dishes." He reached for the menu card, reading it out loud, "Bibimbap, from Korea, is marinated beef, sauteed vegetables, and rice. As well as the fruit salad."

Nick half listened to the group discussing the food as he moved his own food around the plate, not eating anything.

"I decided not to dive anymore," said Natalie quietly to Nick. "I've had my fill. How about you skip the dives today and we go explore a beach?" Her words were light, but her eyes implored him to stay.

Nick knew why she was asking. He shook his head. "This is what I came here to do. I didn't know it then, but I do now. I have to go."

"Are you sure, Nick? After everything that's happened, is it really worth the risk?"

Nick stared downward, fully considering the question. "Yes," he said simply. As he lifted his gaze back up to her, his voice had more confidence. "Just this dive, then I'm done. We can explore the beach later."

Natalie nodded and looked back at her uneaten food.

Thomas stood up at his table and signaled for everyone's attention. "Excuse me everyone. May I please have your attention for a few minutes? I need to remind you of the special circumstance that exist. Today is February seventeenth, the anniversary of Operation Hailstorm. As I explained before, many of the family members of those who died still come to pay their respects. Some may be at the dive sites and usually place wreaths on the water. I want to remind you that while you may be enjoying this diving vacation, that you also respect their grief and customs. If you should see any family members nearby, please be as quiet and discreet as possible. I appreciate your cooperation."

Thomas' words had a sobering effect. The group finished their breakfast in silence, then started pushing back from the table. Thomas caught up to Nick as he left the dining area. "Good morning, Nick. How are you doing this morning?"

Nick saw the real question in Thomas' eyes. *If one more person asks me how I'm doing, I'm going to punch something,* he thought, then took a deep breath. "Fine," he said.

"Honestly?" Thomas' eyes showed his doubt and concern.

"Yes, honestly. I'm good." Nick gave a confident and calm smile. "Thank you for caring."

"Nick, I do care about you, but I am also responsible for everyone as well."

"I understand. I really am fine."

"Alright." Despite doubt clouding Thomas' face, he allowedNick to go.

Nat met him at the stairs. "I need a hug before you go."

Without a word, he pulled her into his arms and they held each other for several minutes. When they pulled apart, Nat wiped her eyes. "Okay, go do what you have to do. I'll see you soon."

Nick nodded and went down the stairs. He met the others on the dive deck to plan the next dive.

Frank again took the lead. "We're diving the *Shinkoku Maru* again this morning."

"Great," said Sarah, "I brought my camera today. I've got it set for macro shots. I want to try to capture some of the magnificent coral close up. That way, the incredible vibrancy of the colors can be seen."

"Shall we keep the same hundred foot limit today that we had on Monday?" asked Ray.

"Sounds good to me," Frank answered.

Nick smiled, thinking how good it was to be surrounded by young people. Their energy was contagious.

"Ben, what part of the ship we are diving on?" asked Sarah.

"Monday, we dove on the aft-ship, the back third of the ship, and today we are going for the mid-ship, also known as the middle third of the ship. The bridge is about sixty feet deep and is easy to penetrate. There is a lot to see on the bridge and, like Monday, the marine growth is spectacular. Sarah, you're going to be very glad that you brought your camera today. And you will also be happy to hear that the choppy water isn't as bad, so the ride out will be a lot smoother."

"Wonderful!" said Sarah.

"You may want to go down lower to the deck area and then make your way up the walls of the superstructure. Reserve several minutes for the bridge itself. It is worth it. Again, like Monday, keep an eye out past the wreck. With the well-established marine life, the larger animals also like this wreck." At that point, everyone loaded into the boat.

"What a magnificent day." Sarah said, over the noise of the motor. "The sky is so blue, with only a few small wispy clouds."

Nick listened, but didn't participate in the discussions. He gazed ahead at another boat floating on the water. Two people were aboard this boat, an old woman and a young man, both Japanese, placing wreaths on the water. Nick's good mood faltered as he watched the family in mourning. The rest of his group stopped talking when they saw the other boat.

No one uttered a word until they reached their dive site. Ben tethered the dinghy to the buoy line and turned back to the group. This time, however, Nick was ready first. He caught Ben's eye. "I'm heading down." Then he fell back into the water and disappeared before Ben could respond.

Forty-Four

Natalie stood by the railing. She woke up this morning, acknowledging this was the anniversary of James' death. One more year, in a long line of time. It's odd, she realized, that James's last resting place was somewhere out there.

"Hi, Natalie," said Mary. "Are you alright today?"

"Yes, a bit sad and I guess reflective."

"I'll listen if you want to talk."

Nat smiled at Mary. She could see the genuine support in her eyes. "Yes, thank you. I do." She turned her gaze back out at the lagoon. "The other day, when we talked, I couldn't go on that dive because it was an airplane. I couldn't face the wreckage and would always wonder if that was what my brother might have gone through."

"It's good you didn't see it."

"You know, it's so strange. Nick, James, Shoko, Junichi, Carl, and I all had such different experiences from that war. I felt guilty for so long that I had it so much easier. For me, apart from James being gone, I still went to school and parties, watched football games. We couldn't buy as much at the stores, but mom still made me dresses. I was shielded from so much. I went with mom and dad to the movies once. That's when I saw newsreel footage of the war in Europe. It was so horrible to see what those guys endured, I wouldn't go to the movies again. I couldn't watch it. I wanted to stay in my cocoon. Then the telegram came. I hated my life for a while, knowing my brother sacrificed everything and I gave up nothing."

"Didn't you realize that your life was exactly why he sacrificed everything?"

"Not then. It took a while. Hearing Shoko's story yesterday brought more of my guilt back up. Other than for me, that war didn't discriminate. It dished out horror at some level for everyone who came in contact with it."

"Don't diminish what you went through," said Mary. "Having a loved one disappear from your life without the ability to say goodbye means the grief hangs on, lingering. You didn't have a tangible place where you knew where James' body was, no grave, no urn. You and your family had nowhere to go and talk with James to say the words that you never got to say before he died. When Carl died, did you bury him?"

"Yes, and I went to his grave often to talk with him, to say all the things that I never said when he was alive."

"Exactly. Your parents couldn't resolve James' death. I'm sure there was always a tiny hope that he would make it somehow." Natalie nodded at that. "I'm sure you had to be strong for your mother and father, didn't you?"

"Yes."

"Nat, you may have had it easier during the war, but you paid your price afterwards. Now you've come here to honor your brother and let him go."

Nat stood there quietly for several minutes, then took a deep breath, slowly exhaling. "You know, grief isn't the loss of someone you love. It's the loss of their future that you wanted to share with them. For whatever reason, fate or bad luck, James wasn't meant to have that future."

"Natalie," said Mary, "I don't know if you would appreciate this or not..." Mary hesitated.

"It's alright Mary, say whatever it is."

Mary smiled. "I have a boat today and if you would like to go and place flowers on the water for James, I'll be happy to take you."

Natalie's eyes immediately filled with tears, touched by Mary's kindness. "Yes, I would appreciate that very much."

"Good, then go, get whatever you need, and meet me down on the dive deck. It should be clear of divers by then. We'll go to shore to get the flowers, then out to the lagoon."

Natalie hurried to her room, grabbing her hat, sunglasses, and some money. She reached the dive deck and Mary was waiting by the dinghy.

"Will you please untie us first, then hop in?"

Nat did as instructed and they set off.

Mary had to yell a bit to be heard over the motor. "We will go back to Weno. I have a friend there that will have the best selection of flowers at the hotel. It will take us about fifteen minutes."

Nat responded with a thumbs up. She was feeling better. At long last, she would be able to have some form of a service for James. Some token gesture to bring closure to his life and her grief, releasing James, Carl, and her own guilt. With that thought, she allowed herself to view the lagoon with fresh eyes and see the beauty of the day.

The minutes passed quickly, and they arrived at a dock by the hotel. Mary tied the boat up, then led the way to a flower stand. Although the quantities were small, the selection was wide. "Oh, how beautiful," Natalie said to the stand owner. Thinking for a minute, Nat chose several white and yellow hibiscuses. "I'll take these, please." The lady stated the price and Nat paid her, adding a generous tip on top. "I'm ready," she said to Mary.

Mary said something in the native language to the woman, then led the way back to the boat.

When they got back to the dock, Mary asked. "Do you have any place specifically in the lagoon to do this?"

"No, I don't, and I didn't want to ask Nick any questions. Can we find a place with some calm water that might be away from the wrecks?"

"Yes, I know where we'll go. There's a lovely area on the leeward side of one of the islands. It's not on the route to any of the wrecks. Get in. It will take about ten minutes to get there."

They shoved off and motored to the area. Natalie scrutinized the location. It was indeed well protected and very beautiful. There wasn't any beach here. Instead, a dense rainforest grew up the side of the island. Colorful flowers popped out, decorating the green background. Once Mary stopped the boat, the only sound rose from the birds. A supremely peaceful spot. "This is perfect," said Natalie.

"Would you like me to say anything?"

"No, thank you though." Carefully, she stood up, trying not to rock the small boat. Nat gazed out over the water, tears welling up in her eyes, and murmured to herself. "Thank you, James, for being a good brother. Thank you for being strong and brave. I hope you have found peace in heaven. You will always be missed. I love you." Nat leaned down and placed the flowers on the water. Sitting down in the boat, her eyes took in the island cove, the water, the blue sky, burning the view into her memory. No cemetery could ever be as beautiful as this cove was. Nat didn't bother wiping away the tears. James deserved them. Taking a deep breath, she turned to Mary. "Thank you."

"You and James are welcome. Are you ready?"

Closure. Chapters complete. Lovely memories will live on, but the pain ends. "Yes, I am."

"If you aren't in a rush to get back to the Eagle Ray, would you like to see my little house?"

Natalie smiled at Mary, happier than she had been in a very long time. A friend in need, she thought. "Yes, I would."

Forty-Five

After the dive, Junichi went to his cabin. Shoko knew what he was doing, so let him go alone. He reached into a drawer and pulled out his father's letter.

Junichi,

My father lived on in me, just as I will live on in you, and you will live on in your son. I asked you to take this journey for you, not for me. My opportunity to bring closure to all that happened has passed. But you still have yours.

It is time for you to let me go, as well as everything my life represents. With that, let go of all of your anger about the past. When we keep anger from the past, we deny joy in the future. Let it all end now, so that it does not live on in your son.

You were born in a time of great change between two very different cultures. You had no foundation to begin your life, but your strength has enabled you to forge a path. This is the foundation you have provided for your son. Without this past, you and your son would not have the freedoms you have today. Enjoy those, but make sure your son understands how precious freedom is and to never allow anyone to take it away, nor allow your own fear to give it away.

You have also lived long enough, and have seen much of this world, to understand that every life has difficulties. Your life is no exception. You faced a terrible childhood. But you made it through. You can deem your life successful when you have faced these challenges and persevered through them. You have achieved this success.

That insanity is over. The world is beautiful again. Embrace its beauty. That is the greatest gift you can give yourself and those that you love.

No words can ever express how honored I am to have been your father. I love you, my son.

Kaito

Junichi read through the letter several times, then wiped his eyes. Taking a deep breath, he exhaled, letting the tension release from his shoulders. The knot that lived there for so long began to ease. His father's words echoed in his heart. *There it will end for me.* Then he smiled. It was over.

"No," he said, as his head snapped up. It was over for his father, but not for himself. Nick sprang to his mind. *There it will end for me.* Did Nick feel the same way his father had felt? He had to talk with Nick, to make peace with him.

Junichi ran out of the room, up the stairs, and through the salon to the cabins. He banged on Nick's door, but there was no answer. Then he ran back down the stairs and into the dining room. Not there either. *He's probably on a dive.* He headed out and down the stairs. Thomas was there, at the side, kneeling on the dive deck, putting dive gear into a dinghy.

"Thomas," he asked, his chest heaving, "do you know where I can find Nick?"

When the other man glanced up, Junichi could also see the strain in his eyes. There was a hollowness in his gaze that reflected the pain that was there as well. Junichi had not truly understood how much Eonin had meant to Thomas until that moment. Watching someone, or in this case a friend, breakdown so completely and then taken away, had to be as hard as an actual death. An inclination to give comfort sprung up. He almost reached out his hand to Thomas' shoulder, but stopped. Somehow, the gesture felt fraudulent when he acknowledged his own contribution to the strain. Then he shook himself. Nick came back into his mind. Not certain why, but the urgency to see Nick now was growing.

"He's on a dive," said Thomas. "After the last few days, I would like to know why you want to see him."

"To apologize."

The radio next to Thomas crackled. "Thomas, are you there?"

Thomas jumped to grab it. "I'm here Ben, go ahead."

"Thomas, Nick went in and hasn't come up yet. The others are surfaced watching for his bubbles."

"Right, I'm on my way. Keep watching." Thomas signed off and finished loading the gear.

"Thomas, what was that about?"

"Nick penetrated a ship, alone. I'm going out there."

"I'm coming with you." Junichi immediately went to check his gear and found his tank had already been refilled. Grabbing it all, he rushed back to the dinghy.

"Alright," said Thomas, "you can come. But if we have to go in, you have to follow me. You don't know the wreck. I do." Junichi nodded. Thomas cast off and radioed a friend at one of the land-based dive shops to come out as well.

En route, Junichi did a thorough check of everything, put on his gear, and waited, thinking. Nick went into a ship alone, which was against all the diving rules. There was something about this ship that made Nick do it. In all of Junichi's emotions, he had never once thought of how Nick might be feeling. Everything about Nick gave the impression of a caring, decent man. How would it feel to know you were responsible for so many deaths, to have to live with those memories? He had blamed Nick. Eonin had blamed Nick as well. Shoko was right. This was the last place a veteran of this battle would come for pleasure. Nick came for some reason, and he had added to that burden. Junichi, like Eonin, had immersed himself in the pain from the receiving side of a war, never the giving side. He tried to put himself in Nick's place, to be put in a position where your only job was to kill. A completely foreign and horrid thought.

Ahead, Junichi could see the other boat with the group in the water, looking for Nick. As soon as Thomas stopped the boat, he fell over the side.

Forty-Six

As fast as he felt was safe, Nick descended to the ship. As before, the visibility was good and the swell minimal. He saw an open hatch on the top deck and went in.

Nick had spent a lot of time on military ships, but this was a merchant vessel. He could only hope the general interior layouts were similar. He started looking for stairs. He knew the officer's quarters wouldn't be up on the top deck. He found the stairs. If the Japanese ship was like US ships, the captain's cabin would be down here. He dropped down the stairs to another very dark corridor and pulled out his light. He slowed his movement to minimize disturbing the silt. After adjusting the air in his BC, he rose as he took a breath in and sunk when he exhaled. Good, he reached neutral buoyancy. From this moment forward, he had to float and hover if he wanted the water to stay clear enough to see.

Outside a wreck, disturbing the silt wasn't a problem, as he could swim away. But inside a wreck, the walls and ceilings contained the silt. So if disturbed, it was like shaking up a snow globe. Then he wouldn't be able to see where the exits were or where the pipes, wires, debris, and other hazards were. It would be easy to get stuck on the destruction around a wreck and then run out of air. Nick could control his movements, but not his exhaust bubbles, which were colliding with the silt above him, causing a gentle snowstorm of silt and rust.

Nick turned right, shining his light in all directions, then inched his way down the hall. *Remember, down the stairs, turned right,* he had to remind himself. Nick shined his light around and found sections of walls were missing, some maybe made out of wood; others that seemed to be thinner metal, more easily corroded away. Through the holes, he could see a larger room with scattered debris. The general layout of the room suggested it was probably the mess deck. Swimming with only his hands, he floated down the hall, where he found a shorter corridor that led to a few rooms. Nick turned left. *Remember down, right, left.* On the left was a small cabin with the remains of a single bunk, an officer's cabin. Nick's heart beat faster. He knew he had found the right area. Nick floated on. The next room on the right was a bathroom with a couple of urinals and a large tiled tub, amazingly still intact. This was built for officers. In anticipation, Nick quickly turned left and immediately stopped as the silt began to billow up. *Slow down!* He gently floated to the end of the corridor and shined his light in. An office with a cabin behind it. *My god, this is it!*

His heart beating fast, he took deep breaths to try, but failed to calm himself. Nick inched his way into the office and slowly shined his light around to see scattered debris, covered by thick silt. He hovered over an area that might have been a desk. *JC sat here.* Nick envisioned the captain sitting here at his desk writing in the captain's log. He shined the light down into the silt, gently lowered himself closer to the debris. Much of the wood had decomposed, but there were many rusted metal items about. Nick gently pulled on something sticking out. As the silt slowly fell away, he could see it was a typewriter. He carefully laid it back down. Nick slowly rose and shined the light on the walls. Like the halls, some of the walls were torn out or eaten away. Between the shock of the explosions and the angle of the ship sinking, shelves had fallen, cabinets smashed through walls.

I caused this. Nick's mind took over, feeling the rumble from the torpedo's explosion, the immediate tilting of the ship as the water dragged it down. Shelves collapsing, everything not bolted to the floor went flying, the terror to those inside the ship. *Stop this! Creating these images doesn't help. What's done is done. I did my job that day.* He looked around again at the destruction. *And I did it well!* His stomach churned.

Nick had been as subtle with his movements as possible. However, the silt clouds were forming near the floor and his bubbles were still causing a constant silt/rust storm from above. His mind began registering that his visibility was slowly diminishing.

Nick rose above the clouds and moved to the room he wanted to see the most, JC's cabin. In the office, JC had to be the captain, but in the cabin, he could be a man. Nick wanted to know the man. The cabin was in the same state of ruin. Remains of the bunk lay against the far wall. A sink was still intact on the right. The locker was open on the left. Nick went there and lowered himself down, just hovering over the silt. Nick saw a boot partially buried and, in slow motion, gently picked it up. He just floated there staring at it, something so inconsequential, yet so personal. Heart pounding against his chest, he softly put the boot back down, but his shaking hand caused a bigger silt cloud. He turned to float over to the bunk area. He could see some glass sticking out of the silt. He picked it up and saw it was about five inches wide by seven inches tall. As it wasn't broken, Nick assumed it had been with a picture which would have decomposed quickly. There was no sign of a frame. Maybe it had been made of wood. Was the picture of JC's wife, child, parents or anyone who would die a little themselves at finding out that he wouldn't be returning to them? Nick's hands were shaking so hard he dropped the glass into the silt.

Nick shined his light around again. *Mitchel, what are you looking for? You sank the ship! You knew it then. You knew JC died that day, along with probably every other man on board. What are you hoping to find?* Then it hit him. He wasn't looking for answers. He was coming home. This is why he had retired. He had completed everything in his life. His kids were grown, his business resolved, his beautiful Jeanne was gone. He had come home. He did his job forty-three years ago today. Now it was time for him to join JC, to see Tony, James, Kaito, as well as so many others. He wasn't here to say goodbye; he was here to find them all and say he was sorry for living.

His visibility was getting worse by the minute. His heartbeat now throbbed in his ears and his eyes. The debris in the room was becoming shadowy and vague. He saw a movement to his side. Ben must have come down to get him, to save him. *I don't deserve to be saved.* Nick turned, then froze.

JC floated before him. He wasn't solid as a man, but cloudy as a spectral image. Sinking down into the silt, Nick looked up and met his eyes, the same eyes he had seen that day. JC had come to escort him home. Nick's rapid breathing became labored, his body shivering. *It's time. I'm ready.*

The ghost suddenly shouted, *GO!* Nick jumped back, blowing up the silt. The apparition came closer. *You were meant to live, now GO!* The specter vanished.

Nick's entire body shook, but some sliver of reason returned. *Oh God. What the hell am I doing?* Nick glanced at his gauges: seventy-one feet, bottom time, fifty minutes. *Oh no,* pressure eighty psi. No *wonder you can't breathe. You've sucked your tank dry, you IDIOT! Get the hell out of here.* Nick, in a panic, spun around. Silt exploded up, visibility eliminated. His heart began to hurt. Panic grew. *STOP! CALM DOWN!* Reason fought to take back control.

Nick focused on holding each breath for as long as he could. First priority, conserve what little air you have left. He slowly moved forward with his hands out. When he could feel the wall, he moved his left arm around and didn't feel an opening. Then he moved his right arm out and found the door. When he moved through the door, he shut his eyes. With his eyes open, he tried to see with his eyes; once closed, he saw with his mind. He envisioned the office as he had seen it before. He turned and swam forward again with his shaking hands in front of him. When he found the wall again, he moved his hands to the right but didn't feel the frame. He moved further to the right. It wasn't there! Stop! Go back. He felt his way along the wall, back to the left. Finally, he found the door frame.

Out in the corridor, the visibility was slightly better, but still he stopped. *Down, right, left.* That was what he had done to get here, so he needed to do the opposite to get out. *Right, left, up.* He resisted checking his gauges again, as they would only reinforce the panic he was fighting. One step at a time. Next, get out of the wreck. Breathing was extremely hard now without the pressure in the tank. He was fighting to suck the little remaining air out. His head ached and his lungs burned. He quickly swam and turned right. The corridor had better visibility, so Nick could rely on his eyes again. That helped. He swam faster. The silt behind him no longer mattered. He found the hall to the stairs and turned left. Quickly, he found the stairs and looked up. Relief surged through him as he saw the light at the top. He kicked hard up the stairs and out the hatch. He was clear.

Nick glanced at his gauges again: pressure thirty psi. He was down too long and needed safety stops, but didn't have the air for them. Thomas' warning rang in his mind, *"If you get in trouble, you are on your own. If you need the re-compression chamber, you will die before you get there."* Panic started building again. *YOU IDIOT.* This isn't helping.

Nick had to risk it and shoot for the surface. He began kicking as fast as he could, but the exertion required more air that he didn't have! Nor could he use the remaining air to fill his BC for the ascent. Nick ripped off his weight belt and felt it hit his foot as it sank. Straining, he sucked in as much of the remaining air as possible, then he started to exhale slowly as he shot up. His mind fought with lungs over the need to hold and save that last breath. But a diver knew that could be disastrous as the pressure reduced as he went up, expanding the lungs. Without exhaling, the lungs could expand too much and rupture.

On his way up, he finished exhaling all his air, but nothing came back in. Panic took over. Never had he experienced the total inability to breathe. He looked up, no surface, no boat. Every organ, every limb in his body screamed in pain. *Think! Ben always hung a bottle for emergencies. Ben tied the dinghy to the buoy line. So, look for the...* He became lightheaded, his vision went dark, he saw Tony, James, and Jeanne smiling, welcoming him home. The current pulled him to his friends, his wife. He felt free, calm, at peace. Everything was going to be fine.

Suddenly he was caught in something. He couldn't move! In desperation, he thrashed at it with all his might, but his arms were pinned. He kicked his legs and wrenched his shoulders, trying to free himself, but it held him tight. His regulator slipped from his mouth. His eyes lost their sight, his mind lost its thoughts. JC floated up to him, ready to escort him on.

As he moved to join JC, something hit his mouth, blasted his throat, pounded his chest. His mind fantasized about breathing, the air flowing in and out, reaching to the farthest tips of his fingers and toes. His body joined in the illusion and grew stronger, desperate to breathe deeper, sucking in huge amounts of air. JC faded from view, bubble sounds resonated in his ears. His arms were still bound, but he could breathe! Nick had no concept of time. Seconds, minutes, or hours were irrelevant. He froze; his body focused solely on breathing, willing the oxygen to race through his veins. His eyes began to clear and his captor came into view.

Junichi shook Nick hard. He blinked back. The grip on his arms loosened. Junichi held up his hand, showing the OK sign. All Nick could give was a weak nod. Junichi's shoulders dropped.

Thomas came into view, holding up a slate for Nick to read:

Safety stop, don't move!

Nick nodded again, not that he had the strength to move. Thomas hooked a weight to Nick's BC and swam back up to the dinghy. Nick hung there, breathing with Junichi's spare regulator and, when he finally could, he reached to squeeze Junichi's arm. He stared into the younger man's eyes and tried to convey his appreciation for saving his life.

Forty-Seven

Nick sat on the bunk, leaning against the wall, when he heard a soft knock on the door. "Come in," he said, not surprised to see Thomas.

"How are you?" Thomas asked.

Nick could see the strain in Thomas' eyes. "I'm alright. Look, Thomas, I'm very sorry for putting you through that."

Thomas studied Nick and tried to appraise his condition. "Nick, how are you physically? We need to go through the list. Any aches, pains, anywhere?"

"Only a headache, but not bad. Nothing anywhere else."

"Any dizziness, nausea, ringing in the ears?"

"An upset stomach, but I am pretty sure that is due to my complete humiliation at my stupidity, not the bends. Nothing else."

"Numbness or tingling?"

"No, Thomas. I have a headache and I'm tired. That's all. I didn't monitor the time, but I think you and Junichi kept me down on that safety stop for quite a while, substantially longer than normal. I don't think the bends are a problem."

"Good." Thomas started to walk around the small cabin, taking a deep breath, then exploded. "What the bloody hell were you doing? Were you trying to commit suicide down there? You are too good a diver to not have known what you were doing." Thomas collapsed onto the other bed, his face fell into his hands. "You scared the hell out of me," he whispered.

"I'm so sorry. You *should* be yelling at me." Nick started to speak, then stopped. His shoulders dropped. "To be truthful, I'm not sure what I was thinking," he said.

Thomas sat back up and looked into Nick's eyes. "What happened?" When Nick didn't immediately respond, Thomas prompted further. "How about you start at the very beginning?"

Nick stared into space for a while, putting his thoughts in order. "It started so long ago. After the war, I went on with my life. I married my wonderful wife, my best friend. We have two wonderful kids, and now a granddaughter, who I adore. I had a good career. Life wasn't always easy, but it was always busy.

"Old memories faded. I thought I was grounded enough to understand what happened. I accepted it all and went on. Or so I told myself." He took a deep breath, closed his eyes. "After I lost Jeanne," he said in a whisper, "the nightmares began to come back in full force. I think Jeanne was the wall that held back the war. It invaded so much of my life afterwards that I couldn't design anymore, so I retired. Nothing I did could stop it. So, I was forced to accept that there were events in my life that I had to face." He took a deep breath, still relishing the ability to do so, and knew he would never take breathing for granted again.

"With war comes death. That fact was made clear almost immediately after I joined. When death comes, you distance yourself from it somehow. You sort of detach or compartmentalize your emotions in some way, or you go crazy. One day in training, a friend that I had grown up with was in front of me. Something happened after takeoff. I watched as he went nose down into the icy water. He never made it out. I was next in line to take off, the signal came, and I did. In battles, we would all take off together, and then when we got back, I would look around to see who didn't return. This was routine. I knew them, trained with them, played cards, drank, and joked with them. To survive, I learned that to control my emotions, I had to turn them off." Nick turned, putting his feet on the floor, rubbing his hands on his legs. "During the battle here, another friend, my best friend and wingman, died. Again, I watched him crash.

"When we went into battle, our targets weren't people. We were after a ship, a base, an airfield, or any other strategic facility that would help end that God forsaken war. We talked about casualties, not men. It wasn't personal to a person. We wanted to defeat a country, not a face. As a pilot, I was able to keep that perspective because I was always well past my target before my torpedoes exploded. I don't think I could have made it in the marines or army, fighting on the ground, face to face."

Nick rubbed his temples. "The first night, I told you that during the raid, I came in low and dropped my torpedo." He took another long breath and closed his eyes again, trying to decide how much to tell. Nick knew he had to tell someone, and Thomas had a right to the full story. "I didn't tell you about JC."

"Who is JC?" Thomas asked.

Nick opened his eyes, saw Thomas' frown, but he was relieved to see compassion too. Nick jumped up and leaned over the bed to open the porthole. A warm breeze blew in fresh air, ruffling his hair. "During the raid, I was able to come in a lot lower than normal when I dropped my load. In a normal battle, with their guns firing, all you think about is getting the hell out of there alive after you drop. That day was different. With so little defense, I had more time to think, to see everything. I knew I could come down lower to make sure I destroyed the ship. After I dropped my torpedo, as I began to fly over the ship, I looked down into the eyes of the captain. He saw the torpedo coming and then...he looked up at me. I could see it in his eyes. He knew he was going to die.

"I cleared the ship and, as usual, heard the blast. This blast was different. Never before had my mind so clearly converted a noise into an image. I knew exactly what the explosion did without actually seeing it. In those few seconds, I know where most of those men were when they died. Before that day, all my missions were to attack facilities. That day, I killed a man. At that moment, the war became very personal to me. I could no longer stay detached. At that moment, the young naïve kid I was grew up."

Nick's shoulders sagged after finally saying out loud what he had never wanted to admit to himself. Nick stole a quick glance at Thomas, who still frowned. Nick went on. "I never knew the name of the Japanese Captain I killed, so I called him JC and, for the last 43 years, those eyes have been with me. His were the eyes I saw that represented all the thousands that I never saw. Truk wasn't my last battle. I dropped many more bombs on ships, airfields, islands. I will never know how many more lives I ended."

Thomas' eyebrows dropped lower. "For God's sake, Nick, it was war! Did you feel guilty?" Thomas asked.

"I hope to God that my children and grandchildren never have to experience war. It isn't romantic, as some movies have tried to make it. It is hell on earth. I was young and full of patriotic duty. I had been in battle before. Again, casualties were merely anonymous, faceless enemies. I did my part and was proud of my success. At the same time, I desperately wanted to go home.

"Truk was different. I stared into a man's eyes, then killed him, as if I stood in front of him with a gun and shot him. Right after that, my friend, who I grew up with, was shot down. Never to be seen again." Nick began pacing the small room, arms moving, accentuating his thoughts. "My emotions were not one-dimensional. Yes, I felt guilt, regret, anger, revenge; but I also understood that JC, as well as every other man on that ship, would have killed me first, if they had had the chance. But they didn't have the chance that day. I did. I lived. My friend didn't. I did. Why me? I was lucky enough to live, but I also had to live with what I did, my part in that God forsaken war.

"I also understood the bigger task, the war needed to end and the only way to do that was to win the battles. So, I did my part to win those battles, which meant killing other men. I also understood the atrocities that existed for those who were captured and tortured by the Japanese and I was willing to do whatever was needed to stop those horrors." Nick sat back down, looking at Thomas. "However...doing something you see as your duty doesn't alleviate the scars.

"Through the years I've also come to realize that men are the same the world over and, regardless of their country, some men fight because they have to for peace to return and some men fight because they enjoy it, and thus are capable of brutal acts. Age has given me more experiences to draw from and taught me that life is never black or white. In reality, it is different shades of gray. Was JC like me, there fighting because he had to, but hated it? Or was he there like others, brutal killers? Did he have a wife and children at home waiting for him? Or did I end his chance at these?" Nick took a deep breath. "History has also shown us that not all Japanese wanted to go to war. Was he one of those?

"I, of course, was left with only questions and memories. When the war was over, I left the service and went on with my life. I buried the memories, but I never could completely forget JC. After my kids were grown and my wife passed, the unanswered questions about him began to haunt me to the point of coming here to see him in Truk and face my past."

Thomas was incredulous at Nick's statement. "Maybe I am being a bit thick. Exactly how were you thinking you were going to 'see' him?"

Nick actually laughed at this. "Well, not actually see him, but this is as close to him as I could ever get. This is where it happened, so I thought, I hoped, this is where it could end." Nick shook his head. "Stupid really, in so many ways. I don't know what I could ever have found out about the man in a ship that sank so many years ago. Still, it was the only chance I had. Taking that chance was equally stupid."

"So that night when you told me you did not know which ship you sank, you lied to me."

"No. I didn't know then. I spent a lot of time reading Lindemann's book, following the maps, mentally tracing my flights, reading the details of each wreck in the area. I realized that the ship was the *Shinkoku Maru*. I didn't know it at the time when we dove on it on Monday. But later when I figured it out, I kept remembering the hole in the engine room, from my torpedo. I also saw on the schedule that we would dive on it again today. It was now or never, so I took my only opportunity. I never thought it would play out the way it did." Nick went silent, and the two men sat there for a few minutes.

"Nick, what happened on the dive?"

He rubbed his eyes and forehead. "I wanted to see his cabin, the only place that I could see something of him, as a man. So I researched the wreck and had a plan. I knew I had limited bottom time, so when we got to the site I went in the water immediately, even beating Sarah in." Nick smiled. "I descended and penetrated before Ben could stop me. My heart was beating so fast and obviously I was breathing fast.

"Once inside, what I saw with my eyes and the images that existed in my head started to merge. Half wreck, half my image of the past. I hadn't completely lost my mind. My diving experience was somewhat ingrained. My movements were calm and controlled. I didn't completely silt the place up. I also made sure I remembered which way I turned, so I could get out if I couldn't see. I found the officers' corridor and then JC's office and cabin. I spent most of the time there. I was so engrossed in what I was seeing physically and mentally that I completely lost track of time and, more importantly, air."

"What made you leave?"

Nick didn't immediately respond. Then he closed his eyes and whispered. "To be completely honest, there was a point that I wasn't going to leave." Nick opened his eyes to see Thomas' shock. "Then a voice yelled, 'GO!' When I didn't immediately move, it came again, louder. 'GO, LIVE!'" Nick stood up and paced the floor again. Shaking his head, his arms and hands mirrored his jumbled thoughts. "I don't know if it came from me, inherently wanting to live. Or if it was nitrogen narcosis, and I thought it was from JC's ghost. Or..." Nick stopped, closed his eyes, took a deep breath, and calmed himself down. "Regardless, at that moment, I came back to what little sense I had left and got the hell out of there. Obviously, a bit too late." Nick opened his eyes, giving Thomas a rueful smile.

He lost the smile and sat back down again, looking into Thomas' eyes. "Thank you, Thomas. As I think back on it with reason, I truly do know how lucky I was. I have no doubt that I owe you and Junichi my life." Nick was quiet, realizing words could never, ever convey his appreciation.

For the first time, Nick started to wonder. "By the way, why were you two there, anyway? You specifically told us twice that we would be on our own."

"After everything that happened in the last couple of days, I was surprised that you still wanted to dive this morning. I had a nagging feeling, so I set up a spare dinghy with my gear. Junichi came back from his dive and was asking for you. He asked what I was doing and wanted to help. I had given Ben a radio and let him know to call me immediately if there was any sign of trouble.

"Ben had to be responsible to the others in your group, which is why he could not go after you. He did see you penetrate. When you didn't come up at the appropriate time, he called me as soon as he got back in the dinghy. The rest of your group floated on the water, watching out for you or your bubbles. Once Junichi and I got there, he went in immediately while I was securing the boat. He was on the way down when he saw you shooting up to the surface. He figured you were out of air, so he grabbed you. You started fighting him, then went still. You scared the bloody hell out of him as well. Fortunately, though, you were not completely gone. You came around after you could breathe again." Thomas thought for a moment. "It's strange the way some things work out. If you had not reacted to that video the first night, I would not have arranged a backup plan today..."

Nick stared into Thomas' eyes and finished the unsaid words. "And I would most likely be dead now."

"You need to rest. Mary, I am sure, will send you some dinner later." Thomas got up to leave, looking at Nick with a twinkle in his eyes. "By the way, you owe me for a new weight belt."

Nick burst out laughing, appreciating the irony as Thomas singled out the most insignificant aspect of the debt Nick owed. "Yes, I do."

Forty-Eight

Nick slept hard for hours and woke up to see the sun setting through his porthole. He still had a slight headache, but was relieved to have no other symptoms. Realizing he was hungry, he considered joining the others for dinner, but his humiliation over the events prevented him. Nor was he up to the questions and glances that would come, or to making light dinner conversation to avoid discussing the events. Jumping when he heard a quiet knock, he stood up and opened the door. Nick's eyebrows shot up as his stomach turned over.

"May I come in? I brought you some dinner." Junichi carried a covered tray and a tote bag.

"Please, come in, and thank you." Nick stepped back, but stayed by the door.

Junichi put the tray on the dresser and took off the cover to reveal two plates of food. Nick raised his eyebrows in question.

Junichi smiled. "If you would feel more comfortable, I will leave. If you would like company, I would like to stay."

Nick shut the door, then turned back around. "Junichi, first let me say thank you for saving my life. Please join me."

Junichi nodded and opened the tote bag to reveal two glasses, a bottle of scotch and a bottle of sake. "Would you care for a glass?"

Nick gave a grateful smile. "Definitely, thank you!"

"I had to convince Natalie to allow me to bring your food."

"Does she also want to strangle me?"

Junichi's eyes twinkled. "I believe I heard words to that effect."

"So, you are saving my life twice in one day." Nick laughed, but still peered at Junichi with trepidation.

Junichi smiled and handed Nick a glass of scotch, then poured himself a glass of sake, and sat down. "Nick, I owe you an apology for the words I spoke to you that first night."

"No, you don't."

"Yes, I do. Because you were one of the pilots, I blamed you for what happened here, but in all fairness, my father was shooting back. I know that you did not bomb my father's ship and that you are not to blame for what happened to me." Junichi pursed his lips and took a deep breath. "That newsreel was very difficult for me to see, and I took out my anger on you. I am sorry for that." He gave a slight smile. "I am glad you never stood up. I am not completely sure what I would have done."

"I think you made up for it today," Nick said, smiling. "I also never thanked you for figuring out it was Eonin behind those events or for stopping him when he lunged at me. After I saw your quick action, I was very glad I never challenged your double black belt." Junichi smiled as well. "I do understand if you blame me, though," Nick said softly.

Junichi watched as he swirled the liquid in his glass. "I have been angry for a very long time. For years, I tried to find the benefit of what happened to me, hoping there was some purpose, some value. When that was unsuccessful, I wanted someone to pay. The enormity of it all was too large to identify one person until I realized that you were here. When you confirmed you were one of the pilots, my anger took over. You were here and you should pay for my pain, my father's pain. You were the enemy. Fortunately, I was only angry, not psychotic. Even that night, after I left your cabin, I knew, in my heart, that you were not to blame. But acknowledging that would mean that I was back with no one to be held responsible." Junichi glanced back up at Nick. "I do not blame you. Do you blame me? I am from the country that started the war."

"Of course not. You were a child, not even in the war."

Junichi took a drink. "My father never spoke of the war until a few weeks before he died. Very few people at home spoke about it, or if they did, they would not speak to a child. When my father came home, it was as if everyone wanted to forget the horrors and move on. And, in reality, there was so much work to survive day to day that I can understand why no one looked back. No real details about the war were ever taught in school. So I was on my own to try to understand, and when that failed, I tried to forget. I successfully buried memories. In their place came anger. Though to be honest, as a father myself, I have not spoken to my own son about any of it. To him, it is history and not real."

Nick listened to this, wondering if he had talked about it all so many years ago, would he be sitting here today? He told himself that he was protecting his son by not discussing the war, but Nick had to admit he was hiding. Fighting in a war exacted a toll. Hiding from the memories cost him even more.

Junichi took another healthy drink, then continued. "It is not easy coming from the country that started the war. I have traveled enough and have heard of some of the atrocities that were committed, and like many of my countrymen, did not want to believe them. I was taken by surprise when Eonin told of what my people did here. Thomas confirmed it, giving me more details. My father never spoke of this."

Junichi gave Nick a rueful smile. "I love my country and am very loyal, but I do not agree on much of what some of my countrymen have done. I was reminded of this the other night when one of the young German boys made a comment about how much propaganda was in that video. Those Germans have similar histories to deal with as my people do. Your country does not have a pristine history, either."

Nick nodded. "That is true. I do not like all that we have done, yet I stayed silent as well."

"It is like a large, loving family that suspects one of their relatives is unkind and cruel. How many make excuses or try not to believe what is said until the evidence is so undeniable? Do the family members call the police? What if the evil is in the police? Then who do you call? That was part of what happened in my country and in Germany. There were secret police embedded in towns. Fear kept people quiet."

Junichi reached to refill his glass. Clear liquid spilling from the bottle was the only sound. Outside, the night was calm and silent. Nick assumed everyone was in the dining room. Junichi sat back in his chair.

"Junichi, you asked me, the other night, if I was in Tokyo. Were you there during the fire bombings?"

"Yes."

"Is your mother still alive?"

Junichi smiled. "Yes."

"She must be a very strong and remarkable woman to have endured all that."

Junichi nodded. "She is. She saved us both that night and took care of me and my father all those years. I never heard her complain. Once, years later, I did overhear her and my father talking about the war. She kept calling it insanity, and she was right.

"Did you know that before the war was over and we were afraid the Allies would invade our mainland, our leaders had a plan: Ichioku Gyokusai—The Glorious Death of 100 Million. It is glorious to die for the Holy Emperor of Japan and every single Japanese man, woman, and child should die for the Emperor when the Allies arrive." Junichi shook his head. "They expected almost every citizen to fight to the death. I snuck out of bed one night to overhear my mother and grandfather talking. Hearing that my mother and I would have to fight caused more nightmares. Those atomic bombs were monsters, yet I cannot imagine the death toll if the Allies had invaded."

Nick automatically thought of Anthony or Dana in that position. The idea turned his stomach.

"How do people resist following their so-called leaders?" Junichi asked, his voice low, almost talking to himself. "Such disrespect is tantamount to treason. But is treason still treason when your leaders are insane with power, willing to sacrifice countless countrymen to maintain their position or to further their gain? In this case, is it not the leaders who are the traitors? Not following our leaders in my country meant dishonor, if you were lucky, and death if you were not lucky."

Nick downed the rest of his drink, feeling the liquid bounce around in his empty stomach. This discussion alone was enough to make him sick. At this moment, the garlic creamy parmesan smell wasn't inviting.

Junichi continued. "Estimates of total deaths during World War II range from fifty million to seventy million. These numbers do not include those who were injured, nor the countless lives changed because of the war. Think of this for a moment! That many humans, wiped away in the span of only a few years. Caused by a few, with immense greed for power, and followed by millions and millions of people. Where was the sanity?"

"I know," Nick agreed. "I have had those same thoughts. We humans seem to have a history of this. I'm reminded of the words of Charles MacKay, 'Men, it has been well said, think in herds; it will be seen that they go mad in herds, while they only recover their senses slowly, one by one.' Only herds of men can allow such insanity to exist. Like water buffaloes following each other over a cliff." Nick took a deep breath, wanting another drink but knowing he needed to eat first. "Junichi, can I ask you something?"

"Of course."

"The kamikaze. Did those men really want to die?" Nick's mouth pinched, and he shook his head, showing his confusion. "I mean, it was a voluntary service, wasn't it?"

"In truth, some did. Those were the ones who were fanatical about what was drilled into them. However, many did not. In reality, nothing was voluntary. Many of those men were selected and asked to volunteer. They were given the choice to strongly volunteer, willing to volunteer, or choose not to. You have to remember, our entire culture was one of conformity, saving face. I believe most realized that if they were not enthusiastic, they would bring dishonor on themselves and their families. This was as bad, and worse, than dying. I think most accepted their fate and did the job. I have heard of many, however, that were chained to their aircraft. At this point, they knew they were going to die, anyway. Several kamikazes, for various reasons, usually mechanical failures that would not let them fly, survived the war and came home. It was sad that for many years, they were treated very badly, as failures."

Nick got up and offered Junichi more sake. Junichi raised his glass to be refilled. Nick then added a little more scotch to his own, but didn't drink. "Junichi, why did you come to Truk?"

Junichi rubbed his forehead. "I came because my father asked me to. However, this journey was really for me, for probably similar reasons as you have. To make sense of the past."

"Have you? Can you let this go?"

"Our world has changed so much. I hope we are smarter now, though I wonder. Will we have another war like that one again? Will we label it differently, such as conflict, police action or any other name, to give the impression that it is not a war? Do we still have countries trying to conquer other countries or instead will wars be waged by corporations trying to conquer the masses? Is land even the measure of power anymore? Is it only money? Or is controlling information the real power? Will we allow someone new in power that rounds people up because they believe something different?

"My thoughts go in all directions. I could never blame or hate you. You were one of the fortunate ones. You were meant to live. Instead, I blame the people from all sides who call themselves leaders, but have no vision for good for their people, rather they want only dominance as a pathway to their rule." His shoulders dropped as he let out a sigh. "Nick, why did you come back?"

Nick took a moment, tilting the glass, watching the liquid coat the sides, slide down, then stopped. "Because I lost a part of me here," he said.

"Did you find it?" Junichi asked gently.

Nick studied the younger man. The anger in his dark eyes was now replaced with an almost boyish, pleading curiosity. "No," Nick said, shaking his head, "some things aren't recoverable. But I can say goodbye to it."

"In a way," Junichi said, "you remind me of my father. You both share a quiet strength. You are a good man."

Nick's eyebrows shot up. "On what do you base that judgment? This is the only time we've been civil to each other."

"You came back here," Junichi said. "Long ago, you could have dropped your bombs and walked away. But you did not. This stayed with you so much that you came back to face the full reality of it. You feel the burden. Is that not the most basic definition of good versus bad, our ability to feel? You did nothing wrong, Nick. Neither did my father. History cannot be changed."

Relief swept over Nick at those simple words, needing to hear someone verbalize the words he couldn't say to himself. He smiled, then realized something was missing. "Junichi, you didn't actually answer my question. Have you let go of the past? Have you found peace here?"

"Yes. My father left me a letter that I read this morning. That helped. In an odd way, seeing Eonin's derangement also made me see myself more clearly. I was holding on to the past at the expense of my future. Which is dangerous. Helping you today has released me. Fate is interesting. Coming from opposite sides, we meet and then help each other to find peace. I want to see beauty in my life. Life is for moving forward. Life is for the living." Junichi closed his eyes for a moment, then took a drink.

"I'm glad," said Nick. "How about we finish our dinners?"

With that, the two men finished their now cold dinners of shrimp fettuccine Alfredo. To Nick, it was one of the most wonderful meals he had ever eaten.

Junichi raised his glass. "Nick, let us toast to the hope that people in the future will not allow insanity to reign. Instead, they will choose beauty and peace."

Nick touched his glass to Junichi's. "To smarter days." They both tipped their glasses up and finished their drinks.

Junichi got up. "I'll take the tray back to Mary and tell her you ate well. She was worried. Good night, Nick."

Nick stood up and offered his hand. As the men shook hands. "Good night, Junichi," he said as they shook hands. "I appreciate you coming." Junichi nodded.

After Junichi left, Nick took a hot shower, crawled into bed, and fell into a deep and peaceful sleep.

Forty-Nine

It was still dark outside when Nick woke up. His headache was gone, and so was the ache in the pit of his stomach. It had been a very long time since he felt this calm, this content. He checked his watch: 4:00 am. He had been in his cabin long enough, so he dressed and went into the salon. Unfortunately, there was no hot water for tea yet, but a bottle of water would do. He took the water and headed to the top deck, where his lounge chair was waiting. What little moonlight remained cast a soft glow behind the dark islands and shimmering seas.

So much was going through his mind as he replayed the events of the last few days. He thought through the conversations he had with Junichi, who had been right, that war should never have been started and it had to end for the benefit of all sides. Nick had played a role in that ending. In a strange way, hearing Junichi characterize his descriptions as history helped Nick shift his thinking. Nick had to admit to himself that he had been the one to keep JC current throughout his life. He couldn't, or in reality wouldn't, let go. He never let himself really think about what happened to him and because of him. He distanced himself from the reality during the war in self-preservation. In reflection, now he understood that the distancing that helped keep him alive during the war was the very thing that kept him from fully living now. Reliving memories on the flights here, facing the wreckage from the battle, diving in the wreck, had forced him to see it all. Then, verbalizing the whole story to Thomas had provided a release of the emotions kept in check for so long. Liberated from the pent-up emotions, he could rationally put Tony, James, his other friends, JC, and the countless, faceless others who died from his own bombs in their proper place in the puzzle of his own life.

This effort also enabled Nick to see himself differently. He realized the most important thing of all; he wanted to live. He'd had a choice in that wreck. He could have given up, he could have stayed there. He would never know if he really saw the ghost of JC or whether it was his own subconscious that brought him back to reality, but Nick knew it was his own will to live that got him out of that wreck. He also acknowledged and thanked God for Junichi and Thomas' parts in saving his life. He was meant to live for a while longer.

Nick smiled to himself. He got up from his chair and went to the side of the boat, looking down into the water. The final puzzle piece fell into place. The picture was complete. He was free. *Goodbye, JC, I hope you are at peace.*

Sitting back down, he stared out at the sea, reveling in his feeling of peace. He heard a noise behind him and turned to find Natalie standing there with two cups of hot tea.

"I thought I might find you here. Guess what I have?" She was smiling and held out one of the cups.

"You are an angel. I got up too early." Nick took a sip of the tea. A comforting warmth followed from the hot liquid as it flowed down his throat. "Oh, this is nice, and you got it right, too. Thank you."

"Well, even in the dark, you look good this morning. I gather you are doing alright?"

Nick smiled at her. "Yes, I am doing very well this morning, thank you." He was glad it was dark, which hid his embarrassment. "If you don't mind me asking, what was everyone told?"

"Don't worry, Thomas said that you got a little lost inside the wreck and it took longer to get out. He said you were a little low on air and appreciated the emergency bottle to have for your safety stops. Nothing else. Also, Sarah agreed not to tell the others about you being in the war. It isn't anyone's business. She was very worried about you, as was I."

"I heard you wanted to kill me yourself," he said, smiling.

"Not kill, simply maim. Regardless, Junichi wouldn't let me."

"Thank you, Nat." And thank you, Thomas, he thought to himself. "You know I've been sitting here for a couple of hours thinking. Do you mind if I share my thoughts with you?"

Natalie laughed at him. "It's about time, don't you think?"

He smiled. "Yes." Since it was so dark still, it made it easier to talk without being watched. "Yesterday morning, Sarah asked a couple of questions. At that time, I had no answers to give. Those questions have stayed with me since, as I have struggled to make sense of all that has happened. But I think I finally figured it all out.

"As Sarah was trying to reconcile the incongruousness of this vacation, I was really trying to reconcile the dichotomy of my life. Part of me naively thought I could come on this trip and say goodbye to someone. Another part of me that I kept buried deep inside knew it was much more complicated than a simple goodbye.

"Through the years, I have fixated on the memory of a single individual who died in the war." He turned to Nat. "Not James. It was a man who I looked in the eyes, moments before he died from my bomb. However, I have come to understand that this individual was a single person that represented everyone I knew, and didn't know, who died in that awful war.

"Millions of us pitted against each other because a few sociopaths, safely far away from any battle, were greedy for more power and were willing to sacrifice countless lives for their gain. But that seems to be how human history goes. The overwhelming majority of people are content to live their lives as best they can and put faith in their leaders. But periodically there seems to be some small group of insane people who, in their insanity, are resolute in the notion that their view of the world, controlled by them, is the best view. They then use their power and resources to lie, manipulate, and divide the world to a point of battle. Until somehow the insane are finally identified and defeated.

"It's hard for normal sane people to truly believe this level of evil until it becomes so inexcusably obvious that we are forced to deal with it. I often wonder how long it took the German population to realize the extent of Hitler's insanity, and even worse was the level of evil by his followers, or handlers. We humans have made incredible technological advancements, but human nature doesn't seem to have progressed at all.

"Sarah pondered two questions. The first was: does life always find a way? This world and this universe have been around an amazingly long time and possess such power, well beyond the ability of the human mind to understand, regardless of our research and arrogance. Thus, we humans are a relatively insignificant species, even though as a whole humans like to think otherwise. So yes, I think life will always find a way. It has been for billions of years. These wrecks give ample evidence to this. The death and destruction are slowly, but inevitably, being taken over by such beauty and life. Additionally, citizens of countries who, a few decades ago, were in a death grip against each other now come together at this spot for a wonderful and happy vacation.

"For her other question, as we get older, other experiences help to give a depth of understanding. It's easy to see that life comes in waves with good and bad. Surviving the bad makes us stronger and hopefully wiser. The good makes life worth living and makes the bad worth surviving. So for the question of whether time heals all wounds, that is not as easy to answer. I know of other veterans who spent years in counseling and physical therapy, but still have not 'healed.' The answer depends on both the wound and the person.

"For me, the experiences I had during the war left me with more than memories. They left scars on my soul. Scars don't heal. In coming here, I didn't merely remember. I was forced to relive those experiences, in my mind and in my heart. But this time, I had the advantage of age and," he laughed, "at least a little more wisdom. I've also had some kind and understanding people, like you, helping me. I was one of the pawns in this struggle and, for some reason, was saved to live beyond it. Why, I don't know. But that isn't the question.

"So, does time heal all wounds? I think I would change a word and say that time resolves all wounds, but only if we have the strength and courage to choose life instead of existence. Not always an easy choice."

They sat for some time as Natalie processed all that Nick shared.

"Thank you, Nick, that helps. I'm also happy you found what you needed." She smiled at him and looked over the water.

"How about you? Did you get what you needed from this trip?"

She nodded. "Yes, Mary helped me and I laid flowers on the water for James. I could finally say goodbye." A hint of sunlight was beginning to shine in the distance. Nat turned back to Nick. "What are you going to do when you get home?"

Nick looked at her with happiness radiating from his eyes. "I'm going to visit my granddaughter, Jani, give her a great big bear hug and hear her giggle. Then, I'm going to enjoy living."

With that, the two watched the sunrise, the dawn of a new beginning.

Historical Notes

This book came about because of a scuba diving trip to Truk lagoon in 1996. The live aboard ship hosted four Americans, four Germans, three Japanese, a couple from England and a woman from Scotland. The entire experience there was surreal. One evening on board, the captain of the ship put in a video of the newsreel footage of the bombing. Though the war had been over for decades, watching the action that caused the very wrecks that we were diving on, reminded everyone of the realities of the human cost that was exacted to cause that which we were now enjoying. That video can be found on YouTube: YANKS SMASH TRUK

This book is historical fiction. The historical aspects are true, at least as true as my sources could provide. The characters are fiction or have been fictionalized. The characters of Nick Mitchel and Junichi Takahashi are complete fiction, composites of several men that I have known. Any similarities between any of the characters here to any other person are coincidence only.

While researching information for this book, I discovered many historical events, big and small, that I never knew, but felt showed the many perspectives of that war and that time. All were woven together to form this fictional account. One aspect that I took literary license with was the burial of the kamikaze pilot. The captain of the USS *Bunker Hill* did not grant military honors to the two Japanese kamikaze pilots that attacked that ship. However, the captain of the battleship USS *Missouri* did grant the honors to the pilot that attacked the *Missouri*.

Additionally, as the events of the books are historically correct, there exists the real and brave men who actually had these experiences. Most could not be specifically identified. However, the book Helldiver Squadron (published in 1944) followed the dive bombers of Air Group 17 and lists the names of the two Avenger pilots who are most likely responsible for the sinking of the *Shinkoku Maru,* as well as the name of the Avenger pilot who crashed and went missing during the battle.

For those who wish to read more about the historical events in this book, the following is a listing of those sources that I found:

Bibliography

- Lindemann, Klaus. *Hailstorm Over Truk Lagoon*. Belleville, MI: Pacific Press Publication, Assoc., 1982

- Bailey, Dan E. *World War II Wrecks of the Truk Lagoon*. Redding, CA: North Valley Diver Publication, 2000

- Stewart, William H. *Ghost Fleet of the Truk Lagoon*. Missoula, MT: Pictorial Histories Publishing Co., Inc, 1985

- Olds, Robert. *Helldiver Squadron*. New York: Dodd, Mead & Company, 1944

- Robinson, Willard F. *Navy Wings of Gold*. Victoria, BC, Canada: Trafford Publishing, 2009

- Gillian, Robert. *I Saw Tokyo Burning*. Translated by William Byron. Garden City, N.Y.: Doubleday &

Company, Inc, 1981

- Hoity, Deion. *The night Tokyo burned*. New York: St. Martin's Press, 1987

- Chatham, William (Lt. CMDR,USNR, RET). *"Night Aboard The Carrier." Air Classics* Volume 38 Number 11 November 2002: pages 45-51

- Rendell, Lou. *Walk Around: TBF/TBM Avenger*. Carrollton, TX.: Squadron/Signal Publications, Inc., 2001

- Dower, John W. *"EMBRACING DEFEAT: Japan in the Wake of World War II."* puff. 1999, April 28, 2022 <https://ebookscart.com/embracing-defeat-by-john-w-dower-pdf-download/>

- *Naval History and Heritage Command, H-048-1: Kamikaze Attacks on U.S. Flagships off Okinawa.* Thu May 28, 2020, September 1, 2022 https://www.history.navy.mil/about-us/leadership/director/directors-corner/h-grams/h-gram-048/h-048-1.html

- Kirkpatrick, Tim. *That time when the USS Missouri gave full honors to a kamikaze pilot*. We are the Mighty. January 28, 2019. September 1, 2022 https://www.wearethemighty.com/mighty-history/that-time-when-the-missouri-gave-full-honors-to-a-kamikaze-pilot/

- *2022 Fist of the Fleet History*, July 17, 2022 https://fisthistory.org/

- Schubert, David. *CAG-17 VT-17 Torpedo Squadron*

Seventeen. July 17, 2022 https://vt17.com/blog/

- Davis, John, Mossman, Harvey, Kellies, Brian. *Heroes on Deck* Documentary. January 2, 2022 https://www.heroesondeck.com/

A Request

You can make a big difference!

If there is something, even if small, that stood out to you about this story, it would be very helpful if you would leave a review with the vendor where you purchased the book, Goodreads, Reedsy Discovery, and/or Bookbub. Additionally, if you are an Amazon customer, following me is very helpful.

Reviews give credibility. As a new author, it's very challenging to gain the attention of other readers. That is where you can help. In our electronic world, honest reviews, of any sort, are the most powerful tools in my arsenal to spread the word about this book. Do you read reviews before you purchase? I know I do.

I appreciate any help you could give.
Best Wishes,

Stephanie Woodman

Acknowledgements

I am indebted to the following people for their time and willingness to help bring this story about. William H Chatham (Lt. Cmdr. USNR. Dec.) for sharing his experiences from WWII. Commander M.W. Nickodem, USN (Retired) for his clarification of military aspects. If any errors remain, they are solely my fault. Nami Sanders for sharing her first date with her beloved Mike. Chris Evans for his initial editing and time discussing the story with me. Kay Springsteen for help with the final editing. And to a representative from the local Japanese association for her help in cultural representations.

I would also like to thank my friends and family for their time and constructive feedback: Tracy Gatesh, Terry Wibbels, Nick Woodman, Ron Kelly, Sue Peters, Kevin O'Keefe, Mary McKnight, Dan Greitzer (also for initial cover ideas), Scott Woodman, Cassie Bass, and Dave Rowton. And to Jack Grapes and Lisa Segal for helping an engineer transform.

About the Author

Stephanie Woodman is an avid collector of experiences and a perpetual student of life. Despite her analytical background with a long engineering career and a short tenure as a high school math teacher, Stephanie has a powerful creative side which has manifested itself in her debut novel, *Eye Contact Over Truk*, a decades-long endeavor which was started in 1996 and finished after her retirement in 2021. With the additional life experience, her writing transformed to explore themes of perseverance, forgiveness, grief, loss, life, love, and adventure. This evolution of her story is captured best by Helen Keller's quote: *"Although the world is full of suffering, it is also full of the overcoming of it."*

Outside the realm of literature, Stephanie loves playing pickleball and golf, scuba diving, sailing, traveling the world, and spending time with her son, who is on his own adventure in college.

If you would like more information about Stephanie's work, please visit her online homes and drop her a note at: **woodm anbooks.com**

Book Clubs

Dear Readers,

I've had such fun sharing the backstory of this book with Book Clubs. Discussing ideas, questions, epilogue speculation, and whatever else comes up is a wonderful way to have a party with friends.

If you've chosen *Eye Contact Over Truk* and would like to include me in your meeting, via phone or online, please contact me on my website to schedule the event.

Thank you.

Stephanie Woodman

Discussion Questions

1. Nick tried to bury the past and fought the idea of facing it. If you had been in Nick's position, would you have gone back?

2. Do you think the way Natalie handled Nick's depression was the right way? Have you had a situation with a depressed friend or love one, and if so, how did you help motivate them?

3. Junichi reflected that he and his father spoke of tasks, not nightmares or dreams. When do we really find out about our parents as people with lives full of struggles and successes? When do we let our own children see our full selves?

4. A very specific odor triggered Junichi's memory. This idea came about because smell is the strongest of the five senses to trigger memories. Have you had a case where some smell brought back a memory?

5. Junichi's mother told him that: "you want to be free, though you are not yet clear on what you want freedom from." Have you experienced a time in life when your energy wanted something, but your mind and heart couldn't provide the clarity?

6. Had you heard about the shipwrecks in Truk Lagoon (now known as Chuuk)? How do you feel knowing that these wrecks are now a popular diving site, even though the families of those who died still place wreaths on the water?

7. Was Junichi's anger toward Nick justified? How often do we focus our anger on one person when we can't hold the actual cause responsible?

8. If you were in Nick's position, how would you have responded to Junichi's anger

9. Were you aware of the firebombings in Japan and the extent of the death toll? Planners knew about the high wind forecast when they planned these attacks. Were these justified?

10. On the path to the cave, Nekiniuo said: "...the path ends, but the trail goes on. From here, the hike is much harder." What are the metaphorical implications of these words?

11. Nekiniuo also shared his perspective that many of the intelligent people look at so much, yet see so little. Why do you think he felt that way?

12. In a scene where Nick was alone on deck for a sunrise, he describes his life as a leaf blowing in the wind with no control and no idea of where he would land. Did you ever experience a time when your normal day-to-day life ended, leaving you with an unknown future? How did you react?

13. Part IV starts with the line: "When we face our greatest fear, we find our greatest strength." Do you agree?

14. There are many themes in the book: grief, fear, for-giveness? Which one resonated with you the most and how did it impact you? How do each of these interplay with the others?

15. C.S. Lewis wrote: "I sat with my anger long enough until she told me her real name was grief." Nick, Ju-nichi, Natalie, Shoko, and Eonin suffered grief from their respective experience from that war. What were the similarities and differences of each of their per-spectives?

16. This battle also touched Nekiniuo, but he found clo-sure many years earlier. How did he do this?

17. Who did you think J.C. was and were you surprised?

18. This story wove many historical events: The Corn Belt fleet, Truk, the firebombings, attack on USS *BunkerHill*, Japanese civilians leaping to their deaths, shipwrecks, and life in Japanpost WW2. Which of these did you know about and which were new?

19. Who should play each lead character if this story is made into a movie?

**Turn the page to read Jeannette Crawford's
(Nick's Wife) story in an excerpt from:**

The Choice Within

(Nick makes a few appearances as well)

Available wherever books are sold

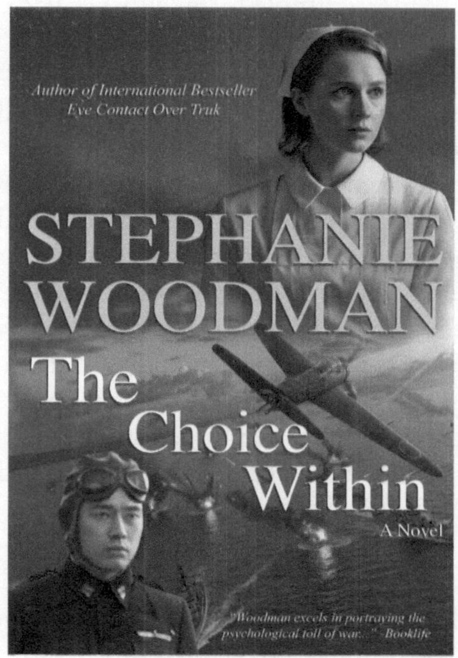

Time

February 9, 1944; Honolulu, Hawaii, USA.

"**W**ill you marry me?"

A deep dimple formed in her left cheek as she focused on writing: *"Breath rate: 12; Temp: 98.7; Pulse: 95."* When finished, Lieutenant Jeannette Crawford glanced up into a pair of very attractive emerald eyes, twinkling like two Christmas wreaths.

Good, he's not serious, she thought, letting a breath escape. The last boy who proposed was so earnest that it almost broke her heart to turn him down. So many soldiers hadn't seen a female in a couple of years—or, at least, one that wasn't for hire—that they fell in love with the first one that was kind, which was often the nurse who took care of them.

"I'm sorry, Captain Herbert, I'm already spoken for."

Though partially true, the phrase wasn't a rejection, which allowed for an honorable retreat. Buzzing from the overhead fluorescent lights filled the empty moment.

She pulled up the blackout shade a little higher, allowing more light from the late-afternoon sun. Tripler General Hospital didn't have any view of the ocean or Diamond Head, but this side of the hospital faced north to the lush green Oahu Mountains, with their flock of White Terns, though sometimes called Fairy Terns, that seemed in perpetual motion. The boys on the other side of the aisle had this view, which broke up the white: white walls, white beds, white sheets and blankets, white pajamas, white floor... At least her wraparound nurse uniform had thin, brown stripes.

"Where is he?" Herbert's smile fell.

"Pacific."

Nick's letters didn't include any details of the battles. Which helped to minimize her imagining the worst. The injuries of the men she treated painted a gruesome picture of what he might endure.

Out of the corner of her eye, she saw Walters, one of the ward medics, wheeling a patient back in from X-ray.

"That covers a lot of water. What island?"

She shook her head. "USS *Bunker Hill*." A full grin formed as she wrapped the blood-pressure cuff around his left arm.

"A carrier? You fell for a squid?! That's treason!" His smile returned. "Please don't tell me he's a flyboy."

She cocked her eyebrow to answer. Air whooshed with each squeeze. With the stethoscope in her ears, she correlated beats to the numbers on the dial.

"Oh, now, here I was thinking you were intelligent."

"Now, now, now." She turned the valve; the air hissed its way out. "You don't want to insult a woman who gives the injections, do you?"

The captain burst out laughing. "No, I don't. I already hurt in enough places. The last thing I need is a new pain in my ass."

"Your wounds are healing well. Soon, you'll transfer to a rehab facility."

Shadows passed over his eyes. "After which I'll go back."

"If you want to talk about it, I'll listen."

"If I told you, then you would have those memories as well." His thick voice dropped an octave. "No one should have those memories."

"It's far better for you to let it out. I can take it."

All teasing disappeared as his eyes latched onto hers. For a fraction of a moment, unspoken details paled as the impact bared itself. "I hope you never have to." He closed his eyes.

She hooked the chart at the end of the bed and took her time walking back to the nurses' desk. Glancing at each patient, she checked their faces, if visible, and tried to let go of the raw pain in those green eyes. Private Sutton sat up, reading. Lieutenants Keith and Clements were talking. Sergeant O'Neill and Jenkins were sleeping, thankfully; they both needed it.

"I had the seventh proposal," she said to the nurse sitting at the desk, writing up the daily report.

"What? You broke my record," said Lieutenant Grace McClure, Jeannette's friend and roommate.

This was as much of a surprise to her. Every day, she watched heads turn to follow Grace's curvaceous body and cute, strawberry-blonde bob hairdo. She couldn't compete with her friend's beauty—not that she had any interest in doing so.

At school, Jeannette always had male admirers. Her father had said it was her intense, chocolate-brown eyes that let the boys know she saw the real person, not the macho image they tried to put out. Her mother said it was her honey-brown hair and cute button nose. To her, it didn't matter. With those boys, she methodically maneuvered them into the position of pal and onto the next girl. She was waiting for the right someone to come into her life. Then, five months ago, Nick Mitchel came.

"Who was it?" asked Grace.

"The captain at the end."

"The one with the gorgeous eyes? He should have asked me; I would have said yes."

Jeannette shook her head, grateful for Grace. She always kept a balance.

"Speaking of great eyes, any news from Mr. Wonderful yet?"

"His letter came—"

She turned her head at the retching sound. "Call a doctor!"

Jeannette ran to Sergeant Jenkins as vomit erupted. "Medic! I'll support his head if you can roll him onto his left side. Ready? Go."

The two held him in place until the purge subsided.

"Okay, bring him back down. Stay here."

Jeannette pulled up the eyelid that wasn't covered in bandages. A large black orb stared out, seeing nothing. She placed her fingers on his carotid. His pulse was increasing, as was hers.

"What have we got?" Dr. Simmons asked, rushing up to the bed.

"Pupil is heavily dilated, rapid pulse, breath rate eight, but erratic." With a clean corner of the sheet, she wiped his mouth.

"Get the resuscitator," he said to the medic as he examined the patient.

Jeannette watched as Dr. Simmons rubbed his knuckle over the patient's sternum.

"No response, dammit. Here," he handed the resuscitator to her, "give him ten to twelve breaths a minute while we wheel him to critical care."

Grace cleared the path. Jeannette held the mask in place and pulled the bellow up, then down, in as normal a rhythm as possible, while she ran along with the bed. Her own pulse raced, more from fear than exertion.

"Dr. Simmons," shouted Jeannette, as they turned into the main hallway, "I'm not getting enough air into him." Jeannette pressed his carotid. "His pulse is weak and slow."

Simmons stopped the bed. Grabbing the resuscitator, he pulled, then pushed hard. The patient's chest barely moved. He tried again. Nothing. With his stethoscope, Simmons listened to his heart. "His heartbeat is faint."

Ticking from the wall clock was all she heard for a few moments. Nothing stopped time.

"He's gone." Simmons stepped back and removed his stethoscope.

Though she had clung to hope, that simple statement wasn't a surprise. "What do you think happened?" Her voice was low and soft.

"I'm guessing an embolism or an aneurysm—either of them with no damn thing we can do." He said the last words with the same impotent frustration that she shared, hers mixed with guilt; the boy had been under her watch.

Dr. Simmons wrote some notes on the boy's chart and handed it to her. His shoulders hung a little lower as he walked away.

"I'll take care of him," Jeannette said to Walters. "Would you please clean up the area around his bed?"

He nodded.

"Walters, thank you for your help."

"I wish it had been more." He shook his head as he walked off. Jeannette watched him leave.

Now alone in the corridor, she turned to the boy lying on the gurney. Thankfully, his eye was already closed; the final stare she saw so often was maybe the hardest part. But then again, there were so many hard parts to this job. Moving his straight brown hair away from his face, she ran her fingers down his smooth cheek. No stubble at all. *So young,* she thought, as were most of them. What little color his face had drained away. His spirit was now on to Heaven.

"I'm sorry, Danny. I'm sorry. No more fighting. We'll notify your parents."

Jeannette folded the soiled portion of the sheet and drew the clean part over his head. On the clipboard, she filled in the information, not bothering to look at the dog tags. She knew his name, as she did for all of them. Sometimes it was all she could do for them. She had met Private Daniel "Danny" Jenkins two weeks ago. Though he regained consciousness a few times between the two surgeries, he just didn't have the strength to fight anymore. A medic walked up as she signed her name on the form.

"Is he ready?"

"Yes, he is." Jeannette handed over the file and watched Danny being rolled out of sight.

"Why don't you take your break now?" said Grace, when Jeannette walked back into the ward.

"It's your turn."

"I'm hoping to leave a little early today. I have a date at the O club, and I'd like a few extra minutes to clean up. Besides, you need a break now."

Jeannette nodded and walked down the hall, mentally replaying all of her actions today, trying to find the one she missed with Danny.

At the entrance to the ambulance drop-off, Dr. Cross and her friend, DeeDee, were hopping from new patient to new patient. Dr. Cross triaged and barked orders, while DeeDee wrote up tags and directed medics to deliver them to the respective wards. Patients outnumbered the staff by a large margin.

Jeannette jumped back to clear the way, watching a medic wheel away a female patient. Female casualties came in from time to time, but weren't normal.

"DeeDee, what's up with her?"

"Nurse from an aid station. They think she might have cerebral malaria. She's going into the isolation ward."

"I hope they're wrong." Of all the diseases that Jeannette treated, cerebral malaria was the scariest and took the most lives with it.

"Me, too. Since you're here, will you please escort this nice man to your ward and get him settled? Here's his chart."

"Do you need me to come back?" Jeannette caught the gentle breeze that rushed in with the next round of patients. Though mixed with exhaust fumes, the sweet smell of flowers was a welcome addition to a room filled with blood and infections.

"No. I'll be sending more your way." DeeDee moved to another incoming litter.

Jeannette pulled over a wheelchair. It was nice to see an ambulatory patient for a change. However, no patient was allowed to walk inside the hospital unless a doctor ordered it.

"I can walk," the lieutenant said, his tired eyes defiant, but the amount he swayed on his feet told a different story.

"Well, of course you can, but are you going to deprive me of the opportunity to drive you in comfort? I promise, no wheelies."

One side of his mouth tilted up. "I can't turn down a pretty girl. And I wouldn't mind the wheelies, but the other patients might get jealous."

"You're right; they would." She placed her hands under his elbows to guide him down and helped get his feet up onto the foot pedals. "So, what's your name, Lieutenant?" Practice had taught her that friendly questions drew out more information about what happened.

"Morris Stout."

"Welcome to Hawaii. What brings you here?" She kept her voice light and upbeat as they maneuvered through the new wounded, trying to ignore the moans and focus on her new patient. His body didn't show any outward injuries, but his skin hung down his face and around his arm bones.

"One of those bastard Zeros shot us down. My co-pilot and I had to take turns in the raft for a while. Not sure how long. It took a while, but they found us."

Jeannette followed his words, piecing together a preliminary list of what he endured: exposure, malnutrition, exhaustion, trauma, and depression.

"Your co-pilot?" she asked softly.

"Didn't make it."

The universal phrase that carried so much meaning. She added guilt to her picture.

"Well, Lieutenant Stout, we have a dry, warm bed that will stay in one place, plenty of good food and water, and a lot of time to sleep. How does that sound?"

"Great. Thank you."

Grace looked up as Jeannette rolled in. "Lieutenant Stout, may I introduce you to Lieutenant McClure? She and I are your day nurses."

"Bed four is ready for you," Grace said, smiling.

Jenkins's bed.

Jeannette caught her breath. *Stop it. It happens in hospitals. Guys come in; guys go out. Focus on the new patient.*

"Sounds like a table at a restaurant," Stout said with a weak smile, as Jeannette pushed him on. "Any chance at a table for two?"

"No chance at all. But we have ice cream." The jokes and innuendos no longer phased her. If a guy didn't joke around, she worried about his mental health. In the end, they all took the gentle rejection in stride.

"Not as good, but I'll take it."

"Here you go. You have a lovely view of the mountains." Jeannette got him settled and started a fresh saline IV, per the instructions on his chart, which also gave a summary that the men had floated for almost two weeks. *They must have had rain for water, or they would have been dead. With rain, they probably also experienced storms and rough seas. I wonder when his friend died.*

She left him asleep to help with the new patients coming through the door. *It seems all forty beds will be full tonight.*

"Now you can take your break," said Grace. "The medics and I can handle this for a while. I suggest going out a different way."

The Sōkeisen

Hirohito 19, February 9; Tokyo, Japan

Why is he here?

"Akira!" shouted Uehara Tetsuo. "Look—"

The ball slammed into his right shoulder the moment he turned.

"—out!"

Akira Tanaka grimaced, rubbing his shoulder, before he picked up the ball and threw it back to his friend. All over the field, young men threw balls to warm up. A sort of symphony played: gentle and hard thumps as the balls hit the various gloves, mixed with the metal-on-metal, ringing sound made by the hammers pounding in stakes to hold down the sandbags, while birds sang along in the background. He wanted very much to go back and join the fun. Instead, he straightened his back and walked toward the short fence that surrounded the field.

Maybe he isn't here to take me home. Far worse possibilities entered his mind. Could something be wrong with his mother? He ran.

"Father, is everyone well?" he asked when he was close enough to be heard.

"Yes," said Takeshita Tanaka, "the family are all well." There was a brief softening around his mouth. Though not so much in his honey-brown eyes—or, at least, what Akira could see of them under the brim of his dark-brown hat, pulled down low.

"So," he asked, looking around the field, "is this how my son spends his Saturday mornings?"

When I should be home working the fields with you? Words his father had made clear before Akira left home at break. As always, he kept his thoughts and desires to himself.

"I thought you said they canceled the season?" His father's eyes followed a ball as it floated from one player to another.

Akira understood the irritation in his father's words, yet surprised to see the older man's eyes droop. To be here this early, his father would have had to get up two hours earlier than normal. His dark herringbone suit, out of place at a dirty baseball field, would soon be hot if those clouds stayed away. He gave his father some credit for his effort.

They had shared the same height for the last two years, yet Akira still lacked the muscular shoulders his father had from years of working the farm. Students don't exert themselves that hard.

"They canceled this season and next year's season. Two of the seniors organized this. They wanted an informal game before the school year ended."

Takeshita's left eyebrow shot up. "An informal game with Keio University?" His voice was full of sarcasm.

How does he know? There were no uniforms; all the players wore old clothes, beaten and torn through the years of work or sliding in the dirt. Ball caps, also old, bore no school emblem. Akira's faded blue pants had rips in both knees, and stains of green and brown marred his dingy white button shirt.

"Did the school administrators approve of this event?" The words came out as a question, but the meaning was an accusation. This event could cause definite trouble if discovered.

"I do not believe so. They asked us to keep this event quiet."

War was now the reason behind the clandestine activities. The military drafted many players and adamantly insisted that baseball was an American pastime, which distracted from the war's seriousness.

Takeshita glanced around at the growing number of spectators. "I believe that part failed. Well, inviting your uncle to umpire should help if they find out."

They both turned to look at Sugihara Tanaka, surrounded by players from both teams, laughing and signing baseballs. A former star shortstop for Waseda University back in the late 1920s, who went on to play for the Tokyo Kyojin until he retired two years ago. He was now Kyojin's infielder coach.

Oh, that is how he found out.

"I hope, for all of your sakes, that the students behave themselves this year. Good luck," he said, then turned away to take a seat on the wooden bleachers.

Did he mean good luck with the game or good luck keeping the students under control? But he refused to ask that question. His jaw clenched all the way to the dugout.

Although Akira would not say so, he also hoped everyone would contain their spirits. Because of inappropriate behavior from student spectators during and after the game, the schools canceled the annual game for several years. Today, such spirit could be disastrous.

"Are you alright, Akira?" asked his uncle. Sugihara wore black pants and a white Kyojin shirt, displaying the shield with an orange outline of the name *"Tokyo"* and the red sun. He also had his black Kyojin cap. Together, he looked like a baseball professional suitable for the umpire position.

"Yes. Did you tell him about the game?"

His uncle nodded. "Underneath my brother's hard exterior, he would want to come to watch you play in the Sōkeisen. Now, go join your team."

Once inside, Akira looked around to count heads. "Where is Hatanaka?" he asked the group.

"He has left the school," said Uehara Tetsuo, in a low voice.

All heads turned to him.

"Did he receive...?" asked Akira.

Uehara nodded.

"But there are only three weeks until graduation," said Akira, his eyebrows drawn down. "Was he not allowed to finish?"

Again, his friend just shook his head.

Reality was a harsh intruder on the day. Another friend gone.

"Teams, please assemble so that we may begin the game," called Sugihara.

Uehara, acting as captain, gave out the assignments, and the group formed a line parallel to the Keio players shooting out from the batter's box toward the pitcher's mound, with Sugihara standing in between.

"First, as I am the umpire, all of my calls are final. I will not accept contradictions.

"Now," he said, speaking in a loud, commanding voice that reached beyond the teams, to the spectators on both sides, "Keio University established baseball fifty-six years ago. Together with Waseda, your programs became the model and foundation of Tokyo's Big Six League. Every year, thousands of people follow your annual rivalry..." he paused, glancing around to both sides, "...until last year.

"While we are not in the traditional, majestic venue of the Meiji Jingu Stadium, today we play on this simple ball field, enjoying these rare warm hours that the natural world has given us. A gift to treasure. A moment in time to keep traditions alive.

"However, today the rivalry is not a contest between long-time opponents. It is a celebration of your schools' history. An opportunity to honor the game that we love. To honor those who cannot be here to play with us. To honor each other. Today, we play with one heart, that which we share with our ancestors through the millennia. Today, we are the heart, the love, the joy of Japan. At the end of this day, the score will be irrelevant; all that matters is that we play with honor."

Akira stood watching his uncle walk off, unconcerned with so many eyes following his steps. His words had elevated this game to a higher level, bringing security and a calm relaxation to his muscles. A warmth spread through him, yet bumps formed on his arms. His eyes scanned the other players, and their facial expressions reflected the wonder of his own feelings. The players all came out of their reverie and smiled at each other.

Excitement surged around the field as Waseda, the home team, took the field.

Akira played right field. He was a good fielder, but not a strong batter. During the 1942 season, though thrilled to make the team, he sat on the bench most of the year. *If Hatanaka had been here today, I would be on the bench.*

With the cancellation of the seasons, the school had not maintained the field. However, in mid-winter, the light-brown grass showed signs of light green. A small gray feather lodged itself between some blades. Patches of weeds grew in the baselines, but not so large as to cause any problems.

Keio's first batter surprised Akira. *If Ozaki is batting first, who is their cleanup hitter?* He ran backwards to be ready. The batter stepped up to the plate.

Horiuchi, a very experienced pitcher, threw the first pitch wide, to the left.

"Outside," yelled Sugihara.

The pitcher dug his shoe into the mound to create a deeper divot before the board. He wound up, kicked his leg out and, as his body fell forward, released the ball. Ozaki swung and hit a hard grounder to the third baseman, who picked it up and threw it to first.

Sugihara ran partway to first and threw both arms out. "Safe!" he yelled after the batter touched the bag. It was such a close call that, under normal circumstances, the coach would have raised a question.

As everyone was resetting their positions, Ozaki walked back toward home plate. "Honorable Umpire, I understand you called me safe. However, the baseman caught the ball before my foot touched the bag. Please accept this one contradiction," he said, with a bow.

Sugihara gave a low bow and held it for a few seconds longer. Then he stood back up and smiled. "Runner, you are out."

Ozaki smiled and walked back to his dugout. A couple of his unhappy team members questioned his action, but the rest nodded.

That simple act of honor set the stage for the rest of the game. Players helped to make close calls. Both sides cheered good plays.

Evidence of the year-long absence from competition was clear on both teams: pitchers threw far more outside balls than center balls, bouncing ground balls missed, and throws to bases went wild. But both teams accepted these mistakes without reprimand. The teams played with joy and freedom, rotating through the full rosters so that everyone played. Gone were the tense moments, the fear of failure. Spectators smiled and laughed.

Inning after inning, Akira watched this continual display of joy, not caring if a ball came his way. He enjoyed watching the plays, the pitches, the secondary game of daring between pitchers and runners trying to steal a base. It was a soft day, suited to a casual game. It all reminded him of when he had been a boy, just learning the game, playing with his friends in a field: no backstops; broken pieces of boards put down as bases, which never stayed in place; ants crawling in and out of their hills, in the line to third base; finding reasons to slide; and the days ending with good-natured arguments on close—and not-so-close—calls.

Late in the eighth inning, a loud crack of the bat and the crowd yelling signaled Akira. His eyes found the moving white speck soaring his way against the blue-and-dark-gray background. Gauging by its speed, it would fly behind him on the left. His eyes glued to the growing speck, he ran both backwards and sideways. With his shorter height, his only chance was to jump for it. Throwing himself forward, extending his left arm, he closed his glove around the ball. After the entire length of his body hit the ground and bounced, he rolled over, holding his glove in the air, then scrambled to his feet to throw the ball to the second baseman, who had come out as the cutoff man. The batter was out, but the runner on first made it to third, then held up. The last out came as the next batter popped up a fly-ball to the shortstop.

Clouds that had built now blew in faster, blocking the sun. As the ninth inning started, the score was four to three in favor of Waseda. With the first batter came fat raindrops, but no one wanted to quit, so the game played on; Sugihara took a break to get a waterproof cover from his bag, then called for the game to resume. Dirt turned to mud, wind blew off hats, runners slipped and fell, and fly-balls mixed in with the downpour were hard to see.

Keio's second batter hit a single and made it to second base because of a wild throw to first. The catcher missed the next pitch, allowing the runner on second to steal third, spraying the baseman with mud as he slid. Then the batter bunted down the third-base line. The baseman looked the runner back, then threw to first, but the throw was late; the man on third scored.

Lightning flashed close by, sending everyone for shelter. Sugihara called the game off, leaving it to endless future arguments about what the outcome might have been if Waseda had had their last bat.

Akira and his father sat in the closest dugout. Sugihara took shelter in the other one, appearing to sign baseballs again. Tension between the two men smothered the fun of the day. How Akira wished he had the freedom to share his heart with his father. To reminisce about the minute details of the game, extending the fun for the rest of the rainy afternoon. But all he could think of was repeating an earlier question.

"How are Mama and Suni?" he asked, glancing into his father's brown eyes before looking out into the rain.

"They are both well. Your grandmother is unwell; it is nothing serious," he added, at Akira's frown. "Your mother is looking after her. Suni is working today."

At the mention of his younger sister working, Akira's stomach contracted. Because of his uncle's financial help and his own good grades, he could go to university. However, the family farm did not earn the money for his sister to continue her education. Once Akira graduated and obtained a position, he hoped he could contribute funds to his family, and also be able to afford to pay Suni's school tuition, if she wished to go—if her father approved.

"Are you corresponding with Miki?"

Akira nodded. "I sent her a letter two weeks ago. She has yet to reply." He turned his head to look back out at the clouds. Miki was another issue between them. His parents had arranged their marriage many years ago. Akira was torn because, in truth, Miki was beautiful and he enjoyed her company; the contention that he was not allowed to find his own bride, to marry for love, ate at him. Breaking the agreement would bring more dishonor to the family. It seemed that everything Akira wanted and dreamed of would bring dishonor to his family.

"The mail is slower these days. I am sure you will get a letter from her soon."

Intent on changing the subject, Akira looked at his father. "You look nice in your brown suit. I appreciate that you came. Can you stay long?"

Takeshita checked his watch. "No. I will need to leave in less than an hour. I obtained a ride in a delivery truck this morning, and the driver will pick me up in front of the school on his way home."

Sugihara came into the dugout at the right time. It amazed Akira how exhausting it was to make small talk with his own father.

"Is there any ink remaining in your fountain pen?" asked Takeshita. For the first time, the older man's face showed some true amusement.

"Yes. Would you like me to sign a ball for you?"

Takeshita shook his head but kept his smile.

"The rain is easing. I believe we should go back to school so that Akira may change into clean, dry clothes."

Akira led them out, forcing himself not to run away from them as fast as he could. He wondered if his father had any idea how much it hurt to watch the casual camaraderie between the brothers, and none existing between the two of them. Why was it so easy to accept his younger brother's choice in careers, but not his own son's choice?

Once they made it to the school, Takeshita looked at them both. "I will remain here in the event that the delivery man comes early."

"Will you wait until I come back to say goodbye?"

"If you hurry."

Akira ran up the stairs, unbuttoning his shirt on the way. Once inside his room, he yanked off clothes, dropping the wet ones wherever they landed. Never had he changed so fast, finishing the buttoning on the way down the stairs.

His uncle laughed when he saw Akira. Even his father had to smile.

"Akira," asked his uncle, "was that a record?"

"I think—"

A honk of a horn interrupted. Akira's heart contracted at the sound. Out of time. Words left unsaid. Emotions unhealed. The space between them grew.

Father and son stood looking at each other, neither knowing what to do. Takeshita broke the tension and took a step forward, putting his arms around his son. Akira reciprocated, but the mechanical embrace allowed only the briefest of touch.

Takeshita turned and opened the exterior door. Looking over his shoulder, he gazed briefly at Akira. "That was a good catch today."

An Opportunity

Three steps out the front door, Jeannette stopped and inhaled the zesty, slight peachy scent of the gardenia trees that scattered around the grounds. Though Grace argued with her, she also noted a hint of coconut from the flower. The calming aroma almost replaced the antiseptic odors embedded in every fiber of her not-so-clean uniform.

A path led a short walk to her bench. At least, it was her spot for every break that Mother Nature allowed—and, in Honolulu, the grand lady was very generous. The bench sat in a dense grassy area under a large monkeypod tree. Last summer, its pink blossoms had formed a twenty-foot-wide umbrella; tiny buds now hinted at the next bloom. Jeannette had sat under this tree at almost every hour of the day and night. On the hardest days, if she could, she arranged her schedule to come out at sunset or sunrise, to absorb its energy and share in its animation, as its leaves closed for the night and opened to the sun.

Today was another perfect day, except for the construction pounding nearby. Grace told her it began the day after Pearl Harbor and it hadn't stopped. Fort Shafter was the Pacific headquarters of the Army. They nicknamed the newest building under construction the "Pineapple Pentagon". Close to it, they filled in a large fishpond for some needed flat space, for a parade ground.

In just over two years, engineers had thrown up many identical, plain, and versatile buildings, expanding the hospital from 450 to the current 563 beds, and adding more. Last month, they had broken ground for a much larger hospital, which would sit up on the foothills, with a spectacular view of the ocean. And the rumor mill said it would be pink, like the Royal Hawaiian Hotel.

Fresh out of nursing school, the Army Nurse Corps sent her here. In her orientation, they stated that the mission of the hospital was to provide a space for solace and recuperation, and it did; her time here had been the most amazing experience she had ever imagined. For most of that time, she worked seven days a week, twelve-hour shifts, with a day off once in a while. The war provided the best medical education—at the expense of the men. She wished so much that this wasn't the case, but her own nursing school in no way prepared her for the diversity of need that she had seen here. During school, she rotated through the various wards. Here, she shifted as needed by the casualties and the staffing required to meet those needs. Beds were not the only area that needed to grow; staff was another. New personnel came in regularly, but the wounded and ill came in faster.

One of the first surprises was treating frostbite cases from the battles in the Aleutian Islands. The next day, she learned to treat jungle rot from the South Pacific; most were on the feet or legs, though she understood it could grow anywhere. Like frostbite, it is painful and can lead to amputations if not treated quickly. And few had that option.

Beyond those, battle wounds, burns, construction accidents, malnutrition, exposure, common illnesses, and diseases she had never heard of all passed through their wards.

But for her, the hardest to treat and see were the psychiatric wounds. Everyone who came into a hospital had some level of mental trauma, but war created its own category.

Mixed in with her medical education was a crash course in the Army regulation of every facet of life. Only in the last few months had she become comfortable with what she was doing, and now could help the new nurses.

She took the letter out of her pocket and ran her fingers over the words. *Please be good news...*

```
Dear Jeanne,
  I miss you so much!
  Today is New Year's Day and the first
day off from work in what seems like
an eternity. I can't explain it, but
time doesn't seem to work the same
over here. Except for New Year's Day,
I think we've worked every holiday.
Some guys have renamed our ship the
Holiday Express. We try to see the
humor, even if we have to create it.
  Hi, back again. James called me away
to come play poker. I need to stop
playing with them, as I don't seem
to be any good at the game. The
challenge is there are only so many
things to do on a ship surrounded by
the ocean. When we get to go to a
base, it's better. I've read most of
the books in the library and played a
lot of basketball in the hangar. I'm
not complaining. If I could just fly
around, that would be great. But my
job doesn't allow that.
  The most fun I have is thinking
about you and our time together. I'm
still embarrassed by my actions in
```

the car. As a pilot, I'm supposed to
be observant. My only excuse is that
I was so blinded by your beauty, I
didn't look to see that the window was
closed.

    The nights we walked along the beach
are my favorite memories to replay.
And staring at the stars at night
takes me back there.

    I'm so glad you're safe in Hawaii
and hope that I'll be back with you
soon.

    Nick

He's safe. With that, her body relaxed.

She looked up at the tree limbs swaying. Green leaves and blue sky became more vivid. Rhythmic whistles from a red cardinal softened to a melody. She reread the letter three times. Her smile grew bigger with each read.

Several jeep ambulances drove up the road, signaling that a new batch of casualties had just landed and her break was over.

Grace met her in the hall, with pinched lips and narrowed eyes; a look Jeannette had seen on her friend's face many times before.

"I came to relieve you. Why are you in the hall?"

"Major Knox asked me to stay and to find you. There is a meeting that we have to attend," she said with a huff.

"What about the ward?"

"She had the next shift come in early."

Jeannette's eyebrows shot up.

Cooler air sent chills through her as she entered the conference room and took an open seat in the back, behind several of her fellow nurses. An army doctor leaned against a table at the front of the room.

"Is this all?" he asked Major Knox.

"Yes. The others are on duty. I will transmit your information to them after their shift." As always, their head nurse was all business. Even though the doctor outranked her, he was wise enough not to question her.

He nodded and stood to address the group. "Thank you all for staying. I am Dr. Frye, and I am here to extend an invitation to an immensely valuable opportunity. We are outfitting a new hospital ship," said Dr. Frye. "The ship is almost ready. I've been involved with the design, which will include three full surgical suites, X-ray, laboratory, a dedicated dietary kitchen with a dietician, seven hundred beds, and clinics for dental, eyes, ears, nose and throat."

On a ship?! That's more beds than we have here.

"We're taking the fight to the enemy, and we need the medical support to do this." Frye shifted his eyes to span the entire group. "This ship will join our existing force, along with new medical staff, who will man station hospitals on key island locations. This is an integral component within a comprehensive plan to provide immediate advanced care to our guys."

Jeannette sat up straighter. *Advanced care at the point where they need it. That will cut out the travel time.*

"The USS *Comfort* is going to be a beautiful and, as her name suggests, very comfortable ship, not only for the patients but also for the staff and crew. It is the first ship to combine the marine expertise of the Navy with the immense medical skill of the Army."

"What does that mean?" asked DeeDee.

"The Navy will run the ship and the Army will run the hospital."

"Would we have any reporting requirements to the Navy?" asked Jeannette.

"No. All aspects of your assignment will report up to the Army Senior Medical Commander, just as you do here. Your staterooms will be comfortable, and the food will be very good—no rations; those Navy boys on the ships eat well. *Com-*

fort will have movies, a library, and a deck isolated from the enlisted men, so that you can enjoy some downtime in the sun."

"You said advanced care," Grace said, her eyes still narrowed; "how close to the battles will this ship go?"

"First, all painting, lighting, and flag designation will comply with the Geneva Convention; the entire crew will also fall under that protection. Second, we intend to keep the *Comfort* well away from the battles until the initial landing areas are secure and the fighting moves inland."

"The nurses in Bataan were supposed to be protected under the Geneva Convention, weren't they?" Grace pointed out in a steely voice.

Jeannette, like every nurse in the Army, had heard about those nurses stationed at a hospital in the Philippines before the war broke out. Though a few women escaped, the Japanese imprisoned seventy-seven of them when they overran the islands. No one knew where they were now.

Dr. Frye lost his initial exuberance. "Yes, they were," he said in a lower voice, then took a deep breath. "This is war; I can't promise you that these missions will be absolutely, without a doubt, safe. These ships are not intended to be put in harm's way, but will harm's way come on its own? It is a possibility." He paused and looked around the room, making eye contact with each woman.

"Our boys deserve the best and fastest help we can give them. This opportunity is of immense importance and comes with risk. I won't lie to you about that. It also requires the right personnel, who have the strength to handle the diversity, constant surprises, weather, fear, as well as the raw emotions of those wounded and scared. What I can promise is that your value will be immeasurable, and you will witness history firsthand."

Again, he paused. "This is a volunteer decision, and we are only looking for another couple of nurses; we have already assigned the rest. I will leave tomorrow before noon, so if you wish to join, give me your answer in the morning. Thank you for your time.”

No one spoke as they left the room.

“Finally,” said Grace. “Let’s get out of here while we can.”

Jeannette followed her, lost in her own thoughts.

Red Card

Akira followed his father out and stood watching until the truck was out of sight, glad that his father could not see the tear running down his cheek.

Sugihara put a hand on Akira's shoulder. "Come with me. You and I will go out for a late lunch."

The two walked in silence for three blocks. Streetcars rumbled alongside. Clouds still covered the sky, but the rain had stopped. Sugihara led them to The Tea House.

Only one table held customers; fewer people had the funds for the luxury of going out to eat. A young woman in a white shirt and light-blue monpe pants directed them to a table. She left and returned with a pot of hot green tea.

"Harusame soup is available today, if you would like it." She said it with her eyes down, which Akira took to mean that was all they had available.

"We would like the soup, thank you," said his uncle. "Also, would you bring us hot sake?"

The young server brightened. "Yes." She bowed as she left.

Wonderful aromas floated about the room, which triggered Akira's stomach to rumble, announcing his hunger, causing his uncle to laugh. Akira looked around. The Tea House had many windows, but with the weather, it was still dark inside. A candle surrounded by a tall, frosted-glass vase burned in the middle of the wooden table, providing extra light.

"You worked up an appetite. You played well today. That catch in the eighth inning was very impressive." He took out a baseball and handed it to Akira, along with his fountain pen.

Akira could not stop the smile that formed. Praise from his uncle was rewarding, but the request to sign a ball was funny. Going along with the joke, he signed his name. "It is hard to write on the curved surface. How do you do this so well?"

"Practice."

The soup was served, followed by the hot sake. Akira filled the sake cups, handing one to his uncle. Raising his cup, he smiled at the man who had been so important to his life. "Kanpai," he said, in toast.

"Kanpai."

Akira admired the presentation of the bowl. The cook had taken time to arrange the tofu cubes and wakame seaweed around the fluffy eggs. Portions were generous, and the vegetable broth with green onions was so flavorful. He also detected a hint of sesame and soy sauce.

"So, what happened between you and your father over your break?"

Akira took a moment to organize his thoughts. "He wants me to come home to help him. I understand; he, Mother and Suni do all the work. I help when I can during the school breaks. The problem is that I do not want to work on the farm."

"What do you wish to do?"

Someone had finally asked. An internal wall crumbled. Every dream he had came tumbling out: "I want to travel and see the world. To sail on large ships, like you did, and visit America." His hands began moving, animating his words. Arms spreading out invited the world into his life. "To visit the castles of Europe, to see their artworks, and walk on the beaches under swaying palm trees on tropical islands. I..."

The light that shone so brightly throughout his words faded as he returned to his reality. "But, as the only son, my responsibility is to take over the farm and take care of my family." His head hung with the last words.

"You say like me, but the only way I could take those trips was because the university and Kyojin paid for them; I cannot afford them on my own. Even if I could find the money for my ticket, I could not take my wife and son; traveling is very expensive, and teachers do not earn the salaries for such luxuries."

Akira looked up, his eyes burning at the betrayal. "So, I should give up my dreams? Do my duty?"

Sugihara shook his head. "No, never give up your dreams. Find another way to achieve them. Perhaps there is another path forward that will help with all of your problems."

Intrigue replaced Akira's anger. "How?"

"Now, just listen to me. Teachers do not earn enough money, but businessmen do."

"What business do you suggest?" asked Akira, turning his palms up.

"Go to your father—not as a son, but as a man with a university education. Pursue a partnership with him and grow the existing business into a large one."

Akira shook his head.

"Stop and think, Akira. Businessmen travel to find new technologies, more efficient processes, and to acquire more property. At this time, the farm does not produce all that it has potential for. However, with more help, manual and mental, it can grow."

"Father would never allow me to be a partner. And how would we pay for this expansion?"

"When someone has a good plan, there are always investors who want to share in those profits. Regarding your father, when you stop seeing yourself as a boy, you can show him the man he has raised you to be. The man Takeshita has been waiting for. The man who has a realistic plan to honor his family and make his own dreams come true."

Sugihara pushed back from the table. "I will leave you to think."

Akira watched him walk to the young server and pay her for the meal, then walk out the door.

He sat at the table for a while longer, keeping the thought that his father would never agree. But then, what other path existed? His uncle had been correct that teaching would not provide the funds for his desires. He had held onto them in a childish wish for what could not happen. With his uncle's words, a new possibility opened.

As he left the restaurant, the young woman gave him a shy smile, which he returned. His steps were lighter now, returning to school. Never had he given any real thought to being a boy, a son, or a man. True, his actions had been those of a boy. When his father had made clear his expectations a month ago, he had not responded—a quiet, rebellious response that belied his age. Frightened of his father crushing his dreams. Was he worthy of more respect when his actions did not justify it? How strong were dreams, if a few words from his father destroyed them? What life did he want, and was it worth fighting his father for?

The clouds were thinner now, as the winds calmed. Cooler now, his thick, black school uniform kept him warm. He climbed the three wide steps up to the school and found his roommate, Uehara, coming out.

"Akira, I was looking for you. Was your visit with your father acceptable? Did he demand you go home?"

"No, he did not. My uncle told him about the game. He only came to watch and had to leave after it was over."

"Good. I was worried; he never looked happy during the game. I am going to the dining hall. Do you wish to join me?"

Akira shook his head. He wanted quiet, to let his thoughts roam.

"Alright." Uehara turned, took a step and stopped. "I am so foolish, I almost forgot. The mail came, and I believe Miki sent you something." He handed over a small package and a couple of letters. "When I get back, do you want to talk about the game?"

"Yes, that will be fun."

With a wave, Uehara walked away.

Uehara had been such a good friend since Akira had come to school. The two had shared everything. Uehara was studying to be a chemical engineer. He wondered what Uehara would think of this new possibility.

He glanced down at the small package. *Miki sent me something. That was thoughtful of her.*

Small rays of sun were seeping through the clouds, inviting him to follow their path. He walked to the Okuma Garden. Because of the rain, it had few people, but a couple of dense pine trees protected the ground from the rain, so Akira could sit and enjoy the afternoon. Several small children from the neighboring school were kicking a ball on the far side of the open field, their teacher watching over them. A pair of Japanese Tits flew in and out of the trees above him, and made him smile; perhaps their sweet song caused it, or perhaps it was their formal attire of black coat, white shirt and black tie.

This had been such a strange day. The early excitement followed by the tension with his father. The wonderful game, which he was sure they would have won if the weather had not stopped it. His uncle's idea. And now the weather, clearing into a nice evening.

Stimulated by the pine fragrance, Akira brought his thoughts back to his future. At twenty-four-years old, he was a man now. After all, his parents planned his wedding to Miki to take place this time next year, after he graduated; he would then be a husband. Akira's eyebrows popped up at that realization. He never thought about the actual wedding; it had always been in the future, but that future was closing in, and bringing him closer to his responsibilities.

Which brought him back to his problem. If he took some different courses this next year, which would teach him about running a business, then that might help him find a clearer path. Would Miki want to travel with him? Regardless—the wife follows the husband. He had never shared his dreams with her, either. She was pretty, though.

I wonder what she sent me.

He picked up the package, running his fingers over the words on the outside. Miki's handwriting. He pulled the string.

"Akira Tanaka?"

He looked up at the stranger, surprised he never heard him walk up. Once on his feet, he bowed. "Yes, I am Akira Tanaka. May I help you?"

"Mr. Tanaka," the man said, pulling an envelope out of his bag and extending it to Akira, "I am with our Military Affairs Office, and I am honored to congratulate you on your opportunity to serve our emperor. Your instructions are on the card."

Akira had reached out to take the envelope, but stopped short at these words.

The man pushed it into Akira's hand, then bowed. "This is a great day for you, is it not?"

Like a robot, Akira nodded his head. "Thank you." Knowing those words were a complete lie, he watched the man until he walked out of the garden.

I am the only son. I should be exempt. This must be some mistake.

Reality hit his body, while the mind continued to question. With shaky legs, he sat back down on the ground. His heart pounded hard against his ribs. Breathing became cumbersome. His hands trembled so hard that he dropped the envelope in his lap.

With a last hope, he opened it and saw the red paper. The order instructed him to report to Tokyo's Naval Conscription

Center on Hirohito 19, February 10, for his physical examination and preliminary testing. It took him a moment to remember that the military required strict adherence to the traditional Japanese calendar system; Emperor Hirohito had been on the throne for nineteen years.

Akira gazed up at the garden in front of him and the buildings behind. All his dreams of traveling, of becoming a teacher or now a businessman, vanished. Only one more year. No more freedom and laughter with friends. No more games of catch.

The Tit stopped singing. The breeze ceased to blow. Sunshine was no longer bright. Cold seeped into his uniform. He had known that this day might come, yet he had pushed it from his mind.

"Akira, are you ill?" asked Uehara as he sat down beside him.

His friend's voice penetrated his daze. Without moving his head, without changing his gaze, Akira handed the envelope to his friend. "It is my time."

Bonus Novelette

Building a relationship with my readers is the very best thing about writing. I occasionally send newsletters that contain more information about the stories, history, characters, as well as details on new releases and special offers. If this is something you are interested in, I invite you to join me.

    If you do signup, I will send you a **free ebook**: *Operation Hailstorm.*   The exciting prequel to *Eye Contact Over Truk*.

For more information and signup, go to woodmanbooks.com